MY SECRET HEART

A DARK HIGH SCHOOL ROMANCE

STEFFANIE HOLMES

MY SECRET HEART

Now you know my secret.

Bit of a doozy, isn't it?

Sorry 'bout that.

The problem is, someone else knows too.

Someone dangerous.
Someone who's already buried me once.
This time, they're determined to finish the job.

Three broken princes stand between me and my doom:
The fallen king with his thirst for vengeance.
The rock god who sings of blood and stars.
The sweet one who's drowning in hate.

Three spoiled princes who own my heart of ice.

Keeping them secret is the only way to save them.

By my betrayal will drive them into my enemy's hands.

Alea iacta est.
Let the die be cast.
Welcome to Stonehurst f**king Prep.

Grab a free copy *Cabinet of Curiosities* – a Steffanie Holmes compendium of short stories and bonus scenes – when you sign up for updates with the Steffanie Holmes newsletter.

JOIN THE NEWSLETTER FOR UPDATES

Grab a free copy *Cabinet of Curiosities* – a Steffanie Holmes compendium of short stories and bonus scenes – when you sign up for updates with the Steffanie Holmes newsletter.

www.steffanieholmes.com/newsletter

Every week in my newsletter I talk about the true-life hauntings, strange happenings, crumbling ruins, and creepy facts that inspire my stories. You'll also get newsletter-exclusive bonus scenes and updates. I love to talk to my readers, so come join us for some spooky fun :)

A NOTE ON DARK CONTENT

This series goes to some dark places.

I'm writing this note because I want you a heads up about some of the content in Stonehurst Prep. Reading should be fun, so I want to make sure you don't get any nasty surprises. If you're cool with anything and you don't want spoilers, then skip this note and dive in.

Keep reading if you like a bit of warning about what to expect in a dark series.

- There is some bullying in the first book, but our heroine holds her own. No heroes in this story threaten or are involved in physical or sexual assault of the heroine.

- Mac is a sexual abuse survivor and she references this past trauma in places.

- Mac also experiences a sexual assault in *My Stolen Life*, but it is stopped by one of her boys.

- There is also a scene where a beloved animal is attacked and hurt. I want you to know that this animal survives and the person who attacked her will be punished.

- Subsequent books contain violence, human trafficking, organised crime, drug use, murder, further examples of animal cruelty (not by Mac or her boys), and further references to sexual assault.

Mackenzie and her boys are deep in a cruel, bloodthirsty world. It's not pretty, but I promise there will be suspense, hot sex, and beautiful, violent retribution. If that's not your jam, that's totally cool. I suggest you pick up my Nevermore Bookshop Mysteries series – all of the mystery and hot book boyfriends without the gore and trauma and violence.

Enjoy, you beautiful depraved human, you :) Steff

To Ms. Gallen,
For stoking the fires of my love for ancient shenanigans

"Let them hate me, so long as they fear me."

– Emperor Caligula (12-41AD)

PROLOGUE: NOT-MACKENZIE
(FOUR YEARS EARLIER)

"Stop twitching like a teenager on a meth binge, Jesus fuck." Antony rocks beneath me. "You nearly took my eye out."

"You want to try balancing on my spindly shoulders while cutting this?" I snap back, sucking my bleeding finger into my mouth as I aim the cutters at the next coil of barbed wire. "Stop whining. If the neighbors hear us, we're done for."

Antony grunts and shifts his weight beneath me, and I tighten my thighs around his neck as a tremble rocks through my body. I'm not shaking because I'm struggling to balance sitting on his shoulders – I've always been pretty good at that sort of thing. I'm a wreck because I'm still living inside the nightmare of waking up in a coffin, of sucking in stale air and knowing my last breath will taste of graveyard dirt and loneliness.

If Antony hadn't found me...

I should be dead right now. My parents are dead. The truth of it hasn't hit me yet. It's a story of something terrible that happened to someone else. When Daddy talked to me about his work, he had the same matter-of-fact tone he used to discuss the weather. Grey skies and drug deals, el Nino and Al Capone – it's all the same to him.

I'm detached from my life, floating in the ocean of my own delusion as I *snap, snap, snap* at the barbed wire.

Is this how Daddy stayed sane? I discard the thought as soon as it comes to me. Daddy was many things, but sane wasn't one of them.

Finally, I have a section of wire cut away that's wide enough for me to slip through. Antony gives me a boost, and I vault over the wall. I tuck my knees to my chest and throw my arms out as I land to cushion the impact the way Antony taught me. It doesn't work. I cry out as my ankle rolls and the force radiates up my leg.

"You okay?" Antony yells, his voice muffled by the high stone wall between us.

"Shut up." The last thing we need is some nosy neighbor overhearing him and calling the cops. Although there doesn't appear to be neighbors nearby. A strip of manmade woodland surrounds the mansion on two sides, closing us off from the rest of Harrington Hill. And those neighbors probably had their own woodlands and fancy gardens and huge fuck-off walls, too.

Rich people love their privacy. Behind their barricades, they can get up to all the illicit things that have lined my family's coffers for centuries.

I lean my weight on my good ankle and stand, taking in my surroundings. I've landed on a tiled bar area – upturned pool furniture scattered around a sunken fire pit and outdoor kitchen festooned with spiderwebs. In front of me, the azure waters of a swimming pool glisten in the moonlight. A blow-up unicorn bobs in the water, its neck bent at an impossible angle as it slowly deflates – a remnant of the life of the girl who grew up in this palace. It's a fitting metaphor for Mackenzie Malloy – the spoiled princess touched by magic who's discovered she bleeds like the rest of us.

Beyond the pool, the house glitters, bright and inviting. Strips of LED lighting glow softly as they illuminate a path across the garden. Dorothy's yellow-brick road through the land of Oz. I see more lights on inside, and hip furniture arranged just-so behind the tinted windows. It looks as if the owners will be home any minute.

I'm itching to explore inside, but I need to find a way to let Antony in first. I duck through an iron gate down the side of the house and into the front yard, picking my way gingerly around evil-ass looking succulents. Whoever did the landscaping has a hard-on for spikes.

Twin iron gates tower above me, topped with more spikes and hung from a pair of stone pillars that could pass as the monolith from *2001: A Space Odyssey*. We already tried a crowbar on the gates, but that wouldn't fly. I spy a metal box screwed into one of the pillars. I kick off the front panel. Inside is a manual override, in case the gate's electronics short during a storm and the rich bastards inside need to send out their servants to restock the cellar with Dom Pérignon and gilt-edged toilet paper. I crank the handle to make a gap wide enough for Antony to fit through, and we're both inside.

Our feet crunch on the stone pathway as we walk toward my future. Or my doom. It's too soon and I'm too fucked-up to know which one yet.

"Welcome to your new home, Claws." Antony gestures to the front door like he's a real estate agent on a property reality TV show. He picks up one of the decorative rocks and lobs it at the window beside the door. The rock bounces off and knocks over a cactus, but there's not a single scratch on the glass.

"Ballistic glass." Antony steps in close to inspect the window.

"And this door is bulletproof. Whoever built this house was expecting trouble."

That makes it the perfect place to hide.

If we can get in.

Antony has a gun tucked into his belt, and I consider the possibility of using it – multiple shots fired at the same location will eventually break ballistic glass. But he doesn't have a silencer and we don't need to announce ourselves to the neighborhood by opening fire. We circle the property to look for another entry point, stomping through the gardens and doing battle with the evil-looking cacti. The spiky bastards emerge victorious – by the time Antony yells in triumph from somewhere up ahead of me, my pajama leg is bristled like a porcupine.

"Look at this." Antony stands in front of the pool, pointing to a box on the wall of the house, beside the outdoor fireplace. It's filled with logs. "Pull those out while I search for a hammer."

I do as I'm told, only dimly registering the splinters that puncture my fingers as I toss the wood into the garden. My leg itches from where the cacti got me, but I fancy I can still taste the graveyard in my mouth, and that's all I can think about.

My pajamas are covered in sweat and sawdust by the time I'm done, but I empty the box. At the rear is another door – I realize this must open inside the house, so the family can stoke an indoor fireplace using the same wood supply. *Clever thinking, Antony.*

I push on the door, but it's stuck fast.

"Step aside." Antony strides across the garden toward me, carrying a sledgehammer over his shoulder. I tug off my pajama pants and sit on the edge of the swimming pool, dangling my legs into the cool water while he swings at the inner door. I think about the newspaper article he showed me in the car on the way here – about the family who used to live here, about the girl who looks just like me who disappeared without a trace – and his plan to use that to our advantage. Any other day I'd have punched Antony for being a crazy mofo. But he has grave dirt under his nails. *My* grave dirt. Crazy has gone out the fucking window.

I was buried alive along with my daddy, who didn't survive. My mother was sliced up in our home, her head nearly severed from her body.

Nothing seems crazy after that.

Antony calls me over. I peer into the dark void of the hole he's made in the wood. Antony steps back. "Ladies first."

It can't be this easy. "How come no alarms have gone off?"

"The family has been missing for at least six weeks. I'm guessing they stopped paying their bills. There's only one way to find out."

I step through the hole. This room isn't lit like some of the others. I can't see a thing except for the shaft of pale moonlight across the floor, but the place has a feeling of oppressive gloom. I turn to help Antony through the gap. He fishes his phone from his pocket and turns on the flashlight, handing it to me so I can shine it around the space.

We stand in a grand living room. Dust dances in the beam of the flashlight as we move through the space. Everything seems eerie without the presence of people – the weird hip furniture takes on the shape of sinister, half-human forms.

A home without occupants is like a husk – a body without a soul. Although it's hard to imagine this house feeling like a home to anyone. It looks more like a modern art museum.

The living room leads into a bar area and a formal dining room that seats twenty. The table looks like the kind you see in medieval artworks where everyone's gnawing on wild-boar legs and someone's getting their head chopped off because they slurped their soup the wrong way.

The thought sends up images of my mother's body, and I swallow down bile.

"This place is unreal," I breathe. I can't resist the urge to run my hands over the table, imagining the meals that had taken place here, the intellectual discussions, the titillating parties for famous movie stars and worldly business-people. Did the same elite guests who attended my parents' dinner parties come here, too – only in different outfits, with a different agenda? Had my father ever set foot within these walls? Had he been responsible for the acquisition of the strange art adorning the cavernous rooms?

Did *he* come here, too? The man who lives in a dark box in my mind? Did he sneak away from one of those parties and make his way upstairs...

Or were these a better class of people – the kind with superior morals? If so, what would they think of this cat creeping through their secrets, ready to sink her claws into their life?

"I can't believe no one else has broken in here." I point to a cabinet on the wall holding a collection of ancient coins. I recognize several designs from my father's books, including a golden *solidus* of Emperor Theodosius I, which Daddy told me is worth around twenty grand. "This place is filled with expensive shit."

"This isn't like our neighborhood, where you need to keep your treasures hidden away." There's a darkness in Antony's voice. We both know he's not talking about Roman coins. "The cops have been swarming all over the place since the family disappeared. Plus there are stories about the family, about what happened to them. Any smart crook is too superstitious to touch it. But we're not here to steal shit. We're here to find you a hiding place."

We move from room to room, taking in the scope of the place – the office lined with mahogany bookshelves stuffed with history books and more ancient artifacts, the bright kitchen with gleaming appliances that looks as though its never been used, the media room with its movie-theatre seats and huge curved screen, the girl's room on the second floor with the shelves of creepy porcelain dolls, the gym and sauna and *motherfucking bowling alley* in the basement. The more I see, the more over-whelmed I feel by the sheer size and opulence and volume of *stuff*. Malloy Manor is not a gift but instead the weight of six feet of earth that will bury me alive.

Yeah, I'm not getting over tonight any time soon.

Finally, overcome by the scale of the house and the exhaustion dragging our limbs, we sink down into the impossibly soft sofas in a living room that's larger than every house I'd ever lived in jammed together. And Daddy was no pauper, so that's saying something.

"Here's how this is going to work," Antony says. "You are going to live here. If anyone comes to the house, you have two choices – hide or pretend you're the ghost of the dead daughter."

I snort. "You're cracked. Are you sure you weren't the one inhaling all that graveyard air? No criminal is going to pass up the chance to loot this Tutankhamun's Tomb because I jump out with a sheet over my head and yell *boo*."

"I wouldn't be so quick to doubt, cousin. You read that article – the Emerald Beach gossip queens are filling in the blanks in the official disappearance story with wild theories. Adding a ghost to the mix will only build on their narrative. If we can make people frightened enough to stay away, and it becomes too much of a focal point for thieves to bother with, you'll be able to live here unmolested for five years."

"Why five years?" *How can I possibly stay hidden here for that long?*

"The State of California recognizes squatters' rights. After five years, when you're over eighteen, you're able to take legal ownership of the property."

"What?" I can't even contemplate it. "This house would be mine?"

"Yup. There are a few stipulations, but I think we can find a way to make it work. Namely, we have to continue to pay the property taxes. And obviously, we'll need to keep services like water and power running so the place doesn't turn into a cesspit of filth. I can get someone I know to hack into the family's accounts and get all the details. You'll need to get a job, and I'll contribute what I can. We might be able to quietly sell off some of these antiques. Once this place is officially ours, we sell it off and pocket the money."

"What about you? If Brutus did this for control of the family, then he's going to clear house. You have to stay here with me. If you go back, you're dead."

Antony's face darkens. "And if I disappear, he'll never stop hunting me, and I'll lead him straight to you. This is only going to work because you happen to look like this Harrington Hills bitch. I don't have a handy doppelgänger, so I'm going back to Tartarus Oaks. I'm not worried about convincing Brutus to trust me. He already believes I'm on his side. That's how I found you tonight."

"You knew he was going to move against Daddy?" My hands ball into fists. "How could you stand by and do *nothing*?"

"Because if I did it would've been both of us in that coffin tonight," Antony shoots back. "I didn't do nothing. I got you out. Protecting you is my job. That's what Uncle Julian wanted. That's why I have to go back – we know there's at least one other person out there who knows what you look like."

His words slice the air in half, severing the chains that tether me to that particular box of memories. I shove them away, sending them bobbing untethered in the vast ocean of my pain. I breathe hard, forcing myself to remember the stale air in the coffin, the panic of feeling those walls closing in on me. I need to not think about what's inside that box.

"This doesn't make any sense." I gesture to the enormous room, desperate to leave the box untethered. "Why is this house just abandoned like this? It's too easy. What if the family isn't dead? What if they come back?"

"The word is that they're not coming back." Antony gives me a wink. I wonder if my father had anything to do with their disappearance.

"What do you know?"

"Nothing more than that, but I trust my sources." There's more to the story, but he won't tell me. Antony takes his oath to my father seriously – if Daddy said he wasn't to tell, then he wouldn't. But I don't like the fact that Daddy's keeping secrets from me in his grave.

I'm not convinced by his assurances. "What about other relatives? Lawyers? Someone trying to sell this place off?"

"Nope. Apparently, no one wants to touch it. And I can help with expert legal advice if they try." Antony cracks his knuckles. "If we do run into any problems, don't forget – you're the spitting image of our young Malloy heiress. You're our secret weapon. If someone tries to claim the house, in rolls Ms. Mackenzie Malloy, haughty-as-fuck, and scares them off. I'm betting we won't need to do that, but it's in our arsenal if required."

Despite my reservations, excitement glissades down my spine at the thought of pulling this off. Maybe it's the lure of gold and antiques and riches around every corner. Maybe it's the fact I woke up in my own grave and I understand that my life will never be the same again. Or maybe it's the idea that I have a chance to make a home for myself on my own terms, that I don't have to follow Daddy's rules or be beholden to our family business. Behind the battlements of Malloy Manor, I could truly be queen.

I pick up a bottle of Champagne from a silver ice bucket on the coffee table. The ice inside has long since melted into brackish water. I start to untwist the cork. "Let's say I agree to this insane idea, and I'm not saying I will. But if I *did*, I'd have one condition."

Antony rolls his eyes. "You are *so* your father's daughter. Saving your ass was a favor. You're supposed to owe *me* one."

"And you're asking me to live alone in this house of horrors and pretend to be a ghost so that in five years we can be million-aires. So yeah, you owe me. Luckily, I think even you'll agree to this. If we pull this off, you're getting out of the family business, Antony." I shudder to think of my cousin buried alive in a pine coffin. My father was one of the most powerful men in Emerald Beach, and that didn't protect him. I won't let Antony share his fate. "We take the money and we pay whatever we need to stop the family coming after us. And we get the fuck out of Emerald Beach forever."

Antony frowns. "You know it's not that easy. I've sworn loyalty to Brutus and can't back out, and you—"

I give up on the bottle and hand it to him. "I know who I am. We'll find a way. A lot can happen in five years. As Daddy would say, *alea iacta est* – let the die be cast."

Antony sighs, but he pops the cork and fills two glasses. "So be it."

I sip my lukewarm Champagne and try to stomp down the terrifying sensation of the coffin walls closing in on me. As cages went, this one was pretty magnificent. *Five years.* Five years of waiting and hiding and hoping. If that's all it takes for a chance at getting out of the hell my legacy has gifted me, then I'm all in.

Just call me Mackenzie Malloy, the Ice Queen of Emerald Beach.

1

ELI

"That's not Howard and Ainsley Malloy in these photographs. You're not Mackenzie Malloy. Who the fuck *are* you?"

Not-Mackenzie freezes, her lips pressing together in a pout that might have been utterly irresistible if she was actually the person she says she is. But she's not. All these weeks, she let me live with the hope of finding her again. But it was all a lie, a confidence trick.

Killer.

Liar.

I don't know which one is worse.

Pain arcs across my chest. I'm splitting in two – my ears ringing, my insides tearing apart.

She's even worse than my father.

Not-Mackenzie's shoulders sag. She doesn't look upset, only resigned. "If I don't explain, you're going to the cops, right?"

The Ice Queen returns. That's all she thinks about – whether I'm spilling the beans on her perfect plan to steal Mackenzie's life. She doesn't care about what this will do to Noah. To Gabe.

To me.

Of course she doesn't. She's not Mackenzie. That's the only way she can be this cruel.

"Noah nearly got *shot,*" I spit at her. My fists clench at my sides. I'm not violent, but I want to punch a hole through Howard Malloy's dark mahogany desk, to hurl furniture across the room, to destroy something precious to her in the same way she'd done to me. I suppose I have in a way – I exposed her secret. Too bad I'm collateral damage. "Damn right I'm going to the cops, unless you give me a compelling reason not to. Since you're a murderer who's committed fraud and theft and possibly a million other things, I don't see that happening. How is it you look so much like her? Is it plastic surgery or natural-born subterfuge? Did you just happen to open a newspaper one day and see an opportunity to con your way into the Malloy coffers?"

"The latter. Eli, I can explain—"

"Hey God Almighty, did you find Mac?" Gabe pokes his head through the door. "My dear, your bar is woefully understocked. I'm trying to teach your gorilla-friend how to make a half-decent martini, but your vermouth tastes suspiciously like floor polish—"

"She's not Mackenzie," I hiss through gritted teeth.

"You going blind, mate?" Gabe's hand on my shoulder is a bolt of fire. His voice is too loud, his gestures exaggerated. He's drunk. I register that I'm supposed to be concerned about this, but I can't make myself care. "Blonde hair, ice-cold eyes, that distinctive and shaggable arse. Of course that's Mackenzie. You need a stiff drink. Let Dr. Gabriel take care of you, my friend, as soon as I locate the old man's vermouth..."

Gabriel's words trail off as he nudges the locket with his boot. He stares at the picture, then at the family portrait in the heavy gilded frame behind the desk, then back at the locket again. His face twists as the recognition sets in. "Mac? What's going on? Why do you have two strangers in your locket?"

Not-Mackenzie shakes her head, her blonde waves tumbling over her shoulders. The movement nearly undoes me. "I can explain. Just give me—"

I struggle for breath. The ringing in my ears obliterates whatever she says next. I don't want to be here in this house, surrounded by my memories and the girl who's grinding them to dust under her spike-heels.

I sense a looming presence behind me. No one looms like Noah Marlowe, especially now he's bulked up. "What's going on? I heard raised voices. Eli never raises his voice."

Not-Mackenzie waves her hand at me. "Help Eli. He looks like he's going to keel over."

Noah's hands go under my shoulders just as my body pitches forward. The locket lurches toward me, those two random faces like mocking clowns at a county fair. Mackenzie says something else, but I can't hear it. My head spins and the room recedes as I fall backward through a tunnel. The darkness swirls around me, and I welcome it. At least in oblivion, my life makes sense.

The last thing I hear before the abyss swallows me is Noah's voice calling, "I got you, man."

Noah and Gabriel must've dragged me back to the ballroom, because when I open my eyes again, I'm slumped on the sofa, staring at a pitch-black cat racing around a multi-story castle. I don't remember the journey – one moment I'm staring at the locket as the floor rushes up to meet me. The next Gabriel, Noah, and I are lined up on the sofa like criminals before the firing squad, facing Not-Mackenzie, who sits upright in a leather armchair, flanked by her two hulking cronies.

My head feels like I slammed it into a wall. I incline it slightly, and my brain bounces off the sides.

Ow. I won't do that again.

"Right." Not-Mackenzie clears her throat. "Now that Eli's done being dramatic... I'll tell you about the locket. But first, you need to know that I didn't kill anyone."

Her voice cracks on the word *kill.* Her voice and eyes are hard, but there's something else – a note of pleading. She wants us to believe her. But that's ridiculous. A sociopath who pretends to be someone else and takes over their life doesn't give a fuck what we think of her.

Noah tosses the locket on the coffee table so hard the chain scratches the wood.

I look to him and take strength from the dark rage in his eyes. Noah's spent so long hating Mackenzie Malloy, it's easy for him to flick that switch to hating this stranger, too. Although... her scent still clings to his body, and I wonder if his hatred has become something else. Has Noah been so consumed by his own fire that he's collapsed and crumbled into himself and emerged anew?

A phoenix can't be born of sin and shadow. It would starve without the fire that feeds it.

Not-Mackenzie wrings her hands, and everything wrong about her stands out. She's always seemed different from the girl I fell in love with all those years ago. She forgot everything about her life, about me, about *us.* She tried to make me believe she had amnesia, but all my reading about her symptoms never quite matched up.

She broke into my house and wrote those things on my walls.

She expected me to protect her even though she's *nothing* to me.

She *branded her initials* into Alec LeMarque's forehead.

No. Not her initials. She tried to make Mackenzie guilty of her crime.

She could be a cold-blooded killer.

Killer.

Killer.

She doesn't deserve to wear Mackenzie's name like a designer scarf.

Gabriel slouches, a tall drink in his hand. He thinks no one's noticed that he stopped drinking since he got back to Emerald Beach, that he's been tossing alcohol into bushes and leaving it out of his own cocktails. He's wrong – I always notice. But he's drinking now, gulping back a tall glass of straight rum like his life depends on it.

It figures. When the going gets tough, Gabriel Fallen retreats into a fantasy world and bars the door behind him.

Beside me, Noah's a coiled spring of rage. But I can feel the edges of it. This rage doesn't belong to Noah – it's on my behalf.

Noah rests his hand on my knee and squeezes his fingers – it hurts because the dude does not know his own strength anymore, but I know that squeeze is a promise. I held Noah together when he descended into hell four years ago. He'd take a bullet for me. I can't count on much in my life, but I can count on that.

"Spit it out," Noah rasps. "The truth. No more hiding behind your fake trauma. The agreement we had isn't worth shit now."

Not-Mackenzie's mouth opens, shuts, opens again.

"Eli deserves the truth," Noah snaps. "If you won't give it to him, we're going to the police."

"I'd be careful with my threats if I were you," Antony says, coming forward to stand beside Not-Mackenzie. He cracks his knuckles, and the amusement in his eyes is menacing. "This is not any ordinary Valley Girl you're talking to. Gentlemen, meet Claudia August, prodigal daughter and rightful heir of the August crime family."

2

CLAUDIA

It's *almost* worth this entire charade just to see their faces when Antony gives them my real name.

I always thought of Gabriel as a dark angel, but even angels have their limits. His eyes swim with a shock that reaches deep into his psyche. He clutches his glass like it's the only thing stopping him from sinking into the floor. His mouth wobbles and tugs, and I'm not sure if he's going to laugh or scream.

Noah Marlowe looks *impressed*. There's shock in his coal-dark eyes, sure, but the corner of his mouth twitches that way it does, like he's trying to smile but it's been so long he's forgotten how. I take that almost-smile as a grudging acknowledgment from a bitter rival that I'd bested him.

Or maybe all I see is the residual lust burning off from our fuck in the panic room. Either way, Noah's not my main concern here.

Eli... sweet, unshakeable Eli bends over and throws up on his shoes.

My own stomach twists as I wrestle with the pain I've caused him. I knew on some level the truth would break him. That's why I tried to push him away. That's why I fucked Noah in the panic room and why I lost my virginity to Gabriel – because I thought Gabriel wouldn't give a shit what my real name is as long as I continue to intrigue him.

Judging from the way my favorite musician's mouth twisted into a frown, I think I misjudged him.

I didn't expect Eli discovering my secret to be such a punch in the gut. It's almost as if I *want* to be Mackenzie Malloy so much – I want to pick up her perfect life where she left off and have the all-American boy with the too pretty smile love me with a fire that hasn't dimmed in ten years.

And now he's lost to me forever.

I stand up and pace the room, my boots clacking on the marble floor. I don't want to speak my secret heart into the world like this. I don't want to break the threads that connect me to these three princes, or give them the ammunition they need to destroy me. But they aren't going to let me get away without an explanation. I can't shove these skeletons back in the closet. Gabriel is a mess and Noah is out for blood and Eli... I can't even look at him right now.

I don't look at them as I speak. I can't. If I have to witness the pain flooding Eli's eyes or Gabriel's broken wings unraveling, I'll break myself. "Antony's telling you the truth. My real name is Claudia August."

My name is Claudia August.

It's been so long since I used that name that it tastes foreign on my tongue. Like a character from a book that I used to enjoy but then grew out of.

Like an evil queen who burns her kingdom to ashes and dust.

"My name is Claudia August," I say again, trying to get used to the sound of it. "I am heir to the August criminal empire. I grew up in Tartarus Oaks, on the other side of the city. My father is Julian August. You might've heard of him."

Both Gabriel and Eli look blank, but Noah's mouth does that twitch again. "Holy shit. Julian August was a big-time crime boss about a decade ago. I believe he used to be in charge of narcotics and human trafficking into the city."

I wonder how Noah Marlowe – the senator's son – knows about this, but it's not my turn for asking questions. "That's him. And he didn't go in for skin of any sort – dead or alive. No prostitutes. No body parts. Our family empire is built on drugs and black-market antiquities. It wouldn't surprise me if Daddy sourced the Roman coins and other artifacts that decorate Howard's study—"

Antony glares at me. *Zip it, Claws.* I swallow again. I am still bound by the family oath, even though I never had anyone to spill secrets to... until now. All I wanted to do was make them understand, to find some way for words to dull the pain that I've inflicted. "All you need to know is that Julian August was a gentleman criminal, a terrible man and a great father. When I was twelve... I... I..."

I was buried alive.

I can't form the words. The trauma holds them on my tongue, so when I swallow I taste the bitterness of graveyard dirt. The memory sits on my skin – my nails stinging from scratching at the wooden lid. I sit on my hands, clear my throat, and try again. "When I was twelve, I saw my parents betrayed and killed, and I knew they'd come for me next. So I ran away from home."

Nothing. No reaction except for Noah crossing and uncrossing his boots on the table.

Antony shoots me a questioning look. I give the slightest shake of my head. I can't talk about the coffin. Not now. Not with that hardness in Eli's eyes. I might be stripped bare, but I wouldn't flay my own skin off in supplication. This story is as close to the truth as I'm willing to get.

"Daddy wanted me to take over his empire. He trained me

from the day I was born to manage the vast underground networks he used for illicit trade. He taught me himself, and he would let me hide in the closet or under his desk when he held meetings with subordinates or enemies. I got my obsession with ancient Rome from him. But this knowledge came with a price. He couldn't allow me to enroll in a normal school. He kept me shut away in the house, and when I attended events with him, it was always in elaborate disguises. Antony was one of the few friends I had who he allowed to see my real face."

"Why?" Noah's back is ramrod straight, his posture perfect. That's Noah Marlowe for you, all buttoned up and perfectly put-together – a mask with perfect edges but made of glass that will shatter in an instant.

"Daddy knew that to be a woman in his world meant I'd become a pawn to be moved around the chessboard and sacrificed at will. Vultures would circle, trying to take my power and carve up our empire amongst themselves. He didn't want that for me, so he kept me to himself so I'd become strong. Daddy barely let me leave the house – I didn't have friends. Antony was the only person outside the house who I was allowed to talk to."

I swallow again. "Daddy trained me to be a queen. On the chessboard, the queen is the ultimate weapon, but only because the player has to be prepared to sacrifice her if the reward was high enough. My eventual marriage would seal an alliance with another important crime family and allow me to hold on to our empire, and Daddy didn't want to show me off on the market too soon. When the king was removed from the table, I knew I'd be collateral damage. The man who killed my parents wanted control of my father's empire – they couldn't yet marry me, and they couldn't risk keeping me alive."

"You sound like you know who took out your parents?"

I nod. "His name's Brutus. He's my uncle, and he was my father's *tribune* – his lieutenant, second in command. But he and Daddy disagreed on certain aspects of the family business. Brutus wanted to get out of the antiquities trade and move into human trafficking – there's more money in it and a bigger local client base. Daddy wouldn't hear of it – it went against his fucked-up moral code. Next thing, my parents end up dead and Brutus is the new *Imperator* of the August empire. It doesn't take Eli's Sherlock Holmes orgasm face to put the pieces together."

Antony shakes his head at me, warning me that I'm saying too much. But I can't. I'm falling to pieces under the intensity of Noah's curiosity and Gabriel's storm-filled silence and Eli's rage.

"When they were killed, I didn't know what to do or where to go. I just knew I had to get away from my crumbling family before my uncle came for me. So I went to Antony, who's always looked after me. Antony owns a fight club called The Colosseum in Tartarus Oaks that brings in a lot of money for the three crime families of Emerald Beach, so he'll always be safe. He showed me a newspaper article about the disappearance of the Malloy family – a mother, father, and their blonde-haired, blue-eyed daughter who looked uncannily like me."

Antony moves from the door to the chair opposite the sofa, flopping down with his huge feet hanging over the end. He flips open his jacket, letting the guys see the gun strapped there. I notice Noah staring at him with a weird expression on his face, almost like he's trying to work something out.

My cousin strokes the weapon like a lover. "I knew we could use Claudia's resemblance to this Valley girl to our advantage. I discovered Malloy Manor was unoccupied. A little digging revealed no relatives would be making a claim on the place. Dear Howard was the black sheep of the family, and there was a belief from media and authorities that he was involved in something shady—"

"He was," Noah rasps, his fists clenching at his sides. "He

released supplements into the market without adequate testing. He killed people."

Antony nods. "Of course he did. He's a rich asshole with no morals. But as your court loss attests, his crimes were perfectly legal. The authorities couldn't get anything to stick to Howard Malloy, and you can't put a man away for being a rich asshole with no morals or all of Harrington Hills would be behind bars. But you don't build a house with bullet-resistant glass and the highest spec security system unless you expect to be invaded, and Howard's family knew that. The Malloys are wealthy enough – they don't need the trouble if the cops found anything untoward. A few quick calls to some of my associates around the country ensured they weren't planning to take possession of the property, although they're still scrapping over the money held in Malloy's investments. That left the house free for us to claim."

"How do you figure that?" Noah sounds genuinely interested.

"Squatter's rights," Antony drawls.

"What the fuck is that shit?" Eli splutters.

"In the state of California, if a squatter occupies a property for five years and the owners don't return to evict them, they're legally allowed to take possession of the property."

"Antony was a law student," I say. *And soon he'll get to be again.* My cousin dangles his leg over the end of the sofa. I notice a bloodstain on the cuff of his jeans, no doubt from his time at the club. Brutus forced him to quit school to run the club, and Antony needed Brutus to trust him, so he obeyed. I can't wait to get him out of there before he's forced deeper into the family business. "He knows all about it."

"That's complete bullshit." Eli's hands ball into fists. "You can't just take Mackenzie's house."

"Why not? She's not using it. I've been here four years. I have to wait until I'm eighteen to apply for ownership, but since I ran away close to my thirteenth birthday, I don't have long to wait now. It's a crazy idea – hiding in plain sight – but it's worked for four years. I had to get a shitty job at a diner and Antony dropped out of school to work for the August family so we could pay the property taxes. We sold a few of the antiques when we got desperate, but we didn't want to risk anyone following up on their provenance. The city doesn't give a shit about the house as long as they get their money. A few kids have scaled the fences, and I get the odd reporter snapping pictures or opportunistic thief consumed by a lust for shiny things. But I just wander past the windows in a white nightgown and stare them down, and they run away pretty fast. It's easy to hide when the world thinks you're a ghost."

I dare a glance at Eli and see he's pale as a ghost himself. I remember him from years ago, his soft fingers curled around the iron gate as he peered inside. I thought he was just another journalist intrigued by the story of the disappearing Malloys, but he was here to protect me, just like he promised.

No, not to protect you. You're not her, and Eli owes you nothing.

I fooled myself into believing Eli cared about *me*. In my weakness, I forgot I was wearing the mask of Mackenzie Malloy. Eli's fire still burns bright for her, and there's no room for anyone else in those baby blue eyes.

I turn back to the other two. I can see the cogs turning in Noah's head as he puts all the pieces into place – all the weird clues I've laid over the last few weeks that he hadn't wanted to fit together. Gabriel finishes his drink and reaches for another, and my fallen angel's true heart sinks into oblivion as the alcohol takes over.

I can't see what Eli's thinking anymore because I won't look at him. If I look I will crumble.

I suck in a breath and continue. "This isn't about turning Malloy Manor into the seat of my criminal empire. We're doing this so we can get *out* of the family – Antony and I. And Queen Boudica. She had such a shitty start to life, I want to give her everything. They're my family and I'll do anything to protect them."

"Then why are you at school?" Noah asks. I know he's thinking about all the tutoring he'd done with me, realizing why I couldn't write an essay to save my ass. "Why are you so determined to stay there if it puts you in danger?"

"One of the neighbors heard me playing music because, for all of Howard Malloy's security measures, he didn't install sound dampening around the media room. Sound travels down the valley to the neighbors, who called the police on me. An officer came to the door and I... I knew what I had to do. I pretended to be her. It worked too well. The cop believed me, but he wanted to check up on me and get me in trouble for being a minor living alone. He demanded to know what school I went to, and I said the first name I could think of – Stonehurst Prep. Now I have to keep up the charade that I'm Mackenzie, so I have to go to school." I shrug. "The rest you know."

"Won't the fact that you pretended to be another person put a stain in your claim for the property?" Noah asks. He doesn't sound angry any longer, more like he's excited to put the puzzle together.

That's usually Eli's role in the group – he's the one who has to solve everyone's problems. But Eli won't be able to think his way out of the mess I've made of his life, and Noah is fucked-up enough that *maybe,* if he tries hard enough, he can sink to my level.

Antony keeps jiggling his foot as he shrugs. "We'll deal with that if it comes up. But it won't come up. This building is a problem for the council. It's a blight on the Harrington Hills landscape. The Malloy legacy degrades the property values and the residents constantly complain. But the council doesn't want to deal with the family – if it's sold to a developer who'll bull-doze the thing and build luxury condos, they'll look the other way."

Eli jerks to his feet. "You're going to *sell* Mackenzie's house?"

"For the last time, she's welcome to stand up and object," I shoot back, rising to my feet to glare at him. His face twists and I fucking hate myself, but he hates me more, and that's exactly what I want.

If Eli hates me, he'll be safe.

His whole body trembles. "This isn't yours to take. You... you... *desecrated* it."

He has his hand over his chest as he sweeps his arm around to indicate the ballroom, and I feel a tinge of annoyance because I'd never had anything that belonged to me in my entire life, but this room, this shard of a life that I clawed for myself from thin-fucking-air, this *is* mine. But the Golden Boy of Stonehurst Prep – who's had everything handed to him on a gold-edged plate – will never understand that.

"Don't be so fucking dramatic. I read Mackenzie's diaries. She hated this house. It was her fucking prison, just like it is mine. You three think you have it so tough, living in your huge houses with your millions of dollars and your free ride through life. I bet you've never even set foot in Tartarus Oaks. You don't know what it takes to survive there." I lift my chin.

Noah bites his lip. He looks over at Antony, and then back at me. He wrestles with something he wants to say, but doesn't. Instead, he asks, "So what did you do to Brentwood that has him trembling in his Brionis at the thought of facing you again?"

"I told you, I don't have anything to do with this Brentwood. If he's a killer, then he's connected to another Tartarus Oaks family, because you can't get a contract in this town without going through Constantine Dio. If he saw Mackenzie Malloy murder someone, that's nothing to do with me."

"But my father thinks you're Mackenzie."

"Exactly." I flop back on my chair. Wordlessly, Gabriel hands me the bottle of rum. I swipe it from his hands and take a swig. "Hence, today's little problem."

"We don't know that for a fact." Antony taps away on his phone. "I'm going out to chat with our friend Brentwood, see if I can straighten this out."

"No no no no no." Eli shakes his head so violently. He has his phone in his hand, and he clutches it against his chest like it's giving him the strength to stand upright. "This isn't right. You can't just sit in her house chatting to hired killers like you're the queen of Sheba, not after someone just tried to kill Noah. I won't let you steal from Mackenzie or put my friends in danger. I'm going to the cops right now. Don't try to stop me."

3

GABRIEL

"Sit down, Captain America," the guy with the buzzcut and the hard jaw says. He doesn't move from his chair and he doesn't stop jiggling his bloody foot, but he *does* flip open the lapel of his jacket and caress the gun inside.

At least, I think that's what happens. I'm a little tipsy. Okay, a lot tipsy. Okay, I'm completely plastered, and the sight of that guy touching his weapon like he's stroking his dick strikes me as *so* bloody hilarious. I double over, convulsing with giggles, until I taste bile in my throat. Now I'm the one who's going to puke everywhere. The thought sends me into another giggling fit.

"What's his problem?" Buzzcut waves the gun in the air. It looks like a toy.

Eli's hands ball into fists, and it's probably the shiteloads of expensive piss I just downed but I fancy I see steam coming out his ears. He's usually the calm one, the one bringing me back to reality when I get stuck in my own head. To Eli, the world has always been easy to navigate – this is right, this is wrong, black and white, Noah's perfect, Gabriel's a fuck-up, nice and simple. And then his father got sent to the clink and Eli's perfectly black-and-white world got sprayed all over with lurid color... kind of like how I'm about to spray my dinner everywhere.

I can't help but feel sorry for the chap. He's just got his life back into some semblance of control. He was going to go to a fancy college where he'd be awarded a gilded stick to shove up his arse. Then along comes Mackenzie Malloy to muss up his perfect golden hair. Only, Mackenzie Malloy isn't Mackenzie Malloy at all.

She's *Claudia.*

A beautiful name for a broken girl with a heart carved in secrets.

I look over to her, frozen on her chair, her icicle eyes darting between her cousin and Eli. *Claudia.* The name suits her. I asked her on my balcony once if she ever felt like an imposter in her own life. Beneath our banter and my lustful preoccupation with her gorgeous arse, I always knew we shared something deeper.

We're both practically royalty.

We are both getting away with shit that's eating us inside.

We are both *liars.*

We might even both be cold-blooded killers.

"This is bullshit. She's a lying bitch, and thanks to her, Noah nearly died today. I'm calling them now." Eli presses his phone to his ear as he heads for the door.

In a flash, Buzzcut and his friend Cave-In Face are on him. I didn't even see them move. One moment Eli's striding across the room with purpose. The next, he's shoved face-first against the wall with Cave-In Face's knee in his back, his arm twisted at such an obscene angle I know he's only one twitch away from snapping it.

"Hand over the phone, Captain America." Buzzcut holds out his hand. "Don't make Tiberius here break your fingers."

Eli scowls, but he holds out his free hand, passes the phone over. Buzzcut throws it on the floor and grinds the heel of his boot into it until it sparks and dies. Buzzcut drops Eli. His knees crack against the floor as he sags into himself, the fight gone out of him.

"You want to pitch a hissy fit, fine. But like it or not, you're part of this. Which means no cops, unless you want to get all of us killed. Against my advice, Claudia doesn't want your body riddled with bullets." Buzzcut glances over at me. "All of you are in this."

I nod. Just when I think I have Mackenzie figured out, she turns out to... not be Mackenzie at all. No way am I walking out on her now.

"I'm staying," Noah says.

Eli glares at us, but he knows he's not the threat in this room. Buzzcut nods to the sofa, but Eli doesn't sit. I don't think he knows how anymore. I'm a horrible fucking person, no question, because I like seeing the Golden Boy look all out-of-sorts. It makes me feel superior for once.

Do you know what else will make me feel superior? More booze. Mmmm, what goes well with rum? But of course, vodka. I swipe a bottle from the trolley and cradle it to my chest like it's my firstborn child. Noah tries to pry it from my fingers, but I snap my teeth at him and he backs off.

My eyes sweep back to Mac—er, Claudia. My cock's hard, throbbing against the seam in my jeans as I try to focus my swimming eyes on her face. I thought she was a crazy rich bitch Ice Queen and that was hot enough, but it turns out she's a crazy gangster heir to a crime empire, and I remember the way she melted into me at Midnight Grotto, and I think we might be written in the stars.

I thrust my hand in the air like we're in class. "Are we allowed to ask questions, Teach? Because my first question is, can Claudia put on her school uniform with the garters?"

"Gabe," Noah warns.

"And my second question is, how do we know it's this Bolly-wood chap instead of old Uncle Brutus who's taking potshots at Mac—er, Claudia?"

"That's what we're trying to figure out." Buzzcut sounds exasperated, which gives me a stab in the gut as it triggers a Dylan memory. Dylan always sounded like that around me, until a few months before his death when he stopped talking to me at all.

"I don't think Brutus will give up on his leadership just because you threatened him." Claudia says this guy's name dully, as though it's no big deal, but something passes through her eyes – the darkness I've seen there sometimes that mirrors my own. I know there's more to her story than she's told us. "If he's figured out who I really am, he'll have to get rid of me. I'm the legitimate heir, and that means everything in our world. A lot of people disapprove of him killing my father. If they knew Claudia August lives, things would get ugly for him."

Not half as ugly as what I plan to do to him, the threat echoes in her voice. I'd like to see what she had in mind.

"But it's also dangerous," she continues. "There will be many who support me as the legitimate heir because they want to use me to carve up my father's empire."

I understand immediately what she's talking about. I come from a completely different world, but it's one that's fueled by the same type of dynastic power. I was supposed to marry a duchess, but instead, I ran away to play in a rock band with my best friend, and I paid for that decision in his blood. Like Claudia, I try to hide in plain sight, but in the end, you can't run from fucking destiny.

"You're talking about a forced marriage," I say. Or, rather, try to say. It takes me a couple of tries to get the words to sound right. I suck on the neck of the bottle. More vodka will make me witty and articulate once more.

"Exactly. If I can't keep my identity secret, I either have to fight Brutus for control of my father's empire or risk becoming the possession of a crime lord," Claudia nods to me. "Neither of these are an option. The Triumvirate isn't getting their mitts on my pussy."

"Absolutely not. That precious jewel belongs to Noah and me." I grin up at Eli. "Sorry, mate. You snooze, you lose."

"*Gabe,*" Noah thunders. Eli looks like he might throw up again.

Buzzcut cracks up. "I'm pleased to see you chose such competent soldiers to protect you, Claws."

I beat my chest. "I'll have you know I'm exceedingly competent where it counts. In the bedroom. So what's this Tricycle?"

"Triumvirate," Noah corrects.

"Thank you, Senator Smarty Pants. What's that thingamy, then? It sounds like a sexy sports car. Or one of those yogurts with extra probiotics."

"It's the three crime families who run the city," Noah says. Claudia raises her eyebrow at him, and he adds, "My dad started a taskforce to stamp out organized crime in Emerald Beach. It's a huge part of his platform."

"Yet he's willing to hire a Dio hitman to take out Mackenzie Malloy?" Buzzfeed— Buzzcut muses. "Interesting."

"I'm not defending him," Noah snaps back.

"Noah's right," Claudia says. "Three families have ruled the criminal underground in Emerald Beach for decades. They form the Triumvirate – a ruling council that sets out rules and manages decisions about the empire. My family is in charge of shipping. We traffic anything illegal, mainly drugs and antiquities. Then there's another family who runs illegal gambling, card games, film sets, anything on the entertainment side. The third family, Dio, are the muscle, the mercenaries, the hired killers." She exchanges a look with Antony, and even in my inebriated state, I can see there's more she's holding back. "None of them know what I look like or that I'm still alive, but if Brutus has figured it out, then someone else can, too. And it throws a fat-ass question mark over other things – I thought Alec was the one who broke into the house and hurt my cat, but now I have to consider other possibilities."

"Whether he did or not, he deserved what he got," Noah rasps. "Could Alec be responsible for today?"

"I don't know. I believe he'd think nothing of shooting at *me*, but he nearly hit the son of a senator. That'd cause all kinds of trouble for him." She narrows her eyes at Noah. "You're his friend. Is this the kind of thing he'd do?"

"I *was* his friend," Noah corrects. "I don't hang out with rapists. It could be Alec. I wouldn't have believed it, but... I didn't believe that stunt he pulled in the desert, either. And you *did* destroy his car and his nose."

She nods. "I did. But then, I can't believe he'd be able to pull one over on Tiberius. But neither does this seem like the work of Brutus or Brentwood. None of it makes sense – why cleverly take out Tiberius to get close to the house, but then completely botch my murder with terrible aim and the wrong weapon?"

The casualness with which she speaks of her own attempted murder makes my cock jerk to attention. The alcohol hums in my veins, my whole body drowning in a sweet warmth that makes the danger and insanity of this conversation seem utterly comical. "What happens now? We whack Brutus and Bollywood, and then what?"

Claudia laughs, and the sound is glass shards tinkling against cold hotel room bathroom tile. Beautiful in the way all pain is beautiful, and instantly sobering. "You've known the truth for all of seven minutes and you've already jumped to whacking."

"What can I say? I'm a fast learner."

"You don't just go around taking out crime bosses on a

whim," Antony snaps. "For one thing, Brutus has gone to ground. How do you plan to get close enough to him to 'whack' him?"

"Also, no one says 'whacking' anymore." Claudia rolls her eyes. "This is politics as much as it's crime. There's an honor code, and we need to be careful how we approach this or we could land the city in an all-out gang war."

"Intriguing," I drawl. Noah manages to wrestle my vodka away. I lurch toward him but misjudge... everything, and end up in a giggling heap on the floor. Possibly it's for the best. I wave goodbye to my vodka as Noah pours it into a potted plant.

I burp loudly and shoot my arm into the air again. "I have another question. Why does he call you Claws?"

She raises a hand, curling her fingers over, her long fingernails dripping blood-red polish. "Because I may be tiny, but if you come too close, I'll scratch your eyes out."

Why do I have a feeling she means that literally?

Why do I find that so damn hot?

CLAUDIA SHOVES Buzzcut and Cave-In Face (I'm too wasted to remember their names) out of the ballroom and pulls the doors shut behind them. She leans against the ornately carved panels, her chest heaving, her blonde curls plastered to her face.

"So..." she looks like she's ready to bolt.

"You're not Mackenzie," Noah says. "You're not *her*."

He looks *relieved*. Such a weird face for Noah Marlowe. It doesn't suit him.

She shakes her head. "I'm not going to apologize again. I'm not sorry I stole her life. It was up for grabs and I did what I had to do to survive. I *am* sorry that I dragged the three of you into this. I checked Mackenzie's room before I started at Stonehurst.

I've been using her old phone for years, so I read all the messages. Apart from Eli's incessant texts that eventually stopped coming, there was nothing that talked about close friends or cute boys, so I thought I was safe if I could keep up her Ice Queen facade. I didn't find her diary until later – the one that talks about her friendship with Eli and the crush she had on Noah. By then, the three of you..."

She trails off, her eyes flicking between the three of us. When they settle on me, she shakes her head. "...I got carried away. I blame Gabriel. I can never refuse the boy who sings the stars."

What does she mean by that?

The phrase catches in the fog of my mind, and it drags another memory from the depths of my addled brain. A memory so warped by time and substance abuse that I can't be certain it's even a memory at all, although the sting of the words branding my skin feels real enough.

It was the night my parents sent their lawyer around to my London hotel to inform me I'd officially been cut off. I knew it was coming, of course. I'd been taking public jabs at their stiff-upper-lip for years, and changing my name was the final nail in my lead-lined coffin. But I thought the Duke of Blackwich might at least have the bollocks to do it in person. I should have known better – my father never wanted to face up to me before. That would mean acknowledging his own failures. I was just an annoyance, a bug to squash under his shoe. So he sent his lawyer over with a wax-sealed letter like we were in fucking Elizabethan times, and just like that, I was out of the family. No title, no inheritance, no invite to carve the Christmas roast. Fuck you very much.

I screwed up the letter and tossed it out the hotel window. "I don't care."

I did care. And I didn't know why I cared so fucking much.

So I decided to drink until I didn't care for real. It took a lot of alcohol. And some random pills I found under the mattress. And no less than four groupies who brought more drugs and did interesting things with the heated towel rails. Then the groupies left and I cried on the floor of the shower until Dylan pulled the curtain aside and found me lying in my own vomit.

"Hel..." I tried to say something, but I couldn't make words happen. "Dyleeeeeeelp..."

"You're disgusting." He nudged my hand with the toe of his boot.

"Wasssssidoooo..."

"What did you do? *What did you do?*" Dylan's voice was a cannonball bashing between my ears. "You have to get on stage in *four hours*, Gabe. I have to sleep in this room that you've completely trashed. Did you even think about that? Course not. You were thinking about Gabriel bloody Fallen and no one else."

"Leeeetteeeeeerr..."

"I know about the letter. I was here when you opened it. Not that you'd remember. You stopped paying attention to me a long time ago." Dylan lifted his boot and ground my hand beneath his heel. I registered on some level that it hurt and that it would make it hard for me to play, but I was too far gone to care.

"So go on, Gabe," Dylan spat as he dug his heel in deeper. I heard something pop in my fingers, and the pain ratcheted up a level that started to register through the haze. "Curl up inside your guitar case and cry. Beg for death because your daddy doesn't love you. Because *no one loves you*. There are a thousand broken souls who've forked over fifty bucks a ticket to hear you scream their pain back to them, who believe you carry the stars down to earth, but you're going to burn out their love the way you do everything else that's good and pure and beautiful. I loved you once, and now you're ashes, Gabriel. You're fucking *ashes*."

I felt like ashes, pieces of me scattered in the wind. The cold of the shower tile touched my cheek, and then the old injury in my hand throbs, reminding me that at least some part of the memory is real. I blink, and when I look at Claudia again, I'm a good deal soberer. Soberererer. Soberish…

Okay, maybe not much soberer. But enough that I can comprehend what she's saying if I focus hard. "…the three of you are staying here until we can clear this up. We'll send Tiberius around to your places if there's anything you need. If you have to leave the house, we'll have someone on you at all times."

I wave my arm in the air. "How will I know which scary blokes are watching out for me, and which ones are coming to kill me?"

Claudia taps the center of her forehead. "If they've got a gun pointed here, they're probably not on our side."

"Helpful as always."

Eli shakes his head. "I can't stay here."

"Not negotiable, Hart. Whoever is after me is shooting at Noah too, so you're all in danger. And we can protect you better if we stick together." Claudia folds her arms and shoots Eli her Ice Queen glare, and I kind of wish he'd push her because I want to see what she'll do to make him obey. I hope it involves whips and—

"I don't care." Eli crosses to the French doors leading out to the pool and tries the latch. It's locked. He pounds on the window with his fist. Noah gets up and rushes toward him. I hobble over as well. My lunch disagrees and I have to stop halfway to grab ahold of the cat castle to stop myself from toppling over. A black paw swipes at my nose from the uppermost turret.

Noah gets Eli around the neck, holding his head down so he can whisper something to him. I topple against them both, wrapping my arms around their shoulders and nearly putting Eli's head through the window. "Cuddle huddle!" I cry.

Noah flashes me his patented ignore-Gabriel look and turns back to Eli. "I know how you feel right now, but—"

"You really fucking don't." Eli's face is red with rage.

"Oh yeah? I don't know what it feels like to be confronted with an ugly truth? Ever since she started at school I've been tied up in knots. She walked in those doors and it all came rushing back – what she did to Felix, how her family attacked us during the trial, how they disappeared and it felt like she escaped justice. And then she's... she's *her*. I liked her. And I've hated myself for liking her because she's a Malloy. But now she's not..." Noah shrugs. "Mackenzie isn't coming back, man. And this house was never hers anyway. I say Claudia can have it, and we should help her."

"I agree." I turn to Eli and lick his cheek. He's too far gone to even react. That's bad.

"Fuck you both." Eli whirls around and stalks toward Claudia, fists raised. She leaps out of the way just in time. He slams into the doors and flees deeper into the house.

4

———

CLAUDIA

I open up three of the guest rooms for the guys – I put Gabriel across the hall from me in a room that's a mirror image of mine. Noah and Eli get rooms on the second floor, overlooking the pool, in the same hallway as Mackenzie's creepy doll bedroom. Their rooms share a bathroom, and I glare at Noah meaningfully as I show him the connecting doors – he'll have to watch out for Eli, make sure he doesn't try to shimmy down a drainpipe or do anything stupid.

As for Eli, he's standing in Mackenzie's old room, sifting through the decapitated dolls as if he expects to find her buried there. I wonder if he's looking for her diary. It's under my bed downstairs. I think about giving it to him and throw up a little in my mouth. I can't bear the idea of seeing her words affect him.

I want to cut Mackenzie Malloy for the hold she has over him, and since I've been pretending to be her for over four years, this is disturbing. Even from her grave or wherever the fuck Mackenzie is now, she rules Eli's heart. And I'm nothing.

Nothing.

I wish it could be different.

I can't watch Eli anymore. I go to the kitchen and pull open cupboards and drawers, looking for complicated food to cook. I need to stay busy. If I stop and stand still for a moment, I'll crash into the fact that they know my secret and I'll fall to pieces.

Antony watches me from the doorway as he barks orders into his phone. He's pulling some of his fighters from the club to watch the house. He tells them they've been hired by Mackenzie Malloy and there will be a cash bonus if they catch anyone trying to harm me or my friends. It doesn't hurt to have a psychopath as a cousin with an army of soldiers at his disposal.

I start chopping carrots, but the knife blurs in my hands. I grip the edge of the counter and try to calm my ragged breath. *Who else knows who I am?*

Because if it's not Brutus coming for me, if it's not Brentwood after Mackenzie, if it's not Alec avenging his ruined face and car, then there's one other possibility for who shot at me today.

And it's terrifying.

I can't think about it. Because thinking about it means unlocking a box of memories I wrapped in chains and shoved out into the ocean. That box has sunk so deep that whenever I flit around the edges of what it contains, I willingly bring up the memories of being buried alive – they're more pleasant than what I keep in that box.

Inside that box is my last secret.

There's another person who has seen my face, who knows that Claudia August and Mackenzie Malloy look alike.

Another person who could unravel our entire plan.

And I have no idea who he fucking is.

All I know is the way his fingers pressed into my throat, how his breath panted hot against my ear, and the way his hands slithered like snakes over my body.

Antony watches me as I lean over the counter, as the knife in my hand quivers. He breaks off his call with an abrupt order to his soldier and slides his arms around me. He forces the paring knife from my hand to wrap me in an awkward hug.

We're not exactly the hugging types, Antony and I. Our idea of bonding is gruesome horror films or a knife-throwing session. My cousin's arms were built for pounding people's faces into pulp, not offering tenderness. When he strokes my hair, it jiggles the lock on that box, and I whip the knife from the table and thrust it at his throat.

Antony grabs my wrist, twisting the knife out of my grasp. He's been down this road with me before. He's the only one who knows what's inside that box. "You can't try to stab me every time you think about it, Claws. One of these days you won't miss."

"I know." My hands clench into a fist. "Fuck."

Antony grabs my shoulders, shakes me hard. To anyone watching it might have looked violent, but I need it to push the box into the depths again. "We knew this might become an issue when you moved into the house. But we're so close. The most likely culprit is Brutus or the senator. One of them will show his hand, and we'll slice it off. I promise."

I don't believe him, but I nod.

"I noticed you didn't tell your friends about him. Or about your little adventure in Lazarus' tomb."

I snort. "They just found out I'm not who I said I was. Now's not the time to delight them with the story of my resurrection or..."

Words dry on my tongue. I can't even speak it aloud.

Antony cocks his head and gives me his monstrous smile, the one he uses before he cracks skulls together. "You know you've just made it infinitely more difficult to keep what we're doing here a secret? Before, only two people knew about your true identity, now we've got the whole Scooby Doo gang, and probably Pretty Boy's social media followers if you don't get his shit under control."

"The guys don't know everything. And they won't tell. I'll make sure of it. What can I do?" I ask. "I need to be part of this."

"Nothing. You're still our ticket out of this mess, remember? You're no good to anyone dead." Antony squeezes me one last time, then drops his grip. "First, we need to figure out if it's Brentwood or Brutus behind this."

"Who else can it be?"

The box bobs to the surface again.

"We'll deal with that if it comes up. If we play our hand too soon with the Triumvirate, we could lose more than just the battle. I'll put some men on your friend Alec, in case he wants to cause more trouble, and we'll need a presence at your school."

"So we should keep going to Stonehurst and pretending everything is normal?"

"Right now, Mackenzie Malloy is your biggest ally." Antony gives me a stern, fatherly look. "As long as she's alive and kicking, you're safe."

ANTONY AND TIBERIUS TURN HOWARD MALLOY's office into their war room. They go through every one of Antony's men – the guys he trains at his gym who he recruits to be runners and soldiers for the Triumvirate – and choose three they'll employ to watch the guys and their families. Antony and Tiberius will watch out for me themselves. This means they don't have to bring anyone else into their confidence about my secret. If our muscle connects the guys to Mackenzie Malloy, Antony can just say she hired him to protect her crew. Nothing should get back to the three families about what's really going on here. Antony's grown to be pretty notorious in Tartarus Oaks – no one will dare fuck with him by breaking their oath.

I offer suggestions, but they talk over me like I'm not there. They may be the closest thing I have to family, but they were raised in a criminal underworld where men run the show – they still see me as the king's daughter who needs protecting, a piece to move around the board with no agency of her own.

Daddy prepared me for this. He said my greatest weapon would be people underestimating me, and as long as I'm prepared to be twice as clever and ten times as brutal, I'd triumph over them all.

I get sick of their macho bullshit, pick up Queen Boudica from where she's scratching the hell out of a table leg, and head for the ballroom to blow off steam.

Sunlight streams in through the French doors as I settle Queen Boudica in her cat castle and unfold my knives from their leather pouch. After that night when I was ten, when a shadowed stranger poured hatred into my veins, Antony said he'd help me make sure no man would ever hurt me again. He spent his nights learning to fight at the club and his days at our house teaching me everything he knew about killing. I can throw a decent punch, and I love a good groin kick – as Noah well knows – but I have a particular aptitude for knives.

I love the weight of the cool metal in my hands, the way the blades balance in my fingers, the almost imperceptible slicing sound they make as they cut air. I keep a small arsenal of cheaper knives I use for throwing, and a few precious blades – like the one Antony gave me – that will only be pried from my cold, dead fingers. I've even pulled three swords down from a display in Howard's office and am learning some techniques with them through YouTube videos.

It's a sword I pick up now, feeling the hilt settle into my hand. This is a German double-handed sword, heavy and powerful –

an original purloined from the Hohenzollern family armory and sold to Malloy, quite possibly by my father. It's strange to think the two men who've most defined my life might've met, might even have bonded over their shared love of old crap.

I see so much of Daddy in Howard Malloy that over the years the two of them have become one in my mind. The easiest part of wearing the mantle of Mackenzie's life was believing the evil things her father had done. I've sat in the closet while Daddy hammered a guy's hands to the wall and carved his crime into his stomach. But there was love in Daddy's cruelty – everything he did was to train me to be a ruthless, effective ruler. To honor his legacy. To surpass him.

There was no love on the pages of Mackenzie's diary.

I take up my position on my practice mats. The tutorials online teach different stances – one foot forward, light on your toes so you can move easily in any direction. But I like to begin with my feet turned inwards, my head bowed, my sword-arm limp and lifeless. My greatest weapon is that people believe I'm a helpless little girl. I picture my attacker coming for me, convinced of his victory. I launch into action, swinging the sword up to catch him in the jaw. The heavy blade doesn't slice the air so much as pummels it into submission.

The power behind this swing will crush his jawbone. As he keels forward I step in, slicing the blade to open his belly before winding the weapon back to punch the pommel into his nose. He drops, and I punch the tip of the blade through his ribs, pinning him to the floor as he writhes in his death throes.

I am my father's daughter.

"Nice work."

I don't even think. At the sound of a voice, I flick a blade from inside my wrist and send it flying. Noah yells as he dives for the floor, crashing over Queen Boudica's cat castle as the blade embeds itself in the wall right where his head used to be.

Queen Boudica leaps onto his back and settles down, as if to say she's claiming my kill for herself.

My chest heaves as Noah scrambles to his feet, holding Queen Boudica in his arms. He inspects the knife quivering in the wall. "You tried to kill me."

"Serves you right for sneaking up on a dangerous woman." I shrug, allowing my fingers to loosen their grip on the blade. I'm wound up so tight there's a horror-movie soundtrack of anxiety-inducing violin music playing on constant repeat in my head. "You startled me. I'm not used to having people in my space."

"Clearly." Noah takes in the room again, his eyes appraising all the things I have come to care about in my solitude – my books, my knives, my music, my cat's happiness. Even though the ballroom is literally the size of a football field, when he stands there like that, it feels tiny, like the walls are pressing us together.

Or maybe that's the memory of his cock inside me as I brace myself against the steel of the panic room.

Yeah, could be that.

"What are you doing in here?" I snap. "I thought you were dealing with Eli."

"I locked him in his room. He's ready to bolt, but now he's not going anywhere unless he's eager to scale the side of the house, and he won't risk it in the middle of track season. Eli's dealt with, at least until he successfully Googles a lock-picking tutorial. I came to find you because I..." Noah touches his hair again. "I thought you might want to talk."

I wind the sword through the air a few times. I feel slow, my fingers made of lead. Noah watches me with his intense gaze. "What gave you that idea? We've just spent the last fuck-knows how long talking, and all that happened was Gabe got drunk, you got weird, and Eli hates me."

"I got weird how?"

"Before, when we…" I trail off. I don't know how to talk about this crap. "I just told you I'm an imposter from a crime family trying to steal a house from the first girl you had a crush on. I just gave you all the ammunition you need to destroy me, and you want me to hand you a gun and induct you into the family. That's weird."

"Damn right I want in. Someone *shot* at us." Noah's hands curl into fists. "I'm helpless, and I hate it. The only time I ever felt helpless was when Felix died. He deteriorated so quickly – he took those performance enhancers for a couple of weeks, and suddenly he's in the hospital, slipping in and out of a coma. And then one day he never woke up. When he died, I descended into this void of darkness, and I was just starting to claw my way out when you came back to school and shoved me back down there again."

I cock an eyebrow. "And now?"

He runs his fingers through his hair. "You're not Mackenzie Malloy. You have nothing to do with my brother's death. And like Gabe says, you're intriguing. You're *Claudia*."

He says my name in that dangerous voice of his, edged with sin and shadow. I've opened the door to a world where his desire for revenge is normal, where his ruthlessness is a gift and not a curse, where he can embrace the dark instead of running from it. I can't blame him for wanting more.

Noah's die had been cast a long time ago – the son of a senator bound for college and the life of avarice and cruelty only the rich can imagine. Now I've come along and stomped on the game board, and he has to start to rebuild with the broken pieces left behind. Noah stares at the sword in my hands, and there's a vicious hunger in his eyes that makes my pulse race.

I drop the sword to my side and step towards him. He locks his eyes on me as I close the space between us, stopping only when my chest is inches from his. The sword clatters to the floor, sending chips of marble pinging across the room.

"You think you want to be part of this world." I slide my hand past his ear, trailing my fingers through his curls. Noah's jaw clenches, his coal-black eyes boring into mine as he fights against his better nature. He always has to be in control, but I can see the need in his eyes, can feel it pulling us together. I felt it back in the panic room – that moment when the tension sent his walls tumbling down and the monster inside was unleashed. Now, his monster rears up again, and the beast inside me snarls and snaps her teeth, ready for more. I cup my hand behind his head. I curl my lips back into a smile. "But are you willing to shed blood for it?"

My fingers clasp the handle of the knife. I yank it from the wall behind him. Noah flinches as the blade whips past his ear, and I laugh. I hold the knife over his heart, blade touching his skin. Noah's chest constricts against the metal. But he doesn't look down. He doesn't break my gaze.

"I will bleed for you." His words are a whisper, but they carry all his power. "I'll kill for you. If you keep Eli and Gabriel safe. If you keep Grace safe."

"Your stepmother?" I remember she was sent to the hospital after finding the words I wrote in Noah's bedroom. His muscles tense as he thinks of her – the monster who loves as only a savage heart can, with brutal intensity and wild possession.

Noah nods. The movement draws the blade across his t-shirt, cutting open the fabric and revealing a hint of the skin beneath. A drop of blood rolls down the blade, scenting the air with violence.

"*Claudia,*" Noah whispers.

We snap.

We crash together, a tangle of lips and hands and heat. It's as if something between us has broken open, and now we can't keep our hands off each other. Noah catches my lip between his teeth, biting until I taste blood. I spill his blood and he spills mine. It's filthy and hot as fuck.

My hand holding the knife gets jammed between us. Noah's fingers wrap around my neck, tightening against my skin as he pulls me closer, grinding our bodies together, thrusting his tongue deep because a taste is not enough. I feel something wet slide over my fingers. I pull back slightly and see that I've nicked Noah again. A red line of blood blooms across his shirt.

Noah looks down at the cut with a cool detachment. "You did warn us that you have claws."

I laugh, and he catches my laugh with his lips, swallowing me until I'm his. He walks me backward across the room, his muscled bulk impossible to resist even if I wanted to which, holy Jupiter, no fucking way. He shoves me down into the sofa, rough and commanding. Yes, this is the monster behind those coal-black eyes. This is the beast locked inside Noah's heart-shaped box.

I grip the end of the sofa as he rolls my skirt up. My thighs still ache from what we did in the panic room, but I'm already wet for him, aching to be filled again.

Noah's body presses against mine. He reaches around and pinches my nipple through my shirt. His fingers are bloody from touching his chest. I moan into the sofa cushion as he bites my neck, claiming me as his. I relish the pain, because I know I need it as much as he does. The two of us thrive in pain, we *revel* in it.

"Condom," Noah rasps. I shake my head. I don't have anything on me. I've never had a reason to before.

Noah freezes. I grind against him, begging him with my body. "No point. I already need to get a morning-after pill."

"But—"

"It's my fucking pussy, Marlowe. Don't argue with me."

I need him *now*.

I see the dark side of Noah creeping in as he accepts this command. He thrusts into me, hard and urgent, filling me up until I can't breathe. His hand fists my hair, yanking my head back to expose my neck. I am under his spell, completely help-less as his strong hands hold me in place, his hips thrusting inside me. I love it. I *crave* it.

"Fuck."

A cry reaches my ears, strangled with pain. It's not mine. It's not Noah. But who...

My eyes fly open. Eli stands in the doorway, staring at me like I've grown two heads. His shoulders shake as he takes in the scene – my neck bent back, my naked chest smeared with Noah's blood as he thrusts into me from behind.

Eli's mouth hangs open, but he doesn't speak. The hurt in his eyes rips every last shred of hope from my soul.

"Eli, wait—" I manage to choke out, my voice still heavy with lust.

Eli lets out a strangled sob, turns on his heel, and storms away. And this time, I know he's gone for good.

5

—————

ELI

I make a beeline for the garage and the secret entrance. Not-Mackenzie runs after me, crashing into the walls and knocking over weird statues as she tries to pull her clothes on. She grabs my shoulder, but I shrug her off. She reeks of Noah. She cries my name, and her voice stirs this desperate need inside me that makes me seethe with hatred.

I hate her.

I hate Noah.

I hate myself.

I jog through the cars and hit the spiral staircase leading down into the tunnel. As my hand closes around the balustrade, something hooks around my foot. An arm flings across my chest and my foot is knocked out from beneath me. I go down in a tangle of limbs. My knee hits the metal railing. My tailbone crunches against the concrete.

Not-Mackenzie is on top of me, straddling me, pinning my arms. The ends of her hair tickle my skin. Everywhere she touches me burns. "Eli, listen to me. You can't leave."

"Get the fuck off me." I rock my hips and roll her over. She tries to pin me between her thighs, wrapping her legs around my back and pulling me closer. She's stronger than I expect, but then, I shouldn't be surprised. I never knew her at all.

My body doesn't know what to do with itself. I've spent every night since she returned to school dreaming about being this close to her. My dick's hard and my eyes swell with tears. In my dreams, she didn't have Noah's cum dribbling down her legs.

She was mine.

My Mackenzie.

I shove her off and run for the stairs. She's behind me, but she doesn't run track. In the tunnel, I quickly gain a lead on her. I slam through the outer door and run through the woods toward my car.

I fumble in my pocket for the key fob. Not-Mackenzie's hands slam against the window. "Eli, wait." Her fists pummel the glass. "I know you're pissed at me, but you're putting your life in danger. Don't go home yet. Just stay and we'll—"

I slam my foot down and roar away. I don't look back. If I see her face – familiar and completely alien to me – I won't be able to control what I do next.

I don't go home. I head out of the city to the place I'd been hiding for the last few nights, ever since I saw Mackenzie with Gabriel. I spent the last three days wishing what I saw hadn't been real.

Be careful what you wish for.

Nothing is real.

Mackenzie's playlist blasts out my speakers. Kurt Cobain sings of claustrophobia and suffocation. The lyrics have never punched me in the gut the way they do today. Emerald Beach feels too small, too shallow to hold all the rage I need to scream into the sky.

Only when I pull into the gates of the Everlasting Hart Ranch does my jaw unclench. Only then do I open my mouth and let the screams out.

I howl and curse and rage as I careen up the uneven drive and jerk to a stop in front of the homestead. This place was Dad's vanity project. Back in Tennessee he always dreamed of owning a ranch. Dad had a lot of dreams everyone called stupid, but he made them all come true – he moved our family to Emerald Beach. He grew the humble funeral home he inherited from his father into a multi-million-dollar death empire, he got on TV, he bought a football team. Dad used the proceeds from the reality show to buy this land – two hundred acres of rolling hills and crumbling outbuildings an hour outside of Emerald Beach. He commissioned an architect to redesign the homestead as luxury accommodation. He'd even been in discussions with the TV executives about a new series following his attempts to do up the ranch and offer overpriced cowboy experiences to Emerald Beach's ultra-rich.

Since he's been in prison, the place has gone to ruin. The construction crew left, the network ghosted him, the ranch-hands he hired moved on. The two racehorses he purchased have either died in a paddock somewhere or run off to literal greener pastures. Mom doesn't care about the ranch, and the land has devalued so much she can't sell it. The homestead at the top of the driveway is over a hundred years old and slowly returning to the land – roof tiles blown off during the last storm litter the ground, and much of the siding is rotted away. Weeds choke the flowerbeds around the porch, and the unforgiving landscape looms on all sides, harsh and unwelcoming, making me feel impossibly small. This wild place is such a contrast to our perfectly manicured lives in Emerald Beach – that's probably why I like it so much.

Out here, I don't have to pretend I've got it all together.

I don't have to be Eli Hart, the Golden Boy of Stonehurst Prep, the son of a celebrity undertaker-turned criminal.

Out here, it's okay to scream.

I crack the car door and collapse against the steering wheel. My lungs hurt. I suck in breaths until I feel lightheaded, then swing a leg out onto the weed-choked driveway.

The house greets me with a silent smile – twin dormer windows in the attic like friendly eyes seeing me without judgment. There's no electricity, no amenities. Just me and my thoughts.

As soon as I climb the rotting porch steps and push open the door, Gizmo bounds from the shadows, protesting loudly that I'd abandoned her. She wraps herself around my legs as I prop the front door open with a large rock.

I hold Gizmo against my chest, letting her jet-engine purr calm my shaking limbs. I head into the house and straight to the root cellar underneath the kitchen, where the last tenants stored their cider. Gabriel isn't the only one who can obliterate his pain with booze.

I grab two demijohns of cider and head back outside, collapsing into the porch swing. It creaks in protest. Gizmo sits next to me and stares reproachfully at the bottle in my hands.

"I saw you eat a dried horse turd out of the grass yesterday. You don't get to judge," I growl as I pull off the stopper and take a deep swig. And another. And another.

But the more I drink, the more I see the image of Mackenzie's neck bent back, her pink lips gasping with ecstasy as Noah plowed into her. Instead of fading into a booze-soaked haze, the memory sharpens into a living nightmare – her face contorting to become a pig, a laughing clown, a tentacled monster, his dick transforming into a giant Viking sword, splattering blood across the walls with every thrust.

Mackenzie isn't back from the dead. Mackenzie is still missing. The girl I've been falling for... everything about her is a lie.

6

CLAUDIA

*W*e eat dinner in the formal dining hall, in what might be the weirdest meal I'd ever had in Malloy Manor. Gabriel lights candles in silver holders and Antony helps me carry out platters of salmon steaks and couscous and a tossed salad. I sit at the head of the table, in the only chair with a carved back and padded arms. On one side, two bloodthirsty cage fighters who've sworn to protect me. On the other side, the rockstar and the bad boy who hold my heart in their hands.

We eat in tense silence, the truth hanging between us a pendulum dropping ever closer.

If Eli were here, he'd be trying to make conversation, to smooth over the tension. But Eli isn't here, and even though my thighs ache from having Noah's cock between them twice today, there's a hole in my chest that only the Golden Boy of Stonehurst Prep can fill.

I know I'm being ridiculous. I have more important things to think about than Eli, like figuring out who wants me dead. But I remember him sitting on the wall outside, watching the house. Watching me. Protecting me.

The only person who's ever protected me before was Antony. Daddy liked to pretend he was protecting me, but he also knew I needed to be strong. He sharpened my mind but he also cut me off from anyone getting close.

I never knew what it meant to have a friend. When I stepped into Mackenzie's life, I thought she was like me – that she'd locked herself away from other people to keep her heart safe. And then I met Eli and I saw that even an Ice Queen could be cherished. I hate myself for my weakness, but I wanted some of that. Just for a moment, it was nice to pretend I deserved to be loved.

The moment's over.

But I can't undo the last six weeks. I'm new to caring about people. I didn't realize it would be like this – this crushing weight on my chest at the thought of losing them.

I want Eli back. Back in Malloy Manor, where we can protect him. And back in my life. In my arms. Back believing the sun shines out of my ass.

It's a pointless, hopeless dream, and that's why it sticks in my throat. Eli's safer if he stays away from me, and now he'll never speak to me again. Mission accomplished. Game over.

I've been reckless. And greedy. Eli won't be the last casualty of my secret heart. I have Gabriel and Noah, and that should be enough. Gabriel's made it clear he doesn't care who I sleep with or what I do, except that I see him watching Noah across the table with a new wariness. Gabe thinks he's been subtle, but he's had too much to drink and subtle isn't exactly his middle name. For all his jokes, he's not happy with what he sees between Noah and me.

I don't believe it's possible, but I might've stripped back the corner of Gabriel's mask to reveal the raw, broken flesh beneath.

And Noah… it's as if my secret has flicked a switch inside him, and all that hate directed at me has exploded outward at the world. Gabe might've been the first person to scrub off a layer of my Ice Queen facade, but everything about him is glamorous and celestial. Whereas Noah is my own darkness reflected back at me – bloody and monstrous and real.

He's been bound by the chains of his grief, his desire to fit into the life laid out for him. But when he whispers my name – my *real* name – he casts off those pieces of his old life and welcomes my legacy with open arms.

I don't want that for him, especially not since our whole plan is focused on getting both me and Antony *out* of the family business. But I can't stop Noah falling into the void. I could use a little company down here in the dark and cold.

Only, I know he's not as simple as that. When we fucked in the panic room, Noah believed I was Mackenzie. I was the person he hated most in the world, and he buried his dick inside me and he made me come and he—

How did my life get so fucking complicated?

After dinner, Gabriel catches my arm as I head to my room. "You slept with Marlowe," he cocks his eyebrow at me. His eyes are pure starlight – as if his body is made of the same magic as his music.

"Very astute." He's more coherent than he was a few hours ago, but the alcoholic haze swims in the corners of his eyes. "I've never seen you drunk before."

Gabe giggles. He sounds maniacal, like a creepy clown. "No, you haven't. Because here's the thing you don't know about me, Claudia. Here's my big secret that I've been oh so good at keeping, just like you. I haven't touched alcohol since Dylan died."

That doesn't make sense. "I've seen you drink. You had rainbow cocktails at Midnight Grotto, and those gross pink things at Daphne's party."

"The bartender at Midnight Grotto knows to only serve me non-alcoholic drinks. As for the pink thing, I dumped it onto

Chad's head when you weren't looking." Gabriel grins. "It was a much better use for the disgusting thing. What a travesty to the art of mixology."

That gets a little snort of laughter out of me. "So why haven't you been drinking? And what does that have to do with you being drunk *now*?"

Why do I remind you of your dead best friend?

"I spent so much of my last tour plastered off my face that I didn't see what was happening to Dylan until it was too late. I could have saved him. I could have... been a friend. But I don't know a thing about friendship. So consider this your warning. All my life, people pretend to care about me because they want something from me, and sometimes I can't face the loneliness. Alcohol is like this shield between me and the world, except that it also shielded me from the one person who tried to love me for myself. I tried to be good. I tried to live with the loneliness, because I owe Dylan that. I fucking *owe* him..." Gabriel lurches forward, slamming his hand into the wall to catch himself before he knocks me over.

"Gabe..." I squeeze my eyes shut. It's hard to look at him like this. That's the most honest thing he's said to me since we met, and he's *drunk*. We can't do this now when he's like this. It's not fair on either of us.

"No, you have to hear this. You have to..." Gabe's voice rises. He sounds panicked. "When you walked into school that first day, I saw... okay, so I saw your shaggable arse, but also, there's this defiance in your eyes. You were staring into the same abyss I face every single day, only it doesn't scare you. You *welcome* it. I wanted to know what that was like, to have that kind of strength."

I try to say something, but Gabriel holds a finger against my lips. His skin burns mine, and the starlight in his eyes takes on an ethereal translucency. Behind it is Gabriel's soul – beautiful and weeping and made of scar tissue. "We never talked about what the Midnight Grotto was. About what it meant to you. And now you're sleeping with Marlowe. Is it because I didn't—"

I shake my head. "Gabe, it's okay. We never said anything about being exclusive. I'm not under any illusions about what that night at the grotto meant. It was sex. It doesn't have to be anything more."

"But you want it to be something more," he purrs. His hand brushes my nipple, and my breath hitches as he draws me into that dark and delicious magic he weaves oh so well.

"I know the score. You're a rockstar. You go on tour and—"

"That wasn't the question." His voice takes on this dangerous edge that sets my body on fire. My nipple hardens under his touch.

"I—"

"What I'm trying to say, Claudia, is that I don't care if you want to jump up and down on Marlowe's cock." Gabriel tries to smile, but it's all wobbly and broken. "I've heard it's a magnificent specimen. I wouldn't mind a go myself if I were that way inclined. I know I'm not enough for you, that Marlowe gives you something I can't. Eli too, if he pulls his head out his arse long enough to admit his feelings. That doesn't bother me, because I know for one night I held you in my arms and saw the stars reflected in your eyes. I want you to know that as of right now, the ladies of Emerald Beach are weeping because Gabriel Fallen is officially off the market. As far as I'm concerned, you're more than enough for me."

Well... fuck.

I can't deal with this.

I can't deal with Gabriel Fallen pouring out his messy, broken soul when I'm already so raw and broken myself.

He leans in, tucking his finger under my chin to tilt my head up. I fall into his scarred soul as his lips brush mine in a kiss that tastes of starlight and raindrops, of hope and regret. It's a kiss that forms a hard lump in my throat even as it melts my body into a puddle.

It takes everything I have to break that kiss and back away from Gabriel. The magic that draws us together sings between our bodies – a song that plucks our secrets from the very air. Tonight, I didn't need kisses. I want to be held, to believe that I can have happiness even though I'm a fraud. But I can't show that weakness, not after all three boys have already stripped me bare of my armor. So I swallow and say, "I need to be alone tonight."

"Claudia—"

Before I say something I'll regret, before the tears stinging my eyes threaten to fall, I rip myself from the arms of a fallen angel and flee to my room. I lock my door behind me.

GABRIEL

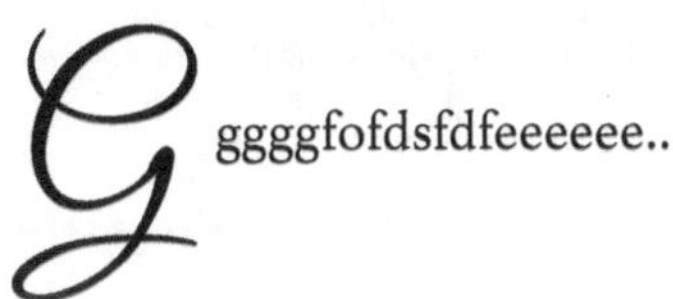

Ggggfofdsfdfeeeeee...

BED IS SQUISHY.

VODKA IS LOVELY.

MAC IS CLAUDIA.

CLAUDIA IS EVERYTHINGGG...

MY HEAD HURTS.

CLAUDIA

I don't sleep. The house is alive with sounds – doors closing, beds creaking, male voices murmuring and breathing in their sleep. I'm not sure which sounds I could truly hear and which were born from my imagination and the raw, needy ache between my legs. All I know is that Malloy Manor would never be silent again.

For so many years I've tried to fill these walls with noise to drive away my loneliness. I've played music at top volume. I've watched every horror film ever made. Sometimes I've screamed until my throat bled. After a while, even the most beautiful song is just empty notes against a cold, lifeless house.

Now that the noise has found me, I'm not sure I'm ready.

When my clock ticks over to 5:32AM, I decide I can no longer abide staying in bed. I pad to the kitchen, Queen Boudica circling my ankles. I put down her food and start the coffee machine. When it's done, I carry my cup to the ballroom.

As my bare feet pad across the cold marble, a dark shape moves at the window. I freeze, my fingers tightening around the handle of my cup. Like a fool, I left my knife on my bedside table. The intruder doesn't look like he's seen me yet. I can throw the hot coffee in his face and then try and get to my knives—

A lamp clicks on, illuminating two faces reclining in the seats at the window, a chessboard open between them. Noah slouches on the sofa, while Gabriel sits on an ottoman, gripping his head with his hands.

"What is it with the two of you sneaking around?" I growl. "One of you is going to end up with a knife in the throat if you're not careful."

"Sorry, Claws." Gabriel smiles, but there's a sadness behind that smile. "I couldn't sleep."

He holds out his palm, and I see that he's holding the broken pieces of my locket. My stomach twists. I stare at the chess game – Noah had set up a classic skewer and pin and placed Gabriel's white king in checkmate before he even knew what hit him.

Noah might be a pampered rich boy, but he understands something of the art of war. I wonder if that's why he hasn't run from me.

And Gabriel... when I look at him again, I see the fallen angel wrestling with his fractured soul. I think of what he said last night, that he sees a strength in me that I never knew existed. I wish I could give some of that strength to him, so he can confront whatever happened with Dylan that has him so tied in knots.

I sit down opposite them. "I don't say this lightly, so don't make me repeat it again. I'm sorry I got you involved in this. I don't want either of you to be hurt. I didn't want to hurt Eli either – at a certain point, it just became inevitable."

Gabriel drops the locket on the table. The CLANG of metal hitting glass ricochets against my skull like a gunshot. I swipe out my hand to collect the pieces, my secret may be out, but I may still need what that locket contains. "Tell us about your parents," he says. "Your *real* parents."

"What's there to tell? My father could snap his fingers and order someone's death. He was soft-spoken, never raised his voice, always had a smile and a joke, but behind that smile was a ruthless streak that made your knees shake. He was obsessed with history – he could trace our family back to the Roman Empire. Our house in Tartarus Oaks was filled with artifacts he purchased on the black market – a bust of Caesar from a dig in Germany, amphorae drawn up from a Mediterranean ship-wreck, drawers and drawers filled with coins and knives. He made sure I had every toy or pretty dress I could possibly want, but I was never allowed the thing I wanted most – a friend. He knew that I was his biggest weakness, and he didn't want me to ever feel weak. He hired tutors so I didn't have to attend school, but he taught me history himself. He made Julius Caesar and Marc Antony and Augustus so real to me that I imagined they were my friends, instead." I smile. "Ms. Drysdale's class has made me see how it's a warped view of history."

"And your mom?"

I shrug. "She was a good crime lord's wife – arm candy in her designer dresses and perfect hair, seen and not heard, but behind the scenes I know she influenced many of his decisions. They would sit beside the fire, sharing a bottle of wine while I read books or drew pictures, talking in low voices about the family business. She brought me books on every subject that interested me. She let me destroy the kitchen trying to make weird delicacies from ancient recipes. She loved to dance – when Daddy was out of the house, she'd put on records and teach me moves. Every weekend they'd leave me in Antony's care and head out to one of their clubs together – the king in his impeccable Armani suit, the queen glittering in precious ancient jewels." I grip the pieces of the locket so tight in my fist the broken edge cuts into my skin. I can't bear their memories being put on display and dissected like this. They were my jailers and I loved them. I love them still. How fucked-up is that? I glare at Gabriel, desperate to change the subject. "What about *your* parents?"

"You forget, I've seen the posters in your room and the stickers on your notebook. You know my story."

I do know his story. At least, what truths Gabriel offers up to the gutter press alongside his carefully-constructed facade. I know his parents are rich and titled, and they publicly disowned Gabriel when he left to pursue his music. I know his surname – Fallen – isn't the name he was born to, but the name he chose to mark his own path in life.

Gabriel. The fallen angel. The dark prince who tries so hard to be good.

I turn to Noah. "What about you?"

Noah shakes his head. "When my father looks at me, all he sees is the son he wishes died in Felix's place."

He speaks in a flat voice, like he's discussing the weather instead of his father's neglect. Noah accepts it as true that he's a consolation prize, but I will never, ever accept that. I don't offer up the platitudes that dance on my tongue. I know how useless they are.

"My father was determined that Felix would be his legacy, his greater achievement. Neither of us was a person to Dad – we're just extensions of his own ambition, and I've always disappointed him. He honestly believed Felix would be president one day, and I can't compete with that. Felix couldn't help being everything Dad wanted, and that made it impossible to hate him – he was the only thing that made living in that house bearable. Felix would never have taken those drugs if Dad hadn't insisted, if he hadn't tried to give his son yet another advantage."

"Was your mom on board with this?"

Noah shakes his head. "Mom tried to speak up, to say she didn't think he should be taking something that hadn't been through proper medical trials. But Dad never listened to anyone. And Felix just went along with it because it made Dad happy. We've spent our whole lives making sacrifices and hiding who we are to make Dad happy, and in the end, it killed the two people I loved most in the world. Now I couldn't give a fuck about Dad's happiness, but in his rage and guilt he can't see that he's killing Grace, too."

"And me." I say it flippantly, but my heart slams against my chest. I hate how much I want him to say that he cares for me with that fierce protectiveness he feels for his stepmother.

Noah's gaze flicks to the empty pool outside, and I know he's thinking of his mother lying in the water, the brick still tied around her ankle. He sinks into the chair, his head falling forward into his hands, dark hair tumbling over his eyes. "If that Brentwood guy doesn't kill you, Dad will find someone else. He's used to getting his way."

"So am I."

Noah lifts his head, his voice cracking. "Claudia, I—"

I cut him off. "I should find something for breakfast."

I flee the ballroom as fast as I can. I don't look back. How can I tell Noah that if his dad is determined to kill me, then I might just have to beat him to the punch?

9

ELI

I sit out on the porch swing, Gizmo in my lap and a dusty bottle of homemade cider from the cellar in my hand. I drink and rage into the nighttime, falling in and out of consciousness until the sun peeks over the horizon.

I consider hiding at Everlasting Hart Ranch forever. I have Gizmo in my lap and enough money in my wallet for a few weeks of food and supplies. No one will miss me. I can drink my way through the cider in the cellar until my skin turns green and I melt into the landscape.

Until I forgot Mackenzie Malloy – the girl I loved who left without a goodbye – and Claudia August – the bitch who stomped my memories into dust.

Gizmo leaps off my lap and bounds toward the outbuildings scattered along the edge of the field behind the shed. There's a big red barn filled with rusting farm equipment, and a bunch of smaller workshops and a tack room for the horses my dad never got to ride. Gizmo wiggles her tiny bum and disappears through a hole in one of the rotting wood boards of the stable block. *She's probably stalking mice, reveling in being a country cat.*

I watch, my eyes swimming and unable to focus, but she

doesn't pop out again the way she usually does. I call out to her. No reply. I debate staggering over to the barn to bring her back when a car pulls down the drive.

At first, I assume it's Noah. I toss the empty cider bottle into the driveway, where it shatters across the gravel. I debate picking up one of the jagged shards of glass, but instead, I curl my hands into fists, ready for a fight. He's not allowed to be here, not after he chose her over me.

As the vehicle nears, I see it's Maria's battered old Honda. My mother begrudgingly pays her a decent wage to keep our house and cook for us (I make sure of that), but Maria doesn't believe in flashy vehicles. She's been driving this same car since we hired her, way back when we first moved to Emerald Beach.

The car narrowly misses the broken glass as it shudders to a stop next to mine. Maria climbs out and runs toward me. I try to rise to meet her, but I forget how much cider I drank. My feet slide in opposite directions and I turn into a jellyfish.

Maria leaps onto the porch and catches me in her arms before I can faceplant into the garden bed. She settles me back onto the swing. I slur, "Thankoo—"

She slaps my cheek.

Either she deliberately pulls her strength or I'm even drunker than I think, because I don't feel it.

"You rotten weasel," she scolds. "I have been so worried. You haven't been home since Friday morning. The school called to say you weren't in class today. I thought maybe you were with your friends, but you are wrong to make me worry."

The way she says it, with a smile in her voice, I know she's really asking if I was seeing a girl. I stare at my hands, wishing they were holding a demijohn of cider. I can't find the words to answer her.

"This isn't like you, Elias Hart, hiding away out here." The swing creaks as she settles in beside me. I resist the urge to lay down with my head in her lap, the way I'd done as a kid when I needed her to soothe the nightmares away. "You haven't showered in days. You smell delightful, did you know that?"

Maria has been part of my life since my earliest memories. She's more a parent to me than Walter or Darlene Hart could ever hope to be. As a kid, I was terrified of my father's job and all the symbols of death that follow our family. Around every corner I imagined restless spirits coming after me. Every minute of every day I worried Death would take the people I loved away from me. It got even worse after I met Mackenzie and saw how even someone as strong as her could be felled by cruelty. When the phone rang in our house, I was certain it was the cops to say Howard Malloy had finally taken his punishments too far. Although why they'd call a ten-year-old boy who was hiding his friendship from the world I didn't know.

Dad called me a sissy. Mom was too busy. Maria held me and sat with me at night and even used some of her own money to drag me to a therapist after Mackenzie disappeared. It didn't help – I wasn't ready to talk or heal, but I'll never, ever forget that she was the one who tried to help me.

As I got older, we've been more like friends, but I can hear the mothering tone creeping back into her voice. "I've been worried about you, Elias."

Claudia's secret dances on my tongue. I desperately want to blurt out the whole sordid story. Something stops me, some tug deep inside my chest that says I need to stay quiet, that carrying this secret alone will keep Maria safe.

"I can't talk about it," I growl into my armpit.

She pats my arm. "It must be a girl. Only a girl can string you out like this. Don't worry, you tell me when you're ready. I'll fetch you a glass of water."

"I don't want water." I want Mackenzie back. I want my father to not be a criminal. I want this nightmare to end.

"Elias Hart. You are drunk. You don't know what you want. I'm here to look after you." She steps into the house, returning a few minutes later with a tall glass of water. I take it and sip. It's heaven on my raw throat.

"Have you moved things around in the kitchen?" she asks. "I was trying to find the saucepan to make you some pancakes, but it seems to have disappeared."

I nod to the broken shards of the demijohn on the driveway. "I don't know. Probably. How can you make pancakes in that kitchen, anyway? The mice probably got into the flour in the cellar."

"I have supplies in the car." She winks. "I know if my Elias is sad about a girl, he needs pancakes."

Pancakes are our comfort food, our secret code. We used to make them together whenever one of us felt sad. Once, I brought Mackenzie around to our place and Maria showed her how to measure the ingredients and flip the pancakes in the frying pan. Mackenzie had never cooked a thing in her life, and she got so frustrated that her pancakes didn't flip that she threw the pan on the floor and smashed the handle. Afterward, when she calmed down, we ate the pancakes Maria cooked smothered in chocolate chips and syrup, and Mackenzie gave me a sticky kiss on the cheek and said I was her best friend.

That's why I made pancakes for Mackenzie at Gabriel's after Noah and I rescued her from the desert. I thought it might help her remember something good and sweet and happy. But you can't remember something when you're living a lie.

"How did you know I was here?" I ask. She'd never come out to the ranch since it had become a ruin – yet another one of Dad's grand plans that has crumbled to dust.

"This is where you go when you're upset. I followed you out here years ago – I needed to know where you were slipping off to for days at a time."

I wince at my stupidity. Of course, Maria would keep an eye on me, make sure I was safe.

Maria folds her arms. "Don't look at me like that. I wouldn't have come if it wasn't important. I know teenage boys need their privacy. I actually thought you might've brought your girl out here."

"Why did you come?"

"Your mother wanted me to find you. She tells me you must be home for dinner tomorrow night. She says she has something to announce."

I rub my head. The last thing I want is to play happy family with my mother across the dinner table. "I plan to not be hungry that night."

Maria shoots me that look of hers, the one that never failed to get me to pick up my toys or finish my homework. "It's not a matter of being hungry. She's your mother."

I stare out across the broken landscape of my father's dream, at fences pushed over, construction materials half-buried in weeds, bare patches where the pasture hadn't been cared for. Beyond all that is the harsh, alien landscape of the desert. Gizmo's face appears around the corner of the barn. She meows at me before turning tail and trotting back inside, as if asking me to come and see what she's found. Out here, with the fresh air and the desert heat bearing down, it's almost possible to believe Emerald Beach doesn't exist, and all my problems are a dream. But Emerald Beach has a way of finding you, and I have lived experience of just how quickly a dream can transform into a nightmare.

10

NOAH

We decide to skip school for a couple of days. Antony needs to prepare protection for Claudia at Stonehurst. Normally, I'd be concerned about falling behind, but I can't muster up a fuck to give. Now that I've had actual bullets whiz past my face, I struggle to see the importance of algebra.

I call in and pretend to be Gabriel's manager needing the rockstar for an urgent meeting, then I hang up and call back, using a deeper voice to impersonate my father saying that I'm taking my son to the office for 'work experience.' I can't believe this shit flies, but you can get away with a lot when your daddy is a senator.

Claudia calls and claims she's ill. The secretary insists she'll need to show a doctor's note when she returns to school. I tell her not to bother – it's an empty threat. The staff knows the students hold all the power.

We eat breakfast in tense silence. I see the clues to Claudia's existence hidden in plain sight – packages of Pop-Tarts and cheap cereal bars lined up on the counter, seasoning and sauce packets stolen from school, cans of beans and minestrone soup stacked in the walk-in. Food Mackenzie Malloy never would have touched. Queen Boudica's food, however, is an expensive organic brand. Gabriel makes a face when he bites into his cereal bar, and goes to dump the rest in the trash. Wordlessly, Claudia grabs it from his hand and finishes it. I guess when you're paying property taxes on a Harrington Hills mansion on a waitress' wage you get used to saving food.

I remember seeing her with her plate piled high in the dining hall – unusual for a girl at a school where everyone is obsessed with looks and health food. Yet another piece of the mystery of Mackenzie Malloy that falls into place, even if it leaves more questions in her wake.

I thought I had the measure of this girl, but Claudia August defies explanation.

Antony enters, pulling on his suit jacket. "I need to get back to Tartarus Oaks and start digging around." He swipes a cereal bar on his way out.

No, you don't, I want to say. *I know my father is behind this. I know because those bullets weren't just meant for Claudia. I'm worth more to him dead than alive.*

I don't say a thing. Claudia's cousin makes me uneasy. There's a hardness in his eyes when he looks at me and Gabriel, like we're here specifically to fuck up his plans.

And there's another reason.

He hasn't recognized me, but I knew his face the moment he stormed into Malloy Manor. He hasn't put it together yet because I was so careful, but I don't know how long I have until he figures it out.

I don't know what will happen when he does.

Claudia's not the only one with a secret that can get her killed.

I watch her kiss her cousin's cheek. Her fingers slide over his lapels, touching the edge of the gun he keeps there. She stiffens.

I wonder if she knows just how powerful Antony is in this city, just what exactly he does for the family business.

After Antony leaves, Claudia goes to her room to brush her teeth, and Gabriel wanders back to the ballroom. I stack the dishwasher, then head deeper into the house to find Claudia. She doesn't answer when I knock on her door, but Queen Boudica tears past me down the hallway and somersaults around a corner. I follow her.

As I wander the hallway, I pass photographs of the Malloys. There's an age gap between thirteen-year-old Mackenzie frowning in her family portrait and the girl I fucked in a panic room, but they really do look similar. That same slight nose, heart-shaped face, and intense ice eyes. The same hair that looks like strands of spun gold, although Claudia could be dying hers. The same defiance burning behind their eyes.

"Meow." Queen Boudica drops to the floor at the door to Howard Malloy's study, rolling over to expose her stomach. I bend down and rub her gingerly, unsure if she'll continue to purr with happiness or if she'll attack my hand. Something bounces on the rug beside me.

A pair of fluffy balls on a string, tied to a stick. A cat toy – an appropriate one if you consider that the girl has spent the last few weeks jerking a string around our balls so all three of us would dance for her amusement.

"She likes it if you wave that around," Mackenzie calls from behind the desk.

Not Mackenzie. *Claudia.* I rub my temple. They really do look a lot alike, at least based on my memories of Mackenzie. This is one serious mindfuck. I stand up and wiggle the balls around. Queen Boudica launches herself from the floor and somersaults through the air to grab them. She rolls onto her back and attacks the balls with claws and teeth.

"This is a very suggestive toy." My own balls twinge with

secondhand anxiety as the cat sinks her claws deeper. Claudia nods, but her attention is focused on her battered old phone with the sparkly case – the one I remember Mackenzie using in second grade. Claudia must've found it in Mackenzie's room. I'm surprised she's managed to keep an iPhone running for so many years, although judging by the way she bangs it on the desk and swears at it, she's losing the battle.

Claudia tosses the phone at the wall in disgust. "I hate this. I hate sitting here doing nothing. We should find Eli."

"I know where he is."

"Enlighten me." She leans across the desk, knitting her fingers together and managing to look both stern and desperate. *Fuck, she's stunning.* My mind goes to a bad place, where I bend her over the desk, my fingers curling around her hair as I pound into her—

I shake my head, trying to force aside all the bad things I was thinking before I acted on my filthy instincts and turned this conversation into a porn film. "Fuck no. Eli needs to be alone right now. He's safe where he is."

"How do you know?" Her eyes flicker with concern. "Whoever shot at us knocked out Tiberius, and you've seen that guy – he's terrifying. All they have to do is follow Eli to wherever he's gone and riddle him with bullets."

The image of it turns my stomach, but I'm not giving up Eli's secret, not after everything he's already lived through this week. My gut churns with guilt. For three days I sat on that swing while Eli poured cider down his throat and spilled his heart into the desert sands, hating myself because I woke up each night with soaked sheets after dreaming of the girl I was supposed to hate. Eli's girl – Mackenzie Malloy who'd had his heart and cock in a vise since he was eight years old.

Now Eli knows the truth. He knows that all this time when I was pretending to be his friend that I thought about nothing else but tasting the secrets of her blush-pink lips. It doesn't matter that she's not Mackenzie – it matters that Eli is my friend, and I fucked him over.

Thinking about Eli's hurt expression when he walked in on Claudia and I makes my dick go soft. I wander around the office, peering at the objects decorating the shelves and the leather-bound books on history and economics. My foot brushes a box on the floor, shoved into the corner behind a chair. It looks as though Queen Boudica has chewed the corner of it. "What's this?"

She shrugs. "Malloy had that hidden in the panic room. I tossed it over there because it was taking up space. It's just a bunch of business papers and shit. I don't understand any of it."

Curious, I flip through the papers. The police searched his office as part of their investigation into Felix's death. They found all his paperwork in order and made no mention of a secret panic room. I wonder if he'd shoved this box inside to hide its contents. The thought drives me to look harder at the papers.

They seem to be mostly related to the Malloy Supplements laboratory in Brawley, reports from his team about testing new products, FDA paperwork, labeling requirements...

A word leaps out at me. *John Marlowe*. My father's name.

I pull out the stapled pages and study them – it's a copy of a contract between my father and Howard Malloy. My father was offering a large sum of money – greater than the amount he'd placed in my trust fund – to secure a shipment of something called 'deer antler velvet' from a New Zealand supplier. It's dated eight months before Felix's death.

The contract is stapled to a series of lab reports and test results. I flip through them, jumping between the tables and pie charts. According to the report, this antler velvet – the soft fuzz that covers the bone and cartilage of a deer's antler as it develops – is used in some traditional medicines. But in high quantities, it has benefits as a performance enhancer and to improve endurance. The report calls the antler velvet a possible 'miracle' drug for athletes but warns that it contains high levels of a particular hormone that could cause harmful side effects and would need further testing.

I've never seen this before. It's completely different from the evidence presented in court. No one ever mentioned deer antler velvet. As I read more and the picture emerges, my veins heat with rage.

That *bastard.*

"Noah?" Claudia moves around the desk. Her hand lands on my shoulder, sending a shockwave through my body. I clench the paper so hard I tear a hole in it.

"I'm going to kill him," I choke out.

"Who?" Claudia whips the paper from my hands. Her eyes widen as she reads, understanding dawning in her icicle eyes. "Shit, Noah. This is about your brother."

"I'm going to wrap my hands around his neck and choke the life out of him," I growl.

"Noah, what's going on?"

"Howard Malloy designed the drug that killed my brother." My whole body shakes with the need to destroy him, to tear his flesh from his bones, to make him feel the pain I'd lived in ever since Felix died. "And my father paid for it. He *funded* it. And when it went wrong, he and Malloy worked together to cover it up."

CLAUDIA

$\mathcal{I}$ stare at the paper in Noah's trembling hand. John Marlowe funded the production of the drug that killed his own son?

That's *insane.*

It makes no sense. What about the very ugly, very *public* court case? Malloy Supplements had the best lawyers in the business – why didn't they just bring up Marlowe's involvement from the onset? Why was he keeping these papers hidden away... unless it was in Howard Malloy's interest *not* to have Senator Marlowe's involvement known. But if they were working together, why would Marlowe hire Brentwood to have Howard and his family killed?

The lab reports leave a big, fat question mark over the entire affair. I feel untethered, lost in the sense that Malloy Manor is working to unravel the secrets Howard built around himself, the secrets that had kept me safe as his child ghost.

This is beyond my ability to puzzle out, and it's not something I can call Antony to get answers from the underground. No, this needs Eli Hart and his Sherlock Holmes orgasm face, Eli who always has the uncanny ability to look right through a problem and see into the messy, broken heart of it. From the way Noah's poring over the papers with an obsessive film over his eyes, I know he's thinking the same thing.

But Eli isn't here, and I've got a dangerously deteriorating Noah Marlowe on my hands. As Noah rereads those lab reports in Howard Malloy's secret box, I see my own madness reflected in him – he needs an outlet for his rage or it will consume him.

Even though I'm curious about what it all means, I know this isn't time for puzzling. I drag Noah into the ballroom and toss a sword at him.

"Go on." I heft my own sword and face him, my feet spread, my fingers loose, feeling the weight of the weapon. "Raise your sword."

"I'm not going to fight you, Claudia." Noah manages to sound both derisive and faintly amused.

"Suit yourself." I swing my sword at his head, not holding anything back. Noah yells as he ducks, throwing his weapon in the air to meet mine with a *CLANG*. He's caught me on the wrong part of the blade, and the momentum throws off his balance. His boot catches the edge of the coffee table, and he staggers backward. I wind against his blade and bring my pommel up, slamming it into his cheek.

"Jesus fuck!" Noah yells as he throws his sword down and grabs his face. "You're *crazy*. That fucking hurt. You could have taken off my head with that blade."

"Damn right. You want to play in my world? You want to sit around in my house and talk about killing your father and getting revenge for your brother? Then grow some testicles. It's all words. It means jack shit unless you're willing to draw blood for your convictions." I flick a knife from my wrist. "You don't know what we're up against, or what it's going to take to bring them down."

His hands ball into fists. "You know nothing about me."

"Then surprise me, Marlowe." I tap the tip of my sword against my toe. "On your feet."

Noah drags himself upright, but he doesn't pick up his sword. He folds his arms across his chest and glares at me with that powerful rage curling. "I'm not fighting you."

"Why not?" I jeer, tossing aside my own sword and moving closer, fists raised. I throw a punch at his head, but he ducks easily. I pummel him with my fists, but he blocks every punch, his huge arms like brick walls in my way. I go in for an uppercut, and Noah grabs my wrist, twisting my body against his and hemming me in with his bulk. His heart thumps against my skin, and the salt and jasmine scent of him makes my stomach flip. I'm not the only one who finds this hot – I can feel Noah's hard cock digging into my leg.

He's fast. Holy fuck he's fast. *Noah Marlowe knows how to fight.* But where did he learn? Not the Stonehurst Prep track team, that's for damn sure.

Well, he never counted on an opponent like me. I reach up and press my lips to his, capturing him in an adrenaline-fueled kiss. My body is alive with the feel of him – all hard muscle pressed against me. Noah moans, attacking my mouth with as much venom as I dish out. As I thrust my tongue deeper into his mouth, I wriggle free of his grip and bring up my knee to get him between the legs.

Sucker—

"Oh, no you don't," Noah growls against my lips as he sweeps my leg out from under me. I go down, dragging him with me. My back hits the mat, driving the wind from my lungs. Noah's on top of me, fighting to pin my hands.

"What the fuck are you doing? I said I won't fight you." He breathes hard, his body heaving. Sweat pours down his face, and the demons in his eyes dance on the surface, certain that any moment they'll be free. Seeing Noah teetering on the edge of control is intoxicating. I wonder how far I can push him, and what I'll find on the other side.

"Tell me why." I mean it to be a command, but he has my hands pinned and he's grinding his cock against my throbbing clit through our jeans, and it comes out more like I'm begging.

"Because I'll *kill* you, Claudia." My real name on his lips is pure poison-laced ecstasy. Noah's shoulders tense again, and before my eyes I watch him shutter himself against the world, putting all those dangerous emotions back into their tiny boxes. But it's too late – I've seen the dangerous side of him.

Noah flings himself away. He stands above me, his chest heaving, and extends a hand to help me up. His fingers lace in mine and send a shock of electricity through my body. Noah feels it too, because he yanks his arm away. My lips ache with the ghost of his brutality. I rub them with my fingers, and when I draw them back, I see blood.

"Don't mind me, lovebirds."

I jump and turn toward the voice. Gabriel grins at me from the designer chair, where he lounges with his feet dangling over the arm, a bowl of popcorn in his lap. He takes a handful of popcorn and shoves it in his mouth. "I'm enjoying the show."

I pick up my knife and wiggle it in his direction. "Don't make me come over there."

"Is that a threat?" Gabriel sets down the bowl and leans forward. There's a hunger in his eyes as he sweeps over my body, taking in the hard peaks of my nipples visible through my thin t-shirt. "I'm not a fighter. I'm a lover. Although for you I might make an exception."

Noah growls, low in his throat. Gabriel chuckles. "Relax, Marlowe. I'm not here to rain on your parade, although this is the most violent game of hide the bishop I've seen in my long life. Claws and I already agreed that I'm cool if she wants to clean out the cobwebs with your womb broom, have a bit of crumpet, take the magic bus to Manchester, stick the llama's head up the lift shaft, give a hot poultice to your Irish toothache..."

"What the fuck is he talking about?" Noah splutters.

"You remember our conversation?" I'm shocked Gabriel can remember anything from last night, let alone that he said *you're more than enough for me.*

"But of course." Gabriel winces. "Well, bits of it. My poor noggin is still smarting."

"You called Noah's cock a 'magnificent specimen.'" I manage a smile, even as my stomach twists with nerves. I knew this conversation would happen eventually – I'd hoped to put it off until after we dealt with the gun-toting crazy threatening my life, but I didn't count on the beautiful train wreck that is Gabriel Fallen. I know how Gabriel feels about me being with Noah, but I can't see Noah Marlowe being into sharing.

Hell, I didn't even know *I* was into sharing until I met three princes who thawed the edges of my ice heart. Even though one of them hates my guts, even though I have no right to ask anything of them, the idea of being forced to choose one of them makes my chest tight.

"I stand by my opinion." Gabriel gestures to Noah, who is still showing signs of... having the Irish toothache, in Gabriel's parlance. "Look at that thing. He could put someone's eye out."

Noah's face reddens. "Stop talking nonsense and tell me what the fuck is going on."

"I hope you're not denigrating the Queen's English, or we shall have words. We're sharing Claudia. I thought that was obvious. She's more than either of us can handle." Gabriel grins. "Welcome to the wonderful world of sexual liberation, friend Noah. Do not cross swords. Please collect your STI kit and bucket of lube when you pass go."

"You're fucking weird." Noah punches Gabriel in the arm. He

locks his gaze on me, his eyes searching. Gabriel smirks and leans back in his chair, satisfied to have sown his own unique brand of chaos. A tense silence captures the room as the two of them wait for me to speak.

I jam my hands into my eyes. Fuck. I don't know how to do any of this relationship shit.

Fingers circle my wrists, tugging my hands free, exposing my rawness for their scrutiny. Noah's dark orbs stare me down, demanding the keys to my secret heart.

"What do *you* want?" Noah rasps in his lordly voice – not a question, a command. My skin whispers with his touch, remembering just ten minutes ago when he pinned my wrists and kissed me like he was punishing me. I try not to focus on how fucked-up I am for loving it, for craving more of Noah's unique fucked-up-edness.

Gabriel rises and stands beside him, swiping his tousled dark hair from his face. His eyes capture a universe disintegrating – behind the pure light of his star is a vulnerability born of rot and decay. He's not as untouchable as he pretends to be. The shit that seems to wash off his skin without a stain is tainting him from the inside. His words from last night stick in my throat as I sense the *need* in them, the desperate desire to be loved despite the rot he refuses to show anyone.

Gabriel and Noah and I... we're all wild animals trapped in our circumstances, bashing our heads against the bars until our skulls bleed. Maybe, together, our rage and our hurt will be enough to break the bars for good.

"I want..." I take a shuddering breath. I can't believe I'm saying these words. "I want to know what it means to be free. I've lived my whole life behind bars built by my father and nailed in deeper by my own hand. I can't promise to have any idea what the fuck I'm doing, because I've never had one boyfriend before, let alone two, and I'm messed-up in the head. And I don't want it if it's going to hurt either of you—"

Noah captures my lips, his tongue dancing over mine. "We're all in cages," he rasps. "But caged animals are the most dangerous."

"Besides..." Gabriel's fingers touch my cheek. He turns my head and tastes my lips, chasing Noah's possessive kiss with one tinged with sweet decay. "Caged bunny rabbits have the best orgies."

Noah whomps him over the head with a pillow, and the pair of them wrestle on the sofa. Their kisses burn on my lips – a promise that they will do everything they can to set me free of my cage. And no matter what, I will protect them.

CLAUDIA

The next morning, Antony's car finally pulls up in the tunnel. He enters the ballroom, cracking his knuckles. "Rise and shine, Claws. Get those dicks out of your nostrils – we're going for a drive."

"You've figured out who shot at us?" That was fast. I ignore his nostril comment.

"Not yet. I *can* tell you that it wasn't Brutus," Antony says. "Or if it was, he was acting alone and he's seriously unhinged. He's still AWOL, and Lucian and Dio have recruited almost every one of his top soldiers. It looks like they've been waiting for him to show weakness so they could seize his empire. Remember, he's still the accursed man – if he shows his face in the city, even his own soldiers might make good on your father's punishment."

"But he could be *anywhere*. He's got Daddy's worldwide network at his fingertips."

"I'm checking, but I don't think he's gone far. Our allies in Rome, in China, in South America – they were loyal to Uncle Julian. They never agreed with what Brutus did but they worked with him because he was their ticket into our market. But now he's a sinking ship and they're rowing their asses away in the lifeboats as fast as they can. They've been distancing themselves for a long time. That's why Brutus has been trying to push into new markets recently."

"How come I didn't know any of this?"

Antony shrugs. "You didn't need to. We're not planning to take back the August empire. Unless the plan has changed?"

I shake my head.

"Good. Because the Triumvirate is on a knife edge right now, and we don't want to get into the middle of that. It's going to be difficult enough to find this guy without raising their suspicions."

"If he's not in charge of the family, who's next in command? Maybe Brutus told them—"

Antony shakes his head. I admire his confidence. He must be more powerful in the family than I realize, if he's able to force Brutus' silence.

"So you think Brentwood's the shooter?"

Antony waves his phone. "That's what we're going to find out. Get in the car. I've got us an appointment with Brentwood, and he gets pissy about tardiness. I need you there to put the shits up him. Bring your loverboys too, since they want to get their hands dirty."

Noah shoots to his feet. I raise an eyebrow in his direction, but I don't question it. Gabriel slouches up, too. "A gangster road trip. How exciting. Where are we going?"

"Not far." The smile on Antony's face is born of blood and violence. "It's time we asked Mr. Brentwood a few questions."

WE DIDN'T EVEN NEED to drive to Brentwood's place – it turns out he doesn't live in Tartarus Oaks, but just around the corner on Santa Casilda Drive. He has one of those ridiculous mock Georgian houses with towering white columns and blue-painted shutters. When we pull up in Antony's car, I see the gates are wide open.

"Is he expecting us?" I ask Antony.

"Nope. So this is interesting." Antony drives in the gate and parks up beside an enormous marble fountain. A statue of Cupid playing his lyre with a pensive expression on his face trickles water from his upturned palm. We climb out of the car. Gabriel wrinkles his nose as he takes in the architectural monstrosity in front of us. He folds a pair of aviator sunglasses from his pocket and slaps them over his eyes.

"You a vampire?" I cock an eyebrow at him.

"I wish. I'm dying of a hangover." Gabriel drank again last night. He runs a finger through the dark hair spilling over his shoulders. Only Gabriel Fallen could roll out of bed after drinking that much alcohol and still look so damn fine.

We ring the bell and wait. No one answers. My skin prickles, and I feel the sting of a pair of eyes on my back. I peer over my shoulder at the neighboring houses, searching for anyone watching us. My stomach twists as I think of those bullets hitting the stucco and pinging off the door as Noah fell on top of me. Was it Brentwood, or was it someone else and they're following me right now? Will they try and finish the job?

I don't like unknowns. There've been too many of them lately.

Antony tries the door handle. It's unlocked. The door swings inward, revealing an opulent foyer bedecked in hideous gilded decor. "Okay, this is fucked. Something's wrong."

Noah and I exchange a glance. Antony draws his gun. I touch the knife in my sleeve. Antony glares at the boys. "You two stay out here. Keep watch."

"No way." Noah shoves his way inside. "We're in this now."

"Careful." Antony thrusts out an arm, stopping Noah in his

tracks. Noah starts to protest, but Antony points to a strip of wire stretched across the hallway about a foot off the ground. "This whole house is booby-trapped."

"You've been here before?" I ask.

"I've done business with Brentwood in the past, on behalf of Brutus. And it's just as well, since I'm now working with a bunch of circus animals— I said, don't touch *anything*." He glares at Gabriel, who's reaching out to pick up one of the glass apples from a bowl on the sideboard. Gabriel jerks his hand back. "I'm not going to end up with an anvil dropped on my head just because you can't keep the monkeys under control."

We move down the hall, peering into the rooms on either side while Antony goes ahead and checks for more booby traps. We don't cross the thresholds, but peer in to check each for... I don't know what for. For some clue as to where Brentwood has gone and why his front door is open.

"He might've made a run for it," Antony says. "And if a guy like Brentwood is on the run from Senator Marlowe, this concerns me."

"Me too," Noah mutters.

The place may be stuffed with antiques, but it's immaculately clean. That's why when I peer into a drawing-room, the first thing I notice is two coffee cups on the table and rumpled cushions on a chair. One of the cups is empty, but the other is still half-filled with liquid, a dirty spoon resting on the side of the saucer. I point them out to Antony. He nods, but doesn't venture a theory.

On the second floor, Antony instructs me to check the guest wing while he takes Noah with him to the master bedroom. I think he just wants a break from Gabe's... Gabiness. This whole week, especially the last forty-eight hours, have been so weird to me. I'm used to things just being me and Antony. I forgot his macho douchebagometer ratchets up to ten whenever there's too much testosterone in the room.

"Your cousin doesn't like me," Gabriel muses as we peer into a guest suite decorated in a gross shade of fuchsia.

"I'm sure he'll come around." I stick my head in to try to see inside the ensuite. As I do, I notice an ax resting on a block tied to a tripwire over the doorframe and quickly snap my head back. "Just do all that male bonding stuff. You know, go to a ball game, toss a pigskin around, BBQ some brisket together."

Gabriel makes a face.

"I'm kidding. If you want to get into Antony's good books, find Brentwood and put a knife through his head."

"Your family is crazy, Claws." Gabriel's hand slides down my side to rest casually and possessively on my hip. "I approve."

"Guys, we found him," Noah calls from the other end of the house. He sounds... weird, but that might just be his voice echoing through the mansion.

Gabriel takes off in the direction of Noah's voice. I yank his arm to stop him from running. "Stay behind me, remember?" I scan every surface for traps and tripwires as we make our way back along the hallway and down another.

"Where are you?" I call out as we face two branching hallways and rows of identical doors. This place is a maze.

"Master bedroom – the door at the end on the left," Antony calls out. "Watch the wire on the bathroom door."

Gabriel and I make our way across the gilded bedroom to where Antony and Noah are inside a palatial ensuite. I have to bend down in the doorway to see the invisible wire catching the light. I lift my foot over it and immediately slide in a puddle of blood.

"Fuck."

Noah slams his body into mine, catching me before I go

down on top of the wire. His warm hands wrap around my waist, and I don't want to leave.

"That was close." I breathe into his neck, inhaling his salt and jasmine scent as I let my heart rate return to normal.

"Mmmm. Watch your step." Noah sets me on my feet again and extends a hand to help Gabriel. "This place is a biohazard."

Massacre is the word I'd use.

My pulse races as I take in the scene. Brentwood lies in a tub of crimson bathwater I'm assuming isn't the result of a Lush bath bomb. Blood splatters the walls and ceiling – great long slashes of the stuff, the marks of a killer who relished his task. Brentwood's stomach is torn open, a mess of gore. But his face is what turns my stomach – his eyes bug out in an expression of pure terror. His tongue lolls to the side of his mouth, sticking out through swollen lips. His cheeks are puffed out, and as I step closer, I see why.

Someone has stuffed pills into his mouth and up his nose – so many they spill out on his tongue. A few bob about on the surface of the water. Several of the capsules have broken open or dissolved, leaving their contents speckling his clothing.

Someone shut Brentwood up good.

13

CLAUDIA

"**W**hat the fuck?" Brentwood is supposed to be Dio's most infamous assassin. How does someone manage to catch him off-guard and do *this*?

"My thoughts exactly." Antony points to the spatter on the wall behind his head. "See how this blood has dried? I think this happened a few hours ago, maybe even last night. The floor's still wet because of the amount of water splashed everywhere."

"There's no way he just... slipped and accidentally stabbed himself?" Gabe shakes his head at Noah's proffered hand. He sits on the end of Brentwood's bed, his skin pale and sickly.

"Sure, Pretty Boy. People slip in the bathtub and eviscerate themselves while choking on a pile of pills all the time." Antony uses the edge of his shirt to pick up an empty bottle bobbing in the water. "Apparently, our friend Brentwood here has been given a crazy overdose of ergogenic aids."

"What's that?"

Antony turns the label around to face me. "Performance enhancers for athletes. And will you look at that... these are a Malloy Supplements special – although according to this warning label, they're not yet approved for the market."

Noah stiffens. Antony glares at him as he shoves the pills into his pocket. "You have something to say, Dark Horse?"

I snort. I can't help it. Antony's nicknames for the guys are so on-the-nose.

"It's just... my brother was killed because he took unapproved supplements made-to-order by Mackenzie's father. I thought my family had it out for the Malloys because Dad blames them for my brother's death and my mother's suicide. But Claudia and I found some papers in Howard's office that show my father was working with Malloy. Maybe he hired Brentwood because he knew Mackenzie was back in her house —" he says this with a sly look in my direction "—and he wants to make sure those papers never see the light of day."

"And according to you, Brentwood refused to go after Mackenzie because of whatever he saw that night," Antony says. "Now he's dead from a drug overdose."

That's too big a coincidence. I turn to Noah. "You think your father did *this?*"

"I don't think he personally shoved these pills down Brentwood's throat." Noah glances up at the blood fanning across the ceiling. He swallows hard. "But yes, I believe this is connected."

"Who else would a senator hire if they wanted someone to disappear?" Antony drags out his phone and starts tapping. "More importantly, who would be able to get the drop on Brentwood?"

I wish Eli was here.

The thought slams into me so hard that I jerk. It's a flush of need that starts in my stomach and pools warmth through my body. This isn't desire. It's something deeper. It's *longing.* I used to feel this tugging in my gut when I watched films about families of teens living their normal lives. Now I feel it for the comfort and steadiness that only Eli Hart can give.

Maybe Eli isn't here, but that doesn't mean I can't borrow a little of his steady, careful nature. Put on my own Sherlock Holmes orgasm face.

I turn back to the bathtub, trying to see the bathroom through Eli's eyes.

"It has to be someone he trusted, because he let them into the house." I think of the coffee cups we saw downstairs. "Probably they were having coffee together and that person put something into Brentwood's drink, then maneuvered him into the bath once he was out cold."

"They'd have to be incredibly strong to get him up here and over that tripwire," Antony says. "I could probably do it if I had to, but it would suck. He's not a small guy. I don't think this was hired out – you'd have to be crazy to incur the wrath of Dio, but... hold on. What's that?"

Antony reaches across the corpse and snaps an object from around Brentwood's neck. He holds it up for us all to see.

It's a gift tag tied on a pink ribbon. It had been wrapped around Brentwood's neck like he was a present under the Christmas tree. It reminds me of a ribbon I used to wear in my hair when I was a little girl – Daddy's favorite color on me. Antony rubs a blood-stained finger on the edge of the tag, reading the words aloud. "A gift for you, baby girl – to show how much I care. Brutus."

Baby girl.

My stomach twists. I sink to my knees as the bile rises in my throat.

I can't breathe.

My eyes slam shut but my eyelids burn with red splotches, with an old wound that's torn open and bleeding inside me.

Baby girl.

That's what *he* said. The man who came into my room that night. The one who's seen my real face.

Baby girl.

Noah drops beside me, grabbing me under the arms and holding me against him. "What's wrong?"

I don't answer him. I can't. My whole body goes slack. Noah's yelling something at me, but I can't hear what over the pounding of my own heart in my ears.

Behind his back, Antony meets my eyes. Realization dawns on him. His jaw sets as he reads the note again.

He turns and smashes his hand into the tiles.

Noah second-hand winces as shards of tile fly from the wall. I guess Brentwood's decorator hadn't used the best glue.

"What's going on?" Gabriel asks. Noah doesn't say anything, but he stares at me with those coal-black eyes and I *know* he sees I'm hiding something.

Antony wipes his bloodied knuckles on the hem of his shirt. He's back in control now. "We know who did this. It's Brutus. He must've found out about the appointment I made with Brentwood. And this note confirms he knows Claudia's real identity."

I'm grateful Antony doesn't tell the rest of the story. "What do we do now?"

"We get the fuck out of dodge before anyone sees us here and reports it to the police. We don't have time to wait around for Dio's clean-up team – we'd have to explain what we were doing here in the first place. Better they believe Brentwood's disappeared." Antony pulls something from his pocket and tosses it to Gabriel. "Pretty Boy, put those on and dig around in his closet. We'll need three pairs of shoes and a pillowcase to stash ours inside."

Gabe pulls on the latex gloves and locates three pairs of shiny Brionis, which he lines up on the carpet. We take turns to slide off our blood-soaked shoes and step into the clean ones. I drop my spike heels into the pillowcase. "I liked these shoes."

"Are we leaving him here?" Noah jerks his head in the direction of the bathroom. But Antony's already on the phone to Tiberius.

We wait in the house until Tiberius arrives with the supplies we need. Antony goes downstairs to guide him through the booby traps. They appear in the doorway, their arms loaded with vats of chemicals and a large kettle.

"You might want to get out of here." Antony plugs the kettle into the power outlet beside the sink and starts boiling. "This will smell delightful."

I sit down on the corner of Brentwood's bed. I don't care about the smell. I'm numb to the world – the only thing that pierces my haze are those words repeating over and over in my head. *Baby girl baby girl baby girl...*

Gabriel wraps me in his arms, pulling me back against the Egyptian linens while Antony and Tiberius get to work.

Noah helps Antony, pouring the boiling kettle over Brentwood's body as Antony mixes the chemicals and uses the plunger to move the slurry forming in the bathtub down the drain. I'm too lost in my pain to pay too much attention, but the fact Noah is so calm and so willing to throw himself into this is... perturbing. He doesn't throw up once, even as Antony asks him to hold Brentwood's limbs while he chops him into pieces so the chemicals will work faster. Gabriel won't even look inside the bathroom, but the smell has him heaving into the pillowcase at least three times.

Gabriel holds me, stroking my hair. He whispers song lyrics into my ears, filling my chest with warmth. But he can't kiss away that cold as I clutch that ribbon between my fingers.

All these years, and the man who hurt me finally has a name.

Brutus.

The accursed man.

The *betrayer*.
He killed my parents.
He broke my spirit.
He will die.

14

CLAUDIA

It takes nearly five hours for the last of Brentwood's remains to flush down the bathtub. Gabriel and I spent most of that time cradled together on the bed, clinging to each other as though every slurp and swirl of the drain washed away the lies that cloaked us.

I'll never be able to scrub the smell out of my skin, nor forget the sludge at the bottom of the bathtub as the potassium hydroxide transformed Brentwood's considerable bulk into a human slurry. Antony picks out the remaining bones that haven't dissolved and throws them in the pillowcase while Noah and Tiberius use bleach to scrub the blood off every surface, until the bathroom shines like new. Tiberius even repairs the broken tiles.

After it's done, Antony drops us back at Malloy Manor, but he won't come inside. "I still have work to do," he says as he starts to wind his window up.

"Wait." I grab the window. "Is it safe for us to go to school tomorrow?"

"Fuck knows, but what's the alternative? Like it or not, you're Mackenzie Malloy now. You need to act as normal as possible until we've got Brutus under control." Antony grins. "Pull up those thigh-high white socks and those garters that drive the Pretty Boy so wild, cousin. You're going back to class."

I give Antony the finger as he laughs and takes off, a pillow-case filled with our bloody shoes and clothes, and the remains of Brentwood that wouldn't fit down the drain.

I know he needs to check in at the club, that our best chance of figuring out who's behind the shooting is to lean into his role in the family and his underground connections. I know that my continued existence is down, in part, to the fact he's been dili-gently careful to not let anyone in Tartarus Oaks know that he occasionally disappears into Harrington Hills to watch horror films with his not-so-dead cousin in a mansion that's only months away from being hers.

I know all this, and still I pace around the ballroom and stare at my broken phone screen every few minutes. I was raised to be a queen. I don't like being helpless, feeling like a monkey in a cage watching the world falling into chaos outside my prison. I especially don't like Antony being out on the front lines in Tartarus Oaks when there's clearly a price on my head.

My agitation only feeds Noah's disquiet. He spends all day poring over the paperwork from Malloy's safe, organizing it into piles and marking certain damning passages with sticky notes. Gabriel and I play music in the ballroom, play with Queen Boudica, and kiss until my lips feel like they're going to fall off. When it gets dark outside and Noah still hasn't left the office, I heat up some soup for dinner and bring it in to him. He's still staring at that pile of papers, trying to force it to offer up the answers he craves.

"There's so much more here than just my brother's case," he says as he shoves aside the bowl without touching it. "Howard Malloy's been using this deer antler velvet in supplements for years – not in his commercially-available products, but in specialized performance enhancers for a select range of clients, many of whom have suffered horrific side-effects. There's enough evidence here that if Howard Malloy ever showed his face in Emerald Beach again, we could put him away in prison for life for gross negligence and manslaughter, not to mention what the sports boards will say if they knew just how many star athletes are taking this stuff..."

"I wonder if that's why he disappeared?" I peer over Noah's shoulder at the piles of paper spread out across the desk. It's weird to think that just a few weeks ago nothing in those files had any relevance to me, and now they might hold the key to neutralizing the person who wants me dead.

If John Marlowe even is responsible for the gunshots. I know Noah believes it, but I'm not certain I do.

Noah fists his hands at his sides. Hopelessness slides into his eyes – a sense that this is too big for him to tackle. For the first time, the spoiled prince must face the fact that wealth can't buy him answers. "We'll never know what happened to the Malloys. I don't believe for a moment that they're dead, but Howard would cover his tracks too perfectly for us to trace."

"I think there's one person who can give us a clue." I toss his leather jacket into his arms. "Let's go."

"Where?"

"To have a chat with your father."

"Wait, Claudia—" Noah bolts out of the chair and races after me as I head back to the ballroom. I grab my own jacket from the back of the couch – it has Gucci emblazoned across the back in rainbow sequins because that's how Mackenzie's mother rolls – and kick Gabriel in the shoulder. My rock god is lying on the floor, staring into nothing, with Queen Boudica curled up in a ball of happiness in his hair.

"Noah and I are heading out for a bit."

Gabe bolts upright, sending Queen Boudica flying. She

lands on her feet, shoots Gabriel a filthy look, and stomps off to her cat castle.

"You can't. Antony said we shouldn't leave the property. What if the shooter—"

"Antony's not the boss. In this house, I'm queen." Gabriel doesn't look convinced. "We'll be careful, I promise. We'll take Tiberius with us, how about that? That leaves you with Horace for protection. And Queen Boudica – she'll scare away anyone who dares come close."

"Tell me about it." Gabriel holds up his hand. His perfect skin is crisscrossed with tiny cuts. "You've taught her well, Claws. What's that line from A Midsummer Night's Dream? *Though she be but little, she is a sadist who will claw your eyes out.* But what's going on? Why would you leave if we don't know it's safe?"

Because I'm sick of being treated like a helpless little lamb. I'm not the lamb. I'm the wolf, and I need this bastard to fear me more than he hates me.

"Noah and I have found something that might give us answers, and I'm not letting Antony do all the dirty work when we can help." Gabriel reaches for his jacket, but I plant my hand against his chest, forcing myself to ignore the heat that sizzles along my arm. "I *want* you with me, but this is something Noah needs to do on his own. Your job is to hang out with my cat. She's a needy bitch."

Gabriel gives me a shaky smile. Queen Boudica leaps from the top of her turret into his arms, and he hugs her to his chest. "I take it Antony knows nothing about this plan? Claudia August asks for forgiveness, not permission?"

I pretend to think. "I've never asked for forgiveness in my life."

15

ELI

Maria waits with me while I sober up. She stops asking me about why I've come to Everlasting Hart Ranch, why I'm drunk, why I don't have my phone, or why I don't want to go back to Emerald Beach. She just sits and pats my knee, and it's fucking heartbreaking because I love her so much and I feel like a disappointment.

I follow Maria home in my car with Gizmo napping on the passenger seat, her belly round with mice from the barn. I allow myself one last look over my shoulder at the crumbling remains of my father's folly.

As Maria exits onto the freeway into the city, I debate pulling off and losing her. But what's the point? There's no escaping my legacy, not even out here in the desert. I see Mackenzie in every beam of golden sunlight, in the sparkling water of the lake.

Back in the city, I pull into the garage and park. Gizmo rolls over sleepily, stretching out a paw to bat my leg. "Mew?"

"I know, you want to go back to the mouse smorgasbord. I don't blame you." I carry her upstairs to my bedroom and set down some food for her. My room is exactly as I left it – the walls stripped bare of all my posters and flags, the windows wide open in an attempt to air out the fresh paint smell. A few days ago I got around to painting over Mackenzie's message in an ice blue, the exact color of her eyes.

YOU WERE SUPPOSED TO PROTECT ME

She made me wretched with guilt that day, and it's not even true. I owe her nothing. She's not Mackenzie. The face I picture before I fall asleep is a mirage.

So why am I letting her get inside my head?

I debate not going downstairs for dinner, but if I don't, Mom will come up here, yelling and ranting. The last time she came into my room, she smashed a lampshade and terrified Gizmo. I couldn't coax her out from beneath the bed for a week.

So I shower and change into a fresh shirt and slacks. My fingers itch to text Noah and check that everything's okay, but then I remember Claudia's cousin smashed my phone.

I remember that nothing will be okay again.

I leave Gizmo in my room with some cat treats and drag my ass downstairs. There's soft jazz music playing in the formal wing of the house. Mom stands behind the drinks cart, one hand patting her blonde curls, as she tosses her head back with laughter. Beside her, a man pours martinis into our finest crystal glasses.

Yeah, this can't be good.

"Eli, honey." Mom beckons me with a manicured finger like I'm a performing pig. "Don't be a wallflower. Come and greet our guest."

She's laying on the Southern charm thick tonight, letting the twang I thought she'd dropped completely back into her voice. I swallow and take a step forward. My legs are made of lead, but I manage to drag myself toward them.

Who is this guy?

My mom has had a steady string of lovers ever since Dad went to prison. That's not new – she was playing around even before the reality TV crews moved in. But she'd never been brazen enough to bring one of her men into our house or to seat him at the table in Dad's chair.

I don't like this.

"Eli, this is Nero Lucian. He works in the entertainment industry. Nero, this is my son, Elias. He's seventeen and he attends Stonehurst Prep, where he's the student council president, captain of the track team and the debate team, as well as a top student."

I don't like my life being reduced to a list of achievements to impress this guy who... who the fuck even *is* he? Nero holds out his hand to me. The expensive fabric of his pinstripe suit tugs across broad, muscled shoulders. His neck is all muscle, and when he squeezes my hand, he crushes my fingers in an iron grip. There's a hint of malice in his friendly eyes, and his smile is all teeth and gums.

Entertainment my ass. You didn't get a body like that yelling at actors.

Nero withdraws his hand, but the smile never leaves his lips. "It's a pleasure to meet you, Elias. Your mother's told me all about you."

Why has she told this guy about me? And why does he give me the fucking creeps?

"She's told me absolutely nothing about you." I meant it to come across as a joke, but I'm no Gabriel, and it sounds accusatory. My mother glares at me, but Nero laughs deep in his belly, his whole body vibrating, sloshing alcohol over the side of his glass. I'm surprised the whole room doesn't shake like an earthquake.

"There's nothing much to tell, my boy." He slaps me so hard on the shoulder that I spill half my drink on the carpet. "I spend my days overseeing my casinos and clubs, and my nights sitting alone in my house drinking my way through my father's Scotch collection."

Nero and Mom fall into an easy conversation about Nero's clubs – apparently, Mom's visited them all – and the private lives of his celebrity patrons. I stare at my drink in stony silence. Nero must notice because he switches his attention to me and bombards me with questions about current affairs, city zonings, my favorite films and TV shows, and what I got up to over the summer. I don't think in my entire time growing up my parents ever asked me so much about myself. I can't wait for this evening to be over.

Maria appears in the doorway. "Dinner is served, ma'am."

Mom leads Nero by the arm into the dining room. We sit down at the table. I move to take the seat at the head of the table, but Nero's too fast. He sits down where my father used to sit. Mom sits beside him. The third place is set on Nero's other side, facing Mom. I deliberately take a seat a few chairs down, sliding the cutlery across the table. Mom flashes her eyes at me, but I pretend not to notice.

"How are your college applications coming along, Eli?" she asks, cutting her beans into demure pieces and popping one in her mouth. My mom believes men don't like to watch women eat. I think of Mackenzie piling her plate high with food in the school cafeteria and feel a stab of pain.

Not Mackenzie. Claudia.

"Fine," I say. *No thanks to you.* I spent the summer working on my application essays and researching programs. I should have started on my letters of recommendation, but I haven't even chosen a program yet. I don't know what I want to do or where I want to go, except that it will be far away from Emerald Beach and Dad's reputation. The idea that this one decision can define the next four-to-eight years of my life weighs on me. I would love to have someone to talk to about it, the way Noah does with Grace, but Mom doesn't care and Dad's of the belief that college is a waste of time. "I never went to no fancy school, and I built a multi-million dollar business with my bare hands," he was fond of saying, as if he were a man of the earth.

And look at you now, I think but don't say.

"So, you're heading to college next year?" Nero says. "A bright boy like you, I'm not surprised. What will you be studying?"

"Veterinary science," I reply. I say it to piss Mom off. Her eyebrows shoot up. She's always assumed I'd go into the family business – taking the shreds of Dad's funerary empire and rebuilding it into something that will continue to keep her in mink coats and Dom Pérignon.

But now the words are out of my mouth, hanging in the air like a dirty secret... I like the taste of them. *Veterinary science.* Caring for sick animals is not exactly the job for the Golden Boy of Stonehurst Prep. But maybe I'm sick of being the steady one who does what everyone else wants without making a fuss.

"Is that a degree at Yale, dear?" Mom is livid, but she won't scold me in front of company. "Because you know that if you want to use your trust fund for college, your father and I have to approve your courses—"

"Now, Darlene, don't you worry. Eli here is a young man; he's got plenty of time to get his head screwed on straight about school. This is the time to follow his *passion*." Nero pounds the table for emphasis. I have to save my glass from spilling. "Passion is everything in life, Eli. Passion and loyalty. Look at me. I never went to college. I followed my *passions* – for spinning the wheel and smiling at Lady Luck, for fine food and wine, for music, for blood and circuses – and now I'm a successful businessman."

The phrase is actually *bread and circuses*. Ms. Drysdale spoke about it in her Political Studies class, how the satirist Juvenal used *panem et circenses* to describe how the common people let base pleasures distract them from the wider picture. I wonder if Nero's use of *blood* is deliberate.

Nero raises his glass and nods at me. "You follow your passion in veterinary science and you may be surprised where you end up. You don't worry, Darlene – smart people like Eli always come out on top."

Seriously, who the fuck is this guy? And why is he sticking up for me?

I expect Mom to fight him. Instead, she reaches across the table and squeezes his hand. "Eli, we need to talk about the future of this family."

I stuff a piece of broccoli in my mouth and deliberately chew while speaking. "What future? Dad's in prison. The business is worthless. I'm leaving for college as soon as I have my diploma in my hands."

"You're exactly right, son. There is no future here for me." Mom fixes me with a strange expression – part defiant, part desperate. "That's why Nero and I are getting married."

I choke on the broccoli, spitting it out on the tablecloth. "That's ridiculous."

"*Manners.* There's nothing ridiculous about being in love." Mom bats her eyelashes at Nero. "You'd know that if you ever dated."

"It *is* ridiculous. You've known this guy a hot minute." I drop my knife on the table. "Oh, yeah, and you're still married to Dad."

"Since when have you been so puritanical, son?" Mom's fake laugh tinkles in the air like glass shards. "I've asked your father for a divorce."

"And he agreed?"

"Under the circumstances, he has little choice." She smiles then, a hint of slyness slithering through her outward charm.

I'm angry, and I don't know why I'm angry. Dad's in prison. He's the one who ruined our lives by breaking the law and defrauding hundreds of grieving families. Why shouldn't I go to veterinary school just to spite him? Why shouldn't Mom move on?

I tell myself all these things, yet the rage simmers under my skin like a kettle boiling over. Nero's grey eyes bore into mine, and I know what I'm feeling is that quality Nero admires so much – loyalty. As much as I hate my father for what he's done, it's a hatred borne of love. I've looked up to him my entire life. He broke something inside me the day the Feds arrested him, something that Mackenzie's disappearance had already cracked open. For all his bluster and bombast, for all the bribes I gave to the wardens and righteous indignation he works up about his appeal, I know that prison is breaking him, and this... this will be the final nail in the coffin of Walter Hart.

Despite everything, I can't bear to see him broken. Because if Walter Hart can't survive in this cruel world, then what hope do I have?

"Eli, you had to know this was coming." Mom reaches across the table to touch my hand. I jerk away. "I'm not going to wait around for fifteen years for your father to get out of prison. Your father agrees. He's already signed the paperwork."

"What about his appeal?"

"We'll still go. As a family."

I know exactly what she's doing. She's leaping off this sinking ship. The civil lawsuits against my father's company will bankrupt us if Mom's spending in his absence hasn't already. If she divorces now, she'll stand a better chance of getting *something* in the settlement. This Nero doesn't look like he's wanting for money. She'll be his arm candy and he'll push his way into our lives, into *my* life, and there's nothing I can do about it.

I shove my plate away. "I'm not hungry."

"Elias Hart, you come back to this table right now—"

She lost the right to act like a mother many years ago, when she gave me to Maria, when designer purses and Botox became more important than playing with me. I've been the good son for too many years, trying desperately to please two people who never considered my needs.

I let them force me and Mackenzie apart.

No more. I've played by the rules my entire life, and all I have to show for it is a father in prison, an uncaring mother, and a gaping hole where my heart should be.

The Golden Boy of Stonehurst Prep is *done with this shit*.

16

CLAUDIA

Since Noah's stepmother ended up in the hospital after my little stunt last month, the Marlowe house has stepped up their security. There's a guard posted at the gate and a state-of-the-art alarm system that will stand up against even Antony's best man.

Fortunately, I have the golden ticket – the son of Senator Marlowe, who's been given the codes and security clearance and free rein to come and go as he pleases. Noah drives up to the gate and punches in a code. The gate swings open, and the security guard runs over and peers in the window. I've wrapped my hair in a scarf and I'm wearing dark glasses on the chance he's been told to shoot Mackenzie Malloy on sight, but the guard doesn't bat an eyelid as he waves us through.

He hasn't even checked underneath the picnic blanket on the backseat, where Tiberius is hiding with his gun strapped across his chest.

We park in the garage – just one vehicle in a bank of fancy-ass cars. The one on the end is covered in a tarp that flaps in the breeze as the door clicks shut. I ease myself out of my door, careful not to clip it against the Mercedes next to us, and pull the blanket off Tiberius.

He groans as he unfolds his bulk and slides awkwardly out of the car. "Did you have to take those speed humps with quite so much enthusiasm?"

Noah is too wound up to appreciate Tiberius' unique sense of humor. He lets out a sound that's part caveman grunt, part tiger growl, but all pissy rich-boy. I itch to slap that expression off his perfect face, but I know he's acting like a shit because he's angry and afraid.

We're in the lion's den.

"Is your stepmother here tonight?" I whisper as Noah punches in a code to turn off the alarms and panic buttons. That done, we make our way through the darkened garage.

Noah shakes his head. "She's staying with her parents. She says she doesn't feel safe in the house anymore. The truth is, she's never been safe here, not from the real enemy."

He leads us through wide hallways and a towering foyer held up by fluted gothic columns. Malloy Manor is flashy in a typical Emerald Beach way, but the decor here is Murder House Chic – heavy wooden furniture, Victorian flocked wallpaper, chandeliers the *Phantom of the Opera* would dismiss as too grandiose. I turn to the sweeping staircase, but Noah tugs me away, leading us instead down a hallway on the eastern wing.

"Shouldn't we go to the bedrooms?" I indicate the sweeping staircase.

Noah shakes his head. "Dad never sleeps there anymore."

We pause outside a half-closed door. I listen hard, but the house is as silent as a tomb. And I'd fucking know. It's got the feel of a tomb, too – the weight of six feet of grave dirt bears down on me as I stare at that door, teetering on the point of no return. Even the palatial rooms manage to feel claustrophobic, and my throat itches with the taste of stale, funereal air.

I will have my revenge on Brutus. I will make him taste the same fear. But it will not be tonight. Tonight is for Noah.

Cold moonlight beams through the window, glinting off Tiberius' pistol as he presses his body against the wall, lifting his chin to wait for Noah's signal. Noah's eyes are two pinpricks of unfathomable blackness. Even in the gloom of the house, he is a creature of shadow and sin. Noah flicks his gaze to the door. His chest heaves. He makes his decision.

Pressing his finger to his lips, he shoves the door inward.

It flings open, bouncing against the wall with a *CRACK* that sounds like a gunshot. My heart leaps in my chest, but I don't rush into the room the way Noah and Tiberius do. A queen takes her time.

I take a moment to glance around me at the room. With the double-height ceiling, stiff furniture, and decorative frieze of romanticized battle scenes, this looks less like a room in a house and more like the stateroom of a Roman palace. A fire blazes from a stone hearth – as if this is the middle of winter in Seattle or something and not fucking California. The flickering light illuminates a portrait that takes up nearly the whole wall – a young man who looks remarkably like Noah. Except for the eyes – they're a beautiful deep blue, like the water of Emerald Beach on a calm, clear day, and there are no secrets inside them. Only kindness.

Felix Marlowe.

I don't have time to appreciate the artwork. Noah's father is on his feet, yelling and reaching for the light. Tiberius grabs his hand and slams it against the table, smashing the Tiffany lampshade and raining shards of glass across the Persian rug. Senator Marlowe grunts as he tries to kick his captor, but his legs are tangled in a blanket he had over his knees and it only takes a few moments for Tiberius to subdue him completely.

Tiberius hauls the senator from the floor and slams him into the wingback chair, pointing the gun at his head. "Don't move a muscle," he says, flicking the safety off with a cocky grin. "Unless you want your brains to decorate that fresco."

"Who the fuck are you? What is this—" The senator's eyes flick to Noah. I see they're the same dark shade, although where Noah's have depth and fire, John Marlowe's are the kind of dark that is cold and heartless. "Son, what is this nonsense?"

I nod to Noah, who flicks on the unbroken lampshade on the opposite side of the fireplace, aiming the bulb at me as I step onto the edge of the rug. *He's been taking lessons from Gabriel on how to make a dramatic entrance.*

"Hello, Senator."

John Marlowe doesn't flinch as he recognizes me. I'll give him credit – he has a near-perfect poker face. But he doesn't know that I've been schooled in how Marlowe men maintain control. He sweeps a hand through his hair, and there's a slight wobble on the edge of his mouth. He's not shitting himself yet, but he's not far away.

"What is this?" He glares at Noah. "Do you know who this girl is?"

Noah moves to stand beside me. He looks down at his father with an expression of complete disdain – I know he's mirroring the way the senator has looked at him for so many years, and I want to slap John Marlowe for it. Noah is amazing, and he should have never been made to feel small while Felix was treated like a god even in death.

He'll never feel small again. Not after tonight.

"Noah, what's the meaning of this?"

Noah says nothing. He lets his dad take in the scene – Tiberius beside the fire, his scarred face wreathed in flame, his finger tapping the trigger. Noah facing him with defiance burning in his eyes, his fingers entwined with his enemy, Mackenzie Malloy. Senator Marlowe flicks his finger beneath the arm of the chair, jabbing a panic button. Little does he know that Noah disabled the alarm. No one is coming to help him.

"What the fuck is this?" Senator Marlowe addresses the question to me. Spits it out like bile.

"You've been trying to have me killed, Senator." I cluck my tongue. "Naughty boy. You should know by now that Mackenzie Malloy can't die. I'm like a ghost haunting your ass."

He tries to launch himself off the chair, but Tiberius shoves him back down. Senator Marlowe seems to accept this. He crosses his legs and picks up the whisky glass from the table beside him, dangling it from his fingers. I see the decanter is nearly drained. "And if I did? It would be only fair. You killed my son."

"Really?" I twirl a strand of blonde hair around my finger. "That's the story you're going with? A thirteen-year-old girl suggests to Noah that her father might have something to help his brother, an idea planted in her head by her own father all so that he has a scapegoat if it goes wrong. Meanwhile, behind the scenes, you and Howard Malloy had a very different arrangement."

That gets a reaction. The senator's jaw tightens. His eyes flick to the door. He's starting to wonder what's taking his security team so long.

Noah's fingers tighten in mine. Still, he doesn't speak. But that's okay – I have swallowed enough venom for both of us. "You see, I know a few things about you, too, Senator Marlowe. I know that you came to my father as one of his elite clients – Howard Malloy might've made his name in cheap supplements made from supposedly ancient wisdom, but his real fortune came from mixing performance enhancers to order. Drugs to make athletes stronger, faster, better, and that couldn't be detected in a drug test. A ticket to stardom that only the super-rich could afford."

"This is absurd. Noah, I don't know what lies this demon girl has fed you, but you can't believe I would endanger Felix's career by doing something illegal. You need to stop this—"

"Oh, Senator Marlowe, don't you worry – Noah and I did our research. We know that supplements made from antler velvet *are* legal. No, what I know is that you paid my father a large sum of money to source a massive shipment from New Zealand so he could use the velvet in far higher concentrations than normal. The lab testing showed incredible results but warned of dangerous side effects. You ignored those warnings. You were determined your son would be on the Olympic team no matter what."

"Being a good father, wanting the best for my children, this warrants you entering my home and putting a gun to my head?" The senator's eyes flick to the door again.

Noah snorts. It's the first sound he's made since we entered the room. I dare a glance over at him, and I can see how tense his muscles are, how the corner of his mouth twitches. His eyes flick to Tiberius' gun, and I can see the lust for violence burning in them.

Noah has imagined this moment for a long time. I bet he never thought Mackenzie Malloy would be at his side. And she is, in a weird way. The Senator believes Mackenzie is the one behind this because of what he did to her, and I stand here for her revenge, too.

"Without waiting for further clinical trials, you gave the supplement to your teenage son. Felix's undiagnosed hormone condition reacted to the concentration of growth hormone in the antler velvet. Your son – Noah's brother – died a terrifying, painful death. You were so determined to make him the best that you killed him, and then you decided to blame a thirteen-year-old girl for your actions so your surviving son would have someone to hate, so that no one would fault you for what you did next."

The senator laughs – a barking sound that has no mirth to it. His finger stabs at the panic button again. "I'd like to see your proof. All you have is a wild story with no basis in fact."

"That's exactly what I have." I hold up a paper. "I have all the evidence right here. It's interesting this never came out in the court case. In fact, it's interesting there even was a court case at all."

"Mom wanted the trial." Noah's eyes flicker to Felix's portrait, and he squares his shoulders. I wonder what it must feel like to stand here with his father at gunpoint, feeling as though his saint of a brother watches from on high. Noah advances on his father, leaning over him. Tiberius holds out the gun, and Noah watches the barrel as it aims at his father's cheek. "You tried to convince her to drop it, but she was so distraught that you had to give in. I'm guessing you and Malloy had some kind of agreement. You'd sue Malloy, but he hid the evidence of your involvement and the initial laboratory reports so no one knew who funded the supplements or just how deadly they were. Just a mistake – a terrible, preventable tragedy. You get to appear the concerned father in front of voters, and the court case acts as one giant advertisement for Malloy's services."

"Only, Daddy gets greedy when he realizes he holds in his hands these documents that can destroy your career," I add. "He decides he's going to blackmail you. Are we close?"

"Answer them." Tiberius jams the revolver into the senator's temple.

"Speaking hypothetically," the senator hisses through gritted teeth as Tiberius' fingers dig into his neck. "If someone wanted a favor from me, such as overturning drug legislation, those papers would be a good way to ensure compliance."

"Mmmm. I thought so." I whip the papers away as Senator

Marlowe reaches for them. "I suspect that's why you hired Brentwood again when Noah told you I was back, and why you sent someone to break into my house, because you were hoping to get your mitts on these papers."

"This is preposterous. I never—" But his face is pale. He's properly scared now.

Good. He should be scared.

I smile, slow and creepy-like. "Ssssh. I don't care to hear you defend yourself. I have the papers, and the only question before us today is, what are we going to do with you?"

Senator Marlowe swipes at me, but I step back just as Noah slams his fist into his father's stomach. The senator doubles over, choking and spluttering and gasping for breath.

"If you wondered why Brentwood isn't reporting back..." I hold up my mobile phone to his face as he fights for breath. "It's because I did this to him."

He whimpers as he takes in the photograph of Brentwood in the bathtub, his mouth swollen with pills and the stab wounds visible above the scarlet water. I feel a little guilty for taking advantage of someone else's handiwork, but Marlowe didn't have the connections Antony did – he was unlikely to find out the truth.

I hold the papers up to the light and squint at them, pretending to consider my options. I love the way Senator Marlowe squirms in the chair, his eyes wide saucers.

"Son, what are you doing with her?" he gasps out, a last-ditch effort to save himself.

Noah's face is dark. "You made me hate her when all this time it was you who killed him. Is that what you're doing in here every night, Dad? Praying to Felix to atone for your sins? Because he's not a god who needs to devour the sins of his disciples. He's *not a god.* He was an amazing human, he was special and kind and good, but he was human and you took him from me."

"Son, I—"

"I'll never forgive you." Noah steps back, jerking his head toward Tiberius. "Do it. Put a bullet between his eyes."

"Son, I—" But the senator can't even finish the sentence. He squeezes his eyes shut as Tiberius presses the muzzle of the pistol in the middle of his forehead. I catch a whiff of something acrid in the air. The senator has pissed himself.

Oh, this is too much fun.

An idea occurs to me. I place my hand over Tiberius' fingers. He drops the gun into my hand.

"Today's your lucky day, Senator." Noah's eyes widen. I slap the senator's cheek with the pistol until he opens his eyes. He's trembling all over, and the smell of urine is getting worse. "Don't look so glum. I'm feeling generous, and I know your wife had a scare recently. I wouldn't want her to be the one to discover your brains decorating the wallpaper. So you and I are going to strike a deal."

"I'm listening."

I love this guy. Even with a gun pointed to his head, he still pretends like I'm the one bowing down to him.

"Call off your hired guns. Brentwood was the best in the business – no one else will get as close to me as he did, and look where that got him. You don't know how many copies of this paper I've made or who I've left them with. As soon as my people hear I'm dead, this gets released to the media. Your political career is over and you'll be looking at time for the perjury your ass committed in the original trial against my father. All I'm asking, in exchange for your continued existence and a flourishing career unhindered by scandal, is that you leave me, and the people close to me, in peace."

He narrows his eyes. He doesn't believe me. "And that's all?"

"Not quite."

Noah's mouth quirks. He looks amused.

"I've done you a favor tonight. Now you owe me one in return." I press my finger to my lips as I step back, keeping the gun pointed at his forehead. "I can't tell you when I'll call on you, but know that you must be ready at any time."

His mouth twists. He hates the idea of owing me. Yes, I like this plan very much.

Finally, the senator nods. I smile and turn to leave. Noah and Tiberius fall into step behind me.

"Oh, and Senator?" I glance back over my shoulder. "One last thing."

His fingernails dig into the fabric of the chair.

BOOM.

The pistol jerks in my hands as I squeeze the trigger. Noah leaps backward, falling over a table. The senator lets out a strangled cry as he jerks his gaze to the portrait of his son, now marred by a single bullet hole placed neatly between Felix's eyes.

"No more living in the past, Senator Marlowe. I'll be calling on you soon." As I turn away I can't help the wild smile playing across my lips. I'd forgotten how good it felt to squeeze a trigger, to feel all that power reverberating through my body as the bullet left the chamber.

I forgot how good it was to see a grown man tremble.

I hand the gun back to Tiberius. He slips it back into his jacket, and we walk out. My knees wobble, but I know Marlowe can't see in the darkness.

We walk down the halls, back through this mausoleum to Marlowe's indifference, and into the garage. We pile into the car and tuck Tiberius under the blanket. My veins throb with heat. That was fucking hot.

Noah remains silent as he drives. I watch him as he makes

each turn precisely, perfectly obeying every road rule. We are opposites in so many ways – he is control, and I am chaos.

"You didn't tell me you were going to ask for a favor." He doesn't look at me.

"I didn't plan it." I shrug. "But a lot of things need to go right for me to get out of this year alive and away from the Triumvirate. He might be able to help me when the time comes. But this isn't about me. Tonight was for you. Tell me what you're thinking."

Noah's hands tighten on the wheel. "I never stood up to him before. Tonight I drew a line in the sand and stomped all over it."

"Are you okay with that?" *Are you okay with me?*

Are you okay with what you will become beside me?

"I'm better than okay. I don't believe for a second he's going to accept owing a Malloy a favor, or seeing his son." Noah's dark eyes blaze with hate. "I've made an enemy of my father. He'll see me buried for this."

CLAUDIA

I strut into school on Wednesday like I'm head witch bitch in a teen horror film before the bloodshed starts.

George is waiting on the front steps, talking to that metalhead stoner guy from under the bleachers. She stares at her shoes, talking a mile a minute, which I think is George's version of flirting. The guy has his back against a pillar, fidgeting with the edge of a band patch on his denim jacket, a waterfall of shimmering black hair obscuring half his face.

Their children will be so adorable.

Wordlessly, I loop my arm through George's and drag her away. Noah and Gabriel flank us as we stalk down the corridor. Heads turn. Vicious whispers assault us from all sides, but I'm surrounded by a Hadrian's Wall of don't-give-a fuck. I'm invincible.

On the inside, I'm a ball of nerves. My spine crawls with spiders. Brutus could be anywhere. He might have eyes on me this very moment, waiting for his chance.

It feels like a literal eternity since I've been inside Stonehurst Prep – since last Thursday, I've stolen a car and rebuilt it around a water fountain, ruined an asshole's life, lost my virginity at a secret underwater club, had sex with another guy twice, been shot at, flushed a man's melted corpse down a drain, threatened a senator, told four people my secrets, and lost the one guy who I'd recently grown to trust would always have my back.

It's been a hell of a week.

At my locker, Gabriel pulls me against him, his lips catching mine in a kiss that has me seeing stars against my eyelids. His hands touch my face, tangle in my hair, and I lose myself in him completely, forgetting that we're in the hallway at a ritzy private school until someone wolf-whistles. I come up for air, panting, in time for Noah to spin me around and slam my back into the lockers. His lips crash into mine, determined to outdo Gabriel. I can't help myself rubbing against him like a cat in heat.

Whistles and catcalls echo down the hallway. When Noah pulls back, I see faces crowding in around him – everyone wanting to get a look at us. Gabriel throws his arm around me and flashes the devil horns as Chad snaps a photo with his phone for the school Facebook page. The two of them have laid claim to me for the whole school to see, making it clear that Mackenzie Malloy has their protection.

In reality, it's the other way around.

Of course, I'm not Mackenzie, but none of the students know that. Nor do they know that our new English teacher – the one with the neck tattoos and the disfigured face – is actually a dangerous mobster who's packing a semi-automatic rifle under his desk.

Tiberius catches my eye as I enter the classroom, and winks at me through the gaggle of girls who've surrounded his desk. Cleo leans over him to straighten the vase of flowers she's brought in – picked from the beds lining the school's driveway, I see. Her skirt rides so far up her tights I get a glimpse of her thong underwear.

And I thought I was a slutty dresser.

Tiberius looks happy with his lot until I mouth, "she's seventeen." He stands up abruptly and shoos everyone to their seats. I turn to head to my usual seat next to Gabriel in the back row, and that's when I see him.

Alec LeMarque.

He's sitting in the middle of the end row, underneath a display about the Stonehurst Shakespearean Society. His shoulders hunch and he focuses his gaze on his books, which is why I didn't notice him at first. He looks completely different from the arrogant asshole who made the mistake of pissing me off. The students forced to sit next to him have turned the edges of their desks away. He may have had his forehead repaired, but he might as well be wearing a scarlet letter – R for Rapist.

I'm not prepared for what seeing him again does to me. My body locks up, my limbs shuddering to a stop so I cause a traffic jam in the aisle. Alec looks up. He brushes his hair from his face and stares me down, and I want to run and also to pummel his head against the wall until his face is mush.

He smiles at me – a sinister smile, devoid of cockiness. This smile isn't saying – *I've come back to taunt you.*

It says, *I've come back to kill you.*

Before I can react, Gabriel leans over Alec's desk. "Don't you dare look at Mackenzie."

"It's a free country, Fallen." Alec flashes Gabe a toothy grin.

"We're watching you. If we hear you've touched a girl in this school, Mackenzie will cut your dick off."

Alec peers at Tiberius, begging him for help. Tiberius reads the situation in my face and leans back in his chair, arms behind his head, a smug smile playing across his scarred face. Alec's smile freezes as he realizes the teacher isn't rushing to help him. He recognizes Tiberius from the night we broke into his house and branded his forehead. His face pales, his shoulders stiffen, his whole body goes limp.

Gabriel lets go of his collar and slides into a seat, deliberately placing himself between me and Alec.

"Hello, students. My name is Mr. Garcia, and I'll be your new English teacher for the rest of the year while Mrs. Berkdale deals with some family business. I know you're excited to get back to your study of Oscar Wilde, so we'll begin by discussing the importance of sin and redemption in Wilde's work, and how it reflects the social and racial landscape of the period—"

"Where is Mrs. Berkdale, really?" Gabriel whispers to me as Tiberius drones on.

"Relax. We didn't bury her in the desert, if that's what you're asking. Antony gave her a generous payment to invent a family emergency and fuck off for the rest of the year. At this moment she's probably enjoying her complimentary piña colada on her flight to Aruba."

"Who's going to believe this guy's an English teacher?"

"Way to make assumptions based on someone's looks, Fallen. He's got a Masters in English Lit from Yale," I shoot back. "He's a mobster because teaching a bunch of spoiled prep-school brats pays shit. Now, back straight and pay attention. You don't want to know what Tiberius Garcia does to naughty Brit boys who act up in class."

Gabriel laughs, but he swivels his chair to face the front of the room and refers to his notes like he's actually taking in what Tiberius says.

I wish I could enjoy Tiberius' English class, not least because Cleo's lame attempts to get his attention were pathetic beyond measure. But even though I don't look into the corner once, I can still feel Alec's presence in the room – a poison gas that I suck with every breath. *How is he back? How can he possibly be back?*

Even though I don't hear a word of what Tiberius says, I notice that even the guys pay more attention than usual, and while there are a lot of meaningful glances, no one dares pass notes or act up. You don't see people who look like Tiberius at Stonehurst Prep, and the guy has a certain... *presence*. Sure, there are jocks – Eli's toned in a lean, crisp way, and Noah is jacked AF – but Tiberius could destroy any of them with his pinkie finger and they knew it.

Most of all, I love Alec LeMarque's white, terrified face.

I watch out of the corner of my eye as Alec pulls his phone from his pocket and texts someone. If he's hoping his daddy will pull some strings for him at the school, he's shit out of luck. Money talks, but violence is louder. I control Stonehurst Prep now.

"What the fuck is he doing here?" Gabriel asks as we shuffle toward our next class.

"I heard military school wouldn't take him." A guy named Mark comes up beside us – one of the jocks who hangs out in Eli and Noah's crowd. I remember him from the desert. He was the one whose cheek I sliced open with my blade. Mark runs a hand through his hair and blinks at me. "Hi, Mackenzie."

He sounds nervous. He should be. I had a feeling he's only being friendly now because he doesn't want to have my initials branded into his forehead. Normally, I hate a suck-up, but we need all the allies we can get in Stonehurst, so I force a smile. "Nice to see you again, Mark."

"See you at lunch." Gabe pats the guy on the shoulder. I can tell he hates doing it, but he knows the rules the same as I do. We need to own this school, and that means making nice with people who watched Alec hold me down over a car hood.

At lunchtime, I slide into a seat at our new table, between George and Noah. Mark and a few of his jock friends take the empty seats around us, while others throw us dirty looks and head to Alec and Cleo's table. All eyes flicker to us, watching where the popular kids choose to form their alliances.

My breath hitches as Eli enters the room. Noah's talking to me, but I don't hear a word as I watch Eli fill his plate at the salad bar. His fingers grip his tray so hard they turn white. His gaze flicks to our table, catching my eyes. He quickly looks away.

I don't think I can stand it if he sits down next to Alec. Noah leans forward, his eyes locked on Eli, as invested in his decision as I am. Eli stalks toward their table but at the last moment, he veers away, dumps his full tray of food into a trash can, and stalks outside.

I shove out of my chair. Noah catches my hand. "Leave him," he says. "He needs space."

Noah needs space. That's how he deals with shit – by bottling it up until he explodes in a fireball of delicious rage. But I don't think that's Eli's way. Eli revels in logic. He loves to solve problems. He wants to be the hero.

Just not for me.

I swallow down the bitter pill of his rejection and bite into my sandwich. I have to let Eli Hart go. It's the only way I can think to keep him safe from Brutus.

WHEN WE ARRIVE at gym class that afternoon, we get another surprise. Mrs. Anderson has gone on 'sabbatical,' and standing at the end of the gym is Antony, wearing sweatpants slung low over his hips and a black tank that shows off his inked, muscled arms.

"I'm Antony Jones, your new gym teacher." Jones is the name the August family uses on public records to keep the heat off us. "Today, we're going to start a new unit on self-defense."

"That's not in the curriculum," Eli points out, wiping his

palms on his tight-ass gym shorts. It figures Eli would have memorized the learning outcomes for fucking *gym*.

"My job is to prepare you for life, and in life it's useful to know how to kick the shit out of someone." Antony cracks his knuckles. You could hear a pin drop, it's so fucking quiet. "No one else with questions? Good. Now, partner up with someone who you'd feel comfortable punching in the face, and we'll start by learning a few basic defensive moves."

George puts her hand up, and I know she's going to pretend to have her period or something to get out of this. I grab her arm and tug her to me. "Got my partner," I call out to Antony.

"Freaks stick together," Cleo mutters as she lines up with Daphne. On the other side of the room, Noah and Gabriel are partnered up. Eli glares at them both, then glances around him, but there's only one person left.

Alec LeMarque.

I glare at Noah. "Do you know what's he doing back at school?"

"I heard from Chad this morning that his father argued his expulsion down to a suspension," Noah whispers back. "After all, it would be unfair to ruin poor Alec's life over a single *mistake in judgment*."

Unfair. Right. I only had to see the online campaign in response to our stunt with his car to know I wasn't Alec's only victim. But I'm determined I'll be his last.

"Excellent." Antony beckons Eli with his finger. "You. Captain America. Come here. Bring your victim—I mean, partner—with you."

There are titters from the girls as Eli stands in front of Antony. Eli's no slouch, but my cousin towers over him, and he's all hard edges and tattoos, whereas Eli is smooth skin and dimples. Antony glares at Alec, who slinks out to join them.

My cousin catches my eye and winks. George whimpers, but I grip her arm. "You won't want to miss this," I whisper.

Alec looks from Antony to me and back again, and I know he's thinking it's too big a coincidence that a second burly-ass substitute teacher has appeared at Stonehurst in the same day, and that teacher has chosen to drag him to the front of the class for a demonstration. He looks to his friends, but none of them will meet his gaze.

"Okay, grasshopper." Antony nods to Eli. "Show us how you throw a punch."

I expect Eli to protest. The head of the student council isn't going to punch another student in class.

Eli snaps his arm out and lands a punch in Alec's solar plexus.

Well, color me surprised.

And turned on. There was a fierceness behind that punch that made my knees weak in the best way. Alec drops to the mats, gasping and wheezing. It's a glorious sound. I try to meet Eli's gaze, but he's staring at his fist like he can't believe it's attached to his body.

"What the fuck, man?" Alec gasps, rolling onto his knees and clutching his stomach as he gasps for air.

"That's excellent. Top marks," Antony says. I can see him struggling to contain his laughter. "The only thing is, you hit him once and then stopped. In a life or death situation, you can't guarantee one blow is going to incapacitate a villain. If he had a weapon, it might've fallen to the ground and he could be heading for it. Like this."

Antony pulls a flick knife from his belt and drops it on the mat. No one's laughing or talking anymore. There's an electric charge in the air – like the heat pulsing whenever I'm around one of the guys, but this one is scented in blood. Alec looks at me with watering eyes, and I see the realization flicker on his face. That's a real knife, and if he wants to make it out of this fight alive, he needs to reach it.

Alec lunges for the knife at the exact time Eli surges forward. He kicks the blade away and stomps on Alec's hand. Alec screams as Eli grinds his heel into Alec's fingers. Eli glances up at Antony, and the expression on his face is unreadable. "Like this?"

"You're a fast learner." Antony kicks Alec in the back. "Once he's on the ground, it's a good idea to go for the kidneys. Anyone else want a go?"

Blood scents the air. I shove George forward. Her eyes widen, but she looks at me and I nod. The secret that hangs between us gives her strength.

"Go on," I whisper. "You may not get justice in a court. But you can have it today."

George's lip wobbles, but she lets go of my arm and steps forward. Eli steps over the mat and takes her hand, then pulls her in front of Antony, who appraises her with his steely gaze. "What's your name, doll?"

"G-G-George," she stammers. "George Fisher."

"Good. Nice to meet you, George Fisher. Now, normally when people teach self-defense they get girls to team up with other girls, but that shit's pointless. I've seen enough catfights in my time to know you ladies have that on lock." Antony kicks Alec in the side again. "Get up, scumbag."

"Can't you choose someone else?" Alec gasps.

"Why would I choose someone else? You're doing great. You'll get an A+ for this assignment. Now, pretend you're a rapist. Lunge at this girl."

The 'r' word sings in the air, heavy with the scent of blood. Alec crawls to his feet. He can barely stand. Antony cracks his knuckles again, and fear flickers in Alec's eyes as he lurches toward George.

For a moment, she's frozen, and I know she's not seeing Alec as he is now, but she's remembering another night, another time he lunged at her and put his hands on her without permission.

"Ms. Fisher."

The authority in Antony's voice snaps George from her trance. She moves her body, although I'm not sure she's even aware she's doing it. Antony's behind her, touching her shoulder as he instructs her.

Alec grabs George's arms, and the look on his face is pleading. But there's no mercy here. He took that from George when he hurt her. She snaps her body around, so his momentum carries him forward, where her upturned knee connects with his crotch with a satisfying *CRUNCH*.

"Yusss!" I punch the air. "Go George."

"A classic move," Noah observes with a wry smile. "She's learned from the best."

Alec's on the ground, moaning, but George has more she wants to say. She kicks him in the side, then again. She doesn't stop kicking. Her face twists into this misshapen roar, and all that is the George I know disappears, and a monster takes over. A monster that Alec LeMarque made.

Cleo keeps looking at Antony like she expects him to call George off, but he simply smiles and taps his foot. Tears roll down Alec's cheeks, and blood spurts from his nose and a cut above his eye. But still, George keeps kicking.

Antony moves around the room until he's standing next to us. "Here's a plot twist for you," he whispers. "It turns out Brentwood wasn't our mystery gunman after all."

"Oh yeah?" I lift an eyebrow. "It was bothering me how messy that was. It didn't seem like Brentwood's style. Please tell me it's not Brutus."

"It's not him. Old Brutey Boy is still AWOL." Antony nods to the prone body of Alec LeMarque. "Your friend Alec purchased a rifle last month. The model matches the bullets I pulled out of the wall."

"Shit," Noah says.

"I admire his cajones. I didn't think he had it in him."

"Anything he had in him is not in him anymore," Antony chuckles. "Consider this an early birthday present."

So Antony was the one who let Alec back in. I wish he'd told me – that was just like my cousin, storming ahead with his own agenda, believing he knew best. It never occurred to him to warn me I might see my would-be rapist in the halls.

I had to applaud his execution, though. I know exactly what my cousin is doing with this little display – showing Alec and the rest of this school who's really in charge.

It's working.

George staggers back, wiping Alec's blood from her face. She slumps, coming back down from the adrenaline I know is coursing through her. She's never looked more beautiful – a warrior goddess restoring balance to the world. As Alec crawls to his feet, blood streaming from his nose, his friends step away from him. Even Cleo wrinkles her nose in disgust. Message received.

She may not really be here, but Mackenzie Malloy's reputation at Stonehurst Prep just got dangerous.

CLAUDIA

"Sooooo... can we talk about homecoming plans?" George slides her tray across from mine. She's gone crazy on the dessert bar today, stacking three slices of different flavored cheesecakes one on top of each other to form a diabetic Tower of Babel.

"Homecoming?" The word snaps me out of thoughts of Brentwood lying in his bathtub with Malloy pills shoved down his throat. I vaguely recall announcements about a dance, and a line outside the cafeteria a couple of weeks ago that blocked access to my preferred lunching bathroom.

"Yeah. It's this weekend. I mean, obviously, you know that, because you're going to be cheering at the big game. I'm not going because..." George gestures to herself. "Obviously."

"Because you're intellectually superior and have no desire to waste your precious brain cells intermingling." I glare at her. "Because *obviously* that's the only possible meaning to your comment."

George stares at her food. "On Saturday, there's a cult horror festival at the Beaumont Theatre. *Happy Birthday to Me, Tokyo Gore Police, Society, Army of Darkness, Braindead, Suspiria.* I thought maybe we could go together... unless you're planning to go to the dance? You might want to find out if you're the homecoming queen."

"Excuse me... *what?*"

"Don't tell me you didn't know." George flips her phone around to show me the homecoming dance news on the school app. There are instructions for parking at the game, the words to the school song, details about the venue, and a place to vote for the homecoming court. Noah, Gabriel, and Eli are on the list for king. My eyes bug out as I look at the list for homecoming queen. There's Cleo, of course, and a couple of other popular girls.

And me.

Mackenzie Malloy.

"This is insane. How did I not know about this?" I know how. I'd been pretty distracted over the last few weeks with boy drama and attempts on my life and shit.

"Anyway." George swallows. "It's fine. You go. I'm used to going to the movies by myself. I prefer it, actually. I don't have to share my popcorn and you won't have to suffer through my terrible jokes, like why do vampires never order at a restaurant—"

"Oooh, who said something about homecoming?" Gabriel slides into the seat beside me. One whiff of his pagan scent and I'm gone. I'm surprised I'm not a permanent pile of goo from hanging around Gabriel Fallen so much. "Because I think we need to strategize. I'll be wearing a pinstripe suit with my skeleton creepers, ala Nick Cave crossed with Jerry Only, so I was thinking to match me you should get some stilettos with a heel made out of a spine. Here, I found a picture... wait until you see this." Gabriel swipes through his phone.

"Fuck off. I'm not going to homecoming." I grab the phone out of his hand and stare at the shoes. They do look fucking *fierce*, but also impossible to walk in. "These aren't shoes, they're torture implements. Don't tell me, you had something to do with my nomination?"

"But of course, Queenie." Gabriel's eyes sparkle with mischief. "If I'm going to be wearing that crown, I need the most shaggable arse in school on the throne next to me."

"If you want a date for the dance, you're supposed to actually ask that person if they want to go with you *first*." I throw my arms around George's shoulder. "As it happens, George and I already have a date – we're going to a horror movie festival at this spooky-ass theatre down in Brawley."

Gabriel looks at me in horror. "Surely you jest? Of course we're going to homecoming. I was going to grab our tickets today."

I turn to George. "Can you believe this?"

George swallows. "It's not a big deal. You should go with Gabriel. Don't worry about me. I'll be fine."

I glare at Gabriel. As George leans over to get something from her bag, Gabriel leans in close. I breathe in his dangerous scent as he presses his lips to my ear and murmurs, "I know you want to see what it's like to have a normal life. Going to homecoming is the most normal high school thing you could possibly do. Besides, whoever's watching you is going to be awfully suspicious if It Girl Mackenzie Malloy doesn't show her face at her own homecoming dance."

He has a point. I glance over at George, who's sliding down in her seat, avoiding looking at us. "Fine. We'll go. On one condition. You're George's date."

George's head jerks up. "What? No. I can't..."

"Hot damn." Gabriel rubs his hands together with glee, before throwing his phone at George. "Even better. George, you'll wear these skeletal death-traps for me, won't you, luv?"

As George and Gabriel start discussing their matching

outfits, I glance across the table at Noah, who is very deliberately cutting his steak into neat squares. I kick him under the table. "Marlowe, I think there's something you want to ask me."

Noah raises his chin, and I peer into those dark orbs. "Honestly? I'd rather be your date for the horror movie festival."

"No way. If I have to miss the festival, you all do." George elbows him in the arm, then suddenly realizes how friendly she's getting with the insanely popular kids who were horrible to her, and stares at her food again. "I mean," she mumbles into her boobs. "Do you what you want, of course, it's totally cool—"

"You are so adorable, George." I reach across the table and spear one of Noah's steak squares, dropping it on my tongue where it melts like an ice cube of meaty deliciousness. Damn, they made such great food here. I spear another, waving my fork at him to emphasize my point. "Let me phrase this another way – you'd better be at my place on Saturday night to pick me up, Marlowe. You'll be wearing a suit, carrying a corsage, and grinning like the Cheshire Cat because you're the luckiest fucking man alive to be escorting Mackenzie Malloy to the homecoming dance. Got it?"

Noah bites the steak off the end of my fork. I watch that jaw of his working, and warmth flushes my body as I remember tasting his blood in our ferocious kiss. I know what he's thinking, because I can read those dark eyes like a book – he's thinking that Noah Marlowe and Mackenzie Malloy at homecoming together will have people talking, and that's going to get back to his father. He's getting used to the fact he doesn't have to be afraid of John Marlowe any longer. He nods, and the corner of his mouth tugs up into that self-satisfied smirk. "I got it."

AFTER WE FINISH EATING, we join the growing line at the home-coming-ticket booth, perusing all the special deals on limousines and crappy seafood restaurants the dance committee has put together. "Leave the pre-prom plans to me," Gabriel throws his arms around George again. "I have ideas."

"That sounds dangerous." I can't help the little dance of excitement in my gut. Even though the last thing I should be thinking about right now is the homecoming dance, all I've ever wanted is the chance to be normal. And going to a dance with my friends and my two fucking gorgeous boyfriends... I couldn't ask for anything more.

Except I wish Eli was part of it, too.

As we take another step toward the table, a guy steps in front of us. "Hey, George, can we talk for a sec?"

It's the metalhead stoner, and he's got his hands shoved in his pockets and his hair pulled in front of his eyes, and I think my chest might burst from the cuteness. George peers up at me with her deer-in-the-headlights look. She needs help that only Mackenzie Malloy can provide.

I fold my arms. "Whatever you have to say to George, you can say in front of her bestie."

I'm smiling, but my reputation precedes me, and stoner dude backs up a step.

"Um... see..." He touches his lips, as though he's holding an invisible good-luck joint. "So, George, here's the thing... I was wondering if you had a date to homecoming because I... I thought maybe we could go together if you're into that kind of thing..."

Gabriel throws his arm around George's shoulder. "She's already got a date, actually."

George looks sick.

"Oh." The guy flicks his gaze to Gabriel, and I see him do a quick math equation in his head regarding his chances of getting out of this with his dignity intact.

"Ignore Gabriel. He doesn't know when to shut his face." I thrust myself between them and hold my hand out to the guy. "Hi. Mackenzie Malloy, class bitch. I hear you want to take my friend George to homecoming."

To his credit, the guy takes my hand and gives it a firm shake. "I'm Isaac Hirst. And yes, I would. But if she's already going with Fallen, I won't intrude—"

"She's not. I apologize for the confusion." I shove a frozen George forward. "The two of you can go buy your tickets together."

George looks like she's going to bolt, but Isaac threads his arm through hers. I see the exact moment his touch registers, because her whole body wobbles and she looks like she's going to faint. I know that feeling – the electrical charge that lights you from the inside. It's how I'm lit up like a Christmas tree 24/7 around Noah and Gabriel. And Eli, although I shove the memory of his touch back down again.

She *likes* this guy.

George and Isaac step up to the table. Cleo gives them this indulgent look as she slots their tickets into a gold-rimmed envelope, like they're two children playing dress-up. "I'm sure you'll have the most *interesting* dress," she purrs at George.

My fingers itch to slap a bitch, but I've got enough to deal with without deepening my feud with Cleo St. James.

We're next. I turn to Gabe and Noah in a panic. As I do, I notice Eli standing near the end of the line, bright ocean eyes boring into me. His body jerks as he sees me looking back, and he turns his head away.

Gabriel grabs me around the waist. "I call bagsy on Mac."

"Bagsy?" Noah makes a face. "You can't just make up words to win an argument. Mackenzie is my date."

"You're the Dark Horse. You need an equine date," Gabriel shoots back. "What about Daphne Ballantyne? She'll happily kick you with her spurs—"

I growl low in my throat. Ain't no one spurring Noah except me. I feel Eli's presence behind me – the itch between my shoulders that says he's listening to every word. "Is there any rule that says you can only have one date?"

"Who cares if there is – you're Mackenzie Malloy." Gabriel looks delighted. "You don't play by the rules."

"Damn right." I throw my arm around both of them just as Cleo gestures angrily at us to hurry up. "What do you say, Marlowe?"

"You're on." Noah waves his black card in Cleo's face.

As Gabriel starts hounding Noah about coordinating their outfits, Eli strides past, his head down. He heard everything. I want him to seethe with jealousy. I want him to stay as far from me as possible. I want his arms around me, but I can't have it. I'm a mess over him, and judging by how rumpled his usually neat uniform is, he's not much better. I watch as he shoves his way through the crowd, nearly knocking down Daphne in his desperation to get away from me.

My good mood deflates like a balloon. I have not one, but two of the hottest guys in school taking me to the dance, so why can't I get the boy with the sunshine smile out of my head?

———

"I HEARD she's taking Gabriel *and* Noah to the homecoming dance."

"That's not allowed. Is that allowed?"

"Cleo says it's not, but that new English teacher took over as faculty advisor for the dance committee and he overruled her.

Have you seen him? He's completely *ripped*. He'd be so fucking hot if it wasn't for his scarred-up face—"

I'll show you a scarred-up face.

I keep my homicidal thoughts to myself. Tiberius can handle his own reputation. Voices swirl around me as I dump my backpack on the bleachers and pick up my pom-poms. I'm used to being the focus of gossip at this school. The minute I step outside Malloy Manor, the whispers claw at my back. At least now I'm in control of the narrative. A few girls even look at me with awe in their eyes.

Damn right, bitches. One guy isn't enough for Mackenzie Malloy.

Antony blows the whistle, and we line up for warm-up drills. I can tell by the smirk on his face as he watches Daphne's ass in her short skirt that he's not sad about being stuck with Mrs. Anderson's after school activities.

As squad captain, Cleo leads us through the halftime routine we'll perform at Friday's game. Football isn't a big deal at Stonehurst – although that might just be because our team is shit. Most of the popular jocks play lacrosse or tennis or are on the track team, and no college recruiters turn up to the games to scout hot talent. But the cheerleading squad is another story. Cleo led the team to take the national championships last year, and before that, they've been state champions ten years running. In the sport of bouncing around like bulimic bunnies, Stonehurst is number one.

I'm glad I spent all that time over the years working out in the ballroom and dancing to Gabriel's music, or I'd struggle to keep up. Today, Cleo is extra brutal, making us repeat every move until it meets her standards. My muscles scream in protest as I lift Daphne onto my shoulders. She kicks me in the ear as she flips. From the smile on her face as I set her down, I'm sure it's deliberate.

"Again," Cleo barks, twisting her head to the side to bat her eyelashes at Antony as she bounces into a series of back hand-springs, flashing her black lace underwear. It's gross.

Antony's phone beeps. He turns away to read the message. Cleo finishes showing off, frowning when she notices Antony isn't even looking. When Antony turns back, the vein in his neck swells and I know I'm in trouble.

"Great work, Ms. St. James. If you can't find a rich sugar daddy, you may have a future in the sports industry yet." Antony nods to the gym door. "Ms. Malloy, can I see you outside for a second?"

Cleo's jealous gaze burns into my back as I follow Antony into the corridor. He slams the gym door and pulls me into a narrow closet that serves as Mrs. Anderson's office. I sit gingerly on the corner of his desk as he slams the door so hard the wood cracks.

"Antony, what the hell—"

"You didn't tell me your fucking boyfriend was connected to the Lucian family," Antony hisses. He slams the trash can against the floor with such force he dents it.

I shake my head. "That's insane. We dealt with Senator Marlowe. No way would he risk it getting out that he's working with one of the gangs—"

"Not him. I'm talking about Captain America. I have Joey watching his house. He says Nero pulled up at his place last night and he hasn't left."

Nero.

No no no no.

Nero fucking Lucian – *Imperator* of the Lucian family. Nero is a cold, calculating motherfucker with a vacuum-cleaner salesman smile. I don't want him anywhere near Eli.

"I swear I didn't know about this." I reach for his phone. "I trust Joey sent pictures."

Antony grunts. I scroll through his messages until I come to the series of images from Joey – it's Nero all right, entering the house, being greeted at the door by Eli's mother – who wears a figure-hugging fishtail dress with silver threads shot through the fabric.

But Eli's family has a housekeeper. Shouldn't she be answering the door?

I keep scrolling. There's Nero kissing her hand, and her beckoning him inside with her index finger. Joey has pictures of Eli arriving home timestamped an hour later. There's a picture through the window of their dining room of the three of them eating dinner together, and Nero's car parked in their driveway overnight.

I'm not the only one with secrets.

"It looks like he's Eli's mother's boy toy," I say with more confidence than I feel. The three of them sitting around the table, Eli's mother reaching across to her son. Eli's back is to the camera, so I can't see his face, but it looks like the perfect happy family portrait. "Eli might not know—"

"I don't care. You've got to get this under control." Antony snatches the phone from my fingers. "If your boyfriend tells the Lucian family who you really are, you know what this could mean—"

"He wouldn't do that." But honestly, I have no idea what Eli will do. I betrayed him and he's hurting. Just because he punched Alec doesn't mean he's forgiven me.

Another thought occurs to me – that this might not be a coincidence. But I don't know what that means exactly. And I won't know until I can find out from Eli, who isn't currently talking to me.

"You need to make sure he keeps his mouth shut," Antony says. "If you don't, I will. And my solution will be permanent."

19

CLAUDIA

alking to Eli proves to be more difficult than I think. The next day, I try to catch him as he heads out to track practice, but he's already on the field when I arrive, doing warm-ups in his tiny shorts and talking to his coach. I head to our last cheerleading practice before the big game, where I drown in Antony's drool as he leads a hellish warm-up drill where skirt hems fly in all directions. He shoved Cleo aside and tries to teach us some boxing moves to inject a little attitude into our carefully choreographed routines. It's hilarious watching Cleo try to keep her squad together without pissing off her new favorite teacher.

I race from practice without changing to try to make it to the track before Eli finishes. I'm too late. The field's empty. Noah emerges from the changing rooms, his dark hair wet from the shower, sticking to his forehead in an adorable way.

"I need to speak to Eli."

"He's already gone." Noah's arm goes around my middle, and he pulls me to him. "He saw you watching him before. I saw you too, in your little skirt, and my thoughts went to a *very* bad place."

I melt against him as his lips envelop mine and his hand slides up my thigh, playing with the edge of my underwear. It's wild how Noah Marlowe can just flick a switch in his head, and all that hate he had for me has burned up in a fire of lust. All it took was a few bitter words and a finger in his ass and he's mine.

I know Eli won't come to me so easily.

This is exactly what you wanted, my sensible half wrestles with me as Noah's finger teases and tempts. *If Eli's not your friend, then he's safe.*

No one is safe with Nero in their house.

Noah tries to slip his finger inside me, but I know if he does that, I'll be gone. And I need his help. "Antony saw Eli's mother inviting a new boyfriend into their home."

"So?" Noah reaches out to grab me again, slamming his chest against mine. He kisses a line along my jaw. "Darlene's had a string of lovers since Walter went to prison. I doubt it's serious."

I wriggle free again. "I don't care who Eli's mother is fucking. But he can't be in the same house as Nero Lucian. It's not safe. If he won't listen to me, can you talk some sense into him?"

"If I promise to try, will you let me kiss you?" Noah growls.

I may be desperate to help Eli, but I'm in Noah Marlowe's arms and I'm only human. His lips sweep mine again, and this time I don't resist. His kiss drags me into fire and brimstone, where his touch sears my skin and melts me against him.

I'm debating dragging him behind the bleachers and doing filthy things to him when he draws back and peers at me, as if he's only just registering what I said. "Who is this Nero guy, anyway? His name sounds familiar."

"He's the current head of the Lucian crime family. They have their greedy-ass fingers in every entertainment company, casino, club, and film studio in the city. You can't play an illegal poker game in this town without lining Nero's pockets. He's got a stake in Antony's club and sponsors his best fighters."

Noah's jaw works. "And he's having dinner at Eli's house?"

"That's what I said. Do you lose your hearing when your little brain is engaged?"

"There's nothing little about it." Noah cups my cheek and kisses me roughly, grinding his hips against mine as if I need any reminding of just how not-little he is. "I'll make sure Eli's safe. But it can wait – right now I need to bend you over the bleachers so the moonlight catches your ice-cold eyes as you come."

20

ELI

I stare at the freshly-painted ceiling in my bedroom. Even with two thick layers of white paint, I still imagine I can see the outline of the words Claudia scrawled there. I roll over and close my eyes, but I see them imprinted on my eyelids.

YOU WERE SUPPOSED TO PROTECT ME

They might've been Claudia's words designed to trap me, but I felt like Mackenzie spoke to me through them. She was the one in all of this who didn't have a voice, and it's my job as her only friend to give her one. I need to stand up for her against what Claudia and Noah and Gabriel are doing. And that starts with figuring out what happened to her four years ago.

My clock reads 3:47AM, but there's no way I'll be falling asleep. No way in hell can anyone sleep with my mother and Nero Lucian banging like a screen door in a tornado. The sounds coming from my mother's room have scarred me for life.

Instead, I've been turning Mackenzie's disappearance in my head for hours, even though I desperately need rest if I'm going to get through school and the homecoming game tomorrow. It seems like everywhere I look at Stonehurst, I'm confronted with my former best friends and Claudia August, the mafia king's daughter with the lies on her tongue.

I've tried to locate Mackenzie before – I even hired a private investigator two years ago, although he turned out to be a scam artist who disappeared as soon as I paid the deposit. Noah said it was my own fault for trusting him. "No one pays for a PI's services up-front."

I guess he's right – I *am* too trusting. I've always wanted to believe the best in people. I was the only person who saw through Mackenzie's Ice Queen bitch witch facade. But now I'm the reason Claudia is getting away with stealing Mackenzie's house. I'm done being the Golden Boy. I'm ready to fight dirty.

To do that, I need weapons. I'm not going into this fight wielding violence – that's not a weapon I know how to use. But I can arm myself with the *truth*.

I searched for the truth for so long and never got anywhere. I know I need help from an outside source – someone who gets off on Sherlock Holmesing their way into dangerous situations.

It occurs to me that I know someone with the exact skills I need. I've already seen the devastating impact of their talents, and I know they can't resist a mystery. I just have to—

My phone rings.

What the fuck? I stare at it as it vibrates across the bedside table. The piercing wail of the ringtone reverberates in my silent room. Gizmo pokes her head from beneath the blankets to glare at the offending device.

Brrrrriiiiing. Brrrrriiiiing.

Why the fuck is calling me at 3:47AM?

Noah's name flashes on the screen. A dark feeling hits my gut. Is he okay? Has something happened?

I grab the phone and moan into the receiver. "This better be fucking important."

"It is. Can you meet me at school in five minutes? I need to practice the hurdles."

Noah *fucking* Marlowe.

We have our first winter indoor meet next month, and it's an important one. College recruiters will be there, and as the team captain, it's my job to make sure we shine. But I can barely muster a single fuck to give about track. It used to be that when I looked up from the starting blocks, I stared into my future – a future far away from my family and fucking Emerald Beach – where I got to live life based on my own values and beliefs. Track was how I would escape my family's obsession with profiting from the grief of others. Now, when I stare down the field, all I see is Claudia August, the ghost of the girl I love.

The last thing I want to do is run through more drills with Noah, especially since he doesn't know how dangerously close I am to kicking him off the team. But something in his voice catches me – a hint of emotion, of desperation. This is Noah Marlowe reaching out, and I'd be a shitty friend if I didn't respond. Even if I do hate his guts right now.

I drag myself out of bed, stuff my uniform and calculus textbook into my gym bag, and pad through the house. I can hear Maria snoring from her room off the back of the kitchen. Mom isn't awake, but even if she was I doubt she'd care where I was going.

My hand turns on the doorknob when a voice says, "Hold on a minute, son."

The deep voice stabs the darkness. My heart hammers in my chest as I look over my shoulder. Nero steps out of the shadows.

What's he doing skulking around the house at 4AM?

"Hi." I nod at him, hoping that I'm not betraying the trembling in my arm. "I'm just on my way to track practice, so I can't stop to chat."

"This is early to be heading to school." He looks faintly amused, as if we've both been caught sneaking snacks from the fridge. As he glides across the floor toward me, I see that he's dressed in his three-piece pinstripe suit, his shoes perfectly shined. He can't have got dressed just to come down and speak to me, so I wonder where he's planning to go at this early hour.

"We have our first meet soon, and college recruiters will be there. Every minute of extra practice matters." Especially now that Dad's civil suits will run our coffers dry and I'll have to pay my way through college.

"You're a very bright boy, aren't you, Elias?" It's not really a question. Men like Nero don't expect an answer. He thrusts his hands in the pockets of his impeccable suit, and I notice a gold watch around his wrist and a small coin hanging from a gold chain around his neck. "I wondered if you might be interested in a job with me after you graduate. I know you're planning for college, but a year or two in the real world might help you decide on your next step."

He sounds so sincere, my hackles immediately go up. Dad would say this guy is slicker than owl shit. "That's nice of you to offer, but I don't think so."

"If you change your mind..." Nero withdraws his hand from his pocket and places a heavy business card in my cold fingers. "I know life's tough on you right now. My father spent time in prison, too. But like it or not, I'm going to be sticking around, and I'd like to think we can be friends."

My fingers close around his business card. I have to admit, I'm intrigued. Nero says his father is a felon, and yet he's obviously a successful guy. No one else I know has dealt with what I've been though – seeing Walter Hart led away in chains, having to talk to him through a glass wall in that piss-soaked room, knowing that when people look at me, they don't see *me* – only my father's crimes.

There are plenty of criminals among the elite in Emerald Beach, but my father was the only one stupid enough to get caught. Despite myself, I slip the card into the pocket of my gym bag. "What kind of work are you talking about?"

"Pretty menial stuff, if I'm honest. All the things my terrible assistant struggles with – managing a schedule, keeping appointments, keeping tabs on my various enterprises. But it would give you a behind-the-scenes look into the industry, maybe make some connections that can help you when you decide on your career."

"Any reality TV shows about rockstar veterinarians?" I raise an eyebrow.

Nero tosses his head back and laughs deep from his belly. I find myself cracking a smile, too. The guy still makes me uneasy, but... "Exactly, son. You never know when the perfect opportunity is just around the corner. Life isn't about what you know – it's *who* you know. A bright boy like you can go a long way if you choose the right friends. But side with the wrong crowd, well..." Nero makes a slicing motion across his throat. He laughs again, his face contorting in the low light of the dimmed chandelier.

As I watch Nero climb into his car and take off into the darkness, I can't help but feel I'd just been given a warning.

* * *

"Where's your gear?" I jog up to Noah. He's sitting on the bleachers, swinging his legs, with a serious Noah expression on his face. It's freezing out – a crisp breeze blows in off the ocean only half a mile down the road. I think about Gizmo snuggled under the covers back home, and wish I was with her. And then I remember the sounds from my mother's room down the hall and Nero giving me his 'man of the house chat' and I amend my wish.

Noah shrugs. "I thought we could have a little talk."

"Fuck off." I throw my gym bag on the ground with as much force as I can. My shoes bounce out and scatter across the grass. "I came because I thought you wanted help with track. If that's not the case, I'm going back to bed—"

Noah stands between me and my bag, folding his arms across his broad chest. I'm struck again by how much he's bulked up. No wonder he's hopeless at track – he's got no hope propelling that sheer wall of muscle forward with any kind of speed. "This is important. We need to talk about Claudia."

"Nope. This is *bullshit*." I shove Noah in the chest. He staggers back a little but doesn't relent. He's a fucking *tank*.

How did I not notice this?

Right – school and prison and civil suits and figuring out how to get out of Emerald Beach. I'm a shitty friend. Something has been going on with Noah for a while, from before Claudia showed up. I've been too distracted to pay attention until now, and it's too late – he's here on her orders. He's lost to me, an enemy of the *real* Mackenzie, who I swore to protect.

Noah folds his arms, and I know I'm not getting through that wall of muscle without breaking a tooth. "What's bullshit is Nero Lucian at your house."

"My mom's new boyfriend. So?"

"Dude, don't you know that guy's the head of one of the crime families in the Triumvirate? He's mortal enemies with the Augusts."

I laugh. "This is ridiculous. She's got you chasing after here like her little lapdog to tell me this bullshit story so I come crawling back to—"

"It's not bullshit, Eli. Do you know what I've been doing since Claudia told me? I've been up for hours poring over the material submitted by my dad's task force. Nero's one of the men they've been following for some time. He runs all kinds of illegal gambling places, prostitution rings, fight clubs, and entertainment venues that serve as fronts for laundering money and stolen goods... anything you can imagine. And you're eating peach cobbler with him."

"This is insane." I ignore Noah's cobbler dig as I sink onto the grass, taking it all in. Nero is a crime lord? How is this my life now? All I ever wanted was a simple life where I help people. Back in Tennessee, Dad would let me help write the eulogies for his clients. That was the only nice thing about his business – I got to make the world a tiny bit better for my being in it. Now my dad's in prison and the girl I love is a lying thief and a mob boss is going to be my stepfather, and that goodness I crave is impossible to reach.

"I know, dude. It's fucked up. So you've spoken to him?"

I nod. "He came to dinner the other night – it was the only reason I came back from the ranch. Maria found me out there and she told me Mom wanted to see me. I thought she wanted to talk about Dad's appeal. Silly me. She's going to *marry* Nero. He'll be my new stepfather."

Noah lets out a string of curse words and kicks the bleachers so hard he splits the wood.

I drop my head into my hands. "He was creeping around the house this morning. He said all this weird shit about me being clever, and asked me to come and work for him. He said something about making sure I was in with the right people."

Noah's hand clamps on my shoulders. "Do you think he's talking about Claudia? He could be trying to make sure you're on his side instead of hers."

"I'm not on her side."

"You can't be on *his* side," Noah insists. "What about your dad—"

"I'm on the side of everyone getting the fuck out of my face with this so I can graduate high school and leave Emerald Beach behind forever," I growl.

"I don't think that's an option anymore." Noah's fingers dig into my shoulder. His eyes burn into mine. "Claudia wants you to move back into Malloy Manor, immediately. Strength in numbers and all that."

"I don't care what she wants."

"I know you're pissed at her, but this is about your life. Nero being here can't be a coincidence. He might be trying to spy on Claudia."

"I'm not going back to the house she's trying to steal from Mackenzie."

Noah looked like he was going to slap me. "For fuck's sake. That bitch has still got you brainwashed."

"Claudia has not—"

"I'm talking about Mackenzie!" Noah yelled. "I never told you this because you're my friend and you've spent your whole life worshipping her, but Mackenzie Malloy treated you like crap."

"You're only saying that because you want me to be okay with Claudia stealing her house, playing happy families like she gives a shit about us—"

"She does give a shit. She especially gives a shit about you even though you're acting like a little bitch right now. No, Eli, I'm saying this because you're mourning the loss of a girl who never existed. It's like you get Mackenzie in your head and you can't think straight. You don't seem to remember her calling you horrible names and letting you take the fall for the pranks she pulled. She scared off every other kid who tried to be your friend because she didn't want to share you. She made you crawl around after her like a lost puppy, and she's not even here and you're *still doing it*."

"What about you?" My hands ball into fists. "You liked her, too. You were jealous of what I had with Mackenzie because you wanted to get into her pants. You couldn't handle the fact that I had something you didn't, and when she came to you about her father's drug trials, you saw a way to finally have one over on me. You always have to be first, best, and brightest, and who cares who you have to step on to do it."

Pain flickers in Noah's dark eyes. I've never twisted a knife between his ribs like this before. The whole reason Noah hates his father is because Old-Man Marlowe forced him to compete with Felix and he could never measure up.

I'd just told him he's his father's son.

Noah's chest heaves as he sucks in breaths. His cheeks flush with color, and I know he's trying to control his anger. Part of me wants to goad him further – I'd love to see Noah Marlowe lose his tenuous grip on control and finally contend with the monster inside. The sensible side of my brain reminds me that Noah could punch his fist right through my ribcage without batting an eye. I remain silent.

"Sure. I liked Mackenzie." Noah's struggling to keep his voice even. "I liked her because I can see myself in her. I'm no better than she is. We're both horrible, twisted people. I've always treated you like shit, bro. And then I expect you to be there for me when I'm hurting. Just like I expected that one day you'd give up Mackenzie for me, or I'd simply take her from you. I let you take care of me after Felix died, and I don't think I ever once asked you how you were coping with your dad going to prison."

"You—you—" I can't form words.

Noah's so close now, his nose touches mine. His face twists in this ugly scowl. "When you thought Mackenzie was back, you drew lines between her old personality and her new one that don't fucking exist. Just because *Claudia* justified Mackenzie's actions by being an actual semi-decent human doesn't make what Mackenzie did to you okay. It's not Mackenzie you fell in love with this time – it's Claudia."

"You didn't know her like I did. Her parents tortured her—"

"Right. And she came to school and tortured everyone else." Noah swipes his hand through his hair. He forgets I can read him, too. I know he's nervous. He wants to change my mind. "She was fucking *evil*. And you know it. What she and Cleo did to George? That wasn't Cleo's idea. Mackenzie let Cleo take the credit because she knew George would tell and Cleo would get in more trouble for being the ringleader. But Mackenzie was always the one pulling the strings. Her leaving you behind with no note, no goodbye – that was the absolute cruelest thing she could do, and that's why you hate Claudia so much. Because she may be the daughter of a mob king, she may be trying to keep Mackenzie's house, but deep down Claudia is the person you wished Mackenzie could be."

Rage burns inside me. "You don't get to tell me who I love or why. You don't know the first thing about love."

"If you say so." Noah thrusts a piece of paper into my hands. "Claudia said to give you that. She said it belongs to you. Ask yourself, did you spend all those nights haunting Malloy Manor because you wanted Mackenzie to come back, or because you wanted a reason to justify her final cruelty?"

I punch him in the nose.

The sting of it slams into my fists. Noah staggers back, clutching his face. Blood spurts down his t-shirt. Anger flashes in his eyes, and for a moment I'm paralyzed with fear. If Noah comes for me, he'll flatten me.

Instead, he lowers his hand, staring me down from those coal-black depths. "Just think about it, Eli."

He stalks away, holding his nose, leaving me alone with the paper and my cold, dark wishes.

I stare down at the paper. I unfold it. It's a page from a notebook – a ragged edge on one side where it had been torn out. Wobbly, childish handwriting crowds on the lines, sometimes spilling over the ends and curling around. Many of the i's and j's had hearts drawn on them instead of dots.

An ache spreads across my chest.

I'd know that handwriting anywhere.

It's a diary entry. It isn't dated, but I remember the day well. It was a few months after our parents declared we weren't allowed to see each other. Dad was at a casket roadshow over the weekend and Mom didn't care what I got up to, so I took Mackenzie out for dinner. We sat at a corner table of this fancy Italian place all the food critics were raving about, the kind of place I thought Mackenzie would enjoy because it's hip and exclusive.

I'm scribbling this in the bathroom. I'm so angry. Eli brought me to a restaurant for dinner. He's excited and keeps asking me how I like the food. I'm going to stab him with my fork.

Everyone around us is at least twenty years older and ugly as sin. The couple behind us hold hands over the table, and a pair of guys at the bar feed each other sick-looking cocktails. I hate them all. They make me sick. Don't they know all this is a lie? No one lives happily-ever-after. The only royals who get to keep their crowns are those who enclose their hearts in ice.

I don't know why we're here, pretending to be adults. Eli folds my napkin on my lap. If he wants me to be one of these air-brushed bimbos making polite conversation, then I'll slit his throat while he sleeps.

Just kidding. But this is weird, and he's been doing lots of other weird things lately. It doesn't matter though – at least Eli-weird is calm and safe. At least Eli lets me yell and break things and do whatever I want. I'll sit through anything if it will keep him by my side.

No matter what I do, Eli will always protect me.

Tears stab at the corners of my eyes. From my pocket, I pull out the strip of photographs of me and Mackenzie at Disney-land. I try to recall the elation of that day, the giddy excitement I felt holding her hand and feeling her body lean against mine as we rode the teacups. This time, what comes back to me are the memories that slipped through the cracks – Mackenzie screaming at a terrified cotton-candy seller until he gave her a free cone. Mackenzie elbowing small children and pulling a girl's hair so we could push past them in the Space Mountain line. Mackenzie guilt-tripping me into doing her homework for her that evening, since I made her skip school.

I think of other things, too. I think of kids scattering whenever Mackenzie walked into a room. I remember finding George hiding in a supply closet, holding a razor blade to the skin of her ankle because Mackenzie told her she'd be better off dead.

I crush the paper in my fingers, screwing it into a tight ball. I throw it at the bleachers, watching it bounce on the wood and fall through a crack.

Claudia lied about who she was. But I've been lying to myself, too.

I needed... I needed to set things straight.

CLAUDIA

"I'm so nervous." George paces the length of our room, her dress swishing around her ankles.

It's the night of the homecoming dance, and we're holed up in a room that's a mirror-image of Gabriel's pad, except decorated in garish burgundy and gold. Gabriel's neighbor is some big shot tech mogul who's hardly ever in the country. He rents his apartment out for events, and Gabriel scored us the place for our dance preparations while he and Noah and Isaac get ready next door.

"You don't look nervous. You're a total bombshell." It's true. George found a vintage '50s dress at her thrift store with a plunging sweetheart neckline that's perfect for her tiny frame. With her shoulders bare and her short pixie cut dyed a brilliant midnight blue, her tattoos are on full display. George has great ink – you'd think she'd be all skulls and bats and roses, but she says she wants to look at her skin and smile, so on one arm are kittens shaped like donuts chasing tiny balls of yarn that twirl around her wrist, and on the other arm is a bunch of different monsters from horror films all having a party and eating giant pieces of cake.

"I don't know how to do this." She flings one of her scuffed New Rock boots into the wall and flops down on the bed.

"Do what?"

"Go to a dance with a boy. What do I even say to Isaac? I can barely talk to anyone, actually. But boys are the worst. I don't even have to be into them and I turn into a hamster. I sat next to Eli the whole game last night and we barely said a word to each other."

"You seemed to be doing fine to me." I shrug, pretending I hadn't noticed or cared she sat with Eli last night at the game (which Stonehurst lost, as predicted. Our cheerleading routine, however, went off perfectly despite Daphne trying to trip me during the opening number). I can still feel the burn of his eyes on me as I spun through my kicks and tumbles, and the stab of jealousy in my chest as Eli and George bent their heads together to whisper to each other.

They looked like they had plenty to talk about.

Even when he hates me, Eli is still the Golden Boy, shunning his many other friends to sit with George – who has no one else and only came in the first place out of loyalty to me. And then, on Wednesday, George didn't show up at our table for lunch. I went looking for her in case Cleo had done something to her, and found her and Eli bent over a desk in the computer lab, laughing at a video of Gizmo on his phone. I snuck away before they could see me.

I'm dying to ask George if Eli said anything about me, but I can't put her in the middle like that, not when I know she carries a candle for Eli and that she's already wound up about the dance.

I don't have to wonder why George has a crush on Eli. Of course she does – he's perfect. I don't know if it's the same kind of heart-pounding, pulse-racing, panty-melting want she has for Isaac, or if it's more of an innocent kid-sister thing born of his kindness. It doesn't matter. He deserves someone like George, someone who won't barge into his life like an iceberg to sink all his hopes and dreams to the bottom of the icy ocean.

I have Noah and Gabriel. I need to let Eli go. He can be with George if he wants to, or any other girl. Even Cleo, if that sack of bitching and Botox makes him happy. He has every reason to never speak to me again.

I wish...

Daddy showed me how to sneak a Roman bust into the country and how to stand on a man's windpipe until he stops breathing. But he never taught me how to mend a broken heart.

To distract myself from imagining what can never be, I yank George off the bed and give her hair a final twist. "There you go. You're ready to knock his socks off."

"Thank you, Mackenzie." George's eyes sweep over my outfit. "Do you need anything else?"

"Nope, I'm good." I'm better than good. I'm *fierce*. The ice-blue fishtail dress George picked out for me hugs my curves perfectly. There's a scattering of beading across the breast and around the hem that catches the light as I move, and the crystal crown she's set into my hair sparkles under the garish lighting. I'm a mermaid – the Ice Queen of the deep.

I text Gabriel to let the guys know we're ready. A moment later, the front door of the condo bangs open. George and I hang over the mezzanine as Gabriel grins up at us, a bottle of Champagne in hand.

Gabriel pours drinks while we crowd around, taking selfies with the horrific decor. My chest does a little flip-flop as I take in my dates. True to his promise, Gabriel is wearing a pinstripe, gangster-style suit – the narrow lines accentuating every sinful curve and muscle of his body. A black skinny tie covered in grinning skulls and a pair of patent leather creepers covered in bones perfect his look. With his freshly-dyed crimson hair and a bone-shaped stud in his labret piercing, Gabe is every inch the bad boy rockstar. Well, *almost* every inch – I notice the drink in his hand is sparkling grape juice.

And Noah... fuck me dead, Noah Marlowe is *magnificent*. His suit and shirt are pure midnight black, matching his eyes and his heart. The only sparkle of color are two dots of blood-red on his cufflinks – rubies sparkling from their gold settings. He steps up to me and hands me a velvet box. I open it to see a matching ruby ring.

I swallow.

I want to say something, but the words catch in my throat.

No one's ever given me a gift like this before. Noah's coal-eyes bore into mine as he removes the ring from its cushion and slips it on my finger. "I wanted to give you something that would remind you of my promise."

I will bleed for you.

Fire leaps beneath my skin as Noah's fingers caress mine. I press my hand against my pattering heart. The metal is cool, grounding. Against my pale skin and the ice of my dress, the color of the red jewel deepens to rich crimson. Our blood. Our promise.

Gabriel admires my finger as I hold the jewel up to the light, admiring it from all angles. "I can't let Marlowe here steal the show." He hands me a larger box. "Everyone at the dance has to know you're my girl, too."

My breath hitches, and I'm afraid I might cry. I lift the lid off the box and gasp. Inside is an amazing corsage made of metal wire and crystal beads – all in glittering ice blue and silver, like the skeleton of a flower. Gabriel points to the matching button-hole on his lapel. His fingers dig under the neckline of my dress, brushing against my nipple as he threads the pin through the fabric. My whole body is alive with fire and need and... something else. I can't speak. My throat's closed over. My heart is dancing and I'm not sure if I'm going to throw up or float away.

"Thank you," I manage to choke out. Gabriel laughs, holding his hand up to Noah for a high five.

"We've rendered Mackenzie Malloy speechless. We're the greatest boyfriends in the universe."

Noah returns the high five with a rueful smile.

"Obviously," Gabe continues, "I'm the superior boyfriend because my dick is so large and my songs make girls cry…"

I let them argue about dick size as I stare down at their gifts – perfect pieces of themselves they've given to me. George grins at me and grabs my phone to take our picture. Isaac has been hanging with Noah and Gabriel, and he got George a corsage too – a more traditional one with real flowers, but instead of a ribbon, it has a little fabric cat face.

I think how much this scene feels like something from a teen movie… the perfect moment where the heroine's heart melts into her shoes. All these years I wished I could be someone I wasn't – the pink princess with the perfect boyfriend and absolutely no dangerous mobsters trying to bury her alive. For tonight I have it – I have the impossible dream. The best friend. The two gorgeous boys who possess my heart. Lungs that still draw breath. And a ballroom filled with students ready to be blown away by my presence.

If only I could scrub the cemetery dirt from beneath my nails. I'll never have a normal life as Claudia. But for tonight, I'm happy to wear Mackenzie's skin.

We drink and laugh and party while we wait for our ride to get here. Noah and George argue about some film they both like, while Isaac and Gabriel choose music for us to dance to. George takes a million pictures with my phone before tossing it back to me. I can't stop looking at the drop of crimson on my finger and the crystal shards on my breast. I tell myself tonight is perfect.

But it's not.

It's incomplete.

I peer down at my phone, my finger hovering over Eli's number. My fingers have a mind of their own. They type a short message, and before I know what I've done, I hit send.

I miss you.

It's the truth. The most true thing I've said to Eli since I met him. I've been hoping he'd call after Noah gave him the diary page, and then hating myself for my hope. I know it's pointless, but I can't let things stand between us without at least telling him how I feel. I owe him that.

The message bar comes up. SEEN. I stare at the screen until the words blur together. There's no reply. I slide my phone into my bra and turn toward the windows just as Gabriel snaps a picture. Noah catches me and spins me under his arm, and between his dark smile and Gabriel singing a drinking song about hating the Irish, and George and Isaac staring adorkably into each other's eyes, and Eli not being here, I feel raw and strange and untethered.

"This is your night," Noah whispers, touching his lips to my forehead. His fingers stroke fire down my bare arms, threatening to undo me completely.

My night. My *right*. But not truly mine. Only by wearing Mackenzie's skin can Claudia August's dreams come true.

"Our ride's here," Gabriel announces. He tugs me to the door. That giddy smile of his drags me out of the strange dark place I'd spiraled into. "Wait until you see this."

Sitting on the road in front of the house is a 1928 Cadillac 341A sedan – the car Al Capone used to drive around in. This was a perfect replica, right down to the armored plating on the sides.

I turn to Gabe in amazement. "You are ridiculous."

"It seemed appropriate," Gabriel grins. "Look, there's even an authentic-looking bullet-hole in the rear window."

Gabriel climbs up front with the driver, while George, Noah, Isaac, and I squeeze in the back. The car drives us around the city while Gabriel pops a Champagne bottle and sloshes it all over us trying to get it into our glasses. George turns the music up, and she and Gabe and Isaac get into a heated battle about their favorite underground LA bands while the city speeds past the windows in a blur of light and color.

I lean back into Noah's arms and wonder if this is what being a normal teenager feels like. It feels pretty sweet.

Then the car pulls up outside the Harrington Hills Country Club and Antony yanks the door open. I can see the outline of his holster through his suit, and I know I'll never get the chance to be normal.

"Satan save me from teenagers," he hisses as he ushers us along the lantern-lined walkway into the club.

"I thought you were happy about this gig." I grin. "All that unfettered cleavage..."

"Don't you start," he growls. "I've been groped so many times already tonight that I'm thinking of lodging a sexual harassment suit."

"What can I say? Ladies love a man in a suit." Antony looks every bit like a future Emerald Beach housewife's wet dream in his dark suit and blue tie that matches his dangerous eyes. If he wasn't my cousin I'd be all over... ew, no, it's too gross to think about—

"Save a dance for me, Mr. Jones." Cleo blows him a kiss as she and her minions slither out to the open courtyard. Antony looks petrified, and I burst out laughing.

I hold out my arms, and Noah and Gabriel take one each. Antony throws open the ballroom doors, and I step into an underwater wonderland.

The theme is 'Under the Sea.' Gabriel hooked the dance committee up with the owners of Midnight Grotto so he could score extra homecoming king points. The ballroom has been transformed into a mini version of the club, complete with bobbing lanterns, shimmering lighting, a shell-encrusted photo booth, and towering coral sculptures as table centerpieces. We move through the dance floor as smoke curls around us and men dressed as Poseidon in loincloths offer shimmering emerald drinks and tiny fish cakes skewered on pitchforks.

Under the bobbing lights, the faceless terrors that are my classmates have been reborn as sea creatures – nymphs and ocean gods, pirates and sirens and water spirits and... Chad is dressed in a giant, fluffy, hammerhead shark costume. A DJ on stage plays annoying house music, but on the stage behind I can see a band setting up.

"The music is terrible." George's cheeks glow with happiness. She leans in close to Isaac, and he looks at her like he's the luckiest guy in the room. I hope they name their firstborn daughter Mackenzie in my honor.

I spy Eli immediately in the middle of a big group of his friends. He looks insanely good in a dark grey suit that's cut to show off his lean muscle. Daphne sashays up to him in a slinky designer dress with the fabric folded over her breasts to look like stylized conch shells. She whispers something in Eli's ear and places a necklace of shells over his shoulders. He searches the room until his blue eyes meet mine.

The whole room disappears. It's just me and Eli, and the vast ocean of lies between us.

I'm the first to turn away. I can't bear reading his pain anymore. It feels intrusive – like I'm hunting around in his private things. His pain doesn't belong to me. I thought giving him that diary page would help him see how important he was to Mackenzie, how much she needed him. I know that's all he ever wanted – to protect her and be part of her life. I want to give him a piece of her for every piece I've destroyed.

I shouldn't have sent him that text. He holds my life in his hands and I don't even care. I should be trying to convince him not to reveal me as a fraud, but all I want is to see the light in his eyes again.

Daphne leads Eli toward the dance floor. He looks back over his shoulder at me, and the edge of his mouth wobbles. The Golden God is crumbling, and it's all my fault.

Noah squeezes my hand. "Come on. We'll make you forget about him."

Gabriel and Noah lead me onto the dance floor. We hang out close to the front as the DJ is ushered off so the band can start their set. Gabriel hooked the school up with his friend's band, Broken Muse. The lights go down, smoke billows across the floor, and three fucking delicious men run on stage. One makes love to a grand piano with bold, sweeping scales. A huge guy bends over a cello, stabbing at the strings with his bow like he's a warrior on a battlefield, while an Ice King with cheekbones that could cut glass pours out his soul on his violin. A girl with a tumble of dark hair appears behind a mixing board, looping their tracks and adding atmospheric samples. The music is this insane mash-up of classical, heavy metal, and industrial. It's wild, reaching right into my bones and jangling them about. I wish Gabe was on stage with them until his hand brushes my hip. I don't want him to ever stop touching me.

"Claudia." He whispers my name against my skin, letting the punishing beat drown out my secret. His body moves against mine, swaying and dipping in time with the sweeping violin. His hands roam freely over me, lighting trails of fire along my skin, and when I grind my ass back against him, I can feel his cock hard for me.

Not to be outdone, Noah sweeps in, his hands closing over

Gabriel's as his shadowed, inky scent steals the air from my lungs. I place my hands around his neck, pulling him in close. He claims my lips in a sin-laden kiss as Gabriel presses his against my neck. Their hands roam unchecked over my thighs, hitching my skirt up.

Bodies swirl around us, and I fancy I catch cruel whispers in the air. But the music pounds and thrashes in my skull, casting a spell over us that won't allow anything else inside. Just me and Gabriel and Noah. We're not dancing so much as fucking with our clothes on. But no teacher dares make us stop.

I'm a passenger in my skin, trapped by the magic they weave with their bodies, their scents. I've been on this dance floor for five minutes and I'm wet and panting for them. If one of them rolled my dress up over my hips, bent me over the edge of the stage, and entered me with a swift thrust, I wouldn't have the power to stop him, even if I wanted to...

And if it was both of them...

I lose the tendril of my evil thought as Gabriel holds my body against his. I tip my neck back, my eyes fluttering open as Noah lays a trail of kisses over my collarbone. In the swirling colors of the room, my eyes catch Eli's. Daphne rocks against him, but his body is stiff and his eyes lock on mine.

His blue irises cloud with emotion, and at first I think it's hatred. But as the music crests into a haunting funereal march, I see the pain that lingers beyond, and I know Eli Hart is not capable of hate. He presses his lips together and pulls Daphne closer, but the movement sends a shudder through his body as his eyes rake over me.

I wish...

I wish I could curl a finger in the air and beckon him over. I wish the Golden Boy would fall to his knees at my feet and worship me. I wish for once he'd toss aside that rigid moral code of his and give himself over to his darker desires.

I wish he'd look at me the way he looked at Mackenzie.

It's too painful to look at him, especially when so much delicious pleasure courses through my body. I draw my gaze back to the stage as the girl steps out from behind the mixing board and picks up a violin. The monster tosses aside his cello and picks up an electric guitar. The raven-haired beauty faces her Ice King as the pianist builds a tense harmony. Their eyes lock, their jaws tense. Their bows hover over the strings. The tension between the two of them is *insane*.

He strikes a note. She plays the same note back to him with flames in her eyes. He plays a series of scales and she throws them back at him, then pretends to slap him across the face with the neck as she lays down a frantic melody, daring him to keep up.

She's the queen of the stage and I love it. And from the way all three of those musicians gaze at her, I think they love it, too.

Gabriel's teeth dig into my neck as he shoves me toward the stage. I can't tear my eyes from the musicians as he drags Noah and me into the shadows of the wings. The hot-as-sin pianist nods at Gabriel and gives him a thumbs up. I'm too distracted to guess at what Gabe's up to until he pushes me against a stack of road cases and rolls my dress over my hips. The cool air hits my bare skin. Gabriel cups my ass, moaning in my ear.

"I couldn't resist that shaggable arse for another moment," he growls, his voice tight with need.

Noah's fingers slide down the seam of my thong. The shadows hide us as he pushes the fabric aside. My heart stutters as fresh heat boils my veins. *I can't believe this is happening. I can't—*

On stage, piano and guitar thrash out a steady riff that pounds in my chest. The raven-haired beauty undulates her body and throws her head back as the pair of them rip into a violin duel. They whip their heads around each other, their limbs entangled as they play faster and faster and...

...Gabriel's fingers slide inside me.

I'm soaking wet, and he feels so warm and so right. His thumb brushes my clit, and my nails dig into the metal case. It's too much... the music and the raw, aching *need* and the well of emotion swelling in my chest.

"Bite me," Noah's lips brush my ear. He cups his hand over my mouth. My teeth sink into his flesh and he grits his teeth, and I know he needs this as much as I do. I want to grab his cock but I'm gone gone *gone...*

The dance floor comes alive as the students are whipped into a frenzy by the violinists' lust-soaked dance – a pagan ritual playing out while Gabriel's fingers play sinful music over my clit.

My eyes sweep the room, and they catch Eli. He's on the far side of the stage, almost in the wings himself. He's alone, his hands in his pockets and misery etched into his features. I know he can see me and what Gabe and Noah are doing to me. I want him to see, I *want* him to see *Claudia* in all her deviant, rotten-to-the-core glory, instead of a shadow of the girl he used to know.

Eli whips his head away, but not before I see the pain bloom in his eyes. I'm so close to the edge that his pain becomes part of me, and I ride it into the onslaught of my orgasm as the wave of pleasure crests over my body.

I collapse against Gabriel, screaming into Noah's hand as the music sweeps over me. I collapse forward into Noah's arms, and as soon as his hands touch my body I know I'm not finished; I'm not nearly done. Tonight I will have my fucked-up teenage dreamland as only I know how.

I smooth down my dress and drag the two of them back into the fray. We dance until my body is once more a Tesla coil of electricity, desperate for release. I'm on the edge of dragging them both behind the grotto and forcing them to do more wicked things to my body when the spell is broken. The band set down their instruments and Ms. Drysdale takes the stage.

"It's time to announce our homecoming court." Ms. Drysdale hands the envelope to Cleo – who slits it with her talon-like nails and pulls out the paper. She reads out the prince and princess from the junior class, a couple of pimply fucks I don't know. Then it's time for the homecoming king.

"Elias Hart." Cleo grins like a lioness surveying her next meal as the spotlight swings across the crowd to Eli. The school breaks out into applause. No one claps as loud as me. I know why Eli won – not only is he hot and popular, but he's *nice*. He doesn't care about social status or what a person can do *for* him – he's friendly to everyone and he genuinely cares about people. When he talks to you, he pays attention with his whole body, and he remembers everything you say. When he laughs, which is often, he lights up the whole room. He'll sit with the weird kid during the football game and not give a fuck who's staring.

"Yay, Eli!" I yell. Gabriel whistles. Eli's eyes seek out mine as he climbs on stage and accepts the crown from Cleo. He waves to the crowd and flashes them his perfect smile, but his eyes are for me only, and they are deep chasms of hurt and regret.

"And now, the moment you've been waiting for... this year's homecoming queen is..." Cleo frowns at the name on the envelope. "Is... Mackenzie Malloy. What the actual *fuck?*"

I'm too busy snort-laughing at Cleo swearing into the microphone to register the name she calls out. That is until Gabriel nudges me. "Go on, Your Majesty. Go get your crown."

I shake my head. "No way. No way did these idiots vote for me."

"Why not? You've shaken up life at Stonehurst with your antics. And remember, you fucked up Alec LeMarque, something everyone has wanted to do for years." The way Noah says the child actor's name in that dark voice of his, I know he's thinking the same as me – that I wasn't the first girl Alec tried to hurt.

"And don't forget, you have the shaggable arse." Gabriel pinches it for good measure. "Plus, you miiiiiiight have had a little help from your favorite lovable scamp."

I punch Gabriel in the arm. "You had something to do with this."

Gabriel winks at me. "I can neither confirm nor deny that I bribed the app developer with backstage passes to the sold-out Broken Muse LA show."

Before I can protest, he shoves my ass toward the stage. I stumble forward but catch myself before I fall over. The steps seem so high, so far, and at the top is...

Eli.

He's playing the game, his mouth a crooked smile as Mrs. Drysdale places a glittering tiara on my head – it's small and fits inside the crown I'm already wearing. Eli looks like he was born to wear a crown. I'm not the right kind of queen for this shit – my kingdom is blood and violence. It should be Mackenzie's honor to stand beside him under the lights, the rulers of this school. And even though I had nothing to do with her disappearance, for the first time since I started wearing her skin, I feel the pinch of guilt.

I don't have any right to Eli. Like everything else in my so-called life, he belongs to *her*.

Mackenzie Malloy is the ghost who will always keep us apart.

The school cheers as I take a seat beside Eli on the thrones festooned with shell garlands. I look out over a sea of faces, and regret churns in my stomach. The tiara slips down over one eye. Cleo and her friends whisper furtively, and I know I'll pay for this slight.

At the back of the room, standing with a grinning Tiberius,

is Antony. His hands remain folded across his chest. He doesn't applaud.

In a room filled with students who voted me queen, only Antony knows that the crown I wear is made of thorns that dig into my skull.

Ms. Drysdale announces the homecoming court dance. Eli holds out his arm for me. He stiffens when I slip my hand in his, but he keeps the facade in place. The band starts up a slow, mournful waltz, and the lights swirl around us – bubbles of purple and ocean blue that cannot hope to match the depth in Eli's eyes.

We descend the steps together, and Eli leads me to the middle of the dance floor. The prince and princess are next to us, swirling through their steps perfectly, chatting away like old friends. My heart is ready to leap out of my throat and smack Eli across his sad, crooked mouth.

Eli looks as if he wants to run, but he's trapped by this charade, too. He's far too kind to make a scene, so he endures my touch as we reach the bottom of the stairs. He drops my arm roughly, pushing me away, but then grabs my hand and knits his fingers in mine. He squeezes, and I want to tell him it hurts, but the hurt is so right.

The fingers of his other hand graze the small of my back, where the dress dips so low he's touching bare skin. He shuffles closer, and his whole body is stiff, corpselike. He shuffles me in a circle, and everything about this would be so awkward and horrible if not for the electric charge of his skin touching mine. There are a million miles between us, and yet I'm aware of every movement, every kiss of his breath on my skin.

"Did you read the diary?" I whisper.

Eli's fingers scrape against my skin as he tugs me close, until my breasts are right against his broad chest. His touch destroys me, but I want to be destroyed and made anew. *I wish that I deserved you.*

"Stop trying to pretend you give a fuck about me," he hisses into my ear. "You're using her words to stop me from going to the authorities. You're protecting your own ass."

"If all I cared about was my own life, I'd kill you," I answer. Eli's fingers crush mine. "Killing you would be sensible. Tidy. But I don't do sensible."

A shudder rocks through Eli's body, and I feel it in my own. This dance is the equivalent of what Noah and I did in the panic room, back when he thought I was responsible for his brother's death. This is Eli stabbing through his pain. I don't know what lies on the other side.

"Do you think giving me a page of her diary is going to make me change my mind about *you*?" his breath rasps. "How do I know you weren't the one who had her killed?"

"I guess you don't know that," I say. "Except on some level you believe my story. I don't think you're going to the cops. If you were, you'd have done it already."

"Maybe I'm waiting for you to make a mistake. Maybe I have FBI agents watching you every moment, waiting for you to take control of that gang so they can swoop in and wipe you all out. You lied to all of us and you nearly got Noah killed, all so you can steal Mackenzie's house."

"I'll give up the house," I say. "I'll move out and let it rot back into the earth if that will make you happy. But not until I know you're safe. Right now, the house and her life is a shield that protects not just me, but you and Gabriel and Noah, too. While Mackenzie Malloy lives, I'll protect you, whether you want me to or not."

The song rises to a crescendo. Eli spins me so fast that the room becomes a maelstrom of bubbles and colors and his deep blue eyes so filled with a pain that rivals my own.

I'm desperate, and falling, and I don't know what else to do. I'm adrift in the ocean of his eyes, and even though I know I should go on fighting it, he pulls me under completely.

I press my lips to his.

Eli tastes better than I could ever imagine – like vanilla cupcakes and summer cocktails and waves lapping on a white-sand beach. For a single, beautiful moment, his lips are hot on mine, his tongue drawing me deeper as our bodies are slammed together by the desperate flood.

Something breaks inside him.

The light goes out of his eyes.

He tears his lips from mine. A cry escapes me. It's like he's cut off my air and I can't breathe. I need him to breathe.

His lips twist into a cruel, sad smirk. "You're *nothing* like her."

The words are a whisper only I can hear, a knife slicing through my heart.

Eli yanks himself away from me. I can't see the blue in his eyes anymore. He turns and bolts, leaving me standing in the middle of the dance floor.

Alone.

CLAUDIA

We clear out of the ballroom pretty quick after Eli's rejection. Tearing up the dance floor loses its appeal, and the eyes of other students following me feel like knives scraping my skin. Not to mention the fact that Gabriel got a text and disappeared somewhere for like twenty minutes, and when he appeared again, he tried to cover up his distress by being extra ridiculous. When I pressed him on it, he said it was his manager harassing him about the new album, but he wouldn't look at me as we walked out of the country club.

George had sent me a text saying she'd ducked out with Isaac to go to the horror movie marathon (adorable) so we didn't need to wait for them. Gabriel hadn't booked our car until much later in the evening, so Antony gives us a ride to the after-party. He can't come inside because everyone thinks he's a teacher, so he sends in another of his fighters instead. A guy named Horace who's seven feet of raw muscle and is immediately pounced on by a horde of sex-crazed Valley girls as soon as he steps inside.

The after-party is at Cleo's house, right at the top of Beaumont Hills, teetering on the edge of a steep cliff overlooking the ocean. It's in full swing when we arrive, despite the fact I'm pretty sure Cleo is still at the dance. I don't know many of the kids here, and I assume most of them are from nearby Beaumont Academy, who had their homecoming dance tonight as well, until Gabriel informs me most of them don't even go to school.

"These are industry people – mostly wannabe models, YouTube stars, and musicians, but agents and PR and producers, too. They know how important it is to be seen at these parties," Gabriel explains. "We're in a clout house."

"A what?"

He points to a guy in wannabe gangster clothing and a plastic crown holding court at the end of the terrace. "See that dude? He's a YouTube star with six million followers. That girl dancing over there makes TikTok videos, and there's a guy in the garden handing out pills of happiness who's one of the biggest gamers on Twitch. Cleo's daddy pays thousands of dollars a month for her to live here so she can work with these big influencers and grow her following."

"That's legitimately insane."

"No argument." Gabriel pulls me to him. "I've been to parties here before, and they're always wild in a manufactured way – everyone competing to be the most extreme, the most fun and quirky and get in with the stars, while the few real people who actually contribute anything of substance get blazed in the treehouse and solve the world's problems. I can't imagine living here – sharing space with people who need you to be 'on' all the time. That's why I have my own place."

I look around the room at all these kids laughing and talking and handing around drinks. There's a DJ set up in the corner and a bunch of sponsored walls set up where photographers snapped groups together. The furniture looks staged – someone's best guess of a funky, homely atmosphere. It comes across forced, fake, a cardboard facade that will crumble at the first sign of trouble – like the people in this room.

I couldn't imagine living in this towering YouTube-shrine, either.

I think of our home back in Tartarus Oaks. Unlike the Lucians and Dios who lived in extravagant mansions to rival Howard Malloy, Daddy didn't like to flash his wealth around in Emerald Beach. (He saved that for the Romanesque villa he was building on Capri, which he never got to finish). We lived in a nice house – modest on the outside, but inside was another story. If Daddy trusted you enough to invite you inside, you'd step into an Aladdin's cave of precious antiquities – every rug and statue and chair had a story behind it, and Daddy knew them all by heart. At mealtimes, he sat in a gilded chair taken from a pharaoh's tomb in Egypt. He'd entertain guests with china and crystal pilfered from the Austrian Hapsburg dynasty. We even had a Picasso hanging above the toilet.

Even though it had been my prison, even though I'd seen firsthand the blood price of those beautiful statues and ancient coins, I felt something in that house, something sweet and tender and brutally possessive, something I hadn't felt again until I met Gabriel and Noah and Eli.

Gabriel is led aside by some music industry people, and Noah suggests we move further along the terrace, where the noise is less oppressive. The breeze whips off the ocean below and carries away the loud voices and pulsing music. I rest my head on Noah's shoulder and look out to the peninsula where Emerald Beach overlooks the bay. Most of it is shrouded in trees, but I can make out a few rows of grey stones, like jagged teeth jutting out from the gaping maw of the underworld. A shiver runs down my spine that has nothing to do with the crisp ocean breeze.

"Hey." Noah touches my hand. With a start, I realize I've been digging my nails into his arm. "What's wrong?"

I shake my head.

"You're freaked out, and you're holding something back." Noah peels my fingers from around his arm, holding his hand tight in mine. "Tell me."

I point a shaking finger toward the peninsula. "See that cemetery down there? That's where I was buried alive."

"What?"

Noah looks completely shell-shocked. I feel a little stab of pride at being able to surprise him. Of all the things he expected me to say, I bet this doesn't come close.

But now I have to finish what I started. My secret hangs in the crisp air, and I need to speak it or it will become a cancer between us. I ball my hands into fists and stare down at the railing. If I keep looking at those rows of teeth being torn up by the relentless ocean, I'll start screaming and I won't be able to stop.

"The night my parents died, I... I didn't tell you everything."

"I figured," Noah says dryly. He really does know me.

"I woke up in the night to the sound of someone in my room. I tried to fight them off, but they already had a hold of me. They dragged me out of bed and pressed a cloth soaked in chloroform into my mouth. As they carried me downstairs, I saw my mother slumped in a chair, still dressed in her clubbing clothes – a beautiful silk dress and stiletto heels. She'd been stabbed multiple times. Her blood arced across the wall behind her and splattered across the window. I could see my reflection in the glass, behind the blood, and I remember thinking in this weird detached way that it almost looked as if I had her blood on my skin, as if I'd been the one to stab her. I must've passed out then because the next thing I knew, I woke up inside a coffin, buried beneath the earth. I—" I clung to Noah as the memories assailed me. "I could *feel* the weight of the dirt on top of me. With every breath, I felt my life slipping away. I tried to claw through the wood, but it was useless. I… I…"

I died that night, on the inside.

"How did you escape?" Noah's arms tighten around me. His voice tightens too, as though there are things he wants to say but he's afraid if he lets the words free they'll become weapons in my hands.

I know that feeling all too well. My stomach tightens as the words form, then die, form and die, on my tongue. I've carried this secret on my own for so long that speaking it aloud feels like giving Noah a piece of my heart, and I shouldn't be dishing out secrets to coal-eyed boys who hated me only a few weeks ago.

Noah dissolved a guy in potassium hydroxide and flushed him down a bathtub drain for me.

I trust him.

"Antony. He saw Brutus' men at our house and followed them. As soon as they left the cemetery he dug me out again. But he couldn't save my father." I choked out the words. "The greatest gentleman crook of our times lies in that cemetery in an unmarked grave."

Noah strokes my hair. It's such a tender, un-Noah-like action that it makes me want to weep. It's something Eli would do. I can't think about Eli now or I'll fall to pieces completely. I snuggle deeper into Noah's embrace, breathing in his intoxicating scent, pressing my ear to his chest to listen to his heart beat rapid-fire for me. Something about the steady rhythm of it reminds me of the music from the dance – the band drawing out the wildness in all of us like a frenzied pagan rite.

"Thank you for tonight," I whisper into the folds of Noah's shirt.

"What for?"

"I went to a real school dance with two hot boys." I lean back and tuck a loose strand of hair behind my ear. I'm still wearing both my crowns. The homecoming one slides down over my ear again and I reach to clip it back in place. "Sometimes I wish I didn't have to wear her skin to have all this. I wish I was the Ice Queen of Stonehurst Prep instead of a mafia queen in hiding. I wish her life could be real for me."

Noah looks out over the people teaming onto the balcony. It looks as if the dance is over for real, as a long line of cars pull up outside, discharging more people in glittering outfits. "Look around. Everyone is living a fake life. We're all wearing a mask. Cleo's a seventeen-year-old living her life on the internet and she has no idea which version of herself is the real one."

"What's real, then?"

"This."

He kisses me. It's rough and raw and beautiful, the kind of kiss that spreads an ache across my chest. Noah's lips part mine, and his tongue threatens to devour my darkness. He is a sin-eater, taking my crimes into himself to sate his own lust for revenge. He slips under my skin to wear my misdeeds as his own.

As Noah wraps his arms around me and pulls me closer, melding our bodies together, I *believe*. For the first time, I believe that he sees what's underneath, the black heart at the center of me, the heart-shaped box I'd carried since Brutus took my parents from me. That it doesn't frighten him. That he could even be falling in love with it.

And that is the biggest lie of all.

I pull away, because he is everything I crave and I will not destroy him. I look into those eyes that reflect my heart-shaped box back at me, and I find the words to break the spell that binds us. "Where's Gabe?"

Noah blinks. I don't think he's heard me, so I repeat the question. As the words leave my mouth, the spell unknits. Noah has let go of my sins, for now.

I haven't seen my rock-god since he was pulled away to talk music. I cast my eyes over the people on the deck. The party has filled up since Noah and I moved out here, and I hardly recognize anyone. I can't see Gabriel anywhere. A knot of worry tightens in my chest. We'd neutralized our enemies, for now, but I didn't like having Gabriel out of sight.

Noah must be thinking the same thing, because he threads his fingers through mine. "Come on. Don't let go." We shove our way back into the fray, checking every group for Gabriel's beautiful face. He's not on the terrace, and I can't see in him the blue-lit swimming pool on the floor below.

Inside, the place is wall-to-wall people. Noah charges ahead, using those broad shoulders of his to force our way through, like his namesake parting the Red Sea. Rising over the music is someone laughing – wild and throaty and slightly unhinged. Gabriel's laugh.

My heart thumps harder.

We find him in the kitchen, gripping the counter as he battles some punk-looking guy at a drinking game. I don't understand the rules, but Gabriel is holding some kind of elaborately-carved horn aloft, sloshing liquid from the brim. The punk recites a poem with his hand across his heart. Both of them have runic symbols scrawled on their cheeks with hot sauce, and the crowd around them roars with laughter, phones raised to capture the magic.

As we draw near, I recognize the punk kid from a popular Emerald Beach band. He's got two bananas strapped to his head, sticking out like horns, and he seems to be improvising a drinking poem. "Fill your cups, feel no distress... your brain cells will soon be less... For what's there to do when you don't wanna think? Join Gabriel Fallen for another drink."

Everyone claps, and Gabriel hands over the horn for the

punk to drink from. A girl reaches up with a squeezy bottle of hot sauce to scrawl another rune on his cheek.

"Claaaaawwws," Gabriel drawls. He throws an arm around my shoulders, not knowing or caring that he's leaned his entire body weight on me, and we're going to topple over at any moment. "Come here, my beauty, my love, my musey muse muse. We're singing bard songs. Songs of drinking! Now that you're here, I feel words of profound wisdom coming to me..." He whips the horn from the punk's hands and holds it out to me. I push it aside but that's a mistake, because Gabriel sloshes it everywhere as he sweeps his arm through the air and pronounces dramatically, "Booze goes in my mouth, and love goes in my heart. But if your hand goes up my ass, you'll get the mother of all—"

"*Gabe.*" Noah barrels into us, dragging Gabriel away before he can finish his poem. Gabe doesn't seem to notice. He raises the horn to his lips and starts guzzling the contents. I remember that conversation we had in the hallway of Malloy Manor, where he told me why he doesn't drink. I slap the horn from out of his hands.

"Fuck, you bitch," the punk swears at me. He's covered in sticky, sweet-smelling alcohol.

"Bollocks. My mead is gone," Gabriel slurs, reaching for the horn. He teeters and falls into me. My knee slams into the cabinets and it fucking hurts, but not as much as the crazed look in Gabriel's eyes.

I don't like seeing him like this – the fallen angel a booze-soaked mess. He said he didn't drink, and yet this is twice in as many weeks he's got completely plastered.

It's because of me.

I remember back in our room in Midnight Grotto, when Gabriel said that when he looks at me, he sees Dylan. I didn't understand what he meant, but I think I'm starting to see.

Gabriel broke something open inside me, some seal that kept all the darkness inside. It was Gabe who broke through my heart of ice first, who saw something in me beyond Stonehurst's head witch bitch.

It never occurred to me that I might've broken something open in him as well. And while I've been dealing with Alec and Noah's dad and avenging Queen Boudica, all his old wounds have started bleeding again. All I do is pour poison into the cuts, so much poison that he's drowning, and I've been too distracted to see it.

I'm the poison.

I've already poisoned Noah and Eli. I've turned the Golden Boy into a ball of anger and hate, and the dark-horse valedictorian into a wannabe mobster.

No more. I may be too late to help Eli, and Noah is in too deep to draw back now, but I won't let the darkness take my fallen angel.

"Gabriel." I touch his cheek. He turns away, moaning a little. Noah shoots me a look – *we have to help him.*

How do you help the boy who sings the stars when the sky falls around him?

"Gabriel, I—"

"Hide and seek!" Gabriel's eyes light up. He flails himself from our arms. "Come on, let's play. I'll hide, and you seek."

I grab for him, but he's gone. He's surprisingly fast on his feet for someone who's totally smashed. He disappears into the crowd. Noah grabs my hand and dives after him.

Noah drags me toward the DJ, but I see a flash of Gabriel's jacket in the opposite direction. I slip my fingers from Noah and follow Gabriel as he disappears up a wide staircase curving up a glass atrium. I haul myself up after him, cursing myself for wearing six-inch stiletto heels.

There's a couple of guys drawing lines of coke on the

windowsill as I hobble past. I can't help but think this party is kind of tame, not what I expected at all from the richest kids. They can do anything they want and all they want to do is forget their lives in a drug-fueled haze. Now, my father's parties... Saturnalia, Lupercalia... those were *wild*. Gangsters know that you party as if tomorrow never comes, because there's always a chance someone might put a bullet between your eyes.

Or bury you alive.

I shiver as I round the corner, and my gaze flicks to the glass walls that look out over the peninsula. The cemetery appears closer, its grave teeth open wide, ready to swallow me whole. I pour on speed and manage to sprint up the last flight of steps without snapping my ankles.

I've reached the top floor, presumably where all the house-mates have their bedrooms. I pass a guy slumped in the hallway, his eyes swimming from some cocktail of drugs, but his ass is too ugly to be Gabe. I peer into the first room. A girl kneels on the bed with a guy pounding away behind her. His hair flops over his eyes, and for a moment I think I see my fallen angel and a knife twists in my heart. But no, no butterflies flutter around his neck. I move on. The next room has a few guys laughing as they crowd around a computer screen, watching what looks like amateur porn. I back out before they notice me. I push the door of the next room open. It's completely dark inside, and nothing moves or stirs. One entire wall is covered with floor-to-ceiling glass, and the cemetery leers up at me with a mocking grin. From this angle, I feel as though I'm toppling forward into its waiting mouth. Or perhaps that's the terror of watching Gabriel fall and not being able to save him. I start to back out, but a voice startles me.

"Claws."

That one word undoes me. It's a silly nickname Antony gave me when we were kids, but Gabriel speaks it with awe and reverence as if he kneels before a goddess. I squint into the gloom, and I spot him. He's slumped in a beanbag chair, facing the window, his features shrouded in shadow. The horn lays on its side at his feet, spilling mead into the expensive carpet.

I rush to him. I go to kneel – I need to look into his eyes – but Gabriel grabs my legs, wrapping me against him. His whole body shudders with a sob. Over his shoulder, the cemetery's mouth yawns wider.

I'm pissed as hell at him for drinking himself into this state. I had plans for after the party, plans involving continuing what he and Noah started on the dance floor. But I can't ignore the crack in his voice. He's breaking apart, and the stars are far away and cold. But I'm here, and I have to do something.

"I killed him." Gabriel's shoulders tremble. "I killed him because I'm a selfish prick. He was my friend, and I didn't listen to him. I was so busy lapping up all the attention that I didn't notice what was up with him until it was too late."

"So what? Being a shitty friend isn't the same as murdering someone." I roll my eyes. "You didn't point a gun at his head and pull the trigger. You didn't stab a knife through his chest."

"I might as well have." Gabriel's eyes roll back in his head. "I'm such a useless prick. No wonder my parents…"

"Your parents what?"

"Nothing. It's nothing. *I'm* nothing."

"You're being melodramatic." I take Gabriel's hands in mine. My eyes adjust to the dim light and I take in the room – the canopy bed draped in red and gold damask, the Middle Eastern antiques, the ornate desk in the corner with lights blinking on a laptop and webcam, and one wall decorated with gold flocked wallpaper decorated with Egyptian hieroglyphs. We're in Cleo's room. I need to get him out of this snake pit. "You're talking bullshit and you know it. What's this really about, Gabe? Is it the text you got tonight?"

"Dylan needed me," he whispers. "And I ignored him. And now you need me, and I—"

I think I understand. Gabriel's *afraid*. He's afraid if he gets close to me, if he loses the bollocks (in his vernacular) and gives himself over to this *thing* that pulls us together, he'll lose me like Dylan. He lay with me in that room while Antony and Tiberius and Noah washed Brentwood down the plughole. He sees just how real the possibility of losing me is.

"I'm not Dylan," I whisper back. "I'm a queen. I'm *your* queen, remember? I'm not going to leave you, Gabriel."

"Maybe that's what you think now, but I'll drive you away. I'll poison you, just like I poison everything good in my life."

I laugh, to cover up my surprise that he thought of himself as poison when really, he's the antidote, the cure. "I've been described as many things, but never *good*."

"You're something else, Claws," Gabriel slurs. His body grows heavy. "I wish..."

His words trail off as he collapses in on himself, slumping against me, completely out of it.

Wonderful.

I sense a shadow hovering at the door. Noah flicks on the light, plunging the looming cemetery into a pitch-black void. "I see you found Gabriel."

"Yup. And his ass is heavy." *And his pain, too.* I smooth back his hair as he clings to me. "I think we should get him home."

Noah slings Gabriel's arm over his shoulder. I take the other arm and together we drag Gabriel to his feet. I start for the door but then remember the raging party going on downstairs. "Is there any way to get him out of this house without everyone seeing him? I don't want his finest hour to end up as Cleo's next YouTube video."

"I don't think we have a choice—" Noah snaps his fingers. "The fireman's pole."

"The...what?"

"Lauri – he's the guy who runs the house – has a fireman's pole in his bedroom that leads down into his gaming dungeon. So he can just roll out of bed and start slaying orcs."

I roll my eyes. "And I thought Malloy Manor was ridiculous. Where is this pole?"

"I think it's the master bedroom." We drag Gabriel to the doorway. Noah looks left and right, then nods to the room at the end of the hall. One of Gabe's creepers slides off but I don't stop to pick it up. This is one long-ass hallway. Sweat rolls down my face, and I know George's fine work on my hair has been destroyed. If Cleo sees me like this it'll be all over social media, but I don't care about myself. All I want is to shield Gabriel from more pain.

The gods smile upon us, because the hallway is empty. No one will see us—

A door flies open and a guy steps out of a bathroom, right into our path.

Not just any guy.

Eli.

His eyes bug out as he takes in Gabriel's state. "Shit. Is he okay?"

"If by 'okay,' you mean 'absolutely shitfaced and probably in need of a stomach pump,' then yeah, sure. He's okay," Noah says. "We're going to try to get him out of the house through the dungeon so no one sees him."

"I'll help." Eli takes Gabriel's arm from around my neck. I let him. I know Eli needs to feel like he's solving the problem. And helping Gabriel is something he can do that doesn't directly impact me. I step back and watch the two of them maneuver Gabriel into the master bedroom, which appears mercifully empty of revelers.

We keep the lights off, but this room overlooks the lit-up

terrace, and the light from below casts an eerie glow over the already surreal space. Everything in the room is circular – a giant, circular window, circular beanbag chairs, circular rug, circular bookshelves that hold plushie toys and sculptures of *Lord of the Rings* characters. There's an insane circular bed that looks like it revolves. And in the corner is a large circular hole in the floor with a shiny fireman's pole sticking through.

I roll my eyes. "Rich people are ridiculous."

Noah sits on the edge of the hole, dangling his legs over the side. "I can't see anyone downstairs, but it's a three-floor drop." He gestures to Eli. "Get him on my shoulders."

"I need you," Eli grunts at me as he shoves Gabe's prone body onto Noah's back.

I need you.

The words wash over me like a wave, sloughing off my skin. I wonder how bitter they taste on Eli's tongue, but he doesn't acknowledge them. I crawl over and support Gabriel's ass while Eli wraps his body around Noah's shoulders like a scarf.

"Will you be able to support him?" he asks, his voice tight with worry.

"I'm about to find out." Noah wraps his legs around the pole and pushes off from the edge.

He grunts as he takes Gabriel's full weight, but he doesn't lose his grip. I hold my breath as Noah spins, knocking Gabriel's knee against the rim as the pair of them disappear into the darkness below.

The temperature in the room rises ten degrees as Eli glares at me from across the fireman's pole. He's changed clothes since the dance, and he looks devastating in a deep blue shirt that matches the exact shade of his eyes. Those twin oceans fix on me, swallowing me into their depths.

"Gabriel..." Eli trails off.

"He needs me. I have to go." I grip the pole between my

thighs, wrapping my hands around it and pushing off from the edge. As I spin toward him, Eli leans over and briefly captures my lips on his.

The kiss is a feather brushing against me. It's almost possible to believe it didn't happen. But my lips will never forget the taste of Eli Hart. I stole his kiss on the dance floor and he's returning the favor – only this feels even more illicit, more soaked in shadow and secrets.

You're nothing like her.

His harsh words sing in the air as I slide away from him. His body disappears from view as the ground swallows me, until he's a memory, a dream. Until all I can see in the darkness is a pair of ocean swept eyes.

"Thank you," I whisper. My whole body trembles as I fight to grip the pole. My body wants to float away. *What just happened?* Eli Hart made it clear that I was dead to him, so why does the ghost of his kiss linger on my lips?

23

NOAH

We drag Gabriel down the road to where Antony waits with the car. He flings the doors open, and Claudia and I roll him into the backseat. "What the fuck happened to him?"

"It's no big deal." Claudia meets my eyes, and I'm not sure if she's just tired or if something else is going on, but I get the message she doesn't want Antony to know the details of tonight's party. "He just had a little too much fun."

"Why does he reek of honey? No, don't answer that. I don't care. If he throws up in my car, you're clearing it up." Antony drives us back to Gabriel's house. I sit with Gabriel on the backseat, holding his sticky, mead-soaked body so he doesn't smash his head into the door every time Antony flies around a corner. My eyes lock on Antony's hands as they grip the wheel. He doesn't know it, but I've seen those hands soaked in blood.

I wonder if Claudia knows what goes on at Antony's club.

I guess she does – she's the queen, after all. She says she's doing all this to give him a second chance, so he can give up the family life and go back to law school. But I've seen Antony throw men into a ring to be torn apart by wild, rabid dogs. How do you go back from that?

Exactly. I swallow. *You can't go back.*

I watched a man dissolved in his own bathtub, his body reduced to brown sludge. The smell of it will be a fixture of my nightmares for the rest of my life. I'm supposed to be heading to Harvard next year, and I watched my girlfriend hold a gun to my father's head.

I can't go back.

Antony's eyes meet mine in the rearview mirror. A shiver rolls down my spine. Does he recognize me?

Does he know I've been flirting with the edges of his world for a long time?

Antony parks the car outside Gabriel's place, and Claudia helps me drag him out of the car. He's still unconscious but breathing normally, which I take as a good sign. I prop Gabriel against the wall and press his thumb against the keypad to open the door. The pair of us stumble inside and throw Gabriel down on the sofa.

"I'm leaving," Antony yells after us. "Don't do anything I wouldn't do."

Claudia leans out the door and throws him the middle finger, but she's grinning. I feel this twinge at the bottom of my spine. The way they are together reminds me of me and Felix, but then I remember that she's Julian August's daughter and Antony is one of the most dangerous men in the city, and the ache of his loss becomes this weird, creeping monster inside me that I don't understand.

The door slams shut, muffling the roll of the ocean and the gentle trickle of Gabriel's fountain.

Once again, I'm alone with Claudia August.

Not Mackenzie Malloy.

The giddy truth of it still lights my veins on fire. All this time

I've been fighting the way I feel about her, battling the monster inside myself until it made me crazy. But this girl isn't Mackenzie, and that means I can embrace the monster. I can set him free, because I'm in love with the biggest, baddest monster of them all.

But she's still a mystery to me, especially after what she told me tonight. I have to untangle the parts of her that are Claudia from the memories and the pretending.

I remember...

I remember a girl who bowled through life like a tornado, destroying everything and everyone in her path. I remember wishing I could be like the Ice Queen, blotting out her pain with cruelty, railing against the rules of civilized society, and using her father's influence and Eli's devotion to get away with it. I wished I had her balls, and that desire to revel in chaos convinced me that I loved her. But I never loved Mackenzie Malloy – I only longed for everything she represented.

I remember when we shoved Claudia into the trunk of Alec's car, the way she screamed and kicked and fought long after it was clear we wouldn't let her out. Now I know that I'd been part of dragging her back into a Hadean punishment – I can't even imagine what it must have been like to wake up in a tomb, to feel the weight of six feet of earth bear down on you and know that you'll never see the sun again, that you're completely and utterly alone.

Claudia August never stops fighting. She never lets her fear consume her.

Except... when we were trapped together in the panic room with someone outside trying to break into her castle, the two of us pressed chest-to-chest in a metal tomb, something drove her into my arms so we could revel in the darkness together. I wonder if the Ice Queen of Stonehurst, the secret queen of the criminal underworld, draws strength from my black heart the way I do from hers.

Claudia watches me as I cross the room to check on Gabriel, those icicle eyes heavy with want. Her golden hair has fallen out of its confines, her crowns askew. The light catches the ring on her finger – a single drop of blood on her perfect skin.

I'll bleed for you.

The promise sings in the air between us, buzzing inside my head along with the remnants of a violin duel.

Claudia swallows, and for a moment I see the girl behind the queen – the girl who's been holed up inside a house for four years with nothing but a cat and a vibrator for company. "I'm going to shower."

Wordlessly, I drop Gabriel's arm and follow her. I stand in the doorway of the bathroom, watching as she faces away from me and slides the dress off her shoulders, all slow and evil. She pulls the pins from her hair, tossing them against the vanity. *Plink, plink, plink.* Her golden hair tumbles down her back as she shimmies out of the dress, kicking it aside and standing in only her thong and heels. My cock is rock hard. My fingers itch to touch her skin, to slide over the curve of her thigh, to stroke her shapely calves and slip those killer heels off her dainty feet. But I hang back. I want to watch her hold her power. I've always had trouble relinquishing control. I need to be in charge, like my father. But I want to surrender to Claudia.

She is my queen, after all.

But maybe...

Maybe she needs the release even more than I do.

Still facing away from me, she kicks off her shoes and steps into the shower. The water cascades down her body, tumbling over her breasts and soaking the thong she's still wearing. A groan escapes my lips.

She turns, pressing her body against the tiles, arching her long neck so her hair cascades over her shoulders. "Noah…"

My name on her lips is the hottest thing I've ever heard. It's partly because I hated Mackenzie for so long, and having someone who looks like her naked and wet for me makes my dick hard. But mostly it's because I want to sink to my knees and worship her.

I'm completely fucked up. But then, so is she.

I don't even register that I've moved. My fingers curl around the shower door handle, and then hot water blasts my body. I'm dimly aware that I'm still wearing my clothes, that I'm probably ruining this expensive suit, but Claudia August has her icicle eyes trained on me, and I have no fucks to give.

When our bodies collide, it's mutually-assured destruction. Our mouths clash in a hail of tongues and teeth. Our twin monsters growl and gnash inside us, two alphas fighting for dominance. I want to crawl inside her; I can't get enough.

She shoves me against the shower wall, ripping the buttons off my shirt in her desperation to get it off me. I cup her ass, feeling the soaking fabric of her thong slide between my fingers. I turn her body and slam her back against the tiles. She wraps her legs behind me and I grind my dick against her as we lay our battle lines with our lips. My shirt tears as she rips it off my shoulders, but who the fuck cares because it's finally on the floor and her hands are all over me, her breasts pressed against mine. Hot skin on skin. I grip her neck, tilting her head back, pressing my fingers just enough that she moans with rapture. The water pounds against us from all angles – it's one of those showers with multiple heads, and every single one of them seems to be angled to heighten sensation. Whoever designed these condos was a sex freak of the highest order. No wonder Gabriel chose to buy this place.

She claws at my belt like a woman possessed. I set her down

so we can get the bastard off. I slip it free and gracelessly tug off my trousers and boxers. Claudia's eyes flood with greed as she grabs for my cock, but I have other plans.

I seize her neck again, and her moan of appreciation tells me exactly what she thinks of rough play. I force her to spin around, and I kick her legs apart, pressing my body against her back to grind her against the faucet. She moans and wiggles, and it's so fucking hot because she can't get away. She's mine. My queen.

Yes, yes, yes...

I hold her clit right over the water stream, putting that relentless pressure on her sensitive spot. The first orgasm tumbles from her almost immediately. Her pretty mouth falls open with this amazing moan and her ass bucks against me as she shudders through her release.

My dick screams at me. He's buried between her ass cheeks with just that thin scrap of soaking fabric between us. He's been patient long enough. Claudia tries to move off the faucet, but I won't let her go that easy. I reach down and tear away her thong, pressing my body tight against her to hold her in place.

"Where do you think you're going?" I growl in her ear as I bury my cock inside her.

She's so tight and hot... hotter than the water cascading down my back. She clenches around me as I slide all the way in. *Fuck.* My whole body strains, and I have to take a moment to breathe slow, to force my monster to yield to my control. I can't move. I'm so fucking gone that I'll come in a moment if I move. And I'm not ready. Not yet.

A stream of expletives fall from Claudia's pretty lips. "What... the... fuck... are you waiting for?" she gasps out, wriggling her ass against me, trying to force me to fuck her. But I don't obey. Not this time. Not when disobeying is so much fun.

I slam her against the faucet, buried inside her but refusing to move, just holding her against the unrelenting water as it pounds her clit into submission.

She comes again, her pussy tightening around me as more curses fall from her mouth. Her hands slide all over the tiles. She slams her ass back – she's trying to fuck me, but I won't give her the room to move.

"Fuck you, Noah Marlowe," she cries out, her words dissolving into screams as the third orgasm rips through her. I hold her cheek against the tiles and attack her mouth with mine. Her eyes are wide and her pussy clenches and I have to breathe, breathe, breathe, so I don't burst, so I can keep going with this exquisite torture.

Claudia's legs aren't working anymore. Her nails scrape down the tiles. I'm the only thing holding her upright, but still I won't let her escape. Her screams become one long orgasm, her pussy clenching around me, squeezing me. She got her wish in the end – she's the one fucking me, tearing my pleasure from me no matter how much I resist.

"Noah..." my name falls from her lips again and again and again as she loses herself completely. Her eyes are feral, glaring at me as if she's deciding whether I'd taste better raw and bloody or fried with cheese and jalapeños.

"It's payback time," I whisper as I slide my finger into her ass. *Now* I thrust.

I buck my hips back and drive into her, slamming her clit into the faucet as my finger moves past the ring of muscle and deeper inside her. I still remember her evil laugh from the panic room as she did the same thing to me, and at the time I hated how much I loved it, how well she knew what would drive me wild. No girl had ever done that before – I was always the one calling the shots.

And even though I've reduced her to a gibbering mess of sobs and screams, as I pound into her, my cock quivering with the delicious pain of resisting her, I know I'm not in control now. Far fucking from it.

This is so so wrong, and so so right.

When the monster inside me finally wins the battle and I explode inside her, I go blind. My vision blanks and white lights dance across my eyes. There's a moment where I lose myself completely. I'm nothing but pain and light and pleasure and Claudia, and I love it. I never want to wake up.

The pleasure ebbs.

The world spins.

I open my eyes. I'm on the bottom of the shower, smushed up against the glass with my legs splayed out in a most undignified position. Claudia stands over me, hands on her hips.

She slaps my cheek. "You're a fucking bastard, Noah Marlowe."

The sting is exquisite. I reel, but she grabs my neck and thrusts her tongue in my mouth. She reaches above her head and removes the spray head from its hook. Light flickers in her ice-cold eyes, and I know I'm in trouble.

I'm completely under her spell.

24

GABRIEL

I wake up in hell.

That's the only logical explanation. I'm boiling hot, tiny demons are sticking pitchforks in my temples, and I'm fairly certain the Devil himself kneels on my chest, slapping my cheeks with a wet fish.

I open my eyes, half expecting to see Lucifer himself leering down at me. What I see is a thousand times better. Or worse, depending on perspective.

Claudia looms over me, wearing only an old Octavia's Ruin tour t-shirt, her homecoming crown, and an expression of extreme agitation. She leans down and slaps me across the cheek. No wet fish, just the cool sting of her skin against mine.

"You're a fucking idiot, Gabriel Fallen."

I try to speak, but my tongue has grown a layer of fur. I kick my legs to crawl out of the sheets, but my limbs have turned into tentacles overnight. All I manage is to kind of slither around in my own filth.

I'm completely fucked up. In more ways than one.

"I bet I smell like a peach," I mumble. Words hurt.

"You smell like the vomit I just saved you from swallowing.

Consider this a royal edict – you're going to drag your ass to the shower and think about the fact that while you were passed out in your own puke Noah screwed me senseless in there. Like, seriously, what other possible use do you have for all those nozzles? Fuck me dead, that was amazing." She tosses her golden hair over her shoulder. "But first, you're going to make yourself presentable, then you and I are going to have a little chat."

I groan. Foggy memories swirl around in my head. The homecoming dance. Making Claudia come while Dorien and his band played. I had such plans for us once we got back to our place. I even have some new toys I bought for the occasion laid out on my bed.

But then I got that email, and I...

I messed everything up. Again.

SLAP.

Claudia hits my cheek again, pulling me back from my dark thoughts. "Owwwwwie."

"Did you even know how much trouble we had sneaking you out of that party last night? Noah slid down a fireman's pole with you over his shoulders. It was quite spectacular." She plucks her phone from her pocket and scrolls through her feed. "Luckily, it seems to have paid off. No photos of you crying or acting like a complete fool have reached the internet, although there's a delightful video of you chugging mead from a Viking horn that's been retweeted by your fan page, but I figure that's just a normal Saturday night for Gabriel Fallen."

"I..." I lean forward to try to catch a glimpse of the video, but the demons in my brain have other ideas. I fall back against the sofa, clutching my head. "Ow, ow, ow, little pitchfork wankers."

"Shower. Now."

I roll out of bed and stumble to the bathroom. Claudia has already laid out clothes for me, so all I have to do is step under the water. I turn the temperature ice-cold, partly because I need to wake up and partly because thinking about what Claudia and Noah did in here makes my dick hard. As I run shampoo through my hair I curse myself for missing it.

By the time I'm showered and dressed I feel a million times better. The pitchfork demons make a tactical retreat and I even whistle a little tune as I saunter out to see Claudia again.

The tune dies on my lips as I catch sight of her icicle eyes.

"Gabriel, look at me." Claudia grabs my wrists, tugging me back down onto the sofa. Those frosty eyes fix on mine. "I need you to understand. You can't do this. I need you, Gabriel. I know you're not used to being needed. I know it's freaking you out. But I'm not going to bullshit you or sing you lullabies and hide what's really going on. You told me yourself people have done that to you for your entire life, and I respect you too much to be one of them. So I'm going to lay it out for you, but you have to *listen*."

I nod. I can't move even if I wanted to – those fierce eyes of hers make it clear that to move is to die, and while I imagine death by Claudia August to be an exquisite way to go, I can't help but be aware of her knee dangerously close to my dangly bits. Noah's warnings about her echo in my ears.

"Just because we sorted out Brentwood and Alec doesn't mean I'm safe. There are bad people who will kill me to keep me from my father's empire, even though I don't want it. I need you to *not fuck shit up* for me because it will end with one of us getting a bullet between the ears. Got it?"

I stare at her, trying to make the words sink in. This is the same speech I've heard a million times before, from my parents, my manager, from Dylan. I mean, it's never been delivered by a hot, badass queen before, so maybe that's all I need to make it stick. I reach out to run my fingers along her thigh. Although she shudders with need as I trail fire across her skin, she slaps my hand away.

"Here's where things are different – I'm not your parents. I'm not Dylan."

How is she reading my thoughts?

"I'm Claudia August, and maybe that doesn't mean anything to you because you know nothing about my world, but trust me, the very mention of my name alone will have men in Tartarus Oaks quaking in their boots. I may have been in hiding for years, but I *am* my father's daughter. I'm Claudia August and I'm here to protect you. I won't leave you. I will do whatever it takes to keep you safe. I will *die* for you. Got it?"

I won't leave you.

They're just words.

Four words that don't even sound that great put together. They're not exactly poetry worthy of being immortalized through the ages.

But on Claudia's lips, they bring tears springing to my eyes.

I know all too well the power of words to heal or maim. I walk out on stage every night and swing words as weapons. Poetry is the knife I wield against my enemies, but it's also the knife I use to cut myself. Every cruel word my parents spoke to me is etched under my skin.

Disgrace. Degenerate. Pervert. A worthless blight on our family name.

Claudia speaks aloud the secret wish of my heart. That someone, somewhere, believes I'm worthy.

I swallow. I can't speak or I'll burst into tears – not the manly kind of tears women find endearing, but heaping great snotty sobs that'll turn Claudia away in disgust. And she's still kneeling over me with no panties on. No bloody way do I want her going anywhere.

I swallow again. The demons do a stabby dance on the inside of my eyeballs. She tilts her head, waiting.

I do the only thing I can do. I kiss her. I claim her lips and I *pour* my pain into her. I open her lips with mine and I open the wound that is my heart and I let her see. I let her see it *all*.

I let her see my father's rage, my mother's cold cruelty. I let her see the duchess throw my guitar over a parapet, smashing it to pieces on the cobbles. I let her see the duke walk in on Dylan and I kissing and throw us both out on our arses. I let her see the empty seats in the audience when I invited them to my Royal Albert Hall concert, and the statement they made to the press when I changed my name. I let her see Dylan's cold, dead, angry eyes when I found him in the hotel bathroom, the scrawled note in his hands.

I let her consume all the dark secrets I held close, all the times I made the wrong decisions, the times I pushed away people who wanted to love me because I was afraid they'd turn into my parents. All the times I believed that *this* would be different, *this* time they would see me, and I was wrong, wrong, wrong.

Claudia's lips open mine. She draws my pain into herself. What she gives in return is the ice of her strength – she cools the pain until it is beyond numb, like holding ice against your skin for too long. It becomes needles that stab and stab and stab but it's not pain, not really, but a euphoria. It's knowing you're alive.

When I pull away, Claudia's cheeks are glistening. "Oh, Gabe." She strokes my face. And I realize it's not her tears wetting her skin, but mine. So much for not crying in front of her.

Behind her, a shadow descends the stairs. Noah. He's been sleeping in my bed, the bastard. I hope he didn't use any of my toys. He's got on a pair of black jeans slung low over his hips, and no shirt. His chest is covered in deep scratches. Claw marks stretching beneath his clover tattoo. And are those... burns?

Envy stabs at me. I am such a bellend. It should be me with Claudia's claws across my skin.

"You lucky bastard," I croak out as he moves into the kitchen and flicks on the coffee machine. "I missed all the fun."

"Serves you right for getting shit-faced," Noah calls from the kitchen.

Claudia puffs out her bottom lip. "I had plans, Gabriel. I'd love to show you sometime."

"How about now?" Nothing like Claudia August's naked thighs to silence the dancing demons in one's head. I stroke her hair, letting the golden strands fall between my fingers. "I had plans, too. You don't know what you missed out on. Marlowe might have that mopey dark horse thing going on, but does he know what to do with a jar of honey and a colonial butter churner?"

"You're ridiculous—"

I don't care that Noah's watching. I lay her back against the sofa and run my fingers down the inside of her thighs. All I want to do is make her feel good. Safe. Wanted.

All the things I'll never be.

I stroke my fingers along her thighs, watching her face as she bites her lip. Her legs fall open and I can see her pussy lips, pink and swollen from the shenanigans she had last night with Noah. Damn, I'm a bellend of the first order for missing that.

I bend down and brush my lips against the inside of her thigh, just touching her skin. I breathe in her scent – peaches and coconut and wild, pure *Claudia* – and lose myself in the utter perfection of her. She is my queen, and it's an honor to kneel for her, to worship her.

I stroke my fingers across her skin, circling nearer but never touching, until she's trembling and bucking her hips. "Gabe..." she growls in frustration.

I chuckle as I kiss along her inner thigh, pausing at her cleft to blow air across her clit. She smells amazing, so I take a moment to breathe her in. It's too much for my queen – she grabs my hair and tries to force my head down, and a string of profanity falls from her pretty lips.

"Now, now, that's no way for a queen to speak."

I stretch out my tongue to taste her, and she tastes like flowers. I pull her clit into my mouth, sucking the delicate bud as she gasps and squirms again. I have to hold her thighs down as I lap at her, reveling in the gorgeous groans of pleasure she makes.

I sense movement and remember Noah's still here. He sets three coffee cups on the table and climbs up behind Claudia. His eyes meet mine, and he lifts an eyebrow. I nod. He slides in behind her, pulling her body onto his and bending over to kiss her neck.

Claudia whimpers as I increase my pace, arching her back to face Noah, who claims her lips in his. I remember the pair of us dancing with her sandwiched between us, and how good it felt to see how happy we made her. Noah reaches under her t-shirt to circle her nipple with his fingers. I thrust a finger inside her, loving how wet and wanting she is. I stroke her G-spot as I circle her clit with my tongue.

Her ass jerks off the sofa and she gasps into Noah's mouth as the orgasm rocks her body. I sit back on my knees, letting my smile dance on my lips. Even hungover as fuck, I've still got it.

Her eyes flick from me to Noah and back again. Noah's hand slips out of her shirt as he meets my eyes and I read his expression. *This is not how I do things.* He slides his legs out from beneath her and goes to stand up. Being here with Claudia, *with me*, is blowing his perfectly ordered Noah world wide open.

Claudia grips Noah's hand so he can't leave. "I don't want to choose," she whispers.

"So don't," I say. Noah raises an eyebrow at me, but I ignore him. "Mr. Straight and Narrow over there might have other ideas, but I don't give a fuck about monogamy. I just want to make you feel good."

I want to dance music in her veins the way she does for me.

"I've never..." Noah runs his fingers through his hair. "You know what? To hell with it."

I can't help snorting a laugh. "What's that you say, Dark Horse?"

Noah laughs darkly. "If you asked me a year ago if I'd be sharing a girl with my friend, I'd say fuck right off. I've never had any desire for swords swinging around while I'm with a girl. But that was before someone shot at me, my dad put out a hit on my girlfriend, and I helped a mobster dissolve a guy in his bathtub. The whole world is fucked up. Why should my relationship be any different?"

I can't help the smile that plays across my lips. "So you're in?"

"I'm in. Just as long as you don't cramp my style."

I snort. "Unlikely. I think I have a few tricks to teach you, young grasshopper."

Claudia laughs. She throws her arms around us both, bringing us together so we're smushed against her, Noah's salty, jasmine scent mingling with hers. It feels... good, but a completely different kind of good to having her writhe under my lips. This was more of a chest-tightening, flame-licking-down-the-spine kind of good.

I kiss Claudia's forehead. On the other side, Noah copies. The crown falls over her ear, and I pull back to set it straight on her head, brushing her hair away from her face to marvel at those wide, blue eyes. They aren't so filled with ice today. There's a warmth there that spreads fire across my chest.

"Every queen needs a harem." I lean back to admire her crown.

"We're not quite a harem. More like a threesome, a triad." Noah decides now is the time to get technical. "We need at least one more..."

Too late, he realizes what he's saying. Claudia's eyes flutter closed. One name dances on her lips. "Eli..."

The name saps the warmth from the room. My chest tightens so hard I struggle to breathe. I know that I'll never be enough for Claudia August. No one man could be. But especially not me. Noah understands her shadow side because he lives in the shadows himself. All I'm good for is a good time and incredible sex. There's a piece missing. We all feel it.

Claudia needs Eli's steadiness. We all do.

I'll never admit it to Eli, but he's a big reason why I moved back to Emerald Beach. I wanted to borrow a little of his quiet strength to get me through Dylan's suicide. He got Noah through losing his brother, I figured he could help me, too. It never occurred to me until *this very moment* that Eli has lost more than all of us, and he had to go through it alone.

Dylan is right. Even when I try to be a good person, I fuck it up with my own selfishness. Eli knows it. One day Claws will realize too, and she'll drop me for good.

25

CLAUDIA

On Monday, we walk into Stonehurst Prep in our usual formation, only this time, we've added Isaac to our group. George is still beaming with happiness from the weekend – she called me on Sunday as I lay curled up in Gabe's arms to tell me every adorable detail of her night. All the other patrons left halfway through the infamous final thirty minutes of *Society*, leaving George and Isaac with the theatre to themselves, with tubs and tubs of uneaten popcorn. Midway through the scene in *Army of Darkness* where Ash fudges the incantation for the *Necronomicon*, Isaac kissed her.

As George squeezes his hand and surges forward in her non-regulation neon-green Docs, I can't help but think falling in love looks damn good on her. I swear she's gained a couple of inches in height overnight, and her skin has a glow to it that can't be credited to makeup or exposure to nuclear fallout.

I feel I've got a little glow on of my own. That's the power of the right guys at your side.

I wear my homecoming crown askew, and a pink bomber jacket with the word *Queen* stitched across the back. It's my boldest uniform violation to date, but no one will dare write me up.

It's official now – I'm the queen of this school. Soon, I'll be the queen of this whole damn city.

My confidence trembles as we hit the throng of students crowding the entrance. Something seems off. I expect things to be different after the homecoming announcement, but I'm not prepared for the wave of weird vibes that hit us as we pass under the Corinthian columns into the main courtyard.

Eyes flicker across me and then look away. Bodies shuffle aside as we move toward the lockers, clearing a wide berth around us as if accidentally touching me might see me sentence them to death. It reminded me a little of the way Daddy's lower-level soldiers sometimes behaved around him, always glancing over their shoulder as if planning their escape. Sad, because it wasn't his cruelty but their lack of trust in his fair judgment that landed them in an alley with their throat slit.

Something is spreading through Stonehurst Prep – a virus so deadly that no vaccine will kill that fucker.

We reach my locker before I figure it out. I note the turn of heads, the mobile phones hidden in shirt sleeves and behind makeup compacts, the sidelong glances that don't quite brush my skin.

They're not looking at me.

They're looking at Gabriel.

This can't be good.

I glance at him, but he's staring forward, his long eyelashes tangled together, his hair flopping over his face. He'd been back to the same old Gabriel ever since our talk on Sunday, no trace of the melancholia that drove him to drink. But now his wide eyes have that manic look in them. He calls out to some of his friends, but they scurry off without a word. I squeeze his hand, but he's somewhere far away again.

"Any idea what's going on?" I whisper to George as we drop her at her locker. For the school freak, she always seems to know the gossip. Probably it's her years of listening through bathroom stalls. But she shakes her head. Of course, she's been too distracted with Isaac. I could have an iceberg sticking out of my head and she wouldn't notice.

I'm stacking my books when someone stops behind me and coughs unsubtly.

"You should have that cough looked at," I quip without turning around. "I'd hate for it to turn into the bubonic plague. I hear enlarged buboes and bleeding from the mouth are all the rage on Instagram these days."

"Oh, Melrose, *hiiiiiiii*." Cleo waves. "I just wanted to say congratulations on being voted homecoming queen. I was *so* glad to see you at the after-party. It's nice that you're trying to cast off the tarnish of being abandoned by your parents by pretending to have a social life."

I roll my eyes. "I loved your bedroom decor. The Ancient Egyptians were such a fascinating people. Did you know they had this special spoon they used in mummification to stick up the nose of their queen and wiggle around until her brain turned into mush? Something about seeing you reminds me of that."

Gabriel snorts a laugh, but that only averts Cleo's attention to him. "Gabriel, I'm surprised to see you at school today," she smirks, leaning against the lockers. "I thought you'd be in prison by now."

"What are you talking about?" I growl.

"Oh, you don't know?" Cleo holds up her phone and clicks a button. A video plays, titled 'Gabriel Fallen's Shocking Confession.' It's me and Gabe, our heads leaned together against Cleo's hieroglyphic wallpaper, talking in low voices. Gabriel's hands ball into fists and he yells, "I killed him."

Shit. *Shit.*

The video doesn't continue with the rest of our conversation, where it's clear Gabriel is talking about his guilt over the way he acted to Dylan, and not actual homicide. Instead, it's sliced together with such skillful editing it twists Gabe's words into something more sinister.

It's a confession.

My heart plummets, and blood pounds in my ears. This is the absolute last thing we need – more attention on us, the media picking at Gabriel, the police snooping around.

"How did you get this?" My hand shakes as I play the video again, watching in horror as the string of comments grows longer and the number of views shoots up. Cleo's bedroom had been completely empty. I made sure of it.

"I can control my webcam from my phone app," Cleo smirks. "As soon as I saw you and Gabriel head upstairs, I followed you. How fortuitous for you to choose my bedroom for your clandestine chat. As soon as I saw you go in, I turned on the camera. I thought I'd capture something R-rated, but this is even better. An actual murder confession." She glares at George. "Not even your little podcast can beat that."

I look at George in surprise. *What's she talking about?* But George is frowning at the film playing on her own phone and doesn't seem to register Cleo speaking to her.

Cleo smirks. "Have fun rotting in jail, Gabe. And Mackenzie, you'd better watch your back, bitch. Because I'm coming for you next."

She whirls on her heel and stalks off.

I punch my locker. The metal warps, leaving a fist-sized dent in the door. Pain blooms across my fingers, but it's nothing on the rage boiling behind my eyes.

Gabriel's face crumples. This angel has fallen so far, he's in hell.

The bell rings. Noah claps his hand on Gabe's shoulder. "I have to go. You two going to be okay? We'll sort this, I swear. The police don't place much stock in social media nonsense."

Gabriel nods miserably. I know exactly what he's thinking – it doesn't matter what the police do when the court of social media has already found him guilty.

As we duck into homeroom, he seems to perk up a bit. His dark expression washes over with his classic Gabriel charm. He leans across his desk and doodles a big dick on the cover of my folder.

"This will be okay, Claws. It'll blow over. You'll see." He smiles, although it's a little wobbly. "It's not as if I'm the first rockstar to ever get drunk and say something stupid on social media. I'll call Dylan's family, make sure they're okay—"

He's cut off as two police officers step into the room. They fix eyes on Gabriel, whose cocksure grin has frozen on his face.

"Gabriel Fallen, you need to come with us."

26

CLAUDIA

*E*very minute of the school day drags for hours.

After the police escort Gabriel off the grounds, Tiberius drags me into his classroom and tells me Antony forbids me to follow him to the station. "There's going to be enough media attention on that boy without Mackenzie Malloy putting herself in the firing line."

He's right, but I hate that he's right. I also hate that Antony sent him to deliver this message instead of finding me himself. We're only supposed to be pretending we don't know each other – he's still my cousin.

I sit through two classes and I can't take it any longer. I can't sit here reading about the civil rights movement while Gabriel's locked in a jail cell. I lean over Ms. Drysdale's desk. "I need to go to the bathroom."

"You know we don't allow students out during classes." She searches my face, and I feel that strange sense of loyalty to her – like I don't want to disappoint her.

"Please. I just got my period. I promise I'll be right back."

And there I go, manipulating her with the girl code. I'm a terrible feminist. She's the only teacher I feel bad about lying to, but Gabriel is more important. She scribbles a hall pass for me and I grab my bookbag and make a run for it. I turn into the hallway leading to the gym lockers, figuring I'll cut through there and run behind the bleachers. I run smack into Noah.

"Ooof." I rub my head. "I thought I hit a brick wall but no, it's just you and your ridiculous muscles."

"You know what they say – if a fish swam into me, it'd say 'dam.'" Noah curls his fingers into a fist and punches his palm.

I groan. "You've been hanging out with Gabriel too much." I try to push past him, but he blocks my path.

"What are you doing? You're supposed to be in history class. I expended a lot of effort to pull your grades up to passing, and you're destroying my hard work."

"And *you're* supposed to be in geography, Mr. Valedictorian." I shoot back.

"Not while Gabriel's in trouble." Noah's eyes darken. "I was going to talk to your cousin, see if he could pull some strings for us."

I make a face. "Antony already sent his patsy Tiberius to inform me we were staying well out of it. I don't think he cares if Gabriel rots in prison alongside Eli's father."

Noah's shoulders heave as he sighs. "Okay, I have to tell you something. And you're not going to like it. But I need you to keep cool and remember we're trying to help Gabriel here."

I lean against the bank of lockers. "What the fuck now?"

"I know something about Antony you don't. Something I was hoping to use to make him help Gabriel."

"I very much doubt you know anything about Antony that could surprise me." I fold my arms. "Go on. Out with it."

Noah runs his fingers through his hair. "Okay, here goes. After Felix died, I was a bit of a mess. You know this, right? Eli did everything he could to try to help me. One of his sensible Eli suggestions was that I find an outlet for my grief. He kept stuffing pamphlets for art therapy classes and meditation seminars into my locker, can you imagine?"

My heart squeezes against my ribs. That's so wonderfully, perfectly Eli. "I can imagine," I whisper.

"Right? Painting flowers and chanting kumbaya in a circle isn't my style. But I thought maybe he was right about needing an outlet. So I..." Noah shoved his hands into his pockets and stared at a spot behind my shoulder. "I started fighting at the Colosseum."

"*What?*"

Seriously, what the actual *fuck?*

This is bad. This is really bad.

Noah grips my shoulders. "Claudia, it's okay. No one knows who I am. I wore a mask every time. No way did I want the guys who hang out there to know they were facing Senator Marlowe's son in the ring. They already fight dirty as it is. Once, a guy tried to pull it off in the ring and...let's say I made it clear the mask stays on."

My heart pounds in my ears. This is too much to process on top of Gabriel's arrest. I drag Noah into the girl's locker room. It's empty. I jam a mop under the door handle to block it, then kick the door in one of the shower blocks open and drag him inside. "Start talking. I need to know everything."

"I joined a boxing club and some of the guys were talking about it – this rough place in Tartarus Oaks where you could fuck people up with no rules and earn a little cash on the side. I went along one night, just to see what it was like. I'd never done anything like that before, but I couldn't hurt the people I hated the most, and I thought... maybe breaking some random guy's nose would help? The first time I stepped into the cage I figured I'd get my ass handed to me and I'd never do something so stupid again, but as soon as I swung the first punch..." He swallows. "It was like something inside me was freed."

"A monster," I whisper.

"Right. A monster." Noah swallows again. "I fought five against one that night, and I left with eight grand in my pocket. One of the guys had to be dragged outside. I don't know if he'll walk again."

I run my hands down his arms, feeling the hard, taut muscle beneath. I remember things Eli and Gabriel said about how much he's bulked out in the last couple of years. Eli thought he'd been on the paleo diet, but really he'd been pummeling gangsters into a bloody pulp in my cousin's underground fight club.

This also explained how Noah knew about the Triumvirate back when the guys figured out my secret. You didn't hang out in a place like that without understanding who was in charge.

"So what does this have to do with making Antony help with Gabriel?"

"Your cousin isn't telling you the whole truth. Or maybe he is and you don't care. I don't know. I..." Noah's fingers dig into my shoulders. "Antony isn't just a club owner. He *rules* that place. You should see the way he struts around, handing down proclamations like a king. He controls the betting; the only skin allowed inside are girls who work for him. If you want to know who's going to fill in the power struggle once you get rid of Brutus, it's him. It was always going to be him."

I bristle. This isn't right. None of this is right. Noah's got it all wrong. Antony and I have a plan – we wait five years, sell the house, then escape with the proceeds to a new life. Antony knows that plan becomes impossible if he's deep in the family business. He knows he has to stay out of the chain of command or they'll never let him leave. He wouldn't—

I think about Antony's expensive suit, the gun he wears strapped across his chest, the way he was able to mobilize men so quickly when I needed him – loyal men who he trusted with at least part of our secret.

I lean against the cubicle wall. My head spins. None of this made sense. Antony wants out of the family business as much as I do. He wants to go back to law school and have a normal life. That was why we're doing all this – because the alternative is revealing my identity and locking ourselves into an all-out gang war, us against Brutus for control of the August empire. And I couldn't count on support – Brutus cleaned house of all Julian's loyal soldiers as soon as he took control of the family. He had to if he wanted to hold onto power, especially while he still bears my father's mark.

Except... Antony is still alive. He always made it clear he'd do what he needed to do to remain in Brutus' good graces. That's why Brutus gave him the club if he dropped out of law school – Brutus needed someone he could trust, and Antony had to prove he could be trusted. If what Noah says is true, maybe Antony is in deeper with Brutus than he ever let on to me.

"Why are you telling me this?" I rub my temples.

"The last time I was there, I saw Antony punish a guy who had crossed your family. He *crucified* him on a giant cross above the cage. Antony drove the nails in himself. One of the fighters told me dirty cops were there that night, being wined and dined by your cousin in the VIP suite. Antony has influence with the police, with city hall. Maybe it's time he used it."

A shiver runs through my body as Noah brings up the crucifixion. That was my father's favorite punishment. Maybe I hadn't been the only one learning from him.

"I need to talk to Antony." I push off from the wall.

"I'll go with you."

"No. I need to do this on my own."

"Claws—" Noah calls after me, but I'm already stalking down the hall.

I know Antony doesn't have a class right now, but when I check his closet office, it's empty. I hear something in the gym – voices talking, the squeak of shoes against the wooden floor. I shove open the roller door.

At first, I can't see anyone. "Ant—er, Mr. Jones?" I call out.

He appears at the edge of the bleachers, shirtless, with a towel slung over his shoulders. "I was doing some weights," he huffs.

"You talk to yourself while you work out? I heard voices."

"I was playing music. That okay with you?" The sword-and-olive branch tattoo on his wrist flashes as he grabs the rings and starts doing pull-ups. My throat closes as I rub the skin on my own wrist. I would have got that same tattoo for my sixteenth birthday if Daddy had lived that long. Instead, I spent my sixteenth birthday watching horror films alone with my cat, while Antony worked at the club.

I'm a queen on the run, and the only family I have left is keeping secrets from me.

"I'm not here to bust your ass. Or maybe I am." I debate how to approach this. I want to ask him about everything Noah told me, but I can't find the words. For so long, it's been me and Antony against the world. He's everything to me, and I can't destroy that bond we have.

I also don't want to rat Noah out to him. I know my cousin well enough to know he won't hesitate to kill first and ask questions never.

Antony glares at me as he sets his feet on the ground. "You're supposed to be in class."

I settle on making demands. I may be in hiding, but I'm still a queen. "I need you to find out what's happening to Gabriel, if they're charging him."

"Even if I had that kind of power, I'm not using it on your pretty boy musician." Antony dribbles a basketball along the edge of the court. I watch him with new eyes, searching for some sign that he's this person Noah claims.

Did he crucify one of Brutus' enemies?

If he's in that deep with Brutus, what did Antony *really* do to make him go to ground?

Has Antony been lying to me this whole time?

But I can't say *anything* without alerting him that Noah's been at his club. Frustrated, I try the baby cousin routine, even though it probably hasn't worked on Antony since I was seven.

"The thing is, I'm starting to wonder if you *do* have power."

Antony snaps his head toward me. "What are you talking about?"

"Just some things I've noticed lately. You're carrying a gun all the time. You're at the club more than ever, and you've got an army of soldiers at your beck and call." I put my hands on my hips. "Things have been different ever since you told me you took care of Brutus, that he's left the city. But the more I think about it, the more I realize it doesn't make sense. You're a low-level soldier – what could you possibly have done to him? Where is he, really?"

Antony leans over, his nose inches from mine. He's breathing heavy, and a vein above his eye throbs. I've seen him angry before, but I've never, *ever* felt that rage directed at me. I want to flinch away, but I won't give him the satisfaction.

"Are you questioning me, cousin?" he sneers. "I've done *everything* to keep you safe, even after you recklessly bring the three stooges in on our secret. And you want to do something reckless again just because your poor pretty boy might have to spend a night in a cell?"

"This isn't about Gabriel anymore." My hands ball into fists. "It's about you keeping things from me. We're the only family we've got, Antony."

"Did it occur to you I might be keeping things from you for

your own good? Secrets can get you killed, Claws. Sometimes it's better to be in the dark."

"I disagree." I fold my arms and glare right back.

Antony sighs. "I don't know where Brutus is. If I knew, I'd have given you his head by now. I'm trying to find him, but I need to search each of his boltholes and feel out the allies who might be hiding him. I have to navigate this carefully – if I ask too many questions or piss off the wrong person, I lose my position in the family, which means we lose access to those assets."

"You're not supposed to have a position in the family." Antony's father is my mother's brother. He's not an August. "You've supposed to run the Colosseum and be Brutus' errand boy. That's it. That's what we agreed. That's the only way you'll be able to escape this life."

"Things change." Antony's jaw clenches. "You've been swanning around that mansion eating caviar and rescuing stray cats. You don't know shit about the real world. If Brutus tells me to do something, I can't say, 'sorry, I promised Claudia August I wouldn't get involved.' The only reason you've managed to stay hidden all these years is because I've kept him on a leash, and I needed to grow close to him to do that. I needed him to trust me. It's the only way I could have got him out of the city. Unfortunately for us, he took my advice too well and didn't tell me where he's hiding."

It all makes sense now. Antony made it sound as if Brutus had left in fear of what Antony would do to him – instead, he convinced Brutus he was in danger, and the rat scampered into a hole to hide. "Why lie to me, then? Why make me think you weren't still in Brutus' pocket?"

"I didn't lie. I said he skipped town to save his ass, and that's true. I let you make assumptions so you wouldn't go blabbing to your boyfriends and get us into even deeper shit."

I bite my lip. I want to defend the guys, but Antony has a

point. Things had gone from weird to worse since I invited them into my life. My head spins as the full impact of what he's saying hits me. "You can't lie to me, Antony. You *can't*. I know the guys are a complication, but they can be an asset, too. Noah has connections of a different kind, and Gabriel... well maybe Gabriel is just pretty to look at. We're too close to fuck this up by keeping things from each other."

He squeezes me tight against him – a brutal embrace, the only kind we know how to have. "All of this has been to keep you safe."

"I know. And I love you for it." My throat closes around the words. I hate that he's been holding all of this on his own shoulders. I hate that I've been hiding inside Malloy Manor when I should have been at his side. "But I'm not a little kid anymore. Don't hide the truth from me because it's ugly."

"I don't think you were ever a little kid." Antony dares a smile.

Not since that night. I dig my nails into his skin as the chains on my box of memories rattle free. "Did you know Brutus was the—"

"No." Antony snaps off the word. It's hard, final. Relief floods me. My knees give out, and I sink into him. He catches me in his arms before I can fall to the floor. I can feel his heart beating against mine. A chain slides free before I can stop it, and a memory slams into me.

After *it* happened, I picked the lock on my bedroom door and crept down the hall. Antony's parents were at my father's party downstairs, so Antony was staying over for the night in one of our guest rooms. I pushed open the door and tried to climb in bed beside him. He saw the blood dripping down my thighs. I thought I needed to be held, but Antony knows me better than I know myself. He threw a jacket over my shoulders and snuck me out of the house. We walked to the Colosseum, deserted now, silent except for the ghosts of the roaring crowds pounding in my ears. Or maybe that was my monster baying for blood.

I'd never been inside the club before – it was where Antony hung out when he wasn't at school or with me, learning martial arts from the fighters who trained there during the day. Antony took me into the cage where they held the fights. I breathed in the blood-soaked air and felt my own blood drying on my skin. Everything innocent and good in me was swallowed up by the monster's fury.

All night Antony stood still as a statue while I punched him, kicked him, screamed at him, tore out his hair. I clawed the skin on his chest into ribbons, mingling his blood with mine until the monster was sated.

Antony *knows* me. He's always been here for me. And to think that for a moment I doubted—

"Fuck, Claws, I had you doubting me this bad?" Antony leans his head against my shoulder. "Of course I didn't know. I figured out the truth when you did – when we saw the note on Brentwood. If I'd known, I'd have crucified that bastard on the spot."

"We need to find Brutus," I growl. I need to see him *suffer*. Crucifixion is too good for the bastard.

"I'm aware," Antony says darkly. "At least we know he's close to the city. Brutus' note means he knows you're still alive, which means he knows I've been helping you. It's both our asses on the line here."

"Good. And don't you forget it. But since you no longer have to hide the fact you're a big bad mafia man, could you maybe contact some of those cops I *know* you've got on your payroll, and figure out what's happening with Gabriel?"

"He's a big boy, Claws. He can sort his own shit—"

"What if I beg?" I make a pouty face and get down on my knees in front of him, clasping my hands like I'm praying.

"Get your ass up before someone sees you." Antony's eyes dart to the door of the gym. He grabs my arms and yanks me to my feet. "There are eyes all over this school. The last thing we need is more incriminating material plastered on the internet."

"It won't happen, because I'm wringing Cleo's stupid neck with my own hands," I growl.

"You're not touching her." Antony grabs my wrist. "I'm serious, Claws. I let you have your fun with the actor. No more pranks. No more games. We're *this* fucking close to getting the house. But if you die, it all goes to shit."

"But Gabriel—"

Antony sighs. "I'll make some calls. I'll find out what's going on. But you can't lose your shit."

Mollified, I duck out of the gym just as students start trickling in for Antony's next-period gym class. As I head to the lockers to change, I pass Noah, his muscles bulging from his tight gym shirt. I can't believe I didn't figure it out before. No way he got that jacked running track.

Noah sweeps me into his arms. "What did he say?" he whispers. "Am I going to be strung up by the nuts and fed to the lions?"

"He doesn't know about you," I whisper back. "He came clean to me, though. You were right, he's higher up than I thought. And what's important is that Brutus still trusts him, which means that keeping Antony where he is now is going to be our best path to finding Brutus."

"How does this Brutus guy know who you are?" Noah asks. "That note said—"

"I know what it said."

"Right. So why is he leaving notes for you on corpses, instead of telling all his underworld buddies your real name?"

The chains around my box rattle. "I'd better hurry or I'll be late for gym, and you know that new teacher's a slave driver—"

"Hey, what happened to Gabriel?"

My mouth dries as I whip my head around. Eli stands in front of us, arms folded, that too-perfect mouth of his cocked in a worried expression. My lips tingle with the memory of that faint kiss he brushed against them at the after-party. The urge to throw myself into his arms ripples through me. I grip Noah a bit tighter.

"Like you care," Noah snaps back.

"Of course I care," the Southern notes twang in his voice. Eli swallows. "I've been running all over hell's half-acre looking for you. It's bad enough he's drinking again, but the police are taking that video seriously—"

"Shove off." Noah slams his hand into Eli's chest, splaying his fingers. It's an enormous hand, and it stops Eli in his tracks. He turns his big eyes to Noah, studying his former friend as if he intends to discern the answer from Noah's concrete features. Tension ripples down Noah's arm. He doesn't shove Eli, but his monster lurks under the surface, and I can tell he's close to snapping. "You don't want to be part of this, remember? Go throw a ball around with your new stepfather."

Eli's face darkens. "Fuck you, Marlowe."

He spins on his heel and stalks off, narrowly missing crashing into George as she bounces out of the girl's locker room. "You were talking to Eli?" She sounds hopeful. "Did he say anything about..."

"The kiss?" I shake my head. In between the seventeen discussions we had about how lovely Isaac's hair is, I told her what happened at the party. "Nope. It must've been a drunken mistake."

"Eli Hart doesn't make drunken mistakes," George declares

as she slips her arm into mine. "I meant to tell you, because I won't see you at lunch—"

"Another art project?" George is applying for a creative arts program that's hella competitive, and she's only got a few months left to finish her application, so she's working on it every hour of the day.

"Yeah. I'm going to need to tape paintbrushes to my hands if I've any hope of getting my portfolio done on time. Which was what I wanted to tell you – I'm not going to be at school tomorrow. I'm doing a workshop on audio-visual installations and optically altering time and space at the Brawley Guerilla Art Institute."

"Sounds weird."

"The weirdest." George beams. "I can't wait. But you'll be okay, right? I heard about Gabriel. Is he going to—"

"He'll be fine," I say with more certainty than I feel. "The Emerald Beach police department is no match for the fury of Mackenzie Malloy."

ANTONY WORKS us so hard during gym that by the time I collapse on the mats for warm-down, I can no longer lift my arms. I'm not the only one groaning in agony, but I am the only one who knows I'm to blame for our punishment. Still, seeing Eli's ass bounce around in those tiny shorts is worth any pain Antony dishes out.

Noah stays behind to talk to some of his track teammates, and George races through her shower to get to the art lab. I take my time under the warm water, using all the fancy products I raided from Ainsley Malloy's bathroom cabinets and listening to Cleo and her snakes gossiping about Gabriel. She's so busy holding court that she doesn't notice me drop laxative powder into her gross green shake. Antony said no more pranks, but he's not the queen of this school – I am.

Job done, I head through the Humanities block toward the cafeteria. The halls are deserted – the Humanities block is the oldest wing of the school. As Ms. Drysdale pointed out, "This patriarchal establishment wasn't built with a heating system because they believed frostbite would turn boys into men." Now, the school admits both sexes, and we all get to enjoy freezing our tits off. I hug my bare arms and hurry along the corridor when I hear a sob coming from Ms. Drysdale's office.

I stop in my tracks, listening hard. I hear a male voice say something, and she interrupts. "You shouldn't be here. What if they ask questions? What if someone recognizes you?"

I flatten my body against the hall. The male voice laughs – it's a friendly laugh, full of bonhomie. I can tell from the pinch in her voice that Ms. Drysdale doesn't consider this guy her friend.

"You don't need to be so tense, Penelope," the male voice says, smooth as silk. "I'm here on a personal errand. My future stepson attends this school, and I wanted to make sure your Principal Foster was taking good care of the boy. I'm looking out for his future; that's the kind of guy I am."

"Yes," she says, her voice flat.

"Imagine my surprise when your name came up in our conversation. Apparently, you're one of his favorite teachers. I'm not surprised – a pretty, intelligent woman like yourself is just his type. If I were a schoolboy, I think you'd be my favorite, too. I think I'd have all kinds of naughty fantasies about you." He pauses, letting that lewd comment sink in. Ms. Drysdale doesn't slam his face into her filing cabinet or lecture him on the patriarchy, which tells me this isn't an ordinary parent/teacher interview.

He laughs again. "So I thought to myself, while I was visiting this fine educational establishment I'll drop in to see my good girl Penelope, and make sure she's keeping well. *Are* you keeping well? How rude of me not to ask."

"Please," she begs. "I'll get the money. I promise. I just need more time—"

The man tsks. "I don't think that's fair, now is it? When you needed my help, I jumped straight into action. I sorted your problem the very same day, did I not?"

She makes a choking noise in her throat. My heart pounds against my chest. I glance along the corridor. There's no one around. The door to Ms. Drysdale's office is firmly shut, but I'm standing in front of a corner where supply cupboards have been built up against an older stone wall. There's a cold draft blowing through the gap between the two, carrying Ms. Drysdale's conversation with it. I flatten my back against the stone and press my ear closer.

"If I fulfilled my end of our bargain, it's only fair that you provide what you owe in a timely fashion. You know what will happen if you're late again. But I'm not without a conscience. I've been watching you closely. I know your situation." He tsks again. "That weasel of an ex of yours has left you in a bit of a mess, hasn't he? I abhor men like that. They should treat their women like the queens they are and protect them from the world's problems, instead of causing them. Don't you worry, Penelope. Don't fret. I'm a creative man. I'm here because I think we can come up with a solution to help you pay this debt."

I hold my breath. The air drops out of the building. I *know* this conversation. I understand perfectly what Mr. Smooth in there *isn't* saying. I've heard a hundred times of it a hundred different times, whenever I hid in my father's office and listened to him argue with his brother. This is exactly what Daddy was trying to keep out of the family business, and what Brutus wanted to invite in.

Someone is trying to make my favorite teacher join the skin market.

When Ms. Drysdale speaks, it's with a power I've never heard her wield before. "I'm afraid I don't follow."

"An intelligent woman like you? I think you follow me perfectly. You know the business I'm in. I deal in all types of pleasure – your ex got you into this mess by indulging his pleasure, perhaps you need to embrace your own to get out of it? I have a clientele with exclusive tastes who'll eat you right up, especially if you pull the buttoned-up teacher act on them. Mmmm, yes. You'd be a premium product, commanding a high price. It would only take a few clients to square us up, no trouble on my end. You might even enjoy yourself."

Invisible bugs crawl over my skin. The box of my memories clatters as the darkness inside pushes to escape. I feel flashes of it flay my skin – the hand pinning me down, the saccharine tang of alcohol and blood, the words rasped against my ear.

Let me show you a man, baby girl.

"Thank you for the kind offer, but I don't think I'll need to take you up on it." Mrs. Drysdale uses the clipped tone she saves for students who don't hand in their assignments. "I'll have your money for you by Christmas, as we agreed."

"Very well." A chair scrapes back. "Tis a pity. You'd make much more working for me than you do wrangling these brats. If you change your mind—"

"I won't."

I duck into the janitor's closet just as Ms. Drysdale's door swings open and a man steps out. My heart pounds as I wait for him to yell at me, but he whistles a jaunty tune as he moves along the hall.

He hasn't seen me.

But I've left the closet door open a crack, and I can see him. He wears an expensive pinstripe suit that pulls at his broad shoulders, and his handsome face is serene, jovial. He looks like a man who loves every minute of his job, especially the minutes he gets to spend shaking down innocent high school teachers.

Through the crack in the door, I watch him stroll down the corridor. My blood boils as my gaze sweeps his face. I've never met this man in person, but I *know* him. He's been in my father's office many times, and he was a fixture at every Triumvirate event I attended in disguise. I'm surprised at myself that I didn't recognize his voice, but it's been so long since my father's world invaded my own that I'd almost started to believe it was all a dream.

No dreams here, only nightmares.

My teacher is being blackmailed by Nero Lucian.

The same Nero Lucian who is determined to sink his paws into my Golden Boy. No, not mine, but that didn't matter, not when the Lucians are involved. I think of what Noah told me about his talk with Eli, how Nero tried to give him a job. It's obvious the stepson Nero spoke of is Eli.

I think of Eli reaching out to us today, and I wonder, I *wonder,* if Eli has enough darkness in his heart that he might consider Nero's offer.

But I can't believe Eli would be involved in extorting Ms. Drysdale. She is his favorite teacher, and there's no way she's done anything to deserve this. But I have to remember that I broke something vital inside Eli when I revealed my lies, and the ruined human I left behind might be capable of anything.

Have I driven the Golden Boy of Stonehurst Prep straight into my enemy's arms?

I wait until I hear the door clang shut, then ease open the closet door and step outside. I debate knocking on Ms. Drysdale's door, but I can't say anything as Mackenzie Malloy that she wants to hear.

I remember when Ms. Drysdale took me to her office after

Cleo stole my clothes. She lent me her own clothing, and I noticed the blanket under her desk, the takeout containers littering the room, the suitcase peeking out from behind the filing cabinet in the corner. Ms. Drysdale is the nicest teacher in this school, the only person who believed me. She clearly lives in her office, and someone was trying to shake her down for money she clearly doesn't have.

Not if I have anything to say about it.

27

CLAUDIA

By the time I reach the cafeteria, I'm a ball of nerves. Today's menu is tofu-centric and I can't stomach it, so Noah and I head to the library. I'm still hopelessly behind in all my classes, and he refuses to write my essays for me, even though that would be easier than trying to teach me four years of high school knowledge in thirty-minute intervals.

THE STONEHURST PREP library is pretty cool. It's a rabbit-warren of curving shelves occupying an L-shaped space between three of the oldest wings – an architectural masterpiece of the old and new, designed by a clever Turkish-American architect with a flair for the dramatic. Sunlight streams in from large skylights, and although we're not supposed to talk in here beyond quiet study, there are plenty of hidden corners where Noah and I can set up camp.

NOAH HEADS to his favorite one now, a little mezzanine behind the computer lab with only one narrow staircase for access. He drags me along behind him, muttering titles of the books he wants to collect for our history assignment. I think he's grateful for something normal to think about. Pity, since I'm about to burst his bubble with the news of what I overheard in Ms. Drysdale's office—

WAIT A SECOND.

WHAT'S THAT?

I STOP IN MY TRACKS, my whole body stiffening. I rub my eyes, but when I remove my hands I see that I'm not mistaken. It's no mirage.

THERE, in front of me, is Eli Hart, looking hot as fuck with a blond curl falling over his eye and his mouth set in a serious line. This in itself is not unusual – Eli's competing with Noah for brainiac of the school, so it's totally normal to see him tucked up in a cozy corner with a pile of beanbags stacked around him like a fort. What *is* unusual is who he's snuggled up with, their heads bent close together as if they're sharing the secrets of the universe.

IT'S GEORGE.

28

CLAUDIA

*G**eorge and Eli?*

The picture of the two of them together haunts me for the rest of the day, duking it out with the image of Gabriel locked in a cell. It doesn't help that Isaac finds me after Women's Studies class and asks me shyly if George is still single. "She keeps ghosting me and not answering my texts, and I've seen her hanging with Eli Hart at school. I thought he had a thing for you, but if he and George are an item, could you tell me? I don't want to harass her if she's not interested."

He sounds so dejected. I assure Isaac that everything is fine and George is still crazy about him, even though I honestly don't know anymore. When I saw them together at the football game, I thought they were being friendly, but now I'm not so sure.

When Isaac is out of sight, I slam my fist into my locker, leaving a second dent in its formally pristine surface.

As soon as the final bell rings, I rush to the gym to see Antony, hoping he's managed to find out something about Gabriel. But he's already left. A text beeps on my phone.

I'm needed at the club. I'll be home tonight with news. Don't go to the station yourself or send the Dark Horse or do anything else stupid. You can't help him.

Goddamn Antony, he knows me too well. There's nothing for me to do but go back to Malloy Manor to stew in my nervous rage.

Noah makes extra-strong coffee for both of us and spreads out his homework across the ballroom. Queen Boudica leaps on his history project, spreading papers everywhere. Noah growls at her, but five minutes later he's on the floor tickling her stomach, his assignment forgotten.

She's got him wrapped around her little paw, which is as it should be. Noah may be a dark prince, but he knows when to bow to a queen.

I tap my ailing phone against the table to make it work (poor thing is on its last legs) and stare down at the pictures I snapped on my phone for potential future purposes. *George and Eli?* I can't believe it. They look so cozy together, smushed up in the bean-bags whispering to each other while they point to something on George's laptop. It could just be an assignment they're working on, but why lie to me about it? And after the football game, too…

I can't see George cheating on Isaac. So *why* did she lie?

She did it so smoothly, too. She's a natural. I should take lessons from her.

At least looking at the pictures is more fun than social media right now. The story of Gabriel's 'confession' has spread across the world. Musicians are posting their own stories and videos from tours with Octavia's Ruin, building a narrative of Gabe as this out-of-control drug fiend who doesn't know his ass from his elbow most of the time. That last part is true enough, and every-thing is just this side of believable that it's tough to read.

If he gets out of this mess, he needs to sort out his shit.

I'm happy to see the band from homecoming, Broken Muse, release a statement on their social media supporting Gabriel and calling for their fans not to judge someone based on clearly doctored social media 'evidence.' But a link in the comments leads me over to Cleo's YouTube channel where she's posted three 'confessional' videos about Gabe that are complete bullshit. Utter bollocks, as Gabe would say. And she's gained another two hundred thousand followers overnight, good for her.

"Argh!" I toss my phone across the room. Queen Boudica looks up from her position on Noah's stomach, studying the flying rectangle as it hits the wall and drops onto her cat bed.

She hops off Noah and trots over to me, climbing into my lap and kneading her sharp claws into my thigh. I stroke her fur and feel a tiny bit calmer. It's been the two of us alone in our palace against the world for so long, and now her world's been flipped upside down alongside mine. But she's taken everything in stride.

Her eyes narrow in concentration as if tearing my thigh to shreds is the most important business in the history of the world. As I bury my fingers in her fur, I graze over the raised scar where that bastard cut her. A hot sizzle of possessiveness courses through my veins. I remember what I'm fighting for.

Queen Boudica didn't know she'd chosen another queen when I took her home from the diner that night. But she's my family, same as Antony and Noah and Gabriel and George and… and Eli, even if he never speaks to me again.

I will not allow their hurt to go unpunished.

I will protect them until my dying breath.

I text Antony for an update, but he doesn't answer. Noah finishes his homework and makes dinner for us both. It's terrible – poor little rich boy has clearly never cooked for himself before, because he makes some kind of inedible chicken salad and burns the grilled cheese, but I'm too agitated to eat anyway. Everything will taste like cardboard until I know Gabriel is safe.

Noah tries to interest me in a game of chess, but he's too

competitive and I can't focus. He puts a movie on and promptly falls asleep on my shoulder. It's a weird mirror moment of the night he rescued me from the desert and I fell asleep on him. Weird but good. It feels so natural, so comfortable, to have his warm body pressed against mine. My heart constricts as I think about how close I've been to losing him, how close I am to losing Gabe. How I've already lost Eli.

I stroke Queen Boudica, who's curled up on top of Noah, and stare out at the empty swimming pool until I hear the garage door click open.

I fling off the sleepers – ignoring their meows and groans of protest – and pounce on Antony as he throws open the fridge. "What did you find out about Gabriel?"

"Fuck, give me a minute. I haven't had a break all day, and in four hours I have to get up again to supervise practice for the worst football team in the history of the universe." Antony frowns as he inspects a container of misshapen brown mush.

"Noah tried to make chicken salad." Antony starts to tear the corner off, but I grab it from his hands and toss it in the trash. "I wouldn't attempt it, trust me."

Antony grabs a package of Pop-Tarts and shoves one in the toaster. He looks worn out, his tie askew, his eyes ringed in black. There are more speckles on his cuff, and I have the sinking suspicion that they're blood. I want to ask him about his night, but after our fight earlier today I know I need to back off. Besides, there's something more important I need to know. "Antony, *please*."

He sighs. "It's not good news. According to my source, the UK police have been in contact. They've had Gabriel as a person of interest in his drummer's murder for some time, and with this story making headlines, they want—"

"Hang on, Dylan committed suicide."

But as I say it, I remember overhearing Daphne gossiping in

the bathroom. *Gabriel and Dylan had a massive screaming argument the day he died, and Gabriel threatened to hurt him—*

"Not according to the police, he didn't," Antony smirks. "Maybe that's not public knowledge yet. But that's what they're saying."

"Fuck." I stare at the glaring lightbulb above his head until white squiggles appear in front of my eyes. Queen Boudica winds herself around my ankles, reminding me with plaintive cries that all the world's problems can be solved by opening another can of tuna.

"Exactly. Even with my connections, there's nothing I can do. He's just going to have to play this out." Antony gives me a weird look as he grabs his Pop-Tart and jams it into his mouth. "I guess we'll find out if you're dating a murderer."

"We've got another problem."

He gives me a look like he's going to throttle me. "I need a drink."

I scoop up Queen Boudica and follow Antony into the ballroom. Wordlessly, he pours a glass of Scotch and hands it to me, then takes the bottle to the sofa, flops down, and chugs it like it's water. I notice he doesn't offer Noah a drink. "Talk," he barks.

"Nero was at school today."

Antony spits Scotch down his lapel. "How the fuck did I miss that?"

"I don't know, but I saw him with my own eyes, coming out of Ms. Drysdale's office. He—"

"She's the one with the tortoiseshell glasses? The hot librarian type?"

I roll my eyes. "Sure. Whatever. I mean, she's the smartest woman I've ever met, she has awesome style and she's really kind, but let's reduce her to a male fantasy stereotype."

"Meow," Queen Boudica agrees. Queens stick together.

"Claws, can we focus on *Nero*, please?"

"He was in her office. I overheard their conversation. He said he was at school checking up on his future stepson." I squeeze my eyes shut. "He means Eli. Apparently, he was speaking to Ms. Foster about Eli. And he threatened Ms. Drysdale. He said she owed him money and if she didn't get it to him by Christmas, she'd be in trouble."

"Sounds like the *smartest person you know* has a bit of a gambling problem."

"It was her ex. I don't know why she's responsible for his debt or why Nero came himself instead of sending a soldier, but it was disgusting. He said he could pimp her out if she wanted to pay off the debt sooner."

Thinking about it makes my skin crawl all over again. *Daddy would've never allowed this in the Triumvirate. He always said the skin market was out of bounds.*

"She should consider it," Antony smirks, sloshing his drink as he leans back into the sofa. "Nero pays his girls well for the shit he makes them do. And he likes to do the shakedowns himself. He relishes lording it over the plebs. But she's not our problem. I'm concerned about Captain America. It sounds like Nero has taken an interest in him. And he knows our little secret."

"He won't tell." I have to believe that.

"Meow," Queen Boudica agrees.

"You know we can't take that chance."

"You're not hurting him. You're not *touching* him," I growl.

"I'll do what needs to be done to keep this family safe." Antony glares at Noah. "That includes you too, now, Dark Horse. I'm giving the two of you until Thanksgiving to sort him out, or I'll invoke a more *permanent* solution."

29

ELI

My favorite guard is on duty again – the comedian who calls me Your Highness. This time I slap a hundred-dollar bill in his hand and tell him not to give me any trouble. He skips my pat-down and I get to keep my phone with me.

Dad's in a good mood. He hums into the mouthpiece as I settle into the hard plastic chair. "This is a surprise. I didn't expect to see you on a school day."

"We have some things to discuss. Mom says you're getting a divorce."

He sighs. Lines crisscross his forehead, and I notice again how much weight he's lost. There's no Southern cooking in prison. "For better or worse, Eli. That's the vow she took. But she's decided this counts as worse than worse. With the appeal coming up I can't risk upsetting her, so I've agreed. I can't fight her *and* my creditors."

I get it. This is the price she's demanded for working on his appeal and pretending to the media we're one big, happy family. Southern women stand by their men, even when they turn out to be scumbag body-brokers like Walter Hart. Just like everything else about our family, our united front is another lie – just a mirage used to broker deals and get a leg up in the world.

Dad squirms in his seat. My silence makes him uncomfortable – Walter Hart believes that everyone adores him, that he's cleverer than anyone else, that he's in control of every situation, but his self-worth doesn't hold up under scrutiny. "You don't want to hear about your old man and his troubles. I've come up with a plan for you to take over the business. We'll reinvent ourselves under a new name, new everything. It'll be brilliant, you'll see—"

"Dad," I clear my throat. I'm not here for him to pull my future out from under me. "Last time I visited, I told you about Mackenzie—"

"That bitch giving you trouble?" His eyes narrow. "I still have connections, son. I can make sure she doesn't bother you—"

"No!" I cry out. His eyes open in surprise. "I mean, that's not what I'm here about. Seeing her has made me think about the past, and I have some questions about things I don't understand. Mainly, why you were so opposed to our friendship in the first place. Why did you and Howard Malloy fall out?"

"We had a deal go sour, son." Dad laughs. "That's how it goes in business. You'll learn when you're in the real world."

I carefully slide the folded photograph I printed out from the pocket of my jeans. I hold it up in front of the glass, in such a way that my father's body blocks the camera in the corner from seeing the image. "Who's the guy in this picture?"

When Dad sees the photograph, his jaw tightens. I know that look. It's the look he gets when he's been caught in a lie or someone cuts through his facade. It means he's in damage control and a load of bullshit is about to fall from his mouth.

"Where did you get this?" His voice is even, but I can see the vein throbbing above his temple.

"A friend found it in an archive of deleted photographs on

your computer," I say, turning the photograph toward me so I can look at it, even though I know exactly what it shows – my father sitting in a plush leather booth at some club with a cigar in his mouth and a woman on his lap wearing a dress so tight I can see her religion. He leans in to talk to a man with a hooked nose and eagle eyes that match his brown designer suit, while another scantily-clad woman drapes herself across his shoulders. I tap the other man in the picture. "My friend knows this guy's name – Brutus August. Apparently, he was high up in the August crime family when this photo was taken five years ago. Care to explain why you're buddies with a crime boss?"

"Son, you need to tell your friend to stop digging around in the past." Dad leans in close, the corners of his mouth pulling back into a smile that's more of a snarl. The skin on my neck prickles. I know this version of my father, and I hate him. "If that picture comes out in the media or makes it into my appeal, I'm up shit creek without a paddle."

I lean forward and slam the picture against the glass. "I'm trying to *help* you. But I need you to tell me the truth."

Dad leans back in his chair. That cold smile never leaves his lips as he taps the edge of the counter. He makes me wait for several moments before he answers. "That man was my contact. He put me in touch with the right people in my line of work. Interested buyers and such."

"Buyers for body parts on the black market."

"Jesus H Christ, son. We're not rehashing this unsavory business—"

"We're just talking. So this guy was your hookup in the underworld?"

It's a long time before Dad nods. "In exchange for introductions, he sometimes asked a favor in return. A coffin to be delivered to a secret location at a moment's notice. A request that I vacate the crematorium for a night and leave the key under the rug for him. Letting his people hide things at the bottom of open graves before a funeral service... that sort of thing..."

I swallow. *He's talking about making bodies disappear. This is... this is even more fucked up than I imagined.* I hold up another picture. "What about this guy? Do you know him?"

Dad peers at the picture. He's trying to look casual, but that vein above his eye throbs and his agitation taints the air. "Him I met a couple of times. That's his club we're at in the first picture. You stay well away from him, boy. That's an order. That man is unhinged."

I slide the photographs back into my pocket. "That's going to be difficult. He's Mom's new fiancé."

OUTSIDE, I fling open my car door and sink into the seat. My whole body shakes. It takes several deep breaths before I can grip the steering wheel and back out of the prison.

A few blocks from the prison, I slide into the parking lot of a shitty diner on the edge of a small wooded park. George leaps from the bushes and throws herself into the car like she's the star in a spy film. Her eyes shine with excitement as she picks leaves and twigs from her blue pixie hair. "You look white as a sheet. What happened in there?"

I pull out of the lot and head toward the freeway. I have to swallow three times before I can answer. "I told him Nero Lucian was engaged to Mom and he went *crazy*. He pounded the glass and smashed the phone into the wall and said the most horrible things. The guards had to drag him away."

The shaking starts again. I jam my elbows into my sides in an attempt to control it. George tilts her head to the side. The empathy pooling in her eyes is real, and that matters to me more than I can say. "I'm sorry, Eli."

"Yeah." My fingers grip the wheel so hard my knuckles are turning white. "Me too."

George taps my shoulder. "Don't keep me in suspense. What did your dad say about the other photograph?"

I knew I could count on George – she's the same old certifiable genius with a devious streak a mile long. After I roped her into my mission during the homecoming game, she hasn't wasted a moment. Under the guise of taking photos before the dance, she managed to upload keystroke software and tracking onto Mackenzie's phone. When I told her about Nero, she dug out all the research she had on my dad and found those two photographs from a deleted file on his computer the police never searched.

"He says the man is his contact. Apparently, he introduced Dad to the right people on the body brokering market and in exchange…" *I can't believe I'm saying this,* "…Dad did some jobs for him. Helping him get rid of bodies, by the sounds of it."

George whistles. "So I *was* right. Your father is in deep with Brutus August. Did you know he's Imperator of the entire August crime family? Apparently, he killed the rightful king, his brother Julian, by *burying him alive.* Isn't that wild?"

"*Imperator?* They're serious about this whole Roman Empire schtick." I hide my shock behind a derisive snort. Claudia said her father was killed by Brutus, but she didn't say *how.* Imagine losing your father like that, knowing that he'd suffocated slowly to death—

No. I shake my head roughly. *I'm not going to feel sorry for her.*

I suck my breath between my teeth. "There's more."

"Spill."

"When they dragged my father out after his fit, the warden noticed the picture of Dad and Brutus on my chair. He tells me Brutus has been to visit my dad in jail. Several times. The last visit was the day before he disappeared."

"Shiiiiiit. Do you see what this means, Eli?" George lifts her laptop onto the back of my chair and taps at the keys. "My research shows Brutus has put it out all around the criminal underworld that he killed Mackenzie's parents. And there he is in that photograph with your father, with a business relationship. And they're still in contact. And with all these sightings of the Malloys over the years, all the internet chatter... I don't believe it's true that he killed the Malloys."

I *know* it's not true, because Noah overheard *his* father talking to that assassin about killing the Malloys. And I know Noah's dad wouldn't be working with Walter Hart. But I can't tell George any of this because... because I'd have to give away *her* secret. And I can't do it.

Not until I know everything.

A new piece of this horrific puzzle has slotted into place. I know now that in addition to being a lowlife, lying scumbag, my father is in deep with Claudia's family. And that he's shit scared of Nero Lucian. What I don't know is what that means, or how it changes things for me.

"What next?" I sigh.

"If you want to keep investigating, I can dig deeper into this Nero guy. We'll keep our eyes on Mackenzie, make sure she's not putting herself in any danger, follow her and see if she leads us to answers. I think the key to finding the truth about her parents is to track down our friend Mr. August."

"You want to rock up to the *Imperator* and just casually ask him if he really whacked them?"

"That might be impossible, since apparently he's disappeared recently himself. But you'll be surprised how much I can learn from behind a computer screen." George grins. "Or maybe you won't. Of course, we *could* just ask Mackenzie—"

"She has amnesia," I say automatically, my instinct still to protect her, to justify her behavior.

"I know. That's so wild," George says. "She doesn't act like it. But then, she's Mackenzie Malloy. She wouldn't want anyone to think she's weak."

I grit my teeth.

"My dad always used to say, hating someone is like burning down your house to get rid of a rat." George watches me. Damn that girl – I know she's smart, but she never misses a beat.

I laugh bitterly. "Clearly, your dad never met Mackenzie Malloy."

"Actually, he did. At one of the parent/teacher interviews my parents set up with the school after she and Cleo…" George shakes her head. "You know what happened. Anyway, after we left the meeting, he said to me, 'You know, when I sat down in the principal's office today, I wanted to throttle that girl for hurting you. But now I just want to give her a hug.' He pointed out all the things I missed because I was so busy hating her – the way she stared at the floor while her father talked over her, the way she flinched away from him when he touched her, the way her mother grabbed her as they left. I found it hard to hate her so much after that, even after all the horrible things she did."

"That's because you're too nice." George doesn't know I'm saying those words to myself. I let Mackenzie walk all over me because I hurt for her. I wanted to be the boy who saved her, and all I am is the boy who let her down.

"I'm not sure about that. I am helping you track down her parents behind her back." George bites her lip. "I don't like lying to her. Whatever happened in the last four years, it's changed her. She's a completely different person."

You can say that again.

I hate lying to George, especially since my lies are fueling her lies, but I hate Claudia for lying to her more. George has been through so much already because of Mackenzie, and she's only helping me now because she cares about her friend. My motives aren't nearly as pure.

I need to *understand*.

I need a battle plan.

I need every piece of ammunition I can get.

30

CLAUDIA

Noah manages to get Gabriel's lawyer on the phone. Apparently, my fallen angel is being held for questioning, and the police aren't fucking around. Inspectors from the UK and the Emerald Beach homicide unit have grilled him non-stop for hours. I can't even imagine what he's going through.

"I can't take this any longer," I growl as Noah hangs up the phone. He pulls me close, pressing his lips to my forehead. If the gesture is meant to comfort me, it's a complete failure. I can feel the tension in Noah's body as he battles with his own helplessness.

"We need something to keep our mind off him." Noah nods to my untouched schoolbooks stacked on the kitchen table. "How about your history assignment?"

I roll my eyes. *Only Noah Marlowe could think about schoolwork right now.* "How about we figure out how to get Eli back on our side so Antony doesn't have him silenced?"

Just saying the words makes my chest ache. *I can't let this happen.* If Eli's caught in the crossfire of Nero's megalomania and Antony's protectiveness... a piece of me will die with him. Eli is everything that's good in the world, and I won't allow his spark to be snuffed out before he's had the chance to burn bright.

Something else concerns me about Antony's ultimatum. I know exactly what he's doing, and it makes my chest ache to think of it. He's thinking like a gangster, unconcerned if we leave a trail of bodies in our wake. But with blood on his hands, how will he ever be able to leave the protection of the family?

This is not happening.

"I can see one solution," Noah growls. "We kill Antony."

My heart thuds. "Don't joke about that shit."

"It's no joke. He's threatening to kill my best friend. I'm not going to pretend I'm okay with that."

"You realize you're sitting there talking about murder?" I study Noah's face. "I don't want this life for you. It might be too late for Antony and me, but you're supposed to graduate high school, leave for some snooty Ivy League college, join a fraternity, and be awarded a giant gilded stick to shove up your ass."

"It's too late for me, too." Noah's dark eyes bore into mine. "I lost my future when Felix died."

I hate that he believes that. I hate that he's so willing to embrace my world. It might look like the perfect outlet for his rage, but before this is over Noah Marlowe will wish he'd never met me.

But right now I need his cold fury. "Antony has given us until Thanksgiving to bring Eli back to us. That's significant. It means he has no intention of killing Eli."

"How do you figure?"

"The Triumvirate runs their separate operations, but twice a year the leaders meet for two significant events – Saturnalia in December, and Lupercalia in March. These are wild parties – celebrations of the family achievements – but also a chance for the soldiers and tribunes to form alliances and build working relationships."

Noah raises an eyebrow. "Like a mafia corporate retreat?"

"Exactly. At each event, the Triumvirate holds a secret meeting where they decide on rules, mete out punishments, and move the pieces around on the chessboard of their empire."

"And Antony thinks Nero is planning something for this meeting?" Noah's eyes glint with understanding.

I nod. "And Antony knows it involves Eli and his family somehow. If Antony really believed Eli is a threat to us, he'd have killed him by now. He wouldn't wait for my permission. He knows if he gets rid of Eli, we lose our connection to Nero, the chance to figure out what he's up to. He wants me to get close to Eli again so we can find out what Nero is planning."

"Why not just tell us the truth, then?"

Because he doesn't trust me anymore.

I try to speak the words, but there's a lump in my throat and I choke on them instead. Antony is everything to me, he's held me through my darkest moments, has literally *dragged me from my grave*. Our parents always taught us that loyalty came before anything else, that family was everything.

It fucking *sucks* that he feels he has to keep this from me, but I understand. Both of us lived through the ultimate betrayal – Brutus breaking his blood oath to kill my father and take over the family. Both of us lost everything because we believed loyalty kept us safe. Antony wouldn't make that mistake again, not even for me.

Noah's looking at me like he expects an answer. I shake my head. I can't find the words.

"Okay, so your cousin wants us to get Eli to tell him what Nero's doing." Noah pulls me close. "We can do that, no problem."

Wordlessly, I burrow into his shoulder, digging the remote from between the sofa cushions and pointing it at the sound system. A moment later, Gabriel's smoky voice wafts from the speakers:

You drank my milk,

sipped my blood,

tore my flesh away.

You crawl between the sheets,

My dreams scattered at your feet.

With bloody lips and wide lovely eyes,

You whisper, love me love me love...

I lose myself in the melancholy song, my heart aching at the crack of Gabriel's voice as he allows his pain to bloom in every note. Even before he died, Dylan's ghost haunts him, pulling him back into his body – the one person Gabriel can never escape.

All I want to do is hold him. I want to tell him he's perfect just the way he is, that his broken pieces are all I could ever need. But he's not here, and I can't reach him, and I hate myself for it.

Noah holds me while the music washes over me, bathing my sins in Gabe's beautiful voice. After a while, he clears his throat. There's a question burning in his mind, and he needs to let it out. "What happens to the August family at this meeting in December? Their leader is AWOL. Who goes in his place?"

"No one can speak for him. Brutus will have to show his face at Saturnalia, or he'll forfeit his rule over our family." I realize then how important that is, that we have a chance to unseat Brutus and deprive him of his power if only we can prevent him from attending that meeting.

Noah is thinking the same thing. "That might be one way to get rid of a number of our problems. We find Brutus and make sure he doesn't get to that meeting. Then it doesn't matter what he thinks he knows about you."

"That's basically my plan. Only, Antony says he doesn't know where Brutus is hiding."

The corner of Noah's mouth quirks up into a smile that's saturated in violence. "Maybe it's time we joined the search."

———

WE DECIDE to ambush Eli at school the next day. We'll drag him somewhere private and *make* him see reason. I'll kiss him until he doesn't know which way is up, if it comes to that. My lips still ache to kiss him – not the stolen kisses from the dance, but a *real* kiss – the kind where we need each other to breathe.

But he's not at school again, and neither is George. I ask Mr. Ross if he's heard from George, and he says he's not allowed to discuss another student's medical history with me. I text her to see if she's okay, and she sends me a photo of her lying in bed making a duck face. Her hair's a mess and she's got a thermometer in her mouth and a glass of orange juice in her hand. *I'm sick. It's a total drag. Miss your face.*

Something about the photograph nags at me. "Look at this." I show it to Noah.

"Oh, poor George." He looks at my face. "You look worried. I'm sure it's just a bug or something. I can take you around there if you want—"

"It's not that. Look at the arm."

"The..." Noah frowns in confusion.

"The arm!" I jab my finger at the photograph. Along the side of the screen, just visible on George's Emily the Strange bedspread, is the very edge of a human arm. One that's definitely not attached to George's body.

"So? It's probably her mother."

"Not unless her mother is a bodybuilder. Look at the

muscle." I draw around the shape of the shoulder with my finger. My throat tightens.

"I bet it's Isaac looking after his girl."

"Isaac has tattoos. That arm is perfectly clean." I know that arm. It's Eli. I *know* it.

Eli's in George's bed.

Fuck.

"Whatcha looking at?" A hand drapes over my shoulder, and a warm cheek grazes mine. "No offense to George, but that is the *worst* amateur porn I've ever seen."

My throat closes as a heady, smoky scent fills my nostrils.

"GABRIEL?"

I whirl around, my heart leaping into my throat.

There he is. Standing around like he never left, like he was never dragged out of school by the cops or stuck in a jail cell for three days. My fallen angel laughs as he wraps his arms around me, pulling me under the spell of his sultry pagan scent. He's wearing his leather jacket over his crumpled Stonehurst uniform, and it crackles as his hands roam over my body as though he's trying to commit my curves to memory.

"Miss me?" His lips pull back into a cocky grin. He's got a week's worth of stubble on his chin, and it suits him.

"That's a stupid fucking quest—" Gabriel swallows my words with his mouth. I gasp as his kiss whips the air from my lungs. He forces my lips open and dives his tongue inside. This kiss is so much more than anything we've shared before – this isn't flirty, playful Gabriel whose body is like a drug I can't get enough of. This is Gabriel who has dragged himself out of the desert and fallen into a lake of crystal clear water. This is my fallen angel getting his wings back.

He pushes me against the lockers, and I don't give a fuck that we're in the middle of school, that all around us people are whispering. I want to crawl into his skin and live inside his scent forever. When I suck his bottom lip and he lets out a beautiful moan, I taste how close I was to losing him, and I plan to cling to him and never, ever let go.

Someone wolf-whistles. Along the corridor, a smattering of students cheer – the same people who only a few days ago were denouncing him as a killer. I want to burn them all, and I will, but not now. Not yet.

Right now, I live for Gabriel's kiss.

His lips are like silk, and his tongue plays a melody only I can hear. His eyes are wide open, like he needs to drink in the sight of me after so much time apart.

Gabriel pulls back a little, gasping for breath. His hair has fallen over his eyes. I reach up to tuck it back so I can topple into those beautiful grey orbs, all stormy at the edges and crystal clear in the middle.

"Don't scare me like that again." My nails dig into his shoulders. "What are you doing here? Did you tunnel your way out with a rusty spoon?"

"Don't tell me, you bribed a guard with a bit of British totty." Noah grins. Even his dark eyes are brighter today.

"I'll have you know, this derriere was in high demand." Gabriel grins as he slaps his ass. "But alas, I was saved from becoming the darling of the prison. They let me go."

"Just like that?"

"Just like that." He doesn't look as happy as I expect. "They don't think Dylan killed himself, but they don't have enough evidence to charge me. The British police are here. They're supposed to be running a joint investigation, although they kind of steamrolled in and took over. They made Cleo hand over her laptop and they found the unedited video. She may even get charged with obstruction of justice, since she's the one who alerted the police to it in the first place."

I can't help the grin spreading across my face. At least two things have gone right today. "So you're cleared of all charges?"

"For now." Gabe frowns. The storms swirl around his eyes. "They want me to stay close by in case they need to ask me more questions. It doesn't matter, anyway. This isn't about Dylan's death anymore. It's about the *story*."

"I don't understand."

Gabriel digs his phone from his pocket and pulls up an email. He tosses the phone to me. I scroll through the email. It's from his record label. I'm too incensed to read past the first sentence, but random phrases leap out at me. "...long history of unreliable behavior...", "...becoming a liability...", "...several warnings..."

"They dropped me," Gabriel says. "With all the stuff that's coming out online and the murder investigation, I'll never find another label. Hell, I won't even be able to find musicians to play with me. Octavia's Ruin is over. And that's not even the worst part. The worst part is it's my own fucking fault. I should have shown you this earlier. Instead, I dealt with it the way I deal with everything – by diving headfirst into oblivion so I could forget. But if I'd said something, maybe none of this would have happened."

He taps on another email and hands the phone to me. I'm shocked to see the sender's name. At first, I think it's a spam email, because who will call themselves 'The Duke of Black-wich.' But then I realize it's Gabriel's father.

Gabriel's father, who he hasn't spoken to since his very public estrangement two years ago.

My hand shakes as I stare at the screen. The email is four words, chilling in their brevity. It reads simply, "Return to England immediately."

CLAUDIA

Gabriel mopes around the manor all week. I watch him like a hawk – he doesn't drink or touch any drugs other than weed, thank the gods, but I almost wish he would because sulky Gabriel is, in his own words, 'a miserable git.' I miss his smiling, flirting, and general annoyingness.

He doesn't book a plane ticket back to Old Blighty, and he doesn't email or call his parents. He also barely attends classes and refuses to help us try to ambush Eli, who's doing a deft job of avoiding us and slamming doors in our faces.

One day I arrived home after cheerleading practice to find Gabe lying on the sofa, in the same position I left him that morning. He wore the shorts he slept in, and he tried to balance a hookah pipe on his chest while Queen Boudica made a sleeping nest out of his hair.

Something inside me snaps. I'm *done* with this version of Gabriel. I need him to sing the stars to me once more.

I go into his room, grab his acoustic guitar, take it back to the ballroom, and toss it onto his lap.

"Bloody hell." He leaps up, earning a filthy look from Queen

Boudica as she slides off the end of the sofa. The hookah pipe rolls across the room. "You scared me."

"Good." I fold my arms and glare at him. "You know what would make you feel better? Writing a song about it."

"Meow," Queen Boudica agrees.

"What's the point?" Gabriel lets the guitar slide off the sofa, joining a litter of candy bar wrappers and random sketches and doodles at his feet. "Without a label, I'm never going to be able to release music again. I'm done."

This is ridiculous. I plant my hands on his knees, leaning in close so he has no option but to face me. "Gabriel, I love you, but pull your head out of your ass."

"I'm British. We say *arse.*" Gabriel gives me a sad smile. "Would you say that again?"

"You know what I mean. So you don't have a label? Big fucking deal. There's this new-fangled invention called *the internet.* Musicians have been using it to get their work in front of their fans for decades now. I know you might not have it in your freaking *castle* back in England, but it's a thing here in America, and it's pretty powerful."

"Not that part." Gabriel's cheeky grin plays across his face, and too late I realize my mistake – when I'm this close to him, he draws me under his spell. "The part about you loving me."

My cheeks heat up. "I didn't mean—"

"Say it again." He brushes my cheek with his finger. His words are tight, teasing, but there's a need in them that makes my heart stutter.

"I love you," I growl out, my chest constricting as the words hang in the air between us. "I fucking love you and you're driving me *insane.*"

Gabriel throws himself at me, capturing my lips in his. Like our kiss in the hallway at school, this kiss carries so much weight and hope and promise. He dances music on my tongue, and for the first time in a long time, I see the stars flicker to life in his eyes again.

"I love you. I thought of nothing else *but* you," he whispers. "You were the light that glinted in the darkness."

"Don't be so dramatic," I say, even though his words make my heart race. "You were in jail for three nights. It's not as if you did twenty-to-life in Sing Sing."

A shudder rolls through his body. "It felt like *three decades*. It was the most horrible place. You wouldn't believe the muck they try to feed you, and the toilet facilities..." he shudders. "No room service. No hot towels or Egyptian cotton sheets. No massage therapist for the crick in my neck I got sleeping on the concrete slab they call a bed! There wasn't even a *mirror*. And then they wanted to take my photograph. I told them not until they got me a stylist because my hair was a *fright*."

I laugh. *He's ridiculous*. I need that now – I need someone to light up the world with their smile. I kiss Gabriel again, taking my time about it, committing every piece of him to memory. Then I slide onto the sofa beside him. "You're out now, and your name is clear. That's something to celebrate."

"I know. I know we have more important things to worry about, but I can't stop thinking about what they said," he frowns. "Dylan was *murdered*. Apparently, he didn't overdose as they initially believed. Someone sedated him so he couldn't fight back, then *injected* him with grey death."

"Grey death? I've never heard of it."

"It's a cocktail of heroin, fentanyl, and pink, and it's so potent you can die just from *touching* it." Gabriel shivers. "They told me it's an excruciating death – he'd have struggled to breathe, his skin would have gone all clammy, and then his heart failed. I can't believe someone would do that to him."

"What about Dylan's note?" Dylan had written such horrible

things about Gabriel. That note seemed designed to make Gabriel hate himself.

"The note's in Dylan's handwriting, but who knows? The police think the note shows the murderer wanted to get to me. Maybe the killer forced Dylan to write it. Or maybe they're good at forging." Gabriel smiles ruefully. "Or maybe Dylan planned to kill himself anyway, and he got someone else to help him make it look like a murder."

"That sounds more like the plot from a thriller novel than real life," I roll my eyes. "But then again, I'm the mafia queen doppelgänger of a rich Valley girl trying using a fake life to take possession of a mansion, so what do I know? And I'm guessing you haven't heard anything more from your parents. Are you going to go back?"

"Because the Duke of Blackwich commands me? Bloody hell, no." But Gabriel looks a little sick.

"But..." I prod.

"But... this is the first time he's contacted me since they disowned me. It can't be for any good reason. I don't like to think about what he'll do if I disobey."

"What if I came with you?"

"I don't know." Gabriel knits his fingers in mine. "My parents are vicious. I'd be throwing you to the lions."

"I've got claws of my own. I'll be fine." I pat his leg. "We'll go together, okay? After things calm down here and I know Eli is safe, you can whisk me away to your castle. And maybe introduce me to that English ale. I'm dying to know what all the fuss is about."

GABRIEL and I spend all evening and night in his room getting reacquainted. Around 2AM he collapses, his body spent, his arms wrapped around me as he snores adorably in my ear. I stare at the wall, unable to sleep, my mind buzzing with everything that's going on.

The walls of the room bend in toward me, and the darkness swirls and twists and becomes the dark of nightmares – the dark of a silk-lined coffin and stifling air and rising panic clawing at my throat. I fight against the memory, but it's too much, and I know I won't be going to sleep any time soon. I slip out from beneath Gabriel. Queen Boudica is curled at the foot of the bed, pressed up hard against him, sapping his body warmth for her contentment as a true queen should.

I pull on his oversized Octavia's Ruin hoodie, holding the collar over my face to breathe his scent in deep. I pad down to the media room, where I choose a horror film, make some popcorn, and stare at the screen without seeing anything until Antony returns from the Colosseum at 3:30AM. He must see the lights on because he appears at the doorway, looking like shit. He tosses his suit jacket over the arm of a chair and flops down beside me, digging his hand into my almost-empty popcorn bowl. There are bags under his eyes and he smells like blood and desperation.

"Rough night?"

Antony loosens his tie. There's a lipstick stain on his collar – a glittering shade of pink that could have been pulled from Mackenzie's makeup bag. "There was trouble tonight. A couple of fights broke out."

"I thought that was the whole point?"

Antony smiles, but it's weak. He really does look tired. "These weren't fighters. A bunch of Lucian higher-ups came tonight to talk shop in the VIP area. They took exception to Brutus' soldiers being there. Relations between the families were already strained because of the changes Brutus was making, but now that his empire may be up for grabs, things are escalating."

I roll over to face him. I want him to see that I'm giving him an opening to start to repair our trust. "You never tell me about what's going on with the families. What's Brutus been doing? What are these changes?"

"You know his beef with Uncle Julian was over wanting to expand into other markets – skin, organs, harder drugs, that kind of thing?" Antony asks. I nod, happy he's talking. "Julian didn't want to touch that stuff, but Brutus had a lot of support within the ranks. There's a lot of money to be made, and money makes people shift loyalties. That's the only reason Brutus was able to take over the way he did and keep himself alive despite being an accursed man – and why Dio and Lucian allowed him to become the new Imperator, even though he broke every law in our code."

"And now?"

"And now the August empire is bigger and more lucrative than ever, but it's been disintegrating around Brutus for a long time." Antony licks salt from his fingers. Queen Boudica peers around the door. She has her lap radar initiated, because she barrels across the room and launches herself into his arms. "The families may enjoy the money he brings in and the new markets he's opened up, but they can't trust him. Why would they? He murdered his own brother. They could replace him with someone they do trust, but why do that when they can just squeeze him out? After what Brutus did, there's no clear line of succession. The Imperators plan to get rid of him and absorb the August family into their own empires."

A seething rage burns in my veins as Antony's words sink in. If Dio and Lucian succeed, our family will be obliterated. Everything my father and our ancestors fought to build will be *destroyed*. All because Brutus couldn't stand being second fiddle to his older brother. For that, he broke the sacred ties of family. *Et in morte fidelitas.* I have my own reasons to hate the man, but now my father's vengeance wraps around my heart and refuses to let go.

It's an irrational desire. I've spent the last four years pretending I'm not Claudia August and trying to escape the legacy of our family. If the August family ceases to exist, Antony and I will be free.

The man who knows my face will die, and take my legacy with him.

Except... I wouldn't be the one to do it.

And that's unacceptable.

Daddy's number one rule – your enemies must die looking you in the eye.

He's taught me well.

I don't expect Brutus to go down easy. He'll be plotting his return in December. He knows what the Imperators are planning, and he'll be ready to pull the rabbit out of his hat. *All it takes is for him to blurt out my secret and everyone I love is in danger...*

I can't wait for him to be drawn out for Saturnalia, especially not with Nero cozying up to Eli. I need to move on Brutus *now*. My hands ball into fists.

I need to taste his blood.

Antony averts his eyes, and I *know* he's holding something back, even as he says, "I believe this might be why Brutus has chosen to come for you now. Perhaps he's known you survived for some time, or maybe he only figured it out when the story of Mackenzie Malloy's return hit the news. Either way, he knows that if he has Julian August's daughter under his power, he can regain control of the family. I think that's why he got rid of Brentwood, to win you over."

"Is that what he thinks?" I growl.

Queen Boudica digs her claws into my leg.

That man held me down, pushed my face into a pillow, whispered 'baby girl' in my ear. I thought he couldn't take anything more from me, but then he took my parents, my name, my whole *life*.

And he thinks he can *win my support*?

Death is too good for him. I'm going to claw his eyes out. I'm going to cut off his dick and make him eat it.

"You still don't know where he is." We need to fix this. I'm tired of looking over my shoulder. I'm sick of letting the locked box of my memories control my life. I am my father's daughter, and Brutus will *pay*.

"I'm working on it. I'm checking all his known boltholes, all his associates and business partners. I can only use so many resources, or Brutus' loyal soldiers will get suspicious. As it is, they can't see why I'd bother with a security job in Harrington Hills that keeps me away at all hours. They think I should give your contract to them and focus on the club. I'm only getting away with it because Brutus isn't here."

"I want to help. I'm sick of being cooped up in here." I stroke Queen Boudica's fur.

"You help by keeping those boys of yours under control. You help by bringing back Captain America so we can figure out what the hell Nero is up to. You help by convincing everyone around you that you're Mackenzie Malloy."

I don't like the way he dismisses me. Daddy never dismissed me. He knew I'd make an amazing Imperator. It's ridiculous that Antony can't seem to remember the training I've had, but I won't fight him on it tonight.

I will, however, find out what's *really* going on at the Colosseum. He's not telling me the full truth, and that's unacceptable. Claudia August won't be made a fool of, especially not by her own flesh and blood.

32

CLAUDIA

"Can you try to not be so..." Noah gestures in Gabriel's general *Gabrielness,* "...you."

He has a point. Noah's wearing boxing shorts, combat boots, and a black hoodie pulled over his hair. A black mask hangs around his neck, ready to be pulled on as we approach our destination. I'm wearing one of Ainsley Malloy's slutty designer dresses in a shade of ice blue that perfectly matches my eyes, a white feather boa around my shoulders, and a black wig and heavy makeup that will ensure no one recognizes Mackenzie Malloy in the crowd. But Gabriel... Gabriel is decked out in about twenty heavy gold chains and a backward baseball cap. He looks utterly ridiculous and it's not exactly an outfit designed to blend in where we're going.

"Claws, he's *mocking* me. Up with this I will not put. Would it be better if I pretended to be you?" Gabriel hunches his shoulders forward and grunts in a deep voice. "I'm Noah. I'm so serious. I'm the living embodiment of Elon Musk's tunnel project – endlessly boring."

"*Gabriel.*" Noah looks tired.

Gabriel jangles his gold chains. "I have no neck and my dick is an airplane filled with accountants."

"A... what?"

"A Boring 747."

I hit Gabe on the shoulder. I crack a smile, but inside I'm a bundle of nerves. I know it's a bad idea sneaking out to the club in the first place. But I have to find out the truth about Antony with my own eyes. Which means I have to take Noah with me, since he can get us in, and Gabriel isn't going to let us go without him. So now I have an entourage that seems determined to be as obvious as possible.

Antony left for the club some hours ago. Tiberius is on guard duty at Malloy Manor tonight. I'd love to tell him the truth, but I think if things went to the wire he'd be loyal to Antony instead of me. Instead, I call him and say that Noah is going back to his place for the night.

"You want me to send one of the guys to watch the place?" he asks.

"Nope. No one's going to be stupid enough to go after the senator's son."

I leave the lights on and a movie running in the theatre room, and some pillows and clothing stuffed under a blanket to form the shape of two people. Anyone peering in the windows to check up on us would assume Gabe and I are conked out in front of the TV.

Instead, I make him leave his cap and half his bling behind, and we climb into Noah's car. Gabe and I crouch down, remaining hidden from view until Noah hits the freeway.

Instead of heading straight to Tartarus Oaks, Noah turns off at Brawley and drives into a lot of storage lockers. He parks the Lambo and opens a roller door to reveal a beat-up old Chevy Caprice, the kind of car manic pixie dream girls take on road trips across America with a suitcase of drugs in the trunk while bats circle overhead.

"Why are we here?" I glare at him as he unlocks the Chevy and climbs behind the wheel.

"I rented this shed a couple of years back when I started fighting. I figured the guys at the club would get suspicious if I showed up in the Lambo, so I park here and drive this instead."

Clever. Noah thinks like a criminal. I don't know whether to be impressed or mortified. I decide on impressed as I watch Noah back the Chevy out of the locker and replace it with the Lambo. Our family could do worse than recruit soldiers like Noah – after all, we offer the same perks as an Ivy League education – wealth, power, status – without the crippling student debt.

But I shouldn't be thinking like that – like my father. I might be a queen, but my father's legacy is a broken, thorny crown.

As we pass over the Acheron bridge into the other side of the city, something inside me releases. This side of the city hasn't felt like an enemy since my parents' murders. We pass familiar shops and looming gated communities where the most powerful criminals in this city make their homes. We circle around the old opera house where Daddy snuck me into secret parties as a waitress, where I observed the inner workings of the Empire I was expected to one day rule.

There's a party there tonight – the building is lit up like Fourth of July, and people mill about outside. Even though the temperature has dropped like crazy, couples dine at the outdoor tables of an entire street of Lucian-owned Italian restaurants, and hold hands as they head down to the boardwalk for a romantic stroll by the ocean.

The life that was stolen from me glitters through the car windows in vibrant colors – red lights twinkling against a starless sky.

Beside me, Gabriel reaches across and squeezes my hand. It's such a tender move, making my heart flip.

I need tonight to go flawlessly. I need answers, and I need the two of them beside me if those answers aren't what I want to hear.

We head away from the nightlife into an industrial district of towering warehouses. The world darkens. I shift in my seat. "We're almost there," Noah says.

The car judders as it bumps over a disused railway line.

I swallow my heart as I squeeze Gabriel's hand tighter. I'm glad he's here. I'll need to borrow strength from both of them.

I'm about to walk back into a world I swore to leave behind.

I'm confronting the empire that might've been mine.

I'm about to see for myself if the man I've loved as a brother has truly become a monster.

33

ELI

"Why have they come all the way out here?" George's knuckles whiten as she grips the wheel. "I don't like this."

"Her cousin has a club on this side of the city. I bet that's where they're going." I don't take my eyes off the Chevy in front of us as they cross the railroad tracks and turn again. Luckily, there are several cars on the road alongside us to disguise our pursuit – far too many for a creepy industrial area in the middle of the night.

It's hard to believe that less than an hour ago I was sound asleep on George's trundle bed with Gizmo smushed into my armpit. George had a ping on her phone that *she* was on the move. She woke me up and we piled into her tiny Beetle car to follow them. We caught them just as Noah pulled out of a storage lot behind the wheel of a beat-up Chevy Caprice. The sight of Noah in a car like that on any other day would've been hilarious, but now it's just creepy, like everything else about tonight.

Why are they all in Tartarus Oaks at 11PM on a school night?

Noah parks up outside a derelict warehouse. We're on the

edge of an abandoned railway yard – nothing else around but rotting train cars and weed-choked scrap. I notice all the parking spots around the Chevy are filled with cars. George drives past and finds a parking spot around the corner. "Get out, quick. We need to see where they're going."

"You worry too much." George holds up her phone, where a blinking pink dot on a street map tracks Claudia's location. "Besides, we can't go to a club dressed like this. They won't let us past the door."

I glance down at my underwear, Stonehurst Prep hoodie, and school dress shoes I shoved on as we ran out the door. I hadn't given a thought to what I'm wearing, and now there's no way I'm getting inside that club. "Fuck, what are we going to do?"

"Luckily for you, I came prepared for covert ops." George wriggles around in the backseat.

"You just *happen* to keep a fake mustache and bag of disguises in your car?" I peer at the pile of clothing strewn across the backseat.

"Duh. I'm a true-crime podcaster working at a vintage clothing store. Of course I do." She emerges holding a pinstripe suit with enormous '70s lapels. "Tada!"

"I'm not wearing that. I'll look like a pimp."

"It's better than looking like a hobo." George tosses the suit toward me.

I sigh. She has a point. I peel off my hoodie and tug on the suit, while George wiggles into a skintight red bodycon dress, tucks her hair beneath a platinum blonde wig, and winds three strings of pearls around her neck. She looks completely ridiculous with her cutesy tattoos on display, but she must've thought of that, too, because she wraps a fox fur stole around her shoulders. "I'm ready. Let's go."

We link arms and run back around the corner to the Chevy.

Claudia and the guys are gone, but we spy a couple of other people heading between a gap between the warehouses. We follow them at a respectable distance and see them heading through an open gate in a high chain length fence into the abandoned railway yard.

"What is this place?" George peers around her as we hike along a torn-up track bed toward the towering roundhouse at the far end of the lot.

It's a train graveyard. Train cars line the tracks on either side, their hollowed bodies rusting in place, empty cabs like soulless eyes watching our journey to the underworld. In places, the tracks have been yanked from the earth, probably by the earthquakes that regularly shake the city. George pulls her stole tighter around her shoulders and stares at me with those giant eyes of hers.

People mill around the narrow entrance into the roundhouse – four lanes of track approaching the turntable around which the sheds housing the locomotives are arranged. I can't see over their heads into the space beyond, but lights and music reach across the desolate yard, drawing us in. As we get closer I notice the people around us dressed to the nines, gold and diamond jewelry on display. Black-clad bodyguards survey the crowd, fingers toying with guns on their belts. My pimp suit fits right in.

We step into the crowd and approach one of the broad-shouldered guards who are nodding people through to the roundhouse. "I've never seen you around here before." He narrows his eyes at me. "This isn't a frat party. It's invitation only."

Fuck.

George throws herself in front of me. "But you remember me, don't you, sugar?" she purrs.

The guard stares at her, licking his lips. George tilts her head to the side, her fingers running along his muscular arm as he taps his pistol. I'm forgotten as he leers down at her. "Why don't you jog my memory?"

George doesn't hesitate – she reaches up and kisses him. He holds her roughly, plunging his tongue into her mouth. He's seven feet of pure muscle and he can break George in half like a twig. When he finally sets her down, George's eyes are as wide as the moon. She staggers a little in her heels but manages to blow him a kiss as she drags me past.

"I'll see you around, sugar," she calls to her new friend. Her nails dig into my arm as she drags us along with the crowd. She wipes the smudged lipstick at the corner of her mouth.

"You told me you've never been here before," I hiss.

"I haven't." She grips me harder, and I feel that she's trembling. "But look around. This place is a den of sin. The whole reason that guy works here is so he can make people bleed and get all the pussy he wants. He doesn't remember me, he just thinks he's getting lucky. Now, come *on*." She tugs me into the fray. "I want a seat near the front."

George is a constant surprise.

As she makes her way through the crowd, I can't help staring around us. When Claudia mentioned Antony's club, I pictured some shitty old warehouse with bad lighting and even worse people. But this... this is another *world*.

The roundhouse surrounds us on all sides – a high building of steel with at least forty open bays. Some still contained rusting locomotives, their noses pointed toward the turntable, but most are filled with people. Women swing from the locomotive skeletons and dance on the gangways. As we pass one bay, I see the inspection pits beneath the tracks have been covered with glass, and couples fuck on piles of snow white cushions while people watch from above.

In the center of the circle, open to the elements, is a round pit that once housed the locomotive turntable. It had been made deeper with concrete walls and enclosed by a steel mesh cage. I notice a trapdoor in the floor of the arena, and a gangplank stretched over the center, hung with a professional lighting rig and a series of hooks and ropes and pulleys. Two large water tanks hooked up to a squat building decorated with three distinct insignia – a sword encircled with a laurel wreath, an eagle, and a she-wolf howling at the moon.

The Triumvirate.

My blood chills. This is Claudia's world – the secret underbelly of Emerald Beach, the dark heart that beats at the center of the city, with a constant flow of blood needed to keep it pumping. I know I don't belong here and yet, after what George found out about Dad, I realize how my own comfortable life has flowed directly from this source. My hands may be clean, but my bank balance sure isn't.

Bleachers have been built into the sloping ground, and closer to the stage are collections of tables. On the other side of the arena, a disused train car serves as a bar. A roped-off area on a raised platform fills up with people dressed to kill – *literally*. I see weapons peeking out from every belt on holsters hidden under expensive furs. This roped-off area has its own bar – a small switcher engine – and appears to be the VIP section. My heart pounds as I recognize Nero and my mother at one of the tables, and I whip my head away, hoping they won't recognize me in this getup.

George pulls me toward the tables near the arena. There don't seem to be designated seats, so we slide into one right next to where the action will take place. A waiter appears almost instantly and I empty the cash from my pockets to get us a couple of drinks. I'm jittery enough without adding alcohol to the mix but I'm not about to ask for an orange juice in this place.

At the table next to us, two men in Armani suits snort

cocaine off a woman's exposed breasts. Beyond them, a woman crawls on her knees underneath a table, wearing nothing but a diamond-studded collar around her neck. She kneels in front of one of the men sitting there and unzips his fly. A waiter approaches their table and offers the men a tray containing small rocks of what looks like cement. "Compliments of the boss." The men use tongs to pick up the tiny rocks and drop them into a glass pipe.

"Holy shit, that's grey death," George whispers. "I've been reading about it. It's a synthetic designer drug containing heroin and a cocktail of opioids. It's so potent you can overdose just from touching it. I read it was only in Georgia and Alabama, but I guess someone has brought it to Emerald Beach."

"How do you know this stuff?"

"The wonders of the internet." George nudges me. "There she is."

I follow her gaze to a table on the opposite side of the arena. *Claudia.* She's wearing a black wig and too much makeup, but I'd recognize those icicle eyes anywhere. She's sitting next to Gabriel, who somehow manages to look both ridiculous and also completely in his element in a pitch-black suit with several gold chains hanging around his neck.

I can't breathe. I can't stop staring at her, trying to fit the pieces together. George is talking to me, but I don't hear a word she says. I don't notice anything is happening around me until the lights over the arena come on and a voice on the loudspeaker who sounds suspiciously like Claudia's cousin announces the first fight.

"Ladies and gentlemen, please take your seats. For our first fight, we're pleased to welcome back a crowd favorite tonight – the indomitable, the impenetrable, the Barbarian!"

A masked figure walks into the arena – a beast of a man wearing only boxing shorts and leather cuffs around his wrists.

His eyes and most of the top of his head are obscured in a monstrous leather mask, with goat horns that curl back to accentuate his height.

He raises his fist to greet the crowd as a great roar descends through the roundhouse. All around me, men and women beat their fists on the tables, stomp their feet, yell and holler and scream. Whoever the Barbarian is, they love him. The figure makes a circle of the ring, soaking in the adoration of his fans. He's completely ripped, his muscles glinting with oil, and his jaw set in a mean scowl. Surprisingly, his skin is bare of tattoos, except for...

...I squint at his chest...

...except for the tattoo over his heart. A four-leaf clover disintegrating in the wind.

"Noah," I whisper.

George turns to me in surprise. I nod at the fighter, my heart leaping into my throat. "That's Noah."

"That's impossible. Noah can't be—"

I have to do something. I start to get up. George reaches across and slams my shoulder down, pushing me back into my seat. "*Sit down,*" she hisses. "There's nothing you can do. Besides, according to that announcement, this isn't his first rodeo. He's an unbeaten champion. He'll be fine."

I wish I had her confidence. How can Noah be a champion? He's never been to this place before tonight...

Oh, fuck.

Noah's been here before.

This is how he bulked out and built all that muscle.

This is how he's coped with the deaths of his mother and brother.

This is what he's become. A fighter. A warrior. A *monster*.

The pieces slide into place as Noah's opponent wanders into the ring. Antony announces him as 'Snakebite.' He's twice

Noah's size and covered head-to-toe in snakeskin tattoos. His head is shaven and his face drawn with the features of a snake – sneaky and mean and *deadly*. In his hand he carries a long leather whip, which he cracks in the air as the crowd bays for blood.

A gong sounds from the edge of the arena, and the two men circle each other. The crowd falls silent. You could hear a pin drop in this place – the only sound is the shuffle of feet against the floor of the arena, the sink of the whip as Snakebite cracks it in the air.

Noah, what the fuck are you doing?

Why risk your future for this—

Snakebite lunges forward, dropping to one knee and flicking his wrist. Noah sidesteps, but he's too slow – the whip wraps around his arm. Gasps and angry yells echo through the crowd, and the reverent silence is forgotten as everyone cries for their pound of flesh. Noah *howls* as the leather pulls taut, his skin red and bulging where the leather digs in. Blood splatters into the sand at Noah's feet. The whip is studded with tiny barbs that dig into Noah's skin as Snakebite sinks his fangs deeper.

That's not fair. Noah doesn't even have a weapon.

I lunge forward, my own fists bared, as if I can somehow leap into the caged arena and save my friend from his own stupidity. George slams me back into my seat.

Snakebite grins as he winds the handle of the whip, sinking its barbs deeper into Noah's flesh. Noah roars, thrashing his arm around and splattering more blood. My stomach churns. *I can't watch this. I can't watch Noah die out there—*

Noah grabs the taut whip with his other hand and *pulls*.

Snakebite clearly doesn't expect this move. He's knocked off balance, stumbling forward, right into Noah's fist.

CRACK.

Snakebite's head wobbles. Blood gushes from his nose,

scenting the air with a metallic tang that drives the crowd into a frenzy. He drops the whip as he staggers back, his evil eyes begging for mercy.

But Noah has no mercy in him. His fists pummel Snakebite's face, reducing the man's features to a bloody, gory, pulp. His jaw loosens as he works the man over – he's *enjoying* this. Judging by the way the crowd reacts – leaping to their feet and screaming his name – they love it, too.

I watch, my body frozen and my stomach churning, as my friend grabs his opponent's skull and smashes it into the concrete wall. Snakebite's eyes roll back into his skull. His body goes limp. Noah tosses him to the ground, now crimson with spilled blood. He grunts as he unwinds the whip from his arm and wraps it around Snakebite's neck. Noah tugs on the end, lifting Snakebite's head up and back, up and back, as the crowd chant his stage name.

Claudia leaps to her feet, her fist pounding the air as she yells in triumph. All around me, the air sings with my friend's victory. I can't move. I'm frozen to my chair by the brutality of it.

As Noah's opponent is dragged from the arena, leaving a trail of blood behind him, Antony himself wanders across the gangway. Two men follow him, dragging another man whose legs are shackled in chains. My pounding heart leaps so fast I'm sure it's going to fly out of my chest. I know we haven't seen the last of the blood to be shed tonight.

Noah disappears from the arena as Antony leans over the edge of the gangway, holding his hand up for silence. It takes a long time for the cheers and roaring to calm down enough for him to be heard. "I'm pleased you enjoyed the return of our favorite champion. Now, we have a special treat for you tonight. An interlude for your amusement. Bring him forward."

Antony's guards hold the man upright so everyone can see him. He's naked save for his underwear, which is already stained with piss. He trembles as he's held aloft for the baying crowd, and he looks as though he might pass out at any moment. Someone has carved up his chest with a blade. As I squint, I realize the bloody cuts form words – a Latin phrase. *Et in morte fidelitas.*

"You might know this man as Tony Moretti, but he does not deserve that name. He is a traitor." Antony spits the word. "He broke the cardinal rule of our family – the rule of blood, of loyalty."

"*Et in morte fidelitas,*" the crowd chant. Across the arena, Gabriel grins as he joins the chant. He's got no idea what's coming, but he loves being swept up in the moment.

But Claudia doesn't clap or chant or even smile. Her cold eyes fix on her cousin.

"He offered information about our business to the police. Because of his betrayal, one of our most loyal soldiers is in custody and we've had to close a lucrative distribution channel." Antony points out people in the crowd, including Nero. "This costs me money, and you, and you. But more importantly, it makes a mockery of everything we fought for, everything we stand for. Where is the honor? *Corvus oculum corvi non eruit* – a crow shall not pull out the eyes of a fellow crow."

The crowd hiss and boo. They watch Antony with greedy eyes, waiting for his next move. Nero nods to Antony, sipping his drink with a smile playing on his lips. Antony acknowledges Nero with a nod in return.

I thought Claudia's cousin merely ran this club for the gangs, but it's clear he's so much more than that. These people may bow to Nero, but they *adore* Antony. They look to him to mete out punishment. He may not be top dog, but he wields power I can't even imagine.

And I've pissed him off. For the first time, I realize that the danger Claudia keeps trying to warn me about may be real, and closer than I ever imagined.

"What do you say his punishment should be?" Antony cries.

The crowd roar as they thrust their fists in the air, thumbs pointing up. I remember the gesture from movies about Ancient Rome – it means death to the defeated gladiator in the ring.

It means this man is condemned.

Antony smiles – it's a cold, cruel smile. "As you wish. Tonight he shall face the punishment fit for his crime. For without adherence to our laws he is no more than a beast, and to the beasts he shall return."

"Damnatio ad bestias," the crowd chants as the guard hoist the man over the edge and drop him into the ring. He lands with a *CRUNCH* on the hard floor, and I can tell from the way he drags his leg that he's broken a bone. "Damnatio ad bestias!"

"Damnatio ad bestias?" George's forehead furrows. "What's that—"

Her words are cut off as the trapdoor in the arena floor begins to slowly swing open.

34

CLAUDIA

"*D*amnatio ad bestias. What's that?" Gabriel's chair creaks as he leans forward, desperate to get a look at what's rattling the trapdoor.

I can't answer him. My tongue has frozen to the top of my mouth. My stomach swirls. *I can't believe I'm watching this.*

I can't tear my eyes away.

The condemned man manages to drag his broken leg to the edge of the ring, his back against the wooden sliding door that admits fighters – the door through which Noah had exited only moments before. He claws at the wood, but it's locked tight.

"Please," he cries, "Please..."

His sobs are drowned out by an inhuman roar – a rumble that pools in my stomach and shudders through my body. It feels as though I'm sitting inside a Marshall stack at one of Gabriel's concerts, only the music coursing through me is drenched in blood.

The roar trembles the earth and reverberates in the air. Something bangs against the trapdoor, sending splinters flying across the ring. The crowd takes up the roar, punching their raised thumbs into the air.

"Claws, what's going on?" Gabriel yells. "What is damnatio ad bestias?"

My insides turn to ice. The three families have practiced this torture for decades, until my father outlawed it, as it requires the purchase of exotic animals that will never see their natural habitat. "Let us enforce our laws," he said. "But let us not disrupt the dominion of beasts to do it." It was one of his least popular reforms.

"It's an ancient Roman punishment," I choke out. Gabriel's fingers circle my wrist. "It's usually reserved for Christians, deserters, and convicts who betrayed the Emperor. Translated, it means 'the condemnation of the beasts.'"

"You mean—" Gabriel's words cut off as the roar explodes into a great and terrible quake that tears through the roundhouse. The trapdoor's hinges fly off and the wooden door is flung away. The whole crowd gasps as a golden shape leaps from the depths and stalks across the arena.

A lion.

A motherfucking *lion*.

The beast circles the ring, his glorious mane trailing behind him, his lips pulled back into a vicious snarl.

"Please, tribune." The man is screaming now. "I promise I'll—"

The man's words dissolve into screams as the lion pounces. The crowd roars their approval as the lion tears off the man's arm, shaking its head and splattering blood across the tables toward the front. A few droplets sprinkle my face, my bare arms.

I stare down at the red dots. I breathe in the metallic tang of the air.

The monster in me awakens. She stirs and shakes off her slumber. She paws the dirt, ready for her next feed, her blood warmed with the sacrifices made in her honor.

I'm Claudia August, and I was baptized in bloodshed.

To the bloodshed I return.

I'm not the only one who revels in this anointing. Blood splatters across Antony's suit as he stares down at the carnage he's wrought.

I have the answer I came here to seek. The traitor called Antony *tribune* – the second in command.

The man who will take over the August family if Brutus is killed.

The traitor's screams cut off as the lion drags his carcass to the center of the ring to feast. The crowd roars, drunk on blood and power, taking the lion's hunger into themselves to become beasts. They claw at each other, hands reaching beneath clothing, zippers rustling and buttons popping as they fight to sate their lust in every imaginable way.

Heat pools in my belly as I drink in the blood, the chaos, the carnage. I look across to Gabriel and I see he's affected too. He jiggles his labret piercing with his tongue, and his eyes are heavy with need. The scent of blood in the air sets off something primal in each of us. I can't wait to get him home so I can fuck him every imaginable way, fucking him like the lioness sinking her claws into her lover.

My cousin raises his arms out wide, his smile giddy as he drinks in the debauchery. The lion tears the traitor's legs off, spraying more blood across Antony's face. He loves it, and so does everyone here. No one is mourning Brutus' absence – they already have a new leader in mind.

On the VIP balcony, Nero snaps his fingers for another bottle of Champagne. He's been lording it over the place all night, with Eli's mother at his side. The smile on his lips turns my blood to ice. Suddenly, I'm not horny any longer.

Every word Antony told me is a lie.

And somehow, it's all part of Nero's plan.

Eli is in danger. I know he is.

"We're done here." I stand up. Gabriel tears his eyes away from the arena. He slides my coat over my shoulders, and we walk down toward the edge of the arena, where the Barbarian emerges from the stalls. He wears a silk robe embroidered with the August insignia – the sword and the laurel – and his terrifying mask remains firmly in place. His arm is bandaged where the whip dug into his skin, but the dressing is already soaked with blood.

Women flock from the audience to surround him, chattering and simpering as they reach out to touch him. One leans down and runs her tongue across his collarbone, licking Snakebite's blood from his skin.

I see red.

He's *mine*.

My monster.

I launch myself forward, forgetting the danger of our situation in my desire to see that woman's blood splattered across Noah's chest. My fingers fly to the knife I've hidden in my sleeve, but Noah's faster. He grabs the woman by the scruff of her coat and flings her away. She crashes into a table, sending glasses and plates of food flying everywhere.

Noah storms toward me as fresh blood stains his bandages. He grabs me roughly and attacks my lips with his. The kiss is fierce – a claiming kiss. He is declaring to everyone present that the Barbarian is spoken for. I wrap my arms around him, grabbing hold of his horns and dragging him closer, making it clear that I have a claim of my own. I taste his opponent's blood on his lips. It's sick and twisted and hot as fuck.

As we draw back, Noah's breath kisses me. "We should leave."

"Agreed. I want to take you home and fuck you senseless." I lick a speck of blood from my lip. I'm molten hot again, desperate for release. My boys can do that to me, especially when they're bathed in the blood and sweat of a fight. "And you can leave the mask on."

Noah's lips turn up into a smile. He throws his uninjured arm around me, and the three of us head back toward the locomotive bars. Nervous now, the women step back as we pass. My gaze flicks across their faces, searching for something I can use when I confront my cousin with this – my father's old allies, the people with weaknesses he taught me to exploit—

Wait a second.

It can't be.

I stop in my tracks. Noah curses as he trips over me. Gabriel tugs my arm, but I don't move.

I'm frozen.

I can't stop staring at a couple jogging toward the exit.

They turned away so quickly, I'm positive they didn't see me. I had only a fleeting glimpse of their faces, but as I take in the shape of their bodies and their distinctive gaits, I'm sure of what I saw.

It's George and Eli.

Shit. Shit shit *shit*.

My head buzzes. George and Eli. How did they find this place? How did they get in? They're wearing ridiculous outfits I'm guessing came from George's thrift store.

They saw Noah fight.

They saw a man torn apart by a lion.

They saw Nero lording it from the VIP lounge.

They saw Antony basking in the adoration of the criminal underworld.

They saw me. They saw me with my old family.

They know enough to go to the police for real this time. But that would be as good as signing their own death warrants. My mind reels as I consider my options if I have a hope of saving them before they do something stupid.

If George came here tonight, she knows everything about me. She knows who I am. I thought Eli would keep my secret, but I guess I'm wrong.

But I might be able to use her. I can't get Eli to listen to me, and we're running out of time. But maybe if I go to George, I'll be able to bring them both around before they do something stupid like doing the right thing.

35

CLAUDIA

Thanksgiving is a week away, and all I can think about is Eli. Antony knows I called his Thanksgiving bluff, but after everything we saw at the Colosseum I feel like there's a ticking clock on Eli's life. Why is Nero determined to get close to his family? How can I get him to trust me again so I can protect him?

He's pretty much never in school now, and when Noah went to his house to ask about him, Nero appeared at the door and said his stepson was at his girlfriend's house.

His girlfriend.

I have one last shot at protecting Eli and George from their own goodness. It means letting go of any hope that Eli might be mine again. He was never mine in the first place – he always belonged to Mackenzie. And now he belongs to George, and I'd make damn sure they have the rest of their lives to be nauseatingly good and kind and beautiful together.

She's better for him than I could ever hope to be.

It doesn't matter that knowing they're together feels like a lion tearing my heart out of my chest. They're both family now, and I'll fight to protect them, no matter the cost. After all, that's the motto of family. *Et in morte fidelitas* – even in death, loyalty remains.

Speaking of family... I haven't confronted Antony with what I know. He's held that secret close to his chest for a reason, and I intend to do the same. It's hard being around him, knowing that every time he leaves the house to return to Tartarus Oaks, he's moving away from the future we plotted together. With every secretive phone call he takes, I feel our home disintegrating around me.

But I'm the one who swung the hammer first by bringing the guys in.

Maybe he's not the only one prepared to wear a crown of thorns.

I need to make a decisive move. I text George and tell her we're hanging out tonight, just us girls, and I won't take no for an answer.

"Where do you think you're going?" Antony seizes my arm as I head toward the garage.

"I'm hanging out with George tonight."

"You think that's wise? Isn't she trying to steal Captain America from you?"

I can't help my jaw clenching. "He's not mine to steal."

"He'd better be." Antony's mouth cocks up into a smirk that takes me right back to the violence of the arena. "You've got five days until I put a hit out on that boy. He's dangerous while he hates you, especially if he's got your ex-friend in his bed."

"You wouldn't dare, and she's not my *ex*-friend."

"I don't care if she's the queen of fucking Sheba. We don't know her loyalties and Brutus is still out there."

I fold my arms. "Let me tell you how this is going to go. I will let you take the lead and boss me around and threaten my friends, even though we both know you're full of shit. But I have never, *ever* had a real girl friend before, and I am not going to let

Brutus frighten me into losing her. Have Tiberius drive me if you need to get to the club. He can watch her house while I'm there, but I am going to see George tonight, and that's final."

Antony shakes his head. He looks pissed as he raises his phone to his ear. "I knew I should never have taught you to have a fucking backbone. Wait here while I figure out how to prevent your reckless ass from getting killed."

IN THE END, Antony drives me over to George's place himself. I'm hoping it's a ploy on his part to get me alone so we can talk. Instead, he cranks a party playlist and raps along with Drake. He's in a good mood, and now I know why. It's almost Saturnalia, and Brutus is nowhere to be found. From what I saw at the club, even if the guy does come back, Antony – who isn't even of August blood – will be the new Imperator and our whole plan is shot to hell.

I will have endured four years alone in that house for *nothing*.

Over my dead fucking body.

George lives in Lethe, one of those forgettable suburbs that sits between the rich assholes of the hills and Tartarus Oaks. She bounces out the door as soon as the car pulls up. Her hair's dyed bright pink this time and clipped back from her face with barrettes shaped like skeleton cats. On anyone else, she might've looked like a five-year-old on molly, but George pulls it off.

"Who's the dish behind the wheel?" She peers over my shoulder. Her tone is light, but I know she knows who he is. She's a damn good liar.

"My cousin Antony. He's a complete pain." I glare at him, and he drives away. I know he's just going to circle the block and sit outside, but George doesn't.

"I'm so glad you're here." She pulls me inside. "When you called I was worried something had happened with Alec."

I force a smile. "No. Not Alec. That bastard has been sent to reform school in Poland. He's out of our lives forever."

"And nothing else is up?"

"Nope." *Except that I need you and Eli to stop whatever you're up to so I can protect you from whatever the fuck Antony and Nero have planned.* "I'm just missing my girl time."

"Yay, me too. I feel like we haven't hung out much lately. So, this is our place. I've lived here all my life. It doesn't have a turret or an indoor bowling alley like Malloy Manor, but I like it." George bounds up the steps onto a small patio crowded with flowering plants and dangling crystals. She holds open the kitchen screen door for me. "I dug out some more clothes from the thrift store to show you."

As I enter the kitchen, a woman glances up from wiping down the counters. She looks like she could be George's older, less-wacky sister, with the same pixie-shaped face, cropped hairstyle, and brilliant green eyes. She wears a cream-colored maxi dress and leather sandals, a feather necklace, and a frown that deepens when she recognizes me.

"Hi, Mackenzie." She leans over the counter and sizes me up. "I'm Anne-Maree. It's nice to see you again."

That look gets my back up, and I'm ready to snap back at her before I realize what's happening here. Mackenzie used to be friends with Cleo, and the two of them bullied George in junior prep. Of course we did. That's what girls like us do to girls like George.

I assume that all kids keep their problems locked away in heart-shaped boxes the way I do. But not George. George is an open book, the pages covered in bold scribbles. Her mother knows Mackenzie bullied her daughter because George would have spilled her guts every day after school, and now that same girl is back in her daughter's life as a so-called friend. George may have decided she's forgiven me, but that didn't mean Anne-Maree Fisher had.

Okay, wow. So that's what parental love looks like.

I'd forgotten.

Daddy always says that love will be your boldest strength and your greatest weakness. Anne-Maree Fisher wears her love with all the ferociousness of a lioness. My heart aches as I shove back memories of my parents that threaten to overwhelm me. I need to focus on George tonight. This might be my last chance.

"Hi, Anne-Maree." I look around the faded kitchen with the crystals and rattan planters hanging in the window, the large spice rack shaped like a tree and filled with ingredients I'd never heard of, and the bright-blue refrigerator bulging under the weight of concert posters and sketches and takeout menus and tarot cards stuck to it with magnets shaped like David Bowie's head. "I love your house."

Anne-Maree nods, but I can tell from her eyes that she thinks I'm bullshitting. I'm not. I've only a foot in the kitchen door and already their house feels warmer, more comfortable, more homely, than anywhere I've ever lived. And that's with Anne-Maree's frosty reception.

"So... Mackenzie, George is telling me you started at Stonehurst this year. It must be hard to catch up at a new school after so much time away."

George shoots her mom a look, and a wordless exchange indicates that I've been a topic of conversation in this house before. It's on the tip of my tongue to say that kids sure can be monsters, but George is safe now that the biggest monster of them all is on her side.

"I'm managing. I'm working with a tutor, and my friend Noah is helping me."

"Mom, are there any snacks?" George opens the fridge. I peer over her shoulder, noticing a lot of kale and microgreens.

"Sure. There are buckwheat muffins and activated cashew nut bites in the cupboard." Anne-Maree slings her purse over her shoulder. "I'm off. I'll be staying over at Paul's tonight. There's money on the counter for pizza – remember, Raphael's does that great cauliflower crust you love. Call me if you have any problems." She shoots me a look, as though she expects me to be a problem.

"We will. Love ya, Mom." George leans up to kiss her mom's cheek. A knife twists in my gut at their easy companionship. For the first time in a long time, I ached for my parents – for my mother's kisses and my father's firm smile when I did something that pleased him. I always thought being alone in the world makes me strong – just the way Daddy taught me. But I'm starting to wonder if loving people gives you something to fight for.

As soon as the door swings shut, George drags me into the living room and lifts the couch cushions to reveal a stack of non-organic, teeth-rotting snackage she stashed there. "My mom's a health-food nut. But don't worry – I got supplies. And I have a chocolate mud cake stashed under my bed. I promise it contains absolutely zero buckwheat."

"You're hilarious. And also my hero." I unclip my purse and angle it toward her, showing her the bottle of port I spent way too much time choosing from the cellar. "I raided Daddy's liquor cupboard. I figured he wouldn't mind."

"I'll get the glasses." George tosses me the remote. "You choose our movie."

As George fills rainbow-colored tumblers with Howard Malloy's forty-year-old port, I scroll through the selection on George's hard-drive. Her tastes are predictably George – lots of horror films, music documentaries, and weird arthouse films mixed in with the Disney and Japanese anime. I dive into the horror section and choose something with lots of blood and gore. George comes back with drinks and a huge-ass chocolate cake wobbling on a stand, a knife sticking out the top. She sets down her goodies and flops down next to me.

"Excellent choice," she beams as she sees my selection. "I don't understand how people have movie nights and watch *Titanic* or whatever. It's horror or nothing."

"I know, right? Horror movies don't get nearly enough credit. They contain lots of important lessons. Like never run through a creepy forest wearing only your nightgown."

"And they teach kids the importance of researching arcane shit in libraries," George adds. "My dad worked on this film, did you know that?"

"No way."

"It was actually his big break in the industry. After this he hooked up with Damien Scott – you know, the director of *Bloody Valentine Massacre* – and his career started going places. I grew up watching horror films with Dad – a new one every Friday night. He once said the most unrealistic thing about horror films for millennials is that they always start with someone buying a house."

I snort. "I started watching them because my real life was such a horror film, they were the only thing that felt real. You should see my room. My parents brought me a porcelain doll every year for my birthday and Christmas. It's like a real horror film set. I can't even sleep in that room anymore."

"Hell yes." George leans forward. "I want to see your creepy doll room. Did you remember, you and Cleo bloodied up one of your dolls and stuck it in my locker?"

I shake my head. "I don't remember anything before my parents disappeared."

"Right, the amnesia."

"You know about that?"

"Eli said something about it." She nods vigorously. "At the game."

"You guys have been hanging out a lot lately."

"Yeah, he's great. I'm helping him with a school project." Her eyes dart away for a moment – an involuntary movement exposing her lie. But I'm way ahead of her – she didn't go to the Colosseum because of a school project.

I'm dying to ask her more about Eli, but I can't figure out how. I can't afford to blow it tonight. I need to build up to confronting her, so I change tack. "George, about me and Cleo..."

"I don't really want to talk about it." She trains her eyes on the screen.

"I understand. I've had the pleasure of making an enemy of Cleo this year. I can only imagine what the two of us were like when we hunted in a pack. It's just that... my doctors say hearing about my past might help unlock memories, and I thought if I knew about memories with you in them..." I shrug. *I'm a genius.* "It's dumb."

"It's not dumb." But George hugs her knees to her chest, gripping a candy bar so tight the wrapper bursts with a *POP*. "I guess... I met the two of you in seventh grade. I'd already changed schools twice because of bullying. Being the weird kid is great in movies but in real life it kinda sucks. On the first day of junior prep, Cleo heard my dad was a film producer, and I think she thought I could help her get her big break in showbiz. She invited me to sit with you at lunch, and then I came to her house after school. The three of us hung out all the time and I thought I'd finally made some real friends. But there was always this tension. You and Cleo were rich and you had all these fancy clothes and you just seemed so much older and wiser and *cooler*. I guess I didn't know why you chose me, and so I always felt like the odd one out. Looking back, I think everything you guys said to me was kind of mocking me. But I didn't notice at the time.

"Anyway, my dad had a movie premiere for one of his projects and I knew Cleo was interested in being a movie star so I thought she'd like to go. My parents were so happy I was making friends, they said I could bring you both along. So I got VIP tickets so we could sit behind the velvet rope with the movie stars and go to the afterparty and everything.

"The two of you spent hours getting ready. When you walked out of Cleo's bedroom, you both looked at least eighteen, and I felt like a dumb little kid. You said when we got to the premiere you might not be able to sit with me because I was an embarrassment."

I wince. "I was a real bitch, huh?"

"Oh yeah." George smiles, but it lacks her usual color. Telling this story puts things about her on display that she wished she could keep hidden. The fact that she's doing it because it will help me... I can't believe she's working with Eli against me. I can't believe she accepts the things he says about me. But actually, if Mackenzie was this big a bitch to her, maybe I can. "I started to get nervous that this was a terrible idea, but it was too late. Dad picked us up from Cleo's house and drove us to the Beaumont Theatre – you know, the weird old cinema in Brawley? There's no red carpet, and the only press there were from *Fangoria* magazine. It was actually really cool – the whole cast was there in full monster makeup, and there was a big crowd of musicians and horror industry people and edgy actors and a cake that bled strawberry *coulis* when Dad cut into it. But you and Cleo in your sparkly outfits looked completely out of place, and everything that I loved about the party you said was dumb or lame or dorky. You kind of laughed it off, but Cleo was *livid*. She screamed at me in front of my dad and his friends. You both dumped the cake over my head and took pictures on her phone. I started crying. The two of you left."

Bitch. I dealt with Alec for George, but Cleo still doesn't know not to mess with me and mine. This might've happened years ago, but I remember George's face as she kicked Alec again and again and again. She might brush it off with a smile, but this stuff has eaten away at her. She's the nicest person in that shitty school and she's been eating her lunch alone in a bathroom for years because of Cleo and Mackenzie.

Now her old bully is sitting on her couch, forcing her to relive this story. She doesn't know that the monsters are on her side now.

"By the time I got to school the next day, you and Cleo had spread the photo around to the entire class. That's it, one cake on my head and I'm the freak forever." She clenches her fists. "That part's okay. I know I'm a freak. I've embraced it. I don't know how to be anything else. But I really, *truly* thought you guys were my friends. I thought maybe this time things would be different. I admired the two of you so much, how strong you are. Especially you."

"There's nothing strong about bullying someone," I say.

"I know your parents were..." George swallows. "I don't know what you remember, but you showed me burn marks on your arm once. From your dad's cigar."

"He was a terrible human." It felt like a betrayal of Daddy to say it, even though in all ways it's true. "He taught me everything I know."

"Do you remember anything now?" George asks.

"I think I'm starting to." Only that I'm going to ruin Cleo for hurting George.

"And you really don't know what happened to you?"

I know exactly what happened to me. I was buried alive and I've been squatting in a rich girl's house for four years, completely alone in the world. And I have to figure out what you and Eli have done and make you not hate me so I can save your asses.

I shake my head. "Nope. It's all a mystery."

"Doesn't it kill you not knowing what happened to your parents?" George bites into a candy bar. "If my mom disappeared, I wouldn't stop until I had answers."

"Yeah, well, unlike your mom, my parents aren't exactly worth finding." I gesture to the true-crime documentaries littering her hard-drive. "I can see you love to play detective."

"You don't know the half of it." George grins. "I was the one who figured out what Eli's dad was doing."

"What?" I plump the pillow behind my head. "Okay, I need to hear this."

"You know my dad died four years ago."

"Fuck. I didn't know. I'm sorry." *Why does the world have to suck so bad for the best people?*

"Yeah, me too." George looks away. "Anyway, after Walter's reality TV show, all the showbiz guys bought pre-paid funeral plans from Memories of the Hart. It was kind of a joke but also, it was like a cool thing to say in the industry, being able to 'go out in style.' Dad decided to get a plan for all of us. He got this horror package with a fake coffin that was rigged to spring open during the funeral ceremony and a skeleton pops out and starts dancing. It was *so* him. So, anyway, we have his body delivered to the funeral home for cremation, and as we're making funeral plans Walter tells us there's a backlog in the crematorium, and we might not have his ashes ready in time for the funeral.

"'It's no problem,' he says, with all his Southern charm. 'This happens all the time. What we do is give you a decorative urn to use in the ceremony, and we'll get those ashes to you as soon as possible.' It's shit, but you know, that's the price you pay for booking the most popular funeral director in the city. Dad wanted Walter Hart and we didn't have the money to go some-where else.

"So we have the funeral and it's sad and for a while, I'm busy helping Mom and trying to get through school and being sad, and then one day I realize it's been months and we haven't heard anything about Dad's ashes. I call Memories of the Hart and got passed around call center operators in Kazakstan. So then I go down to the funeral home to talk to someone in person, and they tell me his ashes aren't ready. At this point I'm annoyed," she grins. I grin back; I can't even imagine George annoyed. "I might have suggested that I'd come back there with a police officer and fire up the oven myself, since it was clearly such a hassle. I think I frightened the secretary. She had a whispered conversation with someone over the phone, then came back and said if I returned on Friday, they'll move them up the priority list and I'd be able to take him home.

"So I go back on Friday, and they have no idea who I am. A different secretary goes into the back room. She's gone a long time. When she comes back, she hands me a shopping bag with a small round container inside." George makes a circle with her fingers. "It's about the size of a pot of hand cream."

"That's it?"

"That's it. It's so small I could fit a whole murdered boy band into one decorative urn. But I figure, they're the funeral direc-tors, they must know. I mean, heaps of stuff is different in real life than it is on TV. Maybe that's only how many ashes you get out of a person? So I bring it home to Mom and we pop his ashes in our urn and forget about it.

"Then, one day, I'm at my aunt's house and she's got my grandfather's urn on the mantel, and I decide to take a peek because..." she shrugs. The grinning skulls on her hoodie bounce. "Because I'm me. I wait until my aunt is out of the room and I tug the lid off and peer inside. She's got *mountains* of ashes.

At least ten times as much as us. And my grandfather was a small guy, so you couldn't say it was a size difference in the bodies or anything. I think back on all the weirdness at the funeral home, and I just..."

"Pull a Sherlock Holmes orgasm face?" I venture.

"What?"

"It's something Gabriel says about Eli. He gets this look on his face when he's trying to figure something out. Like he's excited to swoop in and solve the mystery."

George laughs. "Yes. That's exactly it. I have this feeling something isn't right – and the mystery of it made me not so sad about my dad anymore. I decide to test the ashes. I do a couple of experiments in the school lab. Mr. Ross even gave me extra credit when I explained what I was doing. The results I get were... not great. But I'm not an expert, so I send a sample off to an independent lab, and they come back and tell me that while there are definitely fragments of bone in my container, it's not human remains. Possibly a rabbit, they said. Or a gerbil."

I think about how that must feel to know you've been grieving over the ashes of a gerbil, and I want to gouge out Walter Hart's eyes with a rusty spork. "Then what?"

"I had to tell Mom. It was the hardest thing I've ever done in my whole life. She took it better than I thought." George shrugs. "She looks at the urn and says, 'I never felt like he was really in there.' I tried to make her go to the police with the information, but she just wanted to forget about it. I couldn't forget. So I... I made a podcast about it."

I'm laughing. I can't help it. This entire story is completely crazy, but so incredibly George. "You made a *podcast*."

"Right. A true-crime podcast. It's called, 'My Dad is a Gerbil.' It's quite well-known now, one of the top-20 true crime podcasts on Spotify." A red blush creeps across George's cheeks. "Yet another reason kids at Stonehurst don't like me. A true-crime podcaster doesn't exactly fit in with their preppy, Hollywood-slick image, yet I've got more followers than most of them combined."

Wow. I stare at my tiny friend, her face animated as she talks about her podcast, and I see a whole other side of her. George is so like Eli in some ways – obsessed with the truth, unable to let go of an unsolved puzzle, and desperate to make the world a better place. She's more driven and dedicated than all the wannabe actresses and influencers at Stonehurst, and she does it without endless funding from a trust fund or wealthy parents.

"George Fisher, I am in awe." I hold out my hand. She takes it, and I shake vigorously as I clink our glasses with the other. "You're awesome. I'm honored you chose to hand me a fork that day."

George's face glows. I wish she didn't relish my compliments. No one as cool as George should be so desperate for a friend that she goes back to her ex-bully. Especially not now she knows I'm not really Mackenzie and I'm a whole package of trouble.

"What happened next?" I prod.

"Things get next-level crazy. I'm putting out podcast episodes and researching what might have happened to my dad's body. I start getting emails from other families in Emerald Beach, saying the same things – long waits to get their remains, tiny packages, one lady said her brother's ashes smell suspiciously like cement. *Then*, an FBI agent gets in touch with me. It turns out they were investigating Memories from the Hart. I share my notes with him, and the contact information for all the people who sent in their stories. They were able to get enough evidence from eleven of them to bring down Walter Hart on criminal charges.

"When the story broke at school, it was horrible. I'm so used to being invisible, but now everyone was listening to my podcast, learning all this personal stuff about my dad. Alec hung a dead

gerbil in my locker. It wasn't even the stuff they did at school –
I'm used to being the class freak. They came after me online.
They found old class pictures of mine and Photoshopped them
onto pornography and sent them to the lawyers to discredit me.
They made up insane stories about me."

"Even Eli?"

She shakes her head. "No. Eli was amazing. He tried to get
them to stop. He stood up for me when Alec..."

"What?"

She shook her head.

"George, I know that bastard did something to you. It's safe it
you want to tell me."

George won't look at me. "I've never told anyone before. But I
know what you did to his forehead, and I think you had something to do with gym class, too, and I..."

"Just say the words and I'll make you your own brand." I
point to one of her tattoos. "We could put a cat on it. That'd look
great – Alec walking around with a grinning cat-face burned
into his forehead."

"You're terrifying, Mackenzie Malloy." George slaps my knee.
"I have an idea. Can I make it the topic of my next podcast to
figure out what happened to your parents?"

Here it is.

Her question hangs in the air between us. I watch George's
lip quiver, and I see this is what's she's been angling for all along.

That's what she and Eli are doing together. They're digging
into me, into my family. They're trying to find every one of my
filthy secrets so they can stop me from keeping Malloy Manor.

After homecoming night, after the diary entry, after the kiss,
after *everything*, Eli is still holding on to his hate.

If George starts digging into my life, she's clever enough to
uncover my secrets. And I need to hold them close.

But on the other hand... the entire world believes Mackenzie

Malloy has returned, which means the weird stuff that's happened could be related to her, not the Julian family feud. It would be useful to know what happened to the Malloys – did Brentwood kill Howard and Ainsley? If he didn't kill Mackenzie, like he said, and Senator Marlowe believed they were dead until now, then where is my doppelganger?

If I can convince George to trust me again, even after all the lies, will she still keep digging into the Malloys? But that would put George in the middle of the firing line. And I can't do that to her...

I fucking hate this. She's the only friend I've ever had and I'm still lying to her. Grow some ovaries and get this done. We're running out of time.

I shrug. "Can I think about it?"

"Sure. Want to think about it over a chocolate cake appetizer while I order the pizza?"

I make a face. "As long as there's no cauliflower."

"I promise." George hands me an enormous knife, and I cut into the cake. The knife slides easily – it's nice and sharp. Anne-Maree Fisher takes good care of her knives. I appreciate that. Maybe we will get along okay after all.

George places an order for enough pizza and french fries and garlic bread to feed a Roman legion. She sets her phone down and takes the plate I offer her. I sink my teeth into the moist cake, letting the sugar rush bolster me.

Now, you coward. Do it now.

I set down my cake and pause the movie. "George, we need to talk. I know you said you're helping Eli with a school project, but I know that's not true. I saw you at—"

There's a sharp rap at the door.

"Pizza delivery," a guy calls.

My stomach growls.

"Hold that thought. I'll just get the pizza." George sets down her plate and moves across the kitchen. Her shoulders tense. *She's afraid of what I'm going to say, what I'll do.*

My best friend is afraid of me. She—

Hang on a second.

We only ordered the pizza like five minutes ago. There is no way an Emerald Beach pizza parlor – especially a shitty one in Lethe – will cook a pizza and get it through traffic in that amount of time.

My stomach sinks. "George, wait—"

I'm too late. George's hand hasn't even turned the knob before the kitchen door slams open, sending her flying backward. A guy in a black balaclava shoves his way inside, grabbing George by the neck and slamming her against the wall. The twinkling fairy lights over the sink glint off the gun in his hand as he aims it at George's forehead.

36

CLAUDIA

George.

Fuck.

No.

George's eyes widen as the muzzle touches her skin. The intruder rams the gun into her flesh. She whimpers, her whole body collapsing in on itself, like a hedgehog curling up into a ball. Tears stream down her face, and I can see he's cutting off her airway.

"Listen to me, girl," the guy rasps. "I don't want to hurt you, yeah? But I'm going to need all your tapes. Your laptop, too."

"Who the fuck do you think you are?" I blurt out.

I'm so *angry*. This bastard is *hurting* George.

Et in morte fidelitas.

I'll make him regret pointing a gun at my friend.

The guy turns to me, his hand still wrapped around George's throat. All I can see are hollow eyes that bug out from his head as his gaze sweeps over my body.

All I can think about is making him stop. My fingers close around the handle of the cake knife.

My eyes fix on the gun, on his finger twitching on the trigger. His grip wavers. George slides down the wall.

"Y-y-y-you?" he stutters as he takes me in. He sounds surprised. No, not surprised. *Terrified.* "It can't be. This doesn't make any sense—"

I lunge forward, flicking my wrist and letting the knife fly. The guy catches the movement and swings the gun at me, but he's right about one thing – he doesn't want to shoot anyone. If he did, he wouldn't have hesitated, and I'd have a lovely hole in my chest.

Instead, he gets acquainted with the business end of a blade.

George screams as the knife embeds itself into his neck. His mouth flies open, and blood spurts out. George leaps away as his finger slides off the trigger and he drops the gun. Blood sprays in a graceful arc across the kitchen.

He slumps to the floor.

He twitches a few times, and blood from his severed artery splatters the brightly-colored cushions and duck-egg blue cupboards. After a few moments, he stops twitching.

He's still.

He can't hurt her anymore.

My ears ring with noise that comes from nowhere, from a scream only I can hear.

George sinks to her knees, her hands clasped over her mouth. She makes a sound that's not a cry or scream – kind of like a strangled panda bear or, I don't know, a terrified lizard.

Blood pounds in my ears as the scent hits my nostrils – the unmistakable tang of fresh blood in the air, in a home where that smell is all wrong. It doesn't fit. The scent triggers something inside me – a dream that might be too vivid to be a dream. A memory of my mother slumped in a chair, her own blood decorating the walls, splattered across my face in my reflection in the window. The memory that usually makes me want to shit myself in fear but now, with adrenaline coursing through my body and my friend's heart still beating, makes me strong.

I stand over the guy. Yup. He's officially immortality-challenged. I try to tug the balaclava off his face, but the knife holds it in place so I tear the wool until I can get a good look at him.

He's a kid, not much older than me. I don't recognize him, but I've been out of the criminal world for so long that's not a surprise. I lift a limp arm, peel off his glove, and roll up his sleeve to check for a tattoo on his wrist. Sure enough, I find a small design of an eagle – the *aquila*, the symbol of the Dio family.

He's a hired gun, then. A mercenary in training, working for Nero or... or Brutus. Antony's right. This isn't over.

I slide the gun from the deceased's hand and check the magazine. It's fully loaded. I tuck it into my waistband as I bend down to check on George. Her face is getting whiter by the minute as she takes in the guy's arterial blood splattered in pretty patterns across her kitchen.

"Did he hurt you?" She stares at me blankly, not comprehending. I ask again, "George, you need to answer me. Do you need medical attention?"

Slowly, she lowers her head to stare down at her body. I know the feeling she's experiencing all too well – that sense that something has so completely fucked you over that you've been thrown out of your body. It's now an entity apart from you, watching the world pass by in super slow-motion. She shakes her head. No, she's not hurt. Not on the outside, at least.

The guy gives a little jerk, sending a fresh outpouring of blood across the tiles. George shrieks. I cover her mouth with my hand.

"I have to go outside for a second. Don't move. Don't touch the corpse or go anywhere. I promise you that you're safe now.

I'm not going to let anything happen." Nothing but that blank stare. *This is bad.* "George. I need you to acknowledge me."

A nod. It's small, almost imperceptible. But I'll take it. I pat her shoulder – a hollow gesture, especially since I leave behind a bloody handprint – and rise.

I press my back against the door and lean out, peering into the front yard. The driver's side door of Antony's car is open. Antony's facedown in the oleander bushes. He doesn't move. I can't see anyone else around. The guy's delivery bike is leaned against the telephone pole. I see no other cars driving down the street, no sign anyone else in the neighborhood knows what's going down.

Fuck. Shit.

I run to Antony, my heart hammering. Blood cakes his face, and I panic as I search for a bullet hole or knife wound. There's a jagged cut across his hairline – it looks like he cut it open when he hit the concrete. But I can't see anything else. His breathing is soft, shallow. But he's breathing.

I roll him over, but I can't see blood anywhere apart from the wound on his forehead.

"Antony." I shake his shoulders. "Wake up. Please, fuck, please wake up."

Some dark, depraved god is smiling on me. One eye cracks open, and Antony peers up at me like for a moment he's forgotten who I am. He wraps his arms around me and crushes me against his chest.

I shove him. "What are you doing?"

His body sags and he drops his grip on me. "Sorry, Claws. I just wanted to check you were alive. Ow." He clutches his head. He's moving so slowly. He might have a concussion. "How did I get out of the car?"

"I'd blame the fake pizza delivery guy who came into the house and pointed a gun at George's head."

"Fuck. Wha—" Antony rolls forward, wincing. I place my hand on his chest and shove him back. "It's sorted. All those knife skills you taught me came in handy. The little punk just learned that messing with an August gets you a severed carotid."

Antony rubs his head. "It's coming back to me. I was watching a delivery guy on a bike. He stopped outside and pulled a balaclava over his head. I thought that wasn't normal pizza delivery behavior, so I tackled him." Antony touched the back of his head and winced. "The little fucker got me good."

"Can you get to the house? I'm calling Galen."

"I'll sort it. Don't bother him."

"We need him, Antony. I'm worried about George. She just watched me kill this guy. He's bleeding out all over her kitchen."

As I stagger into the house with Antony in tow, George whimpers, shuffling along the wall into a corner and pressing her face into her shoulder. She's in the first stage of losing-your-shit – believing that if you can't see the blood spurting like a water fountain from the dead guy's neck, it's not really happening.

I settle Antony into a chair and kneel down in front of her.

"George." I slap her cheek, lightly, trying not to frighten her but needing to get her attention. "I know this is fucked-up, right? There's a dead guy on your kitchen floor and I put him there. But I need you to listen to me. I'm going to get this cleaned up, and it'll be like it never happened. But we need your help. Do you understand?"

She stares at me with those wide eyes.

"Don't worry, I'm not going to make you do anything freaky." My voice has gone all high-pitched. I've never had to talk my friend through a cleaning before. "I need to know, do you have any tarps or dropcloths in the house? The kind you use for painting or yard work?"

George raises a shaking finger and points to a key hanging on the end of a set of hooks. "In the shed. Around the back."

"Excellent. Thank you. I'm going to leave you here, but I'm just going to your shed. Nothing will happen to you. Anton— I mean, Mr. Jones is here – he'll look after you while I'm gone."

I grab the keys and head around to the small back yard. Instead of the usual patch of anemic-looking grass, George and her mom's garden is crowded with raised beds bursting with vegetables. There are even fruit trees along the fence line. I open the shed and discover neat rows of gardening tools and a stack of folded tarps. I grab one off the top and carry it back to the house.

Antony and I roll the body in the tarp. We back Tiberius' car into the garage so that we can drag the body into the trunk without George's neighbors seeing. Antony collapses onto the passenger seat and calls Galen while I put my arms around George and hold her while she trembles.

"I'm sorry," I say. "I'm sorry about all this."

I don't know if I've ever uttered those words in my life. But they fell from my lips too easily now, because I meant them.

Galen arrives a few minutes later, with Tiberius in the passenger seat. I open the kitchen door for them. Galen pushes past me and makes a beeline for Antony, while Tiberius hands me a pizza box and inspects the mess in the kitchen.

"I met the delivery guy in the driveway. I assume this is yours. He seemed keen to get rid of it when he saw me, didn't even stick around for a tip." Tiberius' face has that effect on people. His bulk seems impossibly large in the small room, like he's trapped in a dollhouse. He looms over us, studying George with curiosity.

Her lip trembles as she takes in Tiberius' disfigured face. "Mr. Garcia," she chokes out. "Are you here to kill me?"

"What? Fuck no." I grab George's shoulders. "That guy in the garage with Antony is Galen. He's a doctor. Antony and Tiberius have been posing as teachers to protect me, and by extension you. They'll make sure nothing else happens to us."

"But what are they protecting me from? Who was that guy? Why does he want to kill me?"

"He doesn't want to kill you. He wants to kill me," I shrug, although I'm not so sure about that, either. "I promise I'll tell you everything, but right now we need to get this cleaned up."

George settles her head against my chest. "When I said you'd be good material for my podcast, I didn't mean quite like this."

"HAND ME THAT BLEACH."

George's hands shake as she holds out the enormous bottle. I uncap the lid and dump another slosh into my bucket. Tiberius and Galen had driven off with the body, to bury it in the spot in the desert they used for all their dirty work. Antony slumps over the table, nursing my bottle of port, while I get to work cleaning the blood off the cabinets.

"You really don't have to help." I glare at Antony. "Don't mind us. We've got this covered."

"Good to see, Claws."

"This isn't coming off," George's voice rises as she scrubs at the blood on the cushions.

"Do you have any shaving cream?" I ask. "It lifts out the stains."

"My mom's boyfriend might've left some in her bathroom. I'll go look." George runs off, returning a moment later with a big can, which she proceeds to spray everywhere like some over-exuberant barber.

"Usually we torch the place," Antony pipes up, carving off a chunk of chocolate cake and taking a big bite. He kicks the empty pizza box onto the floor. There's a round circle of pink on his fresh bandages that concerns me, but he assures me he's survived worse. "There's less chance of leaving evidence. Claws here vetoed that plan."

"Huh. Fancy that. And I was worried I'd never learn anything useful from a gym teacher." George sprays the rest of the shaving cream over the cushions and dumps them into the laundry. "Why does he call you Claws? I've never heard anyone call you that before."

I sigh. "Yes, you have."

Antony's chocolate-coated fingers freeze in mid-air.

"No, I—"

"George," I lean forward and whisper, so Antony can't hear. "I saw you at the Colosseum. I know Eli told you my real name."

George pales even more, which I didn't know was humanly possible since she's already as white as a ghost. "Okay, so you saw—"

"You and Eli at the club. And I saw a guy get ripped to pieces by a lion. I'd appreciate you not saying anything to Antony, since he'll kill us all if he knows we were there."

I pull away. The word *kill* trembles in the air between us. George's eyes are wide as the moon. "What do you mean, your *real* name? You're Mackenzie Malloy. It says so on your birth certificate, which I got from city hall."

Fuck.

She doesn't know.

Eli didn't tell her.

I don't know what to make of that.

I guess she knows now.

"Eli didn't tell you?" I toss my sponge on the floor. "Then why have the two of you been sneaking around together?"

"Eli knows I'm good at finding things," she says. I remember what she just told me – that she's the reason Eli's dad is in jail –

and I marvel at his capacity for forgiveness. If he can conspire with George... hope flutters in my chest. "He wants to dig up what really happened to the Malloys all those years ago."

"So he could take that information to the police?"

She shakes her head. "I don't think so. Eli's... conflicted. I think he believes you're in some kind of danger."

My heart stutters, but I can't think about Eli now. Not when someone's after George. I cock my head to the side. "What did that guy mean when he demanded your tapes? By chance, has the creator of *My Dad is a Gerbil* discovered some dark secret you intend to broadcast to the world?"

George manages to look both sheepish and a little proud. "I was going to tell you, I swear! I just wanted to find something first so you could see that you could trust me—"

Antony snorts with derision. He's not happy I've brought yet another person into the fold.

"George is ride or die." I cock an eyebrow at her. "Isn't she? Consider carefully before you answer."

George wrinkles her nose, and I know she's weighing the dead body we disposed of against everything that's led up to it. She nods. "I'm ride or die. Please don't let it be die."

"Deal. Remember, you're under my protection now, and I'm a crazy bitch." I hold up the knife we pulled out of the guy's neck. "Want me to cut you a slice of cake to seal the deal?"

"I don't think I can cut anything with that knife again." George stomps on the pedal to open the trash can and drops the knife inside. "Are more of these guys going to come after me?"

"It's hard to say. It depends on what they think you dug up."

"Nothing." George shakes her head. "I mean, not much. Just that Eli's father was involved with a crime boss."

"*What?*"

Antony sighs.

I rub my temple. This is too much.

George leans forward. There's a hint of the old sparkle in her eyes. "There's a photograph of his father with a man named Brutus August who, like, *runs* the Emerald Beach drug and skin trade—"

I sigh. "My uncle. My name is Claudia August."

George shakes her head. "You can't be. Brutus August killed Claudia along with her parents so he could take over the family. And besides, you're Mackenzie. I knew you from junior high, remember?"

I toss my blonde hair over my shoulder. "The resemblance is uncanny, right? It's just one of those weird coincidences. That's why Eli hates me, because he's been in love with Mackenzie since he was a kid and I've stolen her life."

"He doesn't hate you," George says. "Trust me."

I wave a hand, as if I don't care, as if her words don't make my pulse quicken and my heart flutter. "My father never let anyone see my face, he thought it would protect me, so no one in the underworld knows that I can pass for Mackenzie's identical twin. It's a long story and I promise to tell you everything as soon as we make sure you're safe."

The weight of my words fall heavy on George's shoulders. She sags into her seat, her hands nervously tapping the table. "The corpse... the guy who attacked me looked terrified when he saw you. Is that why he tried to kill me? Because I'm your friend?"

Actually, that is weird. The guy seemed surprised to see me, but he *recognized* me. *And* he was here to get rid of George's evidence that Brutus and Walter Hart had dealings.

I turn to Antony. He inclines his head. He's figured it out, too.

Brutus sent that guy to threaten George.

And he showed him what I look like.

That means Brutus is still a threat. He's still pulling strings.

And if we don't get to him soon he could hurt everyone I love, starting with George and probably moving on to...

...Eli.

"What would your mom say if you moved in with me for a while? If you're in Malloy Manor, I can keep you safe."

"She won't like it." George's eyes spark with color. "Maybe... maybe I'll tell her I have a boyfriend."

"Or *maybe* you could just ask Isaac to be your boyfriend and make it a reality?" I grin. "It's the least you could do, since you've been ignoring him so much he thinks you and Eli are an item. He's not moving into the manor, though. Mackenzie Malloy draws the line at Metallica fans."

George tries to smile, but it's not happening.

"We've been friends for a couple of months and I already have you lying to your mother."

George tries to crack a smile, but she clutches her stomach, and I realize she's barely holding down the junk food we ate earlier. "Sorry. You develop a bit of a gallows humor about this sort of thing."

"Is my mom in any danger?"

"I doubt it." Antony hacks off a large slice of cake and shoves it into an organic, reusable lunchbag. "There's an honor code, even among scoundrels like us. Brutus may intend to gut you and leave bits of you all over your house, but he won't hurt your mother unless she gets in his way."

Except we all know Brutus has no honor.

The ghost of his voice rasps in my ear. "Let me show you a man, baby girl..."

My fingers touch the knife in my sleeve.

I need to find him. And deal with him. Before it's too late.

37

CLAUDIA

"Wow." George breathes as I lead her through the garage door into the lofty foyer of Malloy Manor. She turns in a slow circle to take in the sweeping staircases, gaudy chandelier, and the eldritch blown-glass and ceramic statuary the Malloys seemed particularly fond of. "I always wanted to see inside this place."

I lead her into the kitchen, where Noah is banging pots with his uninjured arm and cursing. He's tied a flowery apron over his clothes and it's adorable. I roll my eyes at George. "Don't tell me – you were one of the sickos creeping around the perimeter, peering in the gates hoping for a glimpse of the Malloy ghost."

A faint flush creeps across her cheeks. "Maaaaybe. I wasn't being morbid, I promise. It was for research purposes. I *am* Emerald Beach's favorite true-crime podcaster, you know."

"I know. And I'm going to need to see every piece of research you have on my family and the Malloys. We need to find Brutus and—"

"Claaaaaws, I didn't expect you to be here. I come bearing dinner. Noah says he's cooking again, so I figure we needed supplies." Gabriel wanders in, pointedly ignoring Noah's coal-eyed death glare. He clutches a stack of gourmet food containers that smell divine. He's followed by Queen Boudica, who must smell something fishy because she has her tail up in the air and a hungry look in her eyes. When Gabe sees George, he drops his booty and throws his arm around her. "I knew Claws would drag you here eventually. Welcome to Castle Clawstein. You *must* see the sound system in the media room. It's out of this world."

I am so fucking grateful to Gabe, who fully doesn't give a shit that George is social pariah number one at Stonehurst Prep. He may appear superficial, but he's also an artist – he sees beyond the masks people wear. And what he sees inside George is all the things that make her an amazing friend. Her kindness. Her loyalty. Her badass taste in music.

"Is Eli here?" George's eyes light up.

Noah and I exchange a glance. I shake my head. "He hasn't taken my news as well as you. He wants to be left alone."

"No, he doesn't. That's the whole reason he started this research project," George says. "He wants to protect you. I don't think he knows you can kill a man from across a room with a cake knife."

"Hang on, what?" Noah's eyes narrow, but George and I ignore him.

George's lip quivers. "You shouldn't let Eli be alone if he's in danger."

"I'm working on it. But it's complicated, as you'll learn in a moment." I whip Antony's cake sack from his hands and shove it toward her. "Eat up. This is going to take a while. And you'll need chocolate."

Gabriel passes me a plate of shrimp carbonara. Excellent – carbs. I'll need them to get through this.

As George chews her way through an impressive chunk of cake, I lay the story out for her the same as I told the guys. I leave out the bits I'm not ready to talk about – the coffin, and the man without a face who I now know is Brutus. I've held on to my secrets for so long I feel naked without them, and I need to keep some close.

When I finish, she's practically bouncing with excitement. "Okay, you're definitely the topic of my next podcast."

Noah frowns. "Didn't you just hear what she said? No one can know she's not really Mackenzie—"

"No, I mean, this is how I help, right? I won't put anything on air you don't want out, but I've got a whole network of fans all over the world who can help us with information as long as we're fighting for a noble cause."

Gabriel grins. "I can't think of anything nobler than saving Claw's shaggable arse."

George continues. "Since Eli's dad is connected to this Brutus guy, that gives me reason to start digging through my old files again. Oh, speaking of Brutus, I think I know where he is."

I drop my fork.

She's kidding, right?

We've been looking everywhere for this guy, trying to keep this secret from George, and all along she's had the information we need?

How did she manage to find him when Antony couldn't?

Antony leans forward, and I swear his ears perk up like Queen Boudica when she hears me opening a tuna can.

"Okay, pipsqueak, we're listening."

38

CLAUDIA

"*R*un it by me again how you managed to figure out where Brutus is hiding out?" I growl.

It's Sunday. I'm in the kitchen with George and Gabriel, frying steaks for dinner (or rather, I'm frying. George has her research spread out over the table. Gabriel is pulling spatulas from the drawer and trying to whack my ass with them). We're waiting for Noah to get back from his final winter track meet (fuck knows how he's explained the cuts on his arm from the whip) and Antony to return from the club so we can head out to have a little chat with Brutus.

"It's simple. When I was researching Memories from the Hart, I started looking into what Walter Hart was doing with the bodies he wasn't giving back to grieving families. I thought maybe he was selling the organs, but it turns out that you have to yank them out pretty soon after death for them to be viable. It's more likely he was selling body parts on the medical market."

"Do I want to know what the medical market is?" Gabriel asks.

"It's where your body goes if you donate it to science,"

George explains. "Mostly it's chopped up cadavers medical schools purchase for teaching anatomy to doctors. Demand always exceeds supply, so plenty of schools won't ask too many questions about the provenance of their supplies. It's been like this ever since the earliest days of medicine, where medical students spent their nights robbing graves to supply cadavers for their anatomy lessons—"

Gabriel makes a face. "You take way too much delight in this stuff."

"I know." George grins. "So, anyway, I dug around a little into the medical market, learned some delightful things on the dark web, and I came up with this guy's name – Brutus August. Apparently, he's the guy you call if you want to sell a dead body in Emerald Beach."

Somehow, that doesn't surprise me. "That's my uncle, a real charmer."

Brutus seems determined to stomp on Daddy's legacy. First, he gets out of the antiquities trade, then he doubles down on drugs and starts dealing in skin. He repeals Daddy's rule about *damnatio ad bestias*. Now he's moving cadavers?

Daddy is rolling in his grave.

"From everything I've heard, the guy is terrifying and dangerous and not well-liked," George says. "He's also fucking *good*. There's no evidence he's connected to Memories of the Hart. He's wiped everything clean. I take a chance that Walter Hart isn't that savvy. I got a hacker friend of mine to break into Walter Hart's laptop and download files from a hidden directory. Those photographs show Walter and Brutus together at a party. It's not enough to stand up in court, but it was a clear sign to keep digging. I handed over that photograph along with all my other information to the FBI, but August's name never came up in the trial. I figured he's organized crime so they can't touch him and forgot about it until Eli asks me if I could look into him, along with what really happened to the Malloys. I remember the photograph of his dad with Brutus, so we confront Walter Hart with it and see if we can shake something out of him. Well, Eli confronts him, after he bribes a warden and—"

"Elias Hart bribed someone?" Gabriel bangs the table with glee. "This is bloody brilliant."

"It was terrifying," George shudders. "We needed to sneak Eli's phone into the prison to record their conversation. But it worked – we got confirmation from Walter he worked with Brutus *and* we found out he's been visiting Walter in prison. His last visit was the day he disappeared. That got me wondering if Walter Hart had helped Brutus somehow, so I went digging into his property portfolio and found most of it sold off except a dilapidated ranch about an hour from the city."

I remember Noah telling me he and Eli had a place they went when they needed to be alone. It makes sense that it could be this ranch. *What if Eli's going there right now and Brutus gets hold of him?* I drum my fingers against the counter. We need to hurry up and get out there. "Does Eli know?"

"I haven't told him yet," George says. "He's acting so strange. I was afraid if he knew he'd do something stupid—"

I hear the door to the garage creak open. "Noah, is that you? You need to hear what George —"

Noah leans against the door frame, his arm back in its sling and a faint smile playing on his lips. "I have a surprise for you."

I roll my eyes. "Please tell me it's not more of your cuisine."

Noah grins and steps aside. I hear a weird noise, like a cat meowing with excitement, but it's not Queen Boudica's howl. It's—

A strange black-and-white tuxedo cat careens around the corner. It sees us and tries to about-turn, but it's got too much momentum so it skids across the tiles, collapsing into a ball at my feet and immediately sitting up to wash a paw, trying to convince me it meant to do it all along.

This cat almost looks like—

"That's Gizmo. I told her I'm not going anywhere without her."

That voice.

The frying pan slides out of my hands. Bloody steaks slide across the floor. I do not give a shit.

I step forward on shaking legs. "Eli?"

He's here. My golden boy, looking anything but as he hovers behind Noah, staring everywhere but at me. I itch to throw my arms around him and pull him close, to inhale the warm, summer scent of him and to feel the safety of his arms.

My feet won't move. I can't do it, can't throw myself at him again to have him push me away. He's too important. The whisper of his kiss dances on my lips – the kiss from the party that he freely gave but now hangs around his neck like a noose.

He's here.

He may still hate me, but he's here. I can protect him.

Noah nods to his friend. "Eli says he'll stay here if it means he's away from Nero, but that doesn't mean he'll speak to you."

"I'll take it." A smile spreads across my lips as relief floods my body. *He's here. He's safe.*

For now.

"Mew." Gizmo spies the ruined steaks and barrels over to inspect the remnants of our dinner.

"Nice to see you again, mate." Gabriel embraces Eli, who looks a little shellshocked as he pats Gabriel's back.

"What convinced you to come back?" I ask as I pull more steaks from the freezer.

"We had words," Noah says.

Eli shakes his head. "Actually, it was George."

I raise my eyebrow at my friend, and she winks. With George

in my corner, I truly am invincible. She shuffles some of her papers aside and gestures at Eli to sit down. "Welcome to the madhouse."

Eli slides into the seat. He still won't look at me, but I can't help doing a little dance of joy as I slap the meat down into the frying pan. The last piece of my secret heart had returned to me.

Now, I had to protect them all, at any cost.

39

CLAUDIA

The drive out to Everlasting Hart Ranch is tense. George and Gabriel stay behind at Malloy Manor, with Tiberius watching over them. They both wanted to come, but I feel better knowing they're far away from whatever happens tonight.

I'd feel better if Noah and Eli were back at the manor, too. This is between me and Antony and Brutus. But Noah seems determined to prove he can wade into blood alongside me, and Eli... he's impossible to read. He says he wants to be here, and I don't want to say anything to make him leave again. But he insisted on bringing his kitten with us and he still can't bear to look me in the eye. I know things are still broken between us.

At least he's no longer a danger. At least he's part of the family again.

I just hope he doesn't see something tonight that will make him run. We're about to invade his personal space. His sanctuary. And I don't know what will happen when I see Brutus. I can't turn back from that.

Tough shit.

Brutus invaded it first.

Alea iacta est. He cast the die. Now he needs to play the game to the bitter end.

We pull into the towering gates. Weeds grow up around the stone pillars, and the words on the sign are so battered by the sandstorms that they're nearly indecipherable.

Antony leans over the wheel as he slows the car along the winding, broken driveway. "This place is enormous. It's going to take us hours to search."

"Not necessarily." Eli points to the collection of outbuildings behind the main homestead – three floors of broken panes and battered wood siding looming over us, with two dormer windows like eyes watching our every move. The outbuildings look in even worse condition – the barn had a giant hole in the roof and caved-in doors. "Last time I came out here, Gizmo was hanging around the outbuildings. She came back and didn't want to eat her dinner, which almost never happens. I thought she'd been catching mice, but now I wonder if he's been feeding her, which means she knows where he's hiding."

I peer at the tiny cat pawing at her cage. "You want to get her involved in this?"

Eli puts the cage on the ground and opens the door. Gizmo bounds outside and lifts her pink nose into the air, as if to say, "I'm ready for action."

Eli gives her a nudge with her foot. Gizmo peers up at him with wide eyes. He bends down to pet her but she tears off toward the outbuildings.

Antony slides his gun into his holster. He holds out a second weapon to me. I shake my head, lifting my wrist to show him the knives. I want Brutus to believe I came unarmed, like the silly little girl whose innocence he stole.

I want to get up close and personal.

Noah grabs the gun from Antony. Eli lifts a rotting board in the porch and pulls out a locked case, from which he withdraws an assault rifle. My eyebrows go up. Noah's eyes bug out of his head.

"Why are you looking at me like that?" Eli can't help but grin as he engages the weapon. "I *am* from the South. I practically grew up on a gun range."

"Yes, but—" *Look at you, you've never pointed that gun at someone and considered pulling the trigger.* But before I can say anything, Eli stalks after his cat, keeping close to the dilapidated stone buildings as he points the weapon ahead of him.

I rush after him, my heart leaping into my mouth. I flatten my back against the wall behind him. Eli's body tenses as my arm brushes his. An electric charge shoots through my veins from his touch. Seeing him carry that gun is hot as fuck.

I'm completely messed up.

Luckily, the moon is high and full, and there's no light pollution out here to obscure our vision. We have a clear view of the little tuxedo cat as she explores. Gizmo sniffs around in the weeds for a little bit, then chews on a blade of grass. She looks completely nonplussed with the four of us pressed up against the barn with our weapons at the ready.

Finally, she catches the scent of something and darts off toward one of the furthest outbuildings – a low stone lean-to with a pile of rusting tools stacked out front. She wiggles her ass into a narrow gap in the wall and disappears inside. A few moments later, I hear a voice murmur.

"Here, kitty, kitty. Brutus has some nice tuna for you..."

Fuck.

We found him.

He's really here.

My body tenses. My fingers slide into my sleeve to caress the blade I've hidden there. Antony grips my arm, his eyes boring into mine. He gestures that he and Noah will move around the rear of the building to close off his escape. Eli and I are to follow Gizmo in the front.

I nod, counting to twenty in my head as the pair of them slip away, giving them time to get in position. When I reach one, I tap Eli's hand. He looks over at me. Our eyes meet, and it's like a bolt of lightning striking my soul. He's burning me to a crisp, but I can't stop drawing him in.

We move toward the entrance. I can hear the man murmuring inside, cooing at Gizmo. Eli's finger trembles on the trigger, and I know he's regretting putting his cat in the middle of this. I raise an eyebrow at him, wishing I knew a facial expression or sign language that could convey, "I'll die before I let anything happen to Gizmo."

She's part of the family now.

The air crackles with tension – a storm rolling and tossing around Eli and me. I can't stand it any longer – inside that stone building is the man who threatened George and Eli's lives, who broke into the manor and hurt my cat, who killed my father, who pushed my head into a pillow and—

I step into the doorway. My shadow blocks the moonlight casting a rectangle over the beaten-earth floor. For a moment, I'm blind in the gloom, and panic licks at my chest.

A light flickers. A man coughs. A large oil lantern splutters to life, illuminating the aquiline features and cold blue eyes of a man I once regarded as family. He clutches Gizmo against his chest, a knife held to her throat.

"Welcome, Mackenzie," Brutus purrs, his voice like broken glass. "Or should I say, my dearest niece, Claudia."

40

ELI

My gaze flicks from Claudia to the man holding my cat hostage. They're related, all right. He has the same cold, blue eyes like chipped sapphires, the same proud nose, the same bloodthirsty smile. His fingers tighten around Gizmo, and she hisses and slashes at his face with her claws.

Hold on, girl. I'll save you.

I notice a strange pattern of scars on the back of Brutus' hand. It looks like a tattoo image – a sword wreathed with a vine, one of the insignias from the club – but it's not made with ink. The design has been *burned* into his skin.

My finger slips from the trigger. I'm ready to rush forward and offer myself in Gizmo's place. I'd rather he slit my throat than lay a finger on her, but I know if I move even an inch he'll drive that blade into her flesh. *Don't hurt her. Please don't—*

"Brutus," Claudia's voice is even. She steps toward him, deadly calm.

"I'm surprised it's taken you this long to find me." He coughs again, his words slurred.

As my eyes adjust to the light, I force myself to stay calm, to think my way out of this. Nothing makes sense. I can't imagine this hardened gangster squatting in a shed like an animal, yet that looks like exactly what he's been doing. I observe the objects surrounding him – a camping stove, empty cans, a sleeping bag, water containers, a foul-smelling bucket in the corner, as well as packages of expensive cigars, expensive vodka, and – sitting on a small silver tray on top of an upturned crate – some small grey rocks that look like cement mixture.

Shit.

He's high on grey death and he's got my kitty.

"I've been busy. Contrary to what you believe, you're not the center of the universe." Claudia glides closer, her body so still and her eyes so steady I barely notice the movement.

"That's where you're wrong." Brutus chuckles, staring down at the squabbling kitten in his hands like he only just noticed her there. "I know exactly why you've come. Oh, Aaaaantony?" he calls out in a singsong voice. "My loyal tribune. You've done well. I'll reward you when we return—"

Antony steps out of the shadows – there must've been a rear entrance to the shack. All I can see of him in the gloom is his hard grey eyes glinting and the flickering lantern light striking the barrel as he points his gun at Brutus' face.

Brutus' eyes bug out as he sees the gun in Antony's hands. "What is this?"

"Something we should have done a long time ago," Antony growls. He clicks off the safety.

"Not yet. Put the kitten down, Brutus." Claudia tilts her head to the side, her golden hair spilling over her shoulder. "We've a few things to discuss."

Brutus shakes his head, a crazed smile spreading across his face as he cradles Gizmo against his chest, using her as a kitten shield.

"Gizmo?" I call, the panic clawing at my chest. "Come here, girl."

Gizmo's head whirls around. Her tiny paws slash and scratch as she tries to wriggle free. Brutus grins and holds her by the scruff of her neck, the knife pressing into her fur. I see long cuts on his arm from where she'd got him. "Fancy something as tiny as this spilling so much blood? It reminds me of you, Claudia. I knew from the moment Julian placed a screaming baby into my arms that you were born to be the queen of bloodshed."

"Born to be a queen?" Claudia scoffs. "You didn't believe that when you buried me alive."

"And yet, here you are, still breathing, proving me right." Brutus inclines his head. "You have me surrounded. You want your revenge, and I respect that. You want to get even for what I did to dear Julian. His brand still marks my skin, you know. His punishment for daring to question the great Imperator." His voice rises to a singsong pitch. He sounds completely out of it. "You might even believe you won't face consequences, but I know the truth truth truth. All the ugly secrets daddy never told you. Before one of your trained monkeys spills my blood, allow me to make you this offer."

"Not interested." Claudia tosses her hair, and it's such a classic Mackenzie move it makes my heart clench.

"You will be. I've taken the empire Julian built and made it great beyond his wildest dreams. My brother was an admirable leader, but his insistence on ludicrous rules and moral codes meant he'd eventually be conquered by more unscrupulous men. He placed this mark on me and yet *I'm* the most powerful man in Emerald Beach. I did him a favor by conquering him first. I *saved* his legacy. What use is his moral code in a criminal empire?" His whole body jerks with loud, barking laughter. *He's fucking out of it.* "You of all people understand me. That is why you should rule as my queen."

The temperature in the shack drops ten degrees. Silence envelops us as Brutus' words hang in the air. My gaze flicks to

Claudia's stony face, her icicle eyes shining in the darkness. Behind her head, I fancy I see a shadow moving, a flash of golden light, but it's gone in an instant.

My skin prickles with unease. Claudia said it right when she revealed her secret to us that she was stealing Mackenzie's house because she wanted to get out of her crime family.

So why is she hesitating?

Why is there a flicker of interest in those icicle eyes?

The silence stretches for an eternity, while I watch my beloved kitten tear Brutus' hand bloody trying to escape. Tears prick in my eyes. *Please, get loose and come to me. Give me a clear shot.*

I never thought I could even threaten someone with a gun, but now I don't care about destroying my future. This bastard has my cat. I itch to pull the trigger and let loose on his smug, drug-addled, kitten-hurting face.

But I can't risk hitting Gizmo.

So I wait.

I wait for Claudia to decide my fate.

When Claudia speaks, her voice drips with malice. "You think this is some great, magnanimous offer you've bestowed on me? You're pathetic. You've *lost* your empire. That's why you're hiding in this shithole."

"Hiding?" Brutus cackles. "Oh, baby girl. Sweet, innocent baby girl..."

"*Don't call me that.*" Claudia's voice is death itself. "You crossed the Rubicon when you killed Daddy, but you misjudged your die roll. The *homo sacer* may have faded, but you're still a dead man walking. The Triumvirate wants you gone. Why would I tether myself to a loser like you? You only want me because my name will give you the legitimacy you need to hold on to your throne. You're right about one thing, Brutus. I *am* a queen. And I don't need a man to rule over me, especially not one who turns on his only brother and touches innocent children."

Her breath rasps over those final words, and I *see*. I see her truth blazing in her eyes, the secret heart she's kept locked away even as it burns her from the inside. I *see* this man has taken a piece of her he had no right to take, and that even though she's waited and bided her time for this moment of her revenge, she's not here for herself.

She *needs* to claw his eyes out, to open his chest cavity and lay his organs bare, to drench herself in his blood until it washes away what he did to her. But she won't move because of Gizmo. Because of Noah and Gabriel and Antony. She's here because she will take Brutus' power before she allows him to hurt the people she loves.

She's here because of me.

For the first time, I *see* Claudia.

I *feel* the rush of her formidable love washing over me.

I taste her wicked strength on my tongue.

In that moment, I truly believe she is a queen – beautiful and invincible.

There's a hissing sound as a blade kisses the air.

Brutus *howls* – a broken, inhuman sound.

He drops Gizmo as he's flung backward. My baby girl somersaults across the dirt, lands on her feet, shakes herself off, and trots over to me.

"Mew?" She looks up at me with those big eyes, completely unharmed, inquiring about the food situation. Relief floods me as I pick her up, feeling her tiny heart thundering in her chest. I sit her on my shoulder and turn back to the scene.

Brutus is sobbing and gibbering as his body convulses with pain. A blade sticks straight out of the center of his hand, through the scar of the sword and vine, pinning him to the wooden post. He's trapped. He cries as he tries to pull the blade out, but it's buried up to the hilt and the blood gushing from the wound makes it impossible to grip.

A smirk dances across Claudia's face as she pulls back her arm and lets a second blade loose.

Hissss.

It buries itself into his other arm, near the wrist. Blood spurts like a fountain from the wound, tainting the stale air with its distinctive tang.

Brutus looks up at Claudia with wide eyes. For the first time, I see a flicker of terror behind the drugged haze.

"Claws," Antony drawls. "Do you want me to finish him?"

"No." Claudia holds out her hand toward Noah, palm flat. "We should bury him alive, but I'm not that patient. I'm not giving him another chance to hurt someone. I'll have your gun."

Noah looks like he wants to argue, but he drops the weapon into her hand. She points it at Brutus' head, her finger on the trigger. She looks completely at home with that gun in her hand, her perfect skin streaked with Brutus' blood, her eyes dancing with joy.

"You said you'd make things oh-so-good for me," she hisses. "You said I was your *baby girl*. That's sick, and when animals get sick, we put them down. I was never yours. I'm Julian August's baby girl and I'm all grown up. This time, you're the one who's going to get fucked. I promise I'll make it oh-so-good."

"What are you talking about, you crazy bitch?" He's scared now, his whole body trembling. Blood spurts from his wounds as he jerks his hand, trying to tear himself free. "You crazy-ass bitch. You're just like him, just like Julian, two sides of the same coin. I'll get you for this. You kill me and you doom them. All these spoiled rich boys you love so much. I already ruined that one's father." His eyes fix on me, and a white-hot bolt of rage strikes my chest. "We'll ruin him, too."

Claudia's face is a pale moon. The weapon in her hands remains steady.

The light flickers behind her, and I catch a glimpse of the gold again. But it's only a reflection of her face on a mirrored surface, haloed by her golden hair. A queen of hell with death in her eyes.

"He did it, Claws," Antony says. "You know it was him. There's no other explanation for the note he left on Brentwood's body. He needs to die."

Brutus throws back his head and *shrieks*. He sounds deranged, like a banshee calling down death and destruction. "The note..." he caws. "The fucking *note*."

Claudia's jaw clenches. Her eyes flick to me.

"Eli, get out of here," she says.

I shake my head.

"I'm not warning you again. You don't want to see this."

My feet won't move. I can't turn away. Claudia doesn't ask a third time.

"Alea iacta est," she says.

She pulls the trigger.

The gunshot explodes around me. With it, the final shred of my old life disintegrates into dust.

With it, I lay my life down before my queen.

Blood splatters across the wall in a halo of destruction. Droplets rain down on me, anointing me in this man's life – a life *she* took to save Gizmo.

To save me.

She shot her uncle in the head.

She. Shot. Him. In. The. Head.

Brutus' body slumps forward, still held in place by the blades through his flesh. His head's a mess of blood and gore and... I turn away. I can't look at it.

I turn away, and I see her.

My queen.

She runs to me.

"Eli—"

The air shatters with shards of sound that tear through my skull. *Gunfire.* I can't see where it's coming from or who's shooting. All I see is Claudia running toward me as her reflection runs the opposite way.

That's not right. How—

I freeze as bullets rip through the old tools and paint cans on the shelf behind me. I know I need to move, to protect Gizmo, but it's all happening so fast, I can't think. I can't—

Claudia barrels into me, knocking me down. Her arms go around Gizmo, cradling my cat to her chest as bullets fly over us. My ears ring and my brain rattles in my skull and I don't know if the shack has fallen silent or if I've been deafened by the noise.

All I know is *her.*

Out of the corner of my eye, I see Antony and Noah tear off outside, their weapons raised. Gizmo wiggles out from her arms and Claudia presses her body into me, her heart and mine thundering against each other. Even though my hearing is fucked up, her beautiful voice reaches my ears, as clear as the emerald ocean. "Eli, fuck. I thought you were—"

"I'm alive because of you." Something warm trickles over my shoulder. I put my hand up to feel and come away with blood. Her blood. Claudia winces as I touch a wound in her shoulder.

She took a bullet for me.

I want to get her to safety, to take her to a hospital, to pull that damn bullet out with my teeth. But she won't let go of me. She holds me and I hold her and both of us speak at once as Gizmo jumps all over us in excitement. "Why why why?" I ask. "Why did you jump in front of me? Why did you make yourself a murderer?"

"Because of you. And I would do it again and again." Her

nails dig into my skin. "They have not made enough bullets for the retribution I'll rain down on the people who try to hurt you."

"But—"

She cups my cheeks in her hands, smearing Brutus' blood across my skin. Her touch burns, but a good kind of burn. A cleansing fire that devours me like a phoenix so I can be born anew in the ashes of her love. "Stop talking. You've spent your whole life trying to protect other people. You protected me even when I didn't deserve it, and you protected Mackenzie even though she's a fucked-up bitch who was horrible to you. No one was there for you when you needed them. Well, I'm here now, and I'm not going to let a piece of shit like Brutus ruin your life."

I swallow. There's a raw panic in her eyes – she's not thinking about the man she just killed or the bullet in her arm or the person who shot it. She only cares about me.

No one has ever cared like that.

I cup her hands and bring her face to mine. I kiss her as I've wanted to kiss her since the day she showed up at Stonehurst. I kiss away the distance between us, the secrets and lies that don't mean shit anymore. I taste the blood of the life she spilled for me, and I know that I'll never again see the ghost of a girl I thought I loved in her eyes.

Her face, her lips, her dark heart belong only to Claudia August.

She is mine. And I am hers.

She's my queen, and she's baptized me in blood.

TO BE CONTINUED

I was baptized in bloodshed.
To the bloodshed, I return.

I've ascended my throne. I wear my crown of thorns.

Fancy that? I'm Queen of the August crime family.
I'll rebuild my father's kingdom in blood and fire.
With three broken princes at my side.

Eli, Noah, Gabriel.
My golden boy, my dark horse, my rock god.
My *family.*
They are mine, and I am theirs.

There aren't enough bullets on earth for the retribution I'll rain down on those who hurt them.

Et in morte fidelitas.
Even in death, loyalty remains.

I'll bleed for them. I'll kill for them.
Stonehurst Prep will never be the same.

My Broken Crown.

Grab a free copy *Cabinet of Curiosities* – a Steffanie Holmes compendium of short stories and bonus scenes – when you sign up for updates with the Steffanie Holmes newsletter.

TRY THIS COMPLETE DARK SUPERNATURAL BULLY SERIES FROM STEFFANIE HOLMES

I should have kept my mouth shut.
I should have let them win.

**Now the kings of the school are out for my blood,
... and they're not the only ones.**

Need more dark, gothic, and delicious reverse harem bully romance in your life?

HP Lovecraft meets *Cruel Intentions* in the paranormal reverse harem bully romance readers are calling, "The greatest mindfuck of 2019". Warning: Not for the faint of heart – this story of three broken bad boys and the girl who stood her ground contains dark themes, crazed cultists, books bound in human skin, high-school drama, swoon-worthy sex, and potential triggers. Grab book 1, *Shunned*, in KU now.

Turn the page for a sizzling excerpt of *Shunned*.

FROM THE AUTHOR

Claudia came to me in a dream. She is... not like any other heroine I've ever written. Even though I've sworn up-and-down that I'd never write contemporary romance (imagine, romance *without* vampires? What even *is* that?) she wouldn't shut up until I told her story.

I wrote her for *you*. Because the world is scary out there – it feels like we're on the cusp of empires rising and falling. I know when I'm scared I so often find myself in the pages of a book. Sometimes I even borrow a little strength and a little audacity from the characters I love. I think we all need as much of those as we can get right now.

I'm in awe of the incredible health workers and other essential staff who've kept the world running and done their best in an impossible situation. If you're one of them, there are no words I can say to thank you enough for your contribution.

I'm just a teller of stories. I can't save lives or keep food on tables or make sure businesses stay afloat. But if I can give you a new world and a new life and a strange mystery to lose yourself in for a few hours, then that's some small way I can help you survive this wild and crazy world.

Writing *My Secret Heart* has been a joy and a pleasure, but as always, it takes a village to bring a book to life. I'd like to thank my cantankerous drummer husband, for reading this manuscript and giving me so many ideas to make it better. And for being my lighthouse. And for making me so many bacon butties and keeping the house stocked with chocolate during lockdown.

To Kit, Bri, Elaina, Katya, and the Noodles, for all the writerly encouragement and advice. To Meg and Eveis for the epically helpful editing job, and to CJ for the stunning covers. To Sam and Iris, for the daily Facebook shenanigans that help keep me sane while I spend my days stuck at home covered in cats.

To you, the reader, for going on this journey with me, even though it's led to some dark places. Warning: if you thought book 2 was tough, book 3 is a doozy.

If you're enjoying *Stonehurst Prep* and want to read more from me, check out my dark reverse harem bully romance series, *Kings of Miskatonic Prep*. HP Lovecraft meets *Cruel Intentions* in this dark paranormal reverse harem bully romance that's definitely not for the faint of heart. Hazel is the most badass FMC I've ever written after Claudia, and I think you'll love meeting her.

You should also check out my other reverse harem academy series, *Manderley Academy*. Book 1 is *Ghosted* and it's a classic gothic tale of ghosts and betrayal, creepy old houses and three beautifully haunted guys with dark secrets. Plus, a kickass curvy heroine. You will LOVE it.

I've also got two other reverse harem series. The Nevermore Bookshop Mysteries is what you'd get if you crossed Agatha Christie with Black Books and added a harem of famous literary men. It's my most popular series to date, and it's a lot more light-hearted and fun (despite all the murder).

If you want to hang out and talk about all things books, my

readers are sharing their theories and discussing spoilers over in my Facebook group, www.facebook.com/ groups/steffanieholmes. Come join the fun. And for updates and a free book of cut scenes and bonus stories, you can www.stef-fanieholmes.com/newsletter

I'm so happy you enjoyed this story! I'd love it if you wanted to leave a review on Amazon or Goodreads. It will help other readers to find their next book boyfriend (not Gabriel, though – he's mine).

Thank you, thank you! I love you heaps! Until next time.
Steff

I was baptized in bloodshed.
To the bloodshed, I return.

I've ascended my throne. I wear my crown of thorns.

Fancy that? I'm Queen of the August crime family.
I'll rebuild my father's kingdom in blood and ashes.
With my three broken princes at my side.

Eli, Noah, Gabriel.
My golden boy, my dark horse, my rock god.
My *family.*
They are mine, and I am theirs.

There aren't enough bullets on earth for the retribution I'll rain
down on those who hurt them.

Et in morte fidelitas.
Even in death, loyalty remains.

I'll bleed for them. I'll kill for them.
Stonehurst Prep will never be the same.

The third installment of the Stonehurst Prep series is a 100,000
mature high school/new adult romance with mafia and
enemies-to-lovers themes.

books2read.com/mybrokencrown

READ THE FIRST CHAPTER OF SHUNNED

Who the hell builds a school on top of an inaccessible cliff?

Whoever built Derleth Academy, my new school. I answered my own question as the car's wheel skidded over the rough gravel on the way up the steep peninsula. A scream escaped my lips as the car lurched toward the edge of the cliff, one wheel spinning completely free.

Muttering under his breath, the driver for the school slammed the car into reverse and backed us onto the road before slamming on the gas again. We continued our wary climb along the narrow gravel path.

Surely the Academy can't be completely *cut-off.* The school had to bring up food and supplies. Parents must visit on the weekends. My driver was certainly giving it his all, tearing around the corners like he was on a Formula ɪ racetrack and not a goat path hugging the side of a mountain. I gritted my teeth and gripped the back of the seat as rocks rolled from beneath the wheels and clattered over the sheer drop into the raging waters below. One wrong move, and we'd tumble down a two-hundred-foot cliff and be dashed against the cliffs so hard and fast that boats would mistake our remains for rock paintings.

Not the way I ever imagined I'd go.

We passed into thick vegetation, the cliff and ocean on one side giving way to looming trees that blocked out the grey sky. I let out the breath I'd been holding. Branches scraped the sides of the car, and my phone beeped with protest as we moved out of cell range. *No contact with the outside world,* the school brochure read. *At Derleth Academy, we foster a competitive academic program requiring the full attention of our students. Distracting technology or personal items will not be tolerated.*

In other words, I couldn't call for help. It was the opening sequence to every horror film, ever.

Not that I had anyone to call. Not anymore.

"Almost there," the driver said, swinging the car around a hairpin corner and launching my stomach into my throat. It was the most words he'd spoken to me the entire trip. "You can see the school through the trees."

I squinted into the forest, trying to make out some kind of building that might pass as a school. But I couldn't see a thing. We rounded another corner and—

Well, that's terrifying.

We rolled between two towering stone pillars obscured by creeping vines, past an ornate sign that read DERLETH ACAD-EMY. A wide, pristine concrete drive flanked by an avenue of towering trees and wide, manicured lawns led up to an imposing stone building, stretching in all directions with narrow arched windows, spiky towers, and a row of leering gargoyles along the roof.

What is this place? It looked more like Dracula's castle than a prestigious preparatory school.

I couldn't believe the wealthiest people in the country sent their children up that winding road to get educated. *Who's the headmistress, Morticia Addams?* But according to the brochure, that was exactly what they did. In droves. Derleth Academy had a waiting list a mile long, and you couldn't even pay to get in. You had to be *invited*.

Somehow, I, Hazel Waite – an overachieving orphan from the wrong side of Philly – ended up on their radar.

I flashed back to the day two weeks ago, when a banging on the door of my dingy apartment dragged me from a deep slumber. A woman with coiffed hair and a designer suit that cost more than a car staggered backward in surprise when I glared at her through the chain wearing only my pajamas and what must have been a terrifying scowl. Well, *she* wasn't the one being dragged from a pleasant Jason Momoa sex dream during the four-hour reprieve between night shift at the diner and cleaning rooms at a retirement home.

"Are you Hazel Waite?" she asked, her brown eyes wide and curious.

"No. Piss off." I glowered, slamming the door in her face. She was probably from CPS, trying to force me into foster care. Fuck that. I only had seven more months to survive before I turned eighteen. No way was I going to spend it in the hell that had killed Dante.

The woman didn't go away. She sat out on the road in her sports car and waited me out. I had to leave for work or I'd lose my job, and it wasn't easy to find work when you were underage and using an obviously fake ID. As soon as I left the house, she ambushed me.

"I'm not here to hand you over to the authorities," she said hurriedly, shoving a thick envelope into your hands. "I'm a scholarship administrator from Derleth Academy in Arkham, Massachusetts. Your current school put you forward for one of our four senior scholarship positions – a fully funded year at a first-class prep school, where our students go on to attend the top colleges in the world. I know the first quarter has already started, but it's taken me this long to track you down. You've only missed a week so far."

I stared at the envelope in my hands, at the red, black and gold school crest – a crooked five-pointed star inside a shield with some kind of Latin phrase beneath it. *This has got to be a joke.*

"I know what you're thinking," the woman said. "It's not a joke or a trick. I promise you that it's not. If you come to Derleth, we will assume guardianship duties until you turn eighteen. You'll be housed, clothed, and have all your schoolbooks and other needs met, as well as receiving a first-class education. You're a promising student, Hazel, and I know you've been dealt a cruel lot in life. This could be where you turn everything around. Don't answer me now. Read over the paperwork, and I'll return tomorrow for your decision."

And now, just ten days after I signed my soul over to this school in exchange for paid tuition, room, and board, I stared up at the imposing facade and wondered if I'd made a terrible mistake.

Sure, my life was miserable. I was drowning in grief, and even working two jobs I could barely pull in enough money to survive. College was out of the question, because I couldn't finish high school without going into foster care. But at least all that was familiar territory. That was the world I'd grown up in – the world of pain and struggle and loss. Derleth Academy was the exact opposite. Every element of this building screamed wealth and privilege and *you don't belong here.*

The driver pulled to a stop on the wide circular drive beside a towering stone fountain. A black woman in a drab grey smock darted out of the shadows of the porch and approached the car. I held my hand out to her. "Hello, I'm Hazel Waite—"

The woman ducked her head, avoiding me. She popped

open the trunk, hauled out my heavy suitcase and bookbag, and hurried off to the house with them before I could offer to help.

Weird much? I swiped a dreadlock off my face. My friend Dante's foster sister had done them for me last year, back when things were perfect and the most I had to worry about was whether my mom would ground me for getting dreadlocks.

An awful feeling twisted in my gut. I wished Mom was here, hating my loss, right now. But she was gone, gone, gone, and so was Dante, and it was just me and this terrifying school and no other options.

Three figures descended the grand stone steps toward me: A woman with translucent skin and a flowing black dress, flanked on either side by two students wearing the Derleth uniform. Fallen leaves skittered away from the woman's hem, and she moved with such poise that she appeared to float over the steps. With her severe features and a gauzy black ribbon pinned in her hair, she looked more like she was attending a funeral. Behind her, the two students – a guy and a girl – glared at me, distrust emanating from their every pore.

The woman stopped on the second-to-last step, peering down her nose at me as if I were a bug that wasn't even worth squashing. "You'll have to do something about that hair. We enforce a strict dress code in my school, Ms. Waite. I'll not have you flouting it on your very first day."

This must be the principal, Hermia West. My Morticia Addams guess wasn't far off. This woman looked like she drank the blood of students to sustain her beauty. The way her grey eyes stabbed right through me sent a cold shiver through my body.

There was nothing in the student handbook about dreadlocks. Although, of course, I'd only skim-read the thing on the bus from Philly. The handbook was boring. And *long.* "I'm sorry, Ms. West. I didn't know—"

"Ignorance is no excuse. That's 3 demerit points for you. And you're to refer to me as Headmistress."

Beside her, the boy sniggered. I turned my gaze to look at him, and my heart nearly stopped. *Wow, he's beautiful.* I had no idea boys that hot existed outside of magazines and Hollywood movies. He stood practically the same height as Ms. West, his broad shoulders accentuated by the tailored cut of his red-trimmed blazer. Prefect and merit badges decorated both lapels. Dark brown curls caught the grey light filtering through the clouds, throwing back beautiful shades of russet and silver. His clean-shaven face and high, majestic cheekbones appeared angelic, but his ice-blue eyes were cold and cruel.

The girl moved closer to him, touching his arm and shooting me a possessive glare, like a cat in heat. She had the appearance of a cat, too – slanted green eyes accentuated with heavy makeup, pointed chin, and the lithe body and long legs of a panther. Beautiful but deadly.

"This is Trey Bloomberg and Courtney Haynes," Headmistress West said. "I've appointed them as your student guides. They will show you the dorm, library, and dining hall, go over your schedule and classrooms, and ensure you understand *all* our rules. You will dine with the student body in two hours' time, and tomorrow you begin classes. I've had a copy of your schedule and the school handbook placed in your room. Memorize them, for failure to comply will result in further demerits. Here's your dorm room key."

In my pocket, my phone gave another defiant chirp. *Great.* I'd practically worn down the battery looking for a signal on the death road.

Headmistress West descended the last step to drop an ancient-looking metal key into my hand. Her pointy black boots lined up with my scuffed Docs. She loomed over me, her disapproval seeping into my bones. "You have a phone in your pocket." It wasn't a question.

"Yes."

Behind her, the boy smirked. I felt naked, exposed. My legs itched to make a run for the woods. Headmistress West held out her hand, unfurling long fingers topped with red-painted nails, the tips pointed like talons. "Hand it over. We don't allow outside technology on campus."

Instinctively, my hand flew to my pocket. "I won't use it to call or text. It doesn't work here, anyway, so what's the—"

"Ms. Waite, failure to obey a teacher's command is an automatic loss of 10 points. You seem most anxious to find out what punishments await the students at the bottom of the class list."

A lump rose in my throat. My phone contained photographs – snaps of my mom smiling demurely or brushing her hair in the mirror before she went out to work at the strip club. Of Dante and I hanging out around the neighborhood, smoking on the rusted playground beside his house, tagging the concrete wall behind the boxing gym on the corner. Every other one of my possessions had been destroyed in the fire. Those photographs were practically all I had left of them.

Trey and Courtney covered their mouths with their hands, barely disguising their laughter. Courtney leaned over and whispered something to Trey. They both cracked up. Despite myself, my cheeks flushed. *Better get used to this.*

Headmistress West, of course, ignored them. She wasn't backing down on this phone thing. My fingers closed around it, the comfortable weight of it in my hand reminding me that it was one of the last connections to my old life.

What does it matter? They're gone. Looking at their photos won't bring them back. But this school could be the only chance I have at a real future.

My hand trembling, I dropped my phone into her talons. As

soon as it left my hand, I itched to get it back. Headmistress West slipped the phone into a fold of her dress, where it disappeared from sight.

"Follow me." The headmistress swirled on her heel and floated up the stairs. Numb, I fell in step behind her. Trey came up beside me. His arm brushed mine, and a jolt of warmth rocketed through my body. I dared a look up at his face. As we moved into the shadow of the porch, the colors in his hair changed, becoming a deep brown and blood red. A curl flopped over his eye, and I noticed flecks of silver on the edges of those arresting blue irises. My fingers itched to reach up and swipe that curl off his face, to touch his smooth skin, feel his cheek move beneath my fingers, to cut myself on his cheekbones. A familiar longing pooled in my stomach, an ache that I'd never been able to sate before, and now never would.

I'd never seen a boy that *perfect*.

Trey's fingers brushed me again. My breath froze in my mouth as his hand lingered on my elbow. To anyone looking at us from a distance, it would appear as though he was helping me, steadying me up the steep steps. The touch on my skin was white-hot, lighting up parts of my body that hadn't felt anything since Dante... since before the fire. *How can this boy with such cruel eyes have this effect on me?*

When he caught me looking, Trey's perfect lips curled back into a sneer. His fingers tightened on my arm, squeezing my skin. Tighter, tighter, until he was cutting off circulation. I yelped in protest.

"You don't belong here," he murmured, his perfect lips forming hateful words. "You should leave now."

He said it so casually, like he was chatting about the weather, and that self-satisfied smirk never left his face. My stomach twisted, the air driving from my lungs as though he'd punched me.

"No thanks," I said brightly, pretending that I misunderstood him. "I'm good."

"We don't want you, and we're used to getting what we want. We're going to eat you alive, new meat." Trey flashed me a smile that was all teeth and violence. The venom in his eyes frightened me. *This is not a guy to mess with.*

Too bad he seemed to already have it out for me, and I hadn't even got inside the school yet. My plan to keep my head down and stay invisible fizzled before my eyes. Already I could see how the school year was going to play out. *We don't want you here.* Trey spoke for the entire student body. He was a King in this school. It was written in his smile, dripping from the menace in his words.

I'd pissed him off. Just by existing. Just by setting foot on the hallowed grounds of his kingdom. *Well, fuck you, Trey Bloomberg.* I could handle a year of insults and loneliness if I got my diploma at the end of it. My life was already hell on earth – if Trey Bloomberg thought he could break me, he'd have to try a lot harder.

I wrenched my arm away from us. "Don't touch me." Behind us, Courtney giggled.

"Yeah, Trey. You should know not to handle garbage. She's a gutter-trash whore who's probably fucked so many guys that your dick wouldn't even touch the sides."

The comment stung. I thought of my sweet mother, all candy smiles and sticky skin as she stripped off her sweat-soaked lace g-string and six-inch heels after her shift and pulled on the cloud-pink pajamas I found for her in a thrift store. A hard lump rose in my throat. I shoved the image aside. *Not now.*

Wait until you get to your room, until you're alone, then you can break down.

"I guess we're not going to be braiding each other's hair," I muttered to Courtney.

"I wouldn't touch that rat's nest on your head if someone hid a *Faberge* egg inside," Courtney sneered. "I bet it's got real eggs in it, though. Insect eggs, laid by the gross things crawling around in there."

Instinctively, my hand flew up to my face, to touch the dreadlock that always fell over my eye, to tuck it behind my ear – a gesture that Dante would so often do when he noticed my loss in my eyes, which was all the time because I liked them unruly. Ever since the fire, I'd been touching my own hair more and more, seeking the comfort of the familiar weight of a hand moving the dreadlocks. But it wasn't the same. It would never be the same.

Courtney wrinkled her face in disgust, while Trey continued to smirk at me. The force of his loathing sank my stomach to my knees. He didn't even know me, but it didn't matter.

At the top of the stairs, the headmistress turned and frowned at me. "Don't dawdle," she snapped. "The school doesn't bite."

"She's wrong," Trey whispered. "Are you ready to find out just how bad we bite?"

The lump of hard, bitterness burned at the back of my throat. They were right. I didn't belong here. I was the poor gutter-trash girl from the wrong side of the tracks, and they were *royalty.* They were the monarchs. *They're going to make my life miserable, and there's nothing I can do.*

Read Shunned now

I should have kept my mouth shut.
I should have let them win.
Now the kings of the school are out for my blood,
... and they're not the only ones.

The fire took everything.
My parents. My best friend. My life.

Now I have a second chance.
I only have to endure one year at this prestigious academy for
rich snobs.
One year of being the charity case no one wanted.
One year of taunts and insults and bullying. Then I'm free.

But I didn't count on Trey, Ayaz, and Quinn.
Arrogant, privileged, dangerous.
Drop-dead gorgeous.
They want me gone.
They want me to suffer.
They're determined to make my nightmares real.

Tough luck, bully boys – I won't hide away.
I'm not afraid.
But maybe… *I should be.*

HP Lovecraft meets *Cruel Intentions* in book 1 of this dark paranormal reverse harem bully romance. Warning: Not for the faint of heart – this story of three broken bad boys and the girl who stood her ground contains dark themes, crazed cultists, books bound in human skin, high-school drama, swoon-worthy sex, and potential triggers.

START READING NOW
books2read.com/shunned

OTHER BOOKS BY STEFFANIE HOLMES

This list is in recommended reading order, although each couple's story can be enjoyed as a standalone.

Nevermore Bookshop Mysteries

A Dead and Stormy Night

Of Mice and Murder

Pride and Premeditation

How Heathcliff Stole Christmas

Memoirs of a Garroter

Prose and Cons

A Novel Way to Die

Much Ado About Murder

Kings of Miskatonic Prep

Shunned

Initiated

Possessed

Ignited

Stonehurst Prep

My Stolen Life

My Secret Heart

My Broken Crown

My Savage Kingdom

Manderley Academy

Ghosted

Haunted

Spirited

Briarwood Witches

The Castle of Earth and Embers

The Castle of Fire and Fable

The Castle of Water and Woe

The Castle of Wind and Whispers

The Castle of Spirit and Sorrow

Crookshollow Gothic Romance

Art of Cunning (Alex & Ryan)

Art of the Hunt (Alex & Ryan)

Art of Temptation (Alex & Ryan)

The Man in Black (Elinor & Eric)

Watcher (Belinda & Cole)

Reaper (Belinda & Cole)

Wolves of Crookshollow

Digging the Wolf (Anna & Luke)

Writing the Wolf (Rosa & Caleb)

Inking the Wolf (Bianca & Robbie)

Wedding the Wolf (Willow & Irvine)

Want to be informed when the next Steffanie Holmes paranormal romance story goes live? Sign up for the newsletter at www.steffanieholmes.com/ newsletter to get the scoop, and score a free collection of bonus scenes and stories to enjoy!

ABOUT THE AUTHOR

Steffanie Holmes is the *USA Today* bestselling author of the paranormal, gothic, dark, and fantastical. Her books feature clever, witty heroines, wild shifters, cunning witches and alpha males who *always* get what they want.

Legally-blind since birth, Steffanie received the 2017 Attitude Award for Artistic Achievement. She was also a finalist for a 2018 Women of Influence award.

Steff is the creator of *Rage Against the Manuscript* – a resource of free content, book, and courses to help writers tell their story, find their readers, and build a badass writing career.

Steffanie lives in New Zealand with her husband, a horde of cantankerous cats, and their medieval sword collection.

Steffanie Holmes newsletter

Grab a free copy *Cabinet of Curiosities* – a Steffanie Holmes compendium of short stories and bonus scenes – when you sign up for updates with the Steffanie Holmes newsletter.

Come hang with Steffanie
www.steffanieholmes.com
hello@steffanieholmes.com